Daniel W. Fisł

MW01674960

The Progressive Practical Arithmetic

SALZWASSER
VERLAG

Daniel W. Fish, Horatio N. Robinson

The Progressive Practical Arithmetic

Reprint of the original, first published in 1864.

1st Edition 2022 | ISBN: 978-3-75259-326-6

Verlag (Publisher): Salzwasser Verlag GmbH, Zeilweg 44, 60439 Frankfurt, Deutschland
Vertretungsberechtigt (Authorized to represent): E. Roepke, Zeilweg 44, 60439 Frankfurt, Deutschland
Druck (Print): Books on Demand GmbH, In de Tarpen 42, 22848 Norderstedt, Deutschland

THE

PROGRESSIVE

PRACTICAL ARITHMETIC,

CONTAINING

THE THEORY OF NUMBERS, IN CONNECTION WITH CONCISE ANALYTIC AND SYNTHETIC METHODS OF SOLUTION, AND DESIGNED AS A COMPLETE TEXT-BOOK ON THIS SCIENCE,

FOR

COMMON SCHOOLS AND ACADEMIES.

BY

DANIEL W. FISH, A.M.

CHICAGO:

1864.

PREFACE.

PROGRESS and improvement characterize almost every art and science; and within the last few years the science of Arithmetic has received many important additions and improvements, which have appeared from time to time successively in the different treatises published upon this subject.

In the preparation of this work it has been the author's aim to combine, and to present in one harmonious whole, all these modern improvements, as well as to introduce some new methods and practical operations not found in other works of the same grade; in short, to present the subject of Arithmetic to the pupil more as a science than an art; to teach him *methods of thought*, and how to *reason*, rather than *what to do*; to give unity, system, and practical utility to the science and art of computation.

The author believes that both teacher and pupil should have the privilege, as well as the benefit, of performing at least a part of the *thinking* and the *labor* necessary to the study of Arithmetic; hence the present work has not been encumbered with the multiplicity of "notes," "suggestions," and superfluous operations so common to most Practical Arithmetics of the present day, and which prevent the cultivation of that self-reliance, that clearness of thought, and that vigor of intellect, which always characterize the truly educated mind.

The author claims for this treatise improvement upon, if not superiority over, others of the kind in the following particulars, viz.: *In the mechanical and typographical style of the work; the open and attractive page; the progressive and scientific arrangement of the subjects; clearness and conciseness of definitions; fullness and accuracy in the new and improved methods of operations and analyses; brevity and perspicuity of rules; and in the very large number of examples prepared and arranged with special reference to their practical utility, and their adaptation to the real business of active life.* The answers to a part of the examples have been omitted, that the learner may acquire the discipline resulting from verifying the operations.

Particular attention is invited to improvements in the subjects of Common Divisors, Multiples, Fractions, Percentage, Interest, Proportion, Analysis, Alligation, and the Roots, as it is believed these articles contain some practical features not common to other authors upon these subjects.

It is not claimed that this is a perfect work, for perfection is impossible; but no effort has been spared to present a clear, scientific, comprehensive, and complete system, sufficiently full for the business man and the scholar; not encumbered with unnecessary theories, and yet combining and systematizing real improvements of a practical and useful nature. How nearly this end has been attained the intelligent and experienced teacher and educator must determine.

CONTENTS.

SIMPLE NUMBERS.

COMMON FRACTIONS.

DECIMALS.

DECIMAL CURRENCY.

COMPOUND NUMBERS.

PERCENTAGE.

RATIO AND PROPORTION.

PRACTICAL ARITHMETIC.

DEFINITIONS.

1. **Quantity** is any thing that can be increased, diminished, or measured.

2. **Mathematics** is the science of quantity.

3. A **Unit** is one, or a single thing.

4. A **Number** is a unit, or a collection of units.

5. An **Integer** is a whole number.

6. The **Unit of a Number** is *one* of the same kind or name as the number. Thus, the unit of 23 is 1; of 23 dollars, 1 dollar; of 23 feet, 1 foot.

7. **Like Numbers** have the same kind of unit. Thus, 74, 16, and 250; 7 dollars and 62 dollars; 19 pounds, 320 pounds, and 86 pounds; 4 feet 6 inches, and 17 feet 9 inches.

8. An **Abstract Number** is a number used without reference to any particular thing or quantity. Thus, 17; 365; 8540.

9. A **Concrete Number** is a number used with reference to some particular thing or quantity. Thus, 17 dollars; 365 days; 8540 men.

NOTES. 1. The unit of an abstract number is 1, and is called *Unity*.

2. Concrete numbers are, by some, called *Denominate Numbers*. *Denomination* means the name of the unit of a concrete number.

10. **Arithmetic** is the *Science* of numbers, and the *Art* of computation.

11. A **Sign** is a character indicating an operation to be performed.

12. A **Rule** is a prescribed method of performing an operation.

Define quantity. Mathematics. A unit. A number. An integer. The unit of a number. Like numbers. An abstract number. A concrete number. The unit of an abstract number. Denominate numbers. Arithmetic. A sign, or symbol. A rule.

NOTATION AND NUMERATION.

13. **Notation** is a method of *writing* or expressing numbers by characters; and,

14. **Numeration** is a method of *reading* numbers expressed by characters.

15. Two systems of notation are in general use — the *Roman* and the *Arabic*.

NOTE. The Roman Notation is supposed to have been first used by the Romans; hence its name. The Arabic Notation was introduced into Europe by the Arabs, by whom it was supposed to have been invented. But investigations have shown that it was adopted by them about 600 years ago, and that it has been in use among the Hindoos more than 2000 years. From this latter fact it is sometimes called the *Indian Notation.*

THE ROMAN NOTATION

16. Employs seven capital letters to express numbers, thus:

Letters,	I	V	X	L	C	D	M
Values,	one,	five,	ten,	fifty,	one hundred,	five hundred,	one thousand.

17. The Roman notation is founded upon five principles, as follows:

1st. Repeating a letter repeats its value. Thus, II represents two, XX twenty, CCC three hundred.

2d. If a letter of any value be placed *after* one of greater value, its value is to be *united to* that of the greater. Thus, XI represents eleven, LX sixty, DC six hundred.

3d. If a letter of any value be placed *before* one of greater value, its value is to be *taken from* that of the greater. Thus, IX represents nine, XL forty, CD four hundred.

Define notation. Numeration. What systems of notation are now in general use? From what are their names derived? What are used to express numbers in the Roman notation? What is the value of each? What is the first principle of combination? Second? Third?

4th. If a letter of any value be placed *between* two letters, each of greater value, its value is to be *taken from* the *united value* of the other two. Thus, XIV represents fourteen, XXIX twenty-nine, XCIV ninety-four.

5th. A bar or dash placed over a letter increases its value one thousand fold. Thus, V signifies five, and $\overline{\text{V}}$ five thousand; L fifty, and $\overline{\text{L}}$ fifty thousand.

TABLE OF ROMAN NOTATION.

I	is	One.	XX	is	Twenty.
II	"	Two.	XXI	"	Twenty-one.
III	"	Three.	XXX	"	Thirty.
IV	"	Four.	XL	"	Forty.
V	"	Five.	L	"	Fifty.
VI	"	Six.	LX	"	Sixty.
VII	"	Seven.	LXX	"	Seventy.
VIII	"	Eight.	LXXX	"	Eighty.
IX	"	Nine.	XC	"	Ninety.
X	"	Ten.	C	"	One hundred.
XI	"	Eleven.	CC	"	Two hundred.
XII	"	Twelve.	D	"	Five hundred.
XIII	"	Thirteen.	DC	"	Six hundred.
XIV	"	Fourteen.	M	"	One thousand.
XV	"	Fifteen.	MC	"	One thousand one hundred.
XVI	"	Sixteen.	MM	"	Two thousand.
XVII	"	Seventeen.	$\overline{\text{X}}$	"	Ten thousand.
XVIII	"	Eighteen.	$\overline{\text{C}}$	"	One hundred thousand.
XIX	"	Nineteen.	$\overline{\text{M}}$	"	One million.

NOTE. The system of Roman notation is not well adapted to the purposes of numerical calculation; it is principally confined to the numbering of chapters and sections of books, public documents, &c.

Express the following numbers by letters:

1. Eleven. *Ans.* XI.
2. Fifteen. *Ans.*

Fourth? Fifth? Repeat the table. What is the value of LVII? CLXXIII? XCVIII? CDXXXII? XCIX? DCXIX? $\overline{\text{V}}$MDCCXLIX? MD$\overline{\text{XXV}}$CDLXXXIX? To what uses is the Roman notation now principally confined?

3. Twenty-five.
4. Thirty-nine.
5. Forty-eight.
6. Seventy-seven.
7. One hundred fifty-nine.
8. Five hundred ninety-four.
9. One thousand five hundred thirty-eight.
10. One thousand nine hundred ten.
11. Express the present year.

THE ARABIC NOTATION

18. Employs ten characters or figures to express numbers. Thus,

Figures,	0	1	2	3	4	5	6	7	8	9
Names and values,	naught or cipher,	one,	two,	three,	four,	five,	six,	seven,	eight,	nine.

19. The first character is called *naught,* because it has no value of its own. The other nine characters are called *significant figures,* because each has a value of its own.

20. The significant figures are also called *Digits,* a word derived from the Latin term *digitus,* which signifies *finger.*

21. The naught or cipher is also called *nothing,* and *zero.*

The ten Arabic characters are the Alphabet of Arithmetic, and by combining them according to certain principles, all numbers can be expressed. We will now examine the most important of these principles.*

22. Each of the nine digits has a value of its own; hence any number not greater than 9 can be expressed by one figure.

* Fractional and decimal notation, and the notation of compound numbers, will be discussed in their appropriate places.

What are used to express numbers in the Arabic notation? What is the value of each? What general name is given to the significant figures? Why? Numbers less than ten, how expressed?

23. As we have no single character to represent ten, we express it by writing the unit, 1, at the left of the cipher, 0, thus, 10. In the same manner we represent

2 tens, or twenty, 20;	3 tens, or thirty, 30;	4 tens, or forty, 40;	5 tens, or fifty, 50;	6 tens, or sixty, 60;	7 tens, or seventy, 70;	8 tens, or eighty, 80;	9 tens, or ninety, 90.

24. When a number is expressed by two figures, the right hand figure is called *units*, and the left hand figure *tens*.

We express the numbers between 10 and 20 by writing the 1 in the place of tens, with each of the digits respectively in the place of units. Thus,

eleven,	twelve,	thirteen,	fourteen,	fifteen,	sixteen,	seventeen,	eighteen,	nineteen.
11,	12,	13,	14,	15,	16,	17,	18,	19.

In like manner we express the numbers between 20 and 30, between 30 and 40, and between any two successive tens. Thus, 21, 22, 23, 24, 25, 26, 27, 28, 29, 34, 47, 56, 72, 93. The greatest number that can be expressed by *two* figures is 99.

25. We express one hundred by writing the unit, 1, at the left hand of two ciphers, or the number 10 at the left hand of one cipher; thus, 100. In like manner we write two hundred, three hundred, &c., to nine hundred. Thus,

one hundred,	two hundred,	three hundred,	four hundred,	five hundred,	six hundred,	seven hundred,	eight hundred,	nine hundred,
100,	200,	300,	400,	500,	600,	700,	800,	900.

26. When a number is expressed by three figures, the right hand figure is called *units*, the second figure *tens*, and the left hand figure *hundreds*.

As the ciphers have, of themselves, no value, but are always used to denote the absence of value in the places they occupy,

---

Tens, how expressed? The right hand figure called what? Left hand figure, what? What is the greatest number that can be expressed by two figures? One hundred, how expressed? When numbers are expressed by three figures, what names are given to each?

we express tens and units with hundreds, by writing, in place of the ciphers, the numbers representing the tens and units. To express one hundred fifty we write 1 hundred, 5 tens, and 0 units; thus, 150. To express seven hundred ninety-two, we write 7 hundreds, 9 tens, and 2 units; thus,

hundreds.	tens.	units.
7	9	2

The greatest number that can be expressed by *three* figures is 999.

EXAMPLES FOR PRACTICE.

1. Write one hundred twenty-five.
2. Write four hundred eighty-three.
3. Write seven hundred sixteen.
4. Express by figures nine hundred.
5. Express by figures two hundred ninety.
6. Write eight hundred nine.
7. Write five hundred five.
8. Write five hundred fifty-seven.

27. We express one thousand by writing the unit, 1, at the left hand of three ciphers, the number 10 at the left hand of two ciphers, or the number 100 at the left hand of one cipher; thus, 1000. In the same manner we write two thousand, three thousand, &c., to nine thousand; thus,

one thousand,	two thousand,	three thousand,	four thousand,	five thousand,	six thousand,	seven thousand,	eight thousand,	nine thousand,
1000,	2000,	3000,	4000,	5000,	6000,	7000,	8000,	9000.

28. When a number is expressed by four figures, the places, commencing at the right hand, are *units, tens, hundreds, thousands.*

Use of the cipher, what? Greatest number that can be expressed by three figures? One thousand, how expressed? How many figures used? Names of each?

To express hundreds, tens, and units with thousands, we write in each place the figure indicating the number we wish to express in that place. To write four thousand two hundred sixty-nine, we write 4 in the place of thousands, 2 in the place of hundreds, 6 in the place of tens, and 9 in the place of units; thus,

thousands.	hundreds.	tens.	units.
4	2	6	9

The greatest number that can be expressed by *four* figures is 9999.

EXAMPLES FOR PRACTICE.

Express the following numbers by figures: —

1. One thousand two hundred.
2. Five thousand one hundred sixty.
3. Three thousand seven hundred forty-one.
4. Eight thousand fifty-six.
5. Two thousand ninety.
6. Seven thousand nine.
7. One thousand one.
8. Nine thousand four hundred twenty-seven.
9. Four thousand thirty-five.
10. One thousand nine hundred four.

Read the following numbers: —

11. 76; 128; 405; 910; 116; 3416; 1025.
12. 2100; 5047; 7009; 4670; 3997; 1001.

29. Next to thousands come *tens* of thousands, and next to these come *hundreds* of thousands, as tens and hundreds come in their order after units. Ten thousand is expressed by removing the unit, 1, one place to the left of the place

---

Greatest number expressed by four figures? Tens of thousands, how expressed? Hundreds of thousands?

of thousands, or by writing it at the left hand of four ciphers; thus, 10000; and one hundred thousand is expressed by removing the unit, 1, still one place further to the left, or by writing it at the left hand of five ciphers; thus, 100000. We can express thousands, tens of thousands, and hundreds of thousands in one number, in the same manner as we express units, tens, and hundreds in one number. To express five hundred twenty-one thousand eight hundred three, we write 5 in the sixth place, counting from units, 2 in the fifth place, 1 in the fourth place, 8 in the third place, 0 in the second place, (because there are no tens,) and 3 in the place of units; thus,

hundreds of thousands.	tens of thousands.	thousands.	hundreds.	tens.	units.
5	2	1	8	0	3

The greatest number that can be expressed by five figures is 99999; and by six figures, 999999.

EXAMPLES FOR PRACTICE.

Write the following numbers in figures: —

1. Twenty thousand.
2. Forty-seven thousand.
3. Eighteen thousand one hundred.
4. Twelve thousand three hundred fifty.
5. Thirty-nine thousand five hundred twenty-two.
6. Fifteen thousand two hundred six.
7. Eleven thousand twenty-four.
8. Forty thousand ten.
9. Sixty thousand six hundred.
10. Two hundred twenty thousand.
11. One hundred fifty-six thousand.
12. Eight hundred forty thousand three hundred.

Greatest number expressed by five figures? Six figures?

13. Five hundred one thousand nine hundred sixty-four.

14. One hundred thousand one hundred.

15. Three hundred thirteen thousand three hundred thirteen.

16. Seven hundred eighteen thousand four.

17. One hundred thousand ten.

Read the following numbers:—

18.	5006;	12304;	96071;	5470;	203410.
19.	36741;	400560;	13061;	49000;	100010.
20.	200200;	75620;	90402;	218094;	100101.

For convenience in reading large numbers, we may point them off, by commas, into periods of three figures each, counting from the right hand or unit figure. This pointing enables us to read the hundreds, tens, and units in each period with facility.

30. Next above hundreds of thousands we have, successively, units, tens, and hundreds of millions, and then follow units, tens, and hundreds of each higher name, as seen in the following

NUMERATION TABLE.

of septillions.	of sextillions.	of quintillions.	of quadrillions.	of trillions.	of billions.	of millions.	of thousands.	of units.
tens units	hundreds tens units	hundreds tens units	hundreds tens units	hundreds tens units	hundreds tens units	hundreds tens units	hundreds tens units	hundreds tens units
9 8,	7 6 5,	4 3 2,	1 0 9,	8 7 6,	5 5 6,	7 8 9,	0 1 2,	3 4 5
ninth period.	eighth period.	seventh period.	sixth period.	fifth period.	fourth period.	third period.	second period.	first period.

How may figures be pointed off? One million, how expressed? Next period above millions, what? Give the name of each successive period.

NOTE. This is called the French method of pointing off the periods, and is the one in general use in this country.

31. Figures occupying different places in a number, as units, tens, hundreds, &c., are said to express different orders of units.

Simple units	are	called	units	of	the	*first*	order.
Tens	"	"	"	"	"	*second*	"
Hundreds	"	"	"	"	"	*third*	"
Thousands	"	"	"	"	"	*fourth*	"
Tens of thousands	"	"	"	"	"	*fifth*	"

and so on. Thus, 452 contains 4 units of the third order, 5 units of the second order, and 2 units of the first order. 1,030,600 contains 1 unit of the seventh order, (millions,) 3 units of the fifth order, (tens of thousands,) and 6 units of the third order, (hundreds.)

EXAMPLES FOR PRACTICE.

Write and read the following numbers:—

1. One unit of the third order, four of the second.
2. Three units of the fifth order, two of the third, one of the first.
3. Eight units of the fourth order, five of the second.
4. Two units of the seventh order, nine of the sixth, four of the third, one of the second, seven of the first.
5. Three units of the sixth order, four of the second.
6. Nine units of the eighth order, six of the seventh, three of the fifth, seven of the fourth, nine of the first.
7. Four units of the tenth order, six of the eighth, four of the seventh, two of the sixth, one of the third, five of the second.
8. Eight units of the twelfth order, four of the eleventh, six of the tenth, nine of the seventh, three of the sixth, five of the fifth, two of the third, eight of the first.

Units of different orders are what?

32. From the foregoing explanations and illustrations, we derive several important principles, which we will now present.

1st. Figures have two values, Simple and Local.

The **Simple Value** of a figure is its value when taken alone; thus, 2, 5, 8.

The **Local Value** of a figure is its value when used with another figure or figures in the same number; thus, in 842 the simple values of the several figures are 8, 4, and 2; but the local value of the 8 is 800; of the 4 is 4 tens, or 40; and of the 2 is 2 units.

NOTE. When a figure occupies units' place, its simple and local values are the same.

2d. A digit or figure, if used in the second place, expresses tens; in the third place, hundreds; in the fourth place, thousands; and so on.

3d. As 10 units make 1 ten, 10 tens 1 hundred, 10 hundreds 1 thousand, and 10 units of any order, or in any place, make one unit of the next higher order, or in the next place at the left, we readily see that the Arabic method of notation is based upon the following

TWO GENERAL LAWS.

I. *The different orders of units increase from right to left, and decrease from left to right, in a tenfold ratio.*

II. *Every removal of a figure one place to the left, increases its local value tenfold; and every removal of a figure one place to the right, diminishes its local value tenfold.*

Thus,

6 is 6 units.
60 is 10 times 6 units.
600 is 10 times 6 tens.
6000 is 10 times 6 hundreds.
60000 is 10 times 6 thousands.

First principle derived? What is the simple value of a figure? Local? Second principle? Third? First law of Arabic notation? Second?

4th. The local value of a figure depends upon its place from units of the first order, not upon the value of the figures at the right of it. Thus, in 425 and 400, the value of the 4 is the same in both numbers, being 4 units of the third order, or 4 hundred.

NOTE. Care should be taken not to mistake the local value of a figure for the value of the whole number. For, although the value of the 4 (hundreds) is the same in the two numbers, 425 and 400, the value of the whole of the first number is greater than that of the second.

5th. Every period contains three figures, (units, tens, and hundreds,) except the left hand period, which sometimes contains only one or two figures, (units, or units and tens.)

33. As we have now analyzed all the principles upon which the writing and reading of whole numbers depend, we will present these principles in the form of rules.

RULE FOR NOTATION.

I. *Beginning at the left hand, write the figures belonging to the highest period.*

II. *Write the hundreds, tens, and units of each successive period in their order, placing a cipher wherever an order of units is omitted.*

RULE FOR NUMERATION.

I. *Separate the number into periods of three figures each, commencing at the right hand.*

II. *Beginning at the left hand, read each period separately, and give the name to each period, except the last, or period of units.*

34. Until the pupil can write numbers readily, it may be well for him to write several periods of ciphers, point them off, over each period write its name, thus,

Trillions,	Billions,	Millions,	Thousands,	Units.
000,	000,	000,	000,	000

Fourth principle? What caution is given? Fifth principle? Rule for notation? Numeration?

and then write the given numbers underneath, in their appropriate places.

EXERCISES IN NOTATION AND NUMERATION.

Express the following numbers by figures: —

1. Four hundred thirty-six.
2. Seven thousand one hundred sixty-four.
3. Twenty-six thousand twenty-six.
4. Fourteen thousand two hundred eighty.
5. One hundred seventy-six thousand.
6. Four hundred fifty thousand thirty-nine.
7. Ninety-five million.
8. Four hundred thirty-three million eight hundred sixteen thousand one hundred forty-nine.
9. Nine hundred thousand ninety.
10. Ten million ten thousand ten hundred ten.
11. Sixty-one billion five million.
12. Five trillion eighty billion nine million one.

Point off, numerate, and read the following numbers: —

13.	8240.	17.	1010.	21.	370005.
14.	400900.	18.	57468139.	22.	9400706342.
15.	308.	19.	5628.	23.	38429526.
16.	60720.	20.	850026800.	24.	74268113759.

25. Write seven million thirty-six.
26. Write five hundred sixty-three thousand four.
27. Write one million ninety-six thousand.
28. Numerate and read 9004082501.
29. Numerate and read 2584503962047.
30. A certain number contains 3 units of the seventh order, 6 of the fifth, 4 of the fourth, 1 of the third, 5 of the second, and 2 of the first; what is the number?
31. What orders of units are contained in the number 290648?
32. What orders of units are contained in the number 1037050?

ADDITION.

MENTAL EXERCISES.

35. 1. Henry gave 5 dollars for a vest, and 7 dollars for a coat; how much did he pay for both?

ANALYSIS. He gave as many dollars as 5 dollars and 7 dollars, which are 12 dollars. Therefore he paid 12 dollars for both.

2. A farmer sold a pig for 3 dollars, and a calf for 8 dollars; how much did he receive for both?

3. A drover bought 5 sheep of one man, 9 of another, and 3 of another; how many did he buy in all?

4. How many are 2 and 6? 2 and 7? 2 and 9? 2 and 8? 2 and 10?

5. How many are 4 and 5? 4 and 8? 4 and 7? 4 and 9?

6. How many are 6 and 4? 6 and 6? 6 and 9? 6 and 7?

7. How many are 7 and 7? 7 and 6? 7 and 8? 7 and 10? 7 and 9?

8. How many are 5 and 4 and 6? 7 and 3 and 8? 6 and 9 and 5?

36. From the preceding operations we perceive that

Addition is the process of uniting *several* numbers of the same kind into *one* equivalent number.

37. The **Sum** or **Amount** is the result obtained by the process of addition.

38. The sign, $+$, is called *plus*, which signifies *more*. When placed between two numbers, it denotes that they are to be added; thus, $6 + 4$, shows that 6 and 4 are to be added.

39. The sign, $=$, is called the sign of *equality*. When placed between two numbers, or sets of numbers, it signifies that they are equal to each other; thus, the expression $6 + 4 = 10$, is read 6 *plus* 4 is *equal to* 10, and denotes that the numbers 6 and 4, taken together, equal the number 10.

Define addition. The sum or amount? Sign of addition? Of equality?

CASE I.

40. When the amount of each column is less than 10.

1. A farmer sold some hay for 102 dollars, six cows for 162 dollars, and a horse for 125 dollars; how much did he receive for all?

OPERATION.

	hunds. tens. units.
	102
	162
	125
Amount,	389

ANALYSIS. We arrange the numbers so that units of like order shall stand in the same column. We then add the columns separately, for convenience commencing at the right hand, and write each result under the column added. Thus, we have 5 and 2 and 2 are 9, the sum of the units; 2 and 6 are 8, the sum of the tens; 1 and 1 and 1 are 3, the sum of the hundreds. Hence, the entire amount is 3 hundreds 8 tens and 9 units, or 389, the Answer.

EXAMPLES FOR PRACTICE.

	(2.)	(3.)	(4.)	(5.)
	pounds.	rods.	cents.	days.
	132	245	312	437
	243	321	243	140
	324	132	412	321
Ans.	699			

6. What is the sum of 144, 321, and 232? *Ans.* 697.
7. What is the amount of 122, 333, and 401? *Ans.* 856.
8. What is the sum of 42, 103, 321, and 32? *Ans.* 498.
9. A drover bought three droves of sheep. The first contained 230, the second 425, and the third 340; how many sheep did he buy in all? *Ans.* 995.

CASE II.

41. When the amount of any column equals or exceeds 10.

1. A merchant pays 725 dollars a year for the rent of a

Case I is what? Give explanation. Case II is what?

store, 475 dollars for a clerk, and 367 dollars for other expenses; what is the amount of his expenses?

OPERATION.

	hunds. tens. units.
	725
	475
	367
Sum of the units,	17
Sum of the tens,	15
Sum of the hundreds,	14
Total amount,	1567

ANALYSIS. Arranging the numbers as in Case I, we first add the column of units, and find the sum to be 17 units, which is 1 ten and 7 units. We write the 7 units in the place of units, and the 1 ten in the place of tens. The sum of the figures in the column of tens is 15 tens, which is 1 hundred, and 5 tens. We write the 5 tens in the place of tens, and the 1 hundred in the place of hundreds. We next add the column of hundreds, and find the sum to be 14 hundreds, which is 1 thousand and 4 hundreds. We write the 4 hundreds in the place of hundreds, and 1 thousand in the place of thousands. Lastly, by uniting the sum of the units with the sums of the tens and hundreds, we find the total amount to be 1 thousand 5 hundreds 6 tens and 7 units, or 1567.

This example may be performed by another method, which is the common one in practice. Thus:

OPERATION.

```
 725
 475
 367
----
1567
```

ANALYSIS. Arranging the numbers as before, we add the first column and find the sum to be 17 units; writing the 7 units under the column of units, we add the 1 ten to the column of tens, and find the sum to be 16 tens; writing the 6 tens under the column tens, we add the 1 hundred to the column of hundreds, and find the sum to be 15 hundreds; as this is the last column, we write down its amount, 15; and we have the *whole amount*, 1567, as before.

NOTES. 1. Units of the same order are written in the same column; and when the sum in any column is 10 or more than 10, it produces *one or more units* of a higher order, which must be added to the next column. This process is sometimes called "carrying the tens."

2. In adding, learn to pronounce the partial results without naming the numbers separately; thus, instead of saying 7 and 5 are 12, and 5 are 17, simply pronounce the results, 7, 12, 17, &c.

Give explanation. Second explanation. What is meant by carrying the tens?

42. From the preceding examples and illustrations we deduce the following

RULE. I. *Write the numbers to be added so that all the units of the same order shall stand in the same column; that is, units under units, tens under tens, &c.*

II. *Commencing at units, add each column separately, and write the sum underneath, if it be less than ten.*

III. *If the sum of any column be ten or more than ten, write the unit figure only, and add the ten or tens to the next column.*

IV. *Write the entire sum of the last column.*

PROOF. 1st. Begin with the right hand or unit column, and add the figures in each column in an opposite direction from that in which they were first added; if the two results agree, the work is supposed to be right. Or,

2d. Separate the numbers added into two sets, by a horizontal line; find the sum of each set separately; add these sums, and if the amount be the same as that first obtained, the work is presumed to be correct.

NOTE. By the methods of proof here given, the numbers are united in new combinations, which render it almost impossible for two precisely similar mistakes to occur.
The first method is the one commonly used in business.

EXAMPLES FOR PRACTICE.

(2.)	(3.)	(4.)	(5.)	(6.)
miles.	inches.	tons.	feet.	bushels.
24	321	427	1342	3420
48	479	321	7306	7021
96	165	903	5254	327
82	327	278	8629	97
250	1292	1929	22531	10865

Rule, first step? Second? Third? Fourth? Proof, first method? Second? Upon what principle are these methods of proof founded?

(7.)	(8.)	(9.)	(10.)
hours.	years.	gallons.	rods.
347	7104	3462	47637
506	3762	863	3418
218	9325	479	703
312	4316	84	26471
424	2739	57	84

11. $42 + 64 + 98 + 70 + 37 =$ how many? *Ans.* 311.

12. $312 + 425 + 107 + 391 + 76 =$ how many? *Ans.* 1311.

13. $1476 + 375 + 891 + 66 + 80 =$ how many? *Ans.* 2888.

14. $37042 + 1379 + 809 + 127 + 40 =$ how many? *Ans.* 39397.

15. What is the sum of one thousand six hundred fifty-six, eight hundred nine, three hundred ten, and ninety-four? *Ans.* 2869.

16. Add forty-two thousand two hundred twenty, ten thousand one hundred five, four thousand seventy-five, and five hundred seven. *Ans.* 56907.

17. Add two hundred ten thousand four hundred, one hundred thousand five hundred ten, ninety thousand six hundred eleven, forty-two hundred twenty-five, and eight hundred ten. *Ans.* 406556.

18. What is the sum of the following numbers: seventy-five, one thousand ninety-five, six thousand four hundred thirty-five, two hundred sixty-seven thousand, one thousand four hundred fifty-five, twenty-seven million eighteen, two hundred seventy million twenty-seven thousand? *Ans.* 297303078.

19. A man on a journey traveled the first day 37 miles, the second 33 miles, the third 40 miles, and the fourth 35 miles; how far did he travel in the four days?

20. A wine merchant has in one cask 75 gallons, in another 65, in a third 57, in a fourth 83, in a fifth 74, and in a sixth 67; how many gallons has he in all? *Ans.* 421.

21. An estate is to be shared equally by four heirs, and the portion to each heir is to be 3754 dollars; what is the amount of the estate? *Ans.* 15016 dollars.

22. How many men in an army consisting of 52714 infantry, 5110 cavalry, 6250 dragoons, 3927 light-horse, 928 artillery, 250 sappers, and 406 miners?

23. A merchant deposited 56 dollars in a bank on Monday, 74 on Tuesday, 120 on Wednesday, 96 on Thursday, 170 on Friday, and 50 on Saturday; how much did he deposit during the week?

24. A merchant bought at public sale 746 yards of broadcloth, 650 yards of muslin, 2100 yards of flannel, and 250 yards of silk; how many yards in all?

25. Five persons deposited money in the same bank; the first, 5897 dollars; the second, 12980 dollars; the third, 65973 dollars; the fourth, 37345 dollars; and the fifth as much as the first and second together; how many dollars did they all deposit? *Ans.* 141072 dollars.

26. A man willed his estate to his wife, two sons, and four daughters; to his daughters he gave 2630 dollars apiece, to his sons, each 4647 dollars, and to his wife 3595 dollars; how much was his estate? *Ans.* 23409 dollars.

(27.)	(28.)	(29.)	(30.)	(31.)
476	908	126	443	180
390	371	324	298	976
915	569	503	876	209
207	245	891	569	314
841	703	736	137	563
632	421	517	910	842
234	127	143	347	175
143	354	274	256	224
536	781	531	324	135
245	436	275	463	253

32. A man commenced farming at the west, and raised, the first year, 724 bushels of corn; the second year, 3498 bushels; the third year, 9872 bushels; the fourth year, 9964 bushels; the fifth year, 11078 bushels; how many bushels did he raise in the five years? *Ans.* 35136 bushels.

33. A has 3648 dollars, B has 7035 dollars, C has 429 dollars more than A and B together, and D has as many dollars as all the rest; how many dollars has D? How many have all? *Ans.* All have 43590 dollars.

34. A man bought three houses and lots for 15780 dollars, and sold them so as to gain 695 dollars on each lot; for how much did he sell them? *Ans.* 17865 dollars.

35. At the battle of Waterloo, which took place June 18th, 1815, the estimated loss of the French was 40000 men; of the Prussians, 38000; of the Belgians, 8000; of the Hanoverians, 3500; and of the English, 12000; what was the entire loss of life in this battle?

36. The expenditures for educational purposes in New England for the year 1850 were as follows: Maine, 380623 dollars; New Hampshire, 221146 dollars; Vermont, 246604 dollars; Massachusetts, 1424873 dollars; Rhode Island, 136729 dollars; and Connecticut, 430826 dollars; what was the total expenditure? *Ans.* 2840801 dollars.

37. The eastern continent contains 31000000 square miles; the western continent, 13750000; Australia, Greenland, and other islands, 5250000; what is the entire area of the land surface of the globe?

38. The population of New York, in 1850, was 515547; Boston, 136881; Philadelphia, 340045; Chicago, 29963; St. Louis, 77860; New Orleans, 116375; what was the entire population of these cities? *Ans.* 1216671.

39. The population of the globe is estimated as follows: North America, 39257819; South America, 18373188; Europe, 265368216; Asia, 630671661; Africa, 61688779; Oceanica, 23444082; what is the total population of the globe according to this estimate? *Ans.* 1038803745.

40. The railroad distance from New York to Albany is 144 miles; from Albany to Buffalo, 298; from Buffalo to Cleveland, 183; from Cleveland to Toledo, 109; from Toledo to Springfield, 365; and from Springfield to St. Louis, 95 miles; what is the distance from New York to St. Louis?

41. A man owns farms valued at 56800 dollars; city lots valued at 86760 dollars; a house worth 12500 dollars, and other property to the amount of 6785 dollars; what is the entire value of his property? *Ans.* 162845 dollars.

(42.)	(43.)	(44.)	(45.)
15038	26881	41919	93808
7404	12173	19577	41371
34971	39665	74736	110525
30359	33249	66768	102936
6293	6318	12673	17087
2875	4318	7193	13251
16660	34705	51365	112110
64934	80597	155497	220619
80901	95299	183134	225255
7444	8624	16845	68940
57068	53806	111139	176974
17255	18647	35902	86590
32543	41609	82182	149162
40022	35077	75153	109355
56063	46880	132936	283910
33860	41842	82939	112511
17548	26876	44424	72908
28944	36642	65586	157672
16147	29997	52839	86160
38556	44305	83211	119557
234882	262083	522294	839398
39058	39744	78861	117787
152526	169220	353428	471842
179122	198568	386214	571778
7626	8735	17005	41735
1218099	1395860		

SUBTRACTION.

MENTAL EXERCISES.

43. 1. A farmer, having 14 cows, sold 6 of them; how many had he left?

ANALYSIS. He had as many left as 14 cows less 6 cows, which are 8 cows. Therefore, he had 8 cows left.

2. Stephen, having 9 marbles, lost 4 of them; how many had he left?

3. If a man earn 10 dollars a week, and spend 6 dollars for provisions, how many dollars has he left?

4. A merchant, having 16 barrels of flour, sells 9 of them; how many has he left?

5. Charles had 18 cents, and gave 10 of them for a book; how many had he left?

6. James is 17 years old, and his sister Julia, is 5 years younger; how old is Julia?

7. A grocer, having 20 boxes of lemons, sold 11 boxes; how many boxes had he left?

8. From a cistern containing 25 barrels of water, 15 barrels leaked out; how many barrels remained?

9. Paid 16 dollars for a coat, and 7 dollars for a vest; how much more did the coat cost than the vest?

10. How many are 18 less 5? 17 less 8? 12 less 7?

11. How many are 20 less 14? 18 less 12? 19 less 11?

12. How many are 11 less 3? 16 less 11? 19 less 8? 20 less 9? 22 less 20?

44. Subtraction is the process of determining the difference, between two numbers of the same unit value.

45. The **Minuend** is the number to be subtracted from.

46. The **Subtrahend** is the number to be subtracted.

Define subtraction. Minuend. Subtrahend.

47. The **Difference** or **Remainder** is the result obtained by the process of subtraction.

NOTE. The minuend and subtrahend must be *like numbers*; thus, 5 dollars from 9 dollars leave 4 dollars; 5 apples from 9 apples leave 4 apples; but it would be absurd to say 5 apples from 9 dollars, or 5 dollars from 9 apples.

48. The sign, —, is called *minus*, which signifies *less*. When placed between two numbers, it denotes that the one after it is to be taken from the one before it. Thus, $8 - 6 = 2$ is read 8 minus 6 equals 2, and denotes that 6, the *subtrahend*, taken from 8, the *minuend*, equals 2, the *remainder*.

CASE I.

49. When no figure in the subtrahend is greater than the corresponding figure in the minuend.

1. From 574 take 323.

OPERATION.	
Minuend,	574
Subtrahend,	323
Remainder,	251

ANALYSIS. We write the less number under the greater, with units under units, tens under tens, &c., and draw a line underneath. Then, beginning at the right hand, we subtract separately each figure of the subtrahend from the figure above it in the minuend. Thus, 3 from 4 leaves 1, which is the difference of the units; 2 from 7 leaves 5, the difference of the tens; 3 from 5 leaves 2, the difference of the hundreds. Hence, we have for the whole difference, 2 hundreds 5 tens and 1 unit, or 251.

EXAMPLES FOR PRACTICE.

	(2.)	(3.)	(4.)	(5.)
Minuend,	876	676	367	925
Subtrahend,	334	415	152	213
Remainder,	542	261	215	712

Case I is what? Give explanation.

	(6.)	(7.)	(8.)	(9.)
From	876	732	987	498
Take	523	522	782	178

	Remainders.
10. From 3276 take 2143.	1133.
11. From 7634 take 3132.	4502.
12. From 41763 take 11521.	30242.
13. From 18346 take 5215.	13131.
14. From 397631 take 175321.	222310.
15. Subtract 47321 from 69524.	22203.
16. Subtract 16330 from 48673.	32343.
17. Subtract 291352 from 895752.	604400.
18. Subtract 84321 from 397562.	313241.

19. A farmer paid 645 dollars for a span of horses and a carriage, and sold them for 522 dollars; how much did he lose?

20. A man bought a mill for 3724 dollars, and sold it for 4856 dollars; how much did he gain? *Ans.* 1132 dollars.

21. A drover bought 1566 sheep, and sold 435 of them; how many had he left? *Ans.* 1131 sheep.

22. A piece of land was sold for 2945 dollars, which was 832 dollars more than it cost; what did it cost?

23. A gentleman willed to his son 15768 dollars, and to his daughter 4537 dollars; how much more did he will to the son than to the daughter? *Ans.* 11231 dollars.

24. A merchant sold goods to the amount of 6742 dollars, and by so doing gained 2540 dollars; what did the goods cost him?

25. If I borrow 15475 dollars of a person, and pay him 4050 dollars, how much do I still owe him?

26. In 1850 the white population of the United States was 19,553,068, and the slave population 3,204,313; how much was the difference?

27. The population of Great Britain in 1851 was 20,936,468, and of England alone, 16,921,888; what was the difference?

CASE II.

50. When any figure in the subtrahend is greater than the corresponding figure in the minuend.

1. From 846 take 359.

OPERATION.

	(7)	(13)	(16)
Minuend,	8	4	6
Subtrahend,	3	5	9
Remainder,	4	8	7

ANALYSIS. In this example we cannot take 9 units from 6 units. From the 4 tens we take 1 ten, which equals 10 units, and add to the 6 units, making 16 units; 9 units from 16 units leave 7 units, which we write in the remainder in units' place. As we have taken 1 ten from the 4 tens, 3 tens only are left. We cannot take 5 tens from 3 tens; so from the 8 hundreds we take 1 hundred, which equals 10 tens, and add to the 3 tens, making 13 tens; 5 tens from 13 tens leave 8 tens, which we write in the remainder in tens' place. As we have taken 1 hundred from the 8 hundreds, 7 hundreds only are left; 3 hundreds from 7 hundreds leave 4 hundreds, which we write in the remainder in hundreds' place, and we have the whole remainder, 487.

NOTE. The numbers written over the minuend are used simply to explain more clearly the method of subtracting; in practice the process should be performed mentally, and these numbers omitted.

The following method is more in accordance with practice.

OPERATION.

hunds.	tens.	units.
8	4	6
3	5	9
4	8	7

ANALYSIS. Since we cannot take 9 units from 6 units, we add 10 units to 6 units, making 16 units; 9 units from 16 units leave 7 units. But as we have added 10 units, or 1 ten, to the minuend, we shall have a remainder 1 ten too large, to avoid which, we add 1 ten to the 5 tens in the subtrahend, making 6 tens. We can not take 6 tens from 4 tens; so we add 10 tens to 4, making 14 tens; 6 tens from 14 tens leave 8 tens. Now, having added 10 tens, or 1 hundred, to the minuend, we shall have a remainder 1 hundred too large, unless we add 1 hundred to the 3 hundreds in the subtrahend, making 4 hundreds; 4 hundreds from 8 hundreds leave 4 hundreds, and we have for the total remainder, 487, the same as before.

Case II is what? Give explanation. Second explanation.

NOTE. The process of adding 10 to the minuend is sometimes called *borrowing* 10, and that of adding 1 to the next figure of the subtrahend, *carrying* one.

51. From the preceding examples and illustrations we have the following general

RULE. I. *Write the less number under the greater, placing units of the same order in the same column.*

II. *Begin at the right hand, and take each figure of the subtrahend from the figure above it, and write the result underneath.*

III. *If any figure in the subtrahend be greater than the corresponding figure above it, add* 10 *to that upper figure before subtracting, and then add* 1 *to the next left hand figure of the subtrahend.*

PROOF. Add the remainder to the subtrahend, and if their sum be equal to the minuend, the work is supposed to be right.

EXAMPLES FOR PRACTICE.

	(2.)	(3.)	(4.)	(5.)
Minuend,	873	7432	1969	8146
Subtrahend,	538	6711	1408	4377
Remainder,	335			

	(6.)	(7.)	(8.)	(9.)
	gallons.	bushels.	miles.	days.
From	3176	9076	7320	5097
Take	2907	4567	3871	3809

	(10.)	(11.)	(12.)	(13.)
	dollars.	rods.	acres.	feet.
From	76377	67777	900076	767340
Take	45761	46699	899934	5039

What do we mean by borrowing 10? By carrying? Rule, first step? Second? Third? Proof?

14. 479 — 382 = how many? *Ans.* 97.
15. 6593 — 1807 = how many? *Ans.* 4786.
16. 17380 — 3417 = how many? *Ans.* 13963.
17. 80014 — 43190 = how many? *Ans.* 36824.
18. 282731 — 90756 = how many? *Ans.* 191975.
19. From 234100 take 9970.
20. From 345673 take 124799.
21. From 4367676 take 256569. *Ans.* 4111107.
22. From 3467310 take 987631. *Ans.* 2479679.
23. From 941000 take 5007. *Ans.* 935993.
24. From 1970000 take 1361111. *Ans.* 608889.
25. From 290017 take 108045.
26. Take 3077097 from 7045676. *Ans.* 3968579.
27. Take 9999999 from 60000000. *Ans.* 50000001.
28. Take 220202 from 4040053. *Ans.* 3819851.
29. Take 2199077 from 3000001. *Ans.* 800924.
30. Take 377776 from 8000800. *Ans.* 7623024.
31. Take 501300347 from 1030810040.
32. Subtract nineteen thousand nineteen from twenty thousand ten. *Ans.* 991.
33. From one million nine thousand six take twenty thousand four hundred. *Ans.* 988606.
34. What is the difference between two million seven thousand eighteen, and one hundred five thousand seventeen?

EXAMPLES COMBINING ADDITION AND SUBTRACTION.

52. 1. A merchant gave his note for 5200 dollars. He paid at one time 2500 dollars, and at another 175 dollars; what remained due? *Ans.* 2525 dollars.

2. A traveler who was 1300 miles from home, traveled homeward 235 miles in one week, in the next 275 miles, in the next 325 miles, and in the next 280 miles; how far had he still to go before he would reach home? *Ans.* 185 miles.

3. A man deposited in bank 8752 dollars; he drew out at one time 4234 dollars, at another 1700 dollars, at another 962

dollars, and at another 49 dollars; how much had he remaining in bank? *Ans.* 1807 dollars.

4. A man bought a farm for 4765 dollars, and paid 750 dollars for fencing and other improvements; he then sold it for 384 dollars less than it cost him; how much did he receive for it? *Ans.* 5131 dollars.

5. A forwarding merchant had in his warehouse 7520 barrels of flour; he shipped at one time 1224 barrels, at another time 1500 barrels, and at another time 1805 barrels; how many barrels remained?

6. A had 450 sheep, B had 175 more than A, and C had as many as A and B together minus 114; how many sheep had C? *Ans.* 961 sheep.

7. A farmer raised 1575 bushels of wheat, and 900 bushels of corn. He sold 807 bushels of wheat, and 391 bushels of corn to A, and the remainder to B; how much of each did he sell to B? *Ans.* 768 bushels of wheat, and 509 of corn.

8. A man traveled 6784 miles; 2324 miles by railroad, 1570 miles in a stage coach, 450 miles on horseback, 175 miles on foot, and the remainder by steamboat; how many miles did he travel by steamboat? *Ans.* 2265 miles.

9. Three persons bought a hotel valued at 35680 dollars. The first agreed to pay 7375 dollars, the second agreed to pay twice as much, and the third the remainder; how much was the third to pay? *Ans.* 13555 dollars.

10. Borrowed of my neighbor at one time 750 dollars, at another time 379 dollars, and at another 450 dollars. Having paid him 1000 dollars, how much do I still owe him?

Ans. 579 dollars.

11. A man worth 6709 dollars, received a legacy of 3000 dollars. He spent 4379 dollars in traveling; how much had he left?

12. In 1850 the number of white males in the United States was 10026402, and of white females 9526666; of these, 8786968 males, and 8525565 females were native born; how many of both were foreign born? *Ans.* 2240535.

MULTIPLICATION.

MENTAL EXERCISES.

53. 1. What will 4 pounds of sugar cost, at 8 cents a pound?

ANALYSIS. Four pounds will cost as much as the price, 8 cents taken 4 times; thus, $8+8+8+8=32$. But instead of adding, we may say, — since one pound costs 8 cents, 4 pounds will cost 4 times 8 cents, or 32 cents.

2. If a ream of paper cost 3 dollars, what will 2 reams cost?

3. At 7 cents a quart, what will 4 quarts of cherries cost?

4. At 12 dollars a ton, what will 3 tons of hay cost? 4 tons? 5 tons?

5. There are 7 days in 1 week; how many days in 6 weeks? in 8 weeks?

6. What will 9 chairs cost, at 10 shillings apiece?

7. If Henry earn 12 dollars in 1 month, how much can he earn in 5 months? in 7 months? in 9 months?

8. What will 11 dozen of eggs cost, at 9 cents a dozen? at 10 cents? at 12 cents?

9. When flour is 7 dollars a barrel, how much must be paid for 7 barrels? for 9 barrels? for 12 barrels?

10. At 9 dollars a week, what will 4 weeks' board cost? 7 weeks'? 9 weeks'?

11. If I deposit 12 dollars in a savings bank every month, how many dollars will I deposit in 6 months? in 8 months? in 9 months?

12. At 9 cents a foot, what will 4 feet of lead pipe cost? 7 feet? 10 feet?

13. When hay is 8 dollars a ton, how much will 3 tons cost? 4 tons? 7 tons? 9 tons? 11 tons?

14. What will be the cost of 11 barrels of apples, at 2 dollars a barrel? at 3 dollars?

15. At 10 cents a pound, what will 9 pounds of sugar cost? 11 pounds? 12 pounds?

54. **Multiplication** is the process of taking one of two given numbers as many times as there are units in the other.

55. The **Multiplicand** is the number to be taken.

56. The **Multiplier** is the number which shows how many times the multiplicand is to be taken.

57. The **Product** is the result obtained by the process of multiplication.

58. The **Factors** are the multiplicand and multiplier.

NOTES. 1. Factors are producers, and the multiplicand and multiplier are called factors because they produce the product.

2. Multiplication is a short method of performing addition when the numbers to be added are equal.

59. The sign, ×, placed between two numbers, denotes that they are to be multiplied together; thus $9 \times 6 = 54$, is read 9 times 6 equals 54.

MULTIPLICATION TABLE.

1 × 1 = 1	2 × 1 = 2	3 × 1 = 3	4 × 1 = 4
1 × 2 = 2	2 × 2 = 4	3 × 2 = 6	4 × 2 = 8
1 × 3 = 3	2 × 3 = 6	3 × 3 = 9	4 × 3 = 12
1 × 4 = 4	2 × 4 = 8	3 × 4 = 12	4 × 4 = 16
1 × 5 = 5	2 × 5 = 10	3 × 5 = 15	4 × 5 = 20
1 × 6 = 6	2 × 6 = 12	3 × 6 = 18	4 × 6 = 24
1 × 7 = 7	2 × 7 = 14	3 × 7 = 21	4 × 7 = 28
1 × 8 = 8	2 × 8 = 16	3 × 8 = 24	4 × 8 = 32
1 × 9 = 9	2 × 9 = 18	3 × 9 = 27	4 × 9 = 36
1 × 10 = 10	2 × 10 = 20	3 × 10 = 30	4 × 10 = 40
1 × 11 = 11	2 × 11 = 22	3 × 11 = 33	4 × 11 = 44
1 × 12 = 12	2 × 12 = 24	3 × 12 = 36	4 × 12 = 48

Define multiplication. Multiplicand. Multiplier. Product. Factors. Multiplication is a short method of what? What is the sign of multiplication?

5 × 1 = 5	6 × 1 = 6	7 × 1 = 7	8 × 1 = 8
5 × 2 = 10	6 × 2 = 12	7 × 2 = 14	8 × 2 = 16
5 × 3 = 15	6 × 3 = 18	7 × 3 = 21	8 × 3 = 24
5 × 4 = 20	6 × 4 = 24	7 × 4 = 28	8 × 4 = 32
5 × 5 = 25	6 × 5 = 30	7 × 5 = 35	8 × 5 = 40
5 × 6 = 30	6 × 6 = 36	7 × 6 = 42	8 × 6 = 48
5 × 7 = 35	6 × 7 = 42	7 × 7 = 49	8 × 7 = 56
5 × 8 = 40	6 × 8 = 48	7 × 8 = 56	8 × 8 = 64
5 × 9 = 45	6 × 9 = 54	7 × 9 = 63	8 × 9 = 72
5 × 10 = 50	6 × 10 = 60	7 × 10 = 70	8 × 10 = 80
5 × 11 = 55	6 × 11 = 66	7 × 11 = 77	8 × 11 = 88
5 × 12 = 60	6 × 12 = 72	7 × 12 = 84	8 × 12 = 96

9 × 1 = 9	10 × 1 = 10	11 × 1 = 11	12 × 1 = 12
9 × 2 = 18	10 × 2 = 20	11 × 2 = 22	12 × 2 = 24
9 × 3 = 27	10 × 3 = 30	11 × 3 = 33	12 × 3 = 36
9 × 4 = 36	10 × 4 = 40	11 × 4 = 44	12 × 4 = 48
9 × 5 = 45	10 × 5 = 50	11 × 5 = 55	12 × 5 = 60
9 × 6 = 54	10 × 6 = 60	11 × 6 = 66	12 × 6 = 72
9 × 7 = 63	10 × 7 = 70	11 × 7 = 77	12 × 7 = 84
9 × 8 = 72	10 × 8 = 80	11 × 8 = 88	12 × 8 = 96
9 × 9 = 81	10 × 9 = 90	11 × 9 = 99	12 × 9 = 108
9 × 10 = 90	10 × 10 = 100	11 × 10 = 110	12 × 10 = 120
9 × 11 = 99	10 × 11 = 110	11 × 11 = 121	12 × 11 = 132
9 × 12 = 108	10 × 12 = 120	11 × 12 = 132	12 × 12 = 144

CASE I.

60. When the multiplier consists of one figure.

1. Multiply 374 by 6.

OPERATION.

	hunds. tens. units.
Multiplicand,	374
Multiplier,	6
units,	24
tens,	42
hundreds,	18
Product,	2244

ANALYSIS. In this example it is required to take 374 six times. If we take the units of each order 6 times, we shall take the entire number 6 times. Therefore, writing the multiplier under the unit figure of the multiplicand, we proceed as follows: 6 times 4 units are 24 units; 6 times 7 tens are 42 tens; 6 times 3 hundreds are 18 hundreds; and adding these partial products, we obtain the entire product, 2244.

Case I is what? Give explanation.

The operation in this example may be performed in another way, which is the one in common use.

OPERATION.
374
6
2244

ANALYSIS. Writing the numbers as before, we begin at the right hand or unit figure, and say: 6 times 4 units are 24 units, which is 2 *tens* and 4 *units;* write the 4 units in the product in units' place, and reserve the 2 tens to add to the next product; 6 times 7 tens are 42 tens, and the two tens reserved in the last product added, are 44 tens, which is 4 *hundreds* and 4 *tens;* write the 4 tens in the product in tens' place, and reserve the 4 hundreds to add to the next product; 6 times 3 hundreds are 18 hundreds, and 4 hundreds added are 22 hundreds, which, being written in the product in the places of hundreds and thousands, gives, for the entire product, 2244.

61. The unit value of a number is not changed by repeating the number. As the multiplier always expresses *times*, the product must have the same unit value as the multiplicand. But, since the product of any two numbers will be the same, whichever factor is taken as a multiplier, either factor may be taken for the multiplier or multiplicand.

NOTE. In multiplying, learn to pronounce the partial results, as in addition, without naming the numbers separately; thus, in the last example, instead of saying 6 times 4 are 24, 6 times 7 are 42 and 2 to carry are 44, 6 times 3 are 18 and 4 to carry are 22, pronounce only the results, 24, 44, 22, performing the operations mentally. This will greatly facilitate the process of multiplying.

EXAMPLES FOR PRACTICE.

	(2.)	(3.)	(4.)
Multiplicand,	7324	6812	34651
Multiplier,	4	6	5
Product,	29296	40872	173255

(5.)	(6.)	(7.)	(8.)
82456	92714	28093	46247
3	7	8	9

Second explanation. Repeating a number has what effect on the unit value? The product must be of the same kind as what?

9. Multiply 32746 by 5. *Ans.* 163730.
10. Multiply 840371 by 7. *Ans.* 5882597.
11. Multiply 137629 by 8. *Ans.* 1101032.
12. Multiply 93762 by 3. *Ans.* 281286.
13. Multiply 543272 by 4. *Ans.* 2173088.
14. Multiply 703164 by 9. *Ans.* 6328476.

15. What will be the cost of 344 cords of wood at 4 dollars a cord? *Ans.* 1376.

16. How much will an army of 7856 men receive in one week, if each man receive 6 dollars? *Ans.* 47136 dollars.

17. In one day are 86400 seconds; how many seconds in 7 days? *Ans.* 604800 seconds.

18. What will 7640 bushels of wheat cost, at 9 shillings a bushel? *Ans.* 68760 shillings.

19. At 5 dollars an acre, what will 2487 acres of land cost? *Ans.* 12435 dollars.

20. In one mile are 5280 feet; how many feet in 8 miles? *Ans.* 42240 feet.

CASE II.

62. When the multiplier consists of two or more figures.

1. Multiply 746 by 23.

OPERATION.

Multiplicand,	746	
Multiplier,	23	
	2238	3 { times the multiplicand.
	1492	20 { times the multiplicand.
Product,	17158	23 { times the multiplicand.

ANALYSIS. Writing the multiplicand and multiplier as in Case I, we first multiply each figure in the multiplicand by the unit figure of the multiplier, precisely as in Case I. We then multiply by the 2 tens. 2 tens times 6 units, or 6 times 2 tens, are 12 tens, equal to 1 hundred, and 2 tens; we place the 2 tens under the tens figure in the product already obtained, and add the 1 hundred to the next hundreds produced. 2 tens times 4 tens are 8 hundreds, and the 1 hundred of the last product added are 9 hundreds; we write the 9 in hundreds' place in the product. 2 tens

Case II is what? Give explanation.

times 7 hundreds are 14 thousands, equal to 1 ten thousand and 4 thousands, which we write in their appropriate places in the product. Then adding the two products, we have the entire product, 17158.

NOTES. 1. When the multiplier contains two or more figures, the several results obtained by multiplying by each figure are called *partial* products.

2. When there are ciphers between the significant figures of the multiplier, pass over them, and multiply by the significant figures only.

63. From the preceding examples and illustrations we deduce the following general

RULE. I. *Write the multiplier under the multiplicand, placing units of the same order under each other.*

II. *Multiply the multiplicand by each figure of the multiplier successively, beginning with the unit figure, and write the first figure of each partial product under the figure of the multiplier used, writing down and carrying as in addition.*

III. *If there are partial products, add them, and their sum will be the product required.*

64. PROOF. 1. Multiply the multiplier by the multiplicand, and if the product is the same as the first result, the work is correct. Or,

2. Multiply the multiplicand by the multiplier *diminished* by 1, and to the product add the multiplicand; if the *sum* be the same as the product by the whole of the multiplier, the work is correct.

EXAMPLES FOR PRACTICE.

	(2.)	(3.)	(4.)
Multiply	4732	8721	17605
By	36	47	204
	28392	61047	70420
	14196	34884	35210
Ans.	170352	409887	3591420

What are partial products? When there are ciphers in the multiplier, how proceed? Rule, first step? Second? Third? Proof, first method? Second?

(5.)	(6.)	(7.)
7648	81092	37967
328	194	426

8. How many yards of linen in 759 pieces, each piece containing 25 yards? *Ans.* 18975 yards.

9. Sound is known to travel about 1142 feet in a second of time; how far will it travel in 69 seconds?

10. A man bought 36 city lots, at 475 dollars each; how much did they all cost him? *Ans.* 17100 dollars.

11. What would be the value of 867 shares of railroad stock, at 97 dollars a share? *Ans.* 84099 dollars.

12. How many pages in 3475 books, if there be 362 pages in each book? *Ans.* 1257950 pages.

13. In a garrison of 4507 men, each man receives annually 208 dollars; how much do they all receive?

14. Multiply 7198 by 216. *Ans.* 1554768.

15. Multiply 31416 by 175. *Ans.* 5497800.

16. Multiply 7071 by 556. *Ans.* 3931476.

17. Multiply 75649 by 579. *Ans.* 43800771.

18. Multiply 15607 by 3094. *Ans.* 48288058.

19. Multiply 79094451 by 76095. *Ans.* 6018692248845.

20. Multiply five hundred forty thousand six hundred nine, by seventeen hundred fifty. *Ans.* 946065750.

21. Multiply four million twenty-five thousand three hundred ten, by seventy-five thousand forty-six.

Ans. 302083414260.

22. Multiply eight hundred seventy-seven million five hundred ten thousand eight hundred sixty-four, by five hundred forty-five thousand three hundred fifty-seven.

Ans. 478556692258448.

23. If one mile of railroad require 116 tons of iron, worth 65 dollars a ton, what will be the cost of sufficient iron to construct a road 128 miles in length? *Ans.* 965120 dollars.

CONTRACTIONS.

CASE I.

65. When the multiplier is a composite number.

A **Composite Number** is one that may be produced by multiplying together two or more numbers; thus, 18 is a composite number, since $6 \times 3 = 18$; or, $9 \times 2 = 18$; or, $3 \times 3 \times 2 = 18$.

66. The **Component Factors** of a number are the several numbers which, multiplied together, produce the given number; thus, the component factors of 20 are 10 and 2, ($10 \times 2 = 20$;) or, 4 and 5, ($4 \times 5 = 20$;) or, 2 and 2 and 5, ($2 \times 2 \times 5 = 20$.)

NOTE. The pupil must not confound the *factors* with the *parts* of a number. Thus, the *factors* of which 12 is composed, are 4 and 3, ($4 \times 3 = 12$;) while the *parts* of which 12 is composed are 8 and 4, ($8 + 4 = 12$,) or 10 and 2, ($10 + 2 = 12$.) The *factors* are *multiplied*, while the *parts* are *added*, to produce the number.

1. What will 32 horses cost, at 174 dollars apiece?

	OPERATION	
Multiplicand,	174	cost of 1 horse.
1st factor,	4	
	696	cost of 4 horses.
2d factor,	8	
Product,	5568	cost of 32 horses.

ANALYSIS. The factors of 32 are 4 and 8. If we multiply the cost of 1 horse by 4, we obtain the cost of 4 horses; and by multiplying the cost of 4 horses by 8, we obtain the cost of 8 times 4 horses, or 32 horses, the number bought.

67. Hence we have the following

RULE. I. *Separate the composite number into two or more factors.*

II. *Multiply the multiplicand by one of these factors, and*

What are contractions? Case I is what? Define a composite number. Component factors. What caution is given? Give explanation. Rule, first step? Second?

that product by another, and so on until all the factors have been used successively; the last product will be the product required.

NOTE. The product of any number of factors will be the same in whatever order they are multiplied. Thus, $4 \times 3 \times 5 = 60$, and $5 \times 4 \times 3 = 60$.

EXAMPLES FOR PRACTICE.

2. Multiply 3472 by $48 = 6 \times 8$. *Ans.* 166656.
3. Multiply 14761 by $64 = 8 \times 8$.
4. Multiply 87034 by $81 = 3 \times 3 \times 9$. *Ans.* 7049754.
5. Multiply 47326 by $120 = 6 \times 5 \times 4$.
6. Multiply 60315 by 96. *Ans.* 5790240.
7. Multiply 291042 by 125. *Ans.* 36380250.
8. If a vessel sail 436 miles in 1 day, how far will she sail in 56 days? *Ans.* 24416 miles.
9. How much will 72 acres of land cost, at 124 dollars an acre? *Ans.* 8928 dollars.
10. There are 5280 feet in a mile; how many feet in 84 miles? *Ans.* 443520 feet.
11. What will 120 yoke of cattle cost, at 125 dollars a yoke?

CASE II.

68. When the multiplier is 10, 100, 1000, &c.

If we annex a cipher to the multiplicand, each figure is removed *one* place toward the left, and consequently the value of the whole number is increased tenfold, (**32.**) If two ciphers are annexed, each figure is removed *two* places toward the left, and the value of the number is increased one hundred fold; and every additional cipher increases the value tenfold.

69. Hence the following

RULE. *Annex as many ciphers to the multiplicand as there are ciphers in the multiplier; the number so formed will be the product required.*

Case II is what? Give explanation. Rule?

EXAMPLES FOR PRACTICE.

1. Multiply 347 by 10. *Ans.* 3470.
2. Multiply 4731 by 100. *Ans.* 473100.
3. Multiply 13071 by 1000.
4. Multiply 89017 by 10000.
5. If 1 acre of land cost 36 dollars, what will 10 acres cost? *Ans.* 360 dollars.
6. If 1 bushel of corn cost 65 cents, what will 1000 bushels cost? *Ans.* 65000 cents.

CASE III.

70. When there are ciphers at the right hand of one or both of the factors.

1. Multiply 1200 by 60.

OPERATION.

Multiplicand,	1200
Multiplier,	60
Product,	72000

ANALYSIS. Both multiplicand and multiplier may be resolved into their component factors; 1200 into 12 and 100, and 60 into 6 and 10. If these several factors be multiplied together they will produce the same product as the given numbers, (67.) Thus, $12 \times 6 = 72$, and $72 \times 100 = 7200$, and $7200 \times 10 = 72000$, which is the same result as in the operation. Hence the following

RULE. *Multiply the significant figures of the multiplicand by those of the multiplier, and to the product annex as many ciphers as there are ciphers on the right of both factors.*

EXAMPLES FOR PRACTICE.

	(2.)	(3.)
Multiply	4720	10340000
By	340000	105000
	1888	5170
	1416	1034
	1604800000	1085700000000

Case III is what? Give explanation. Rule.

4. Multiply 70340 by 800400. *Ans.* 56300136000.

5. Multiply 3400900 by 207000. *Ans.* 703986300000.

6. Multiply 634003000 by 40020. *Ans.* 25372800060000.

7. Multiply 10203070 by 50302000.
Ans. 513234827140000.

8. Multiply 30090800 by 600080. *Ans.* 18056887264000.

9. Multiply eighty million seven thousand six hundred, by eight million seven hundred sixty. *Ans.* 640121605776000.

10. Multiply fifty million ten thousand seventy, by sixty-four thousand. *Ans.* 3200644480000.

11. Multiply ten million three hundred fifty thousand one hundred, by eighty thousand nine hundred.
Ans. 837323090000.

12. There are 296 members of Congress, and each one receives a salary of 3000 dollars a year; how much do they all receive?

EXAMPLES COMBINING ADDITION, SUBTRACTION, AND MULTIPLICATION.

1. Bought 45 cords of wood at 4 dollars a cord, and 9 loads of hay at 13 dollars a load; what was the cost of the wood and hay? *Ans.* 297 dollars.

2. A merchant bought 6 hogsheads of sugar at 31 dollars a hogshead, and sold it for 39 dollars a hogshead; how much did he gain?

3. Bought 288 barrels of flour for 1875 dollars, and sold the same for 9 dollars a barrel; how much was the gain?
Ans. 717 dollars.

4. If a young man receive 500 dollars a year salary and pay 240 dollars for board, 125 dollars for clothing, 75 dollars for books, and 50 dollars for other expenses, how much will he have left at the end of the year? *Ans.* 10 dollars.

5. A farmer sold 184 bushels of wheat at 2 dollars a bushel, for which he received 67 yards of cloth at 4 dollars a yard, and the balance in groceries; how much did his groceries cost him?

6. A sold a farm of 320 acres at 36 dollars an acre; B sold one of 244 acres at 48 dollars an acre; which received the greater sum, and how much? *Ans.* B, 192 dollars.

7. Two persons start from the same point and travel in opposite directions, one at the rate of 35 miles a day, and the other 29 miles a day; how far apart will they be in 16 days? *Ans.* 1024 miles.

8. A merchant tailor bought 14 bales of cloth, each bale containing 26 pieces, and each piece 43 yards; how many yards of cloth did he buy? *Ans.* 15652 yards.

9. If a man have an income of 3700 dollars a year, and his daily expenses be 4 dollars; what will he save in a year, or 365 days? *Ans.* 2240 dollars.

10. A man sold three houses; for the first he received 2475 dollars, for the second 840 dollars less than he received for the first, and for the third as much as for the other two; how much did he receive for the three? *Ans.* 8220 dollars.

11. A man sets out to travel from Albany to Buffalo, a distance of 336 miles, and walks 28 miles a day for 10 days; how far is he from Buffalo?

12. Mr. C bought 14 cows at 23 dollars each, 7 horses at 96 dollars each, 34 oxen at 57 dollars each, and 300 sheep at 2 dollars each; he sold the whole for 3842 dollars; how much did he gain? *Ans.* 310 dollars.

13. A drover bought 164 head of cattle at 36 dollars a head, and 850 sheep at 3 dollars a head; how much did he pay for all?

14. A banker has an income of 14760 dollars a year; he pays 1575 dollars for house rent, and four times as much for family expenses; how much does he save annually? *Ans.* 6885 dollars.

15. A flour merchant bought 936 barrels of flour at 9 dollars a barrel; he sold 480 barrels at 10 dollars a barrel, and the remainder at 8 dollars a barrel; how much did he gain or lose? *Ans.* Gained 24 dollars.

DIVISION.

MENTAL EXERCISES.

71. 1. How many hats, at 4 dollars apiece, can be bought for 20 dollars?

ANALYSIS. Since 4 dollars will buy one hat, 20 dollars will buy as many hats as 4 is contained times in 20, which is 5 times. Therefore, 5 hats, at 4 dollars apiece, can be bought for 20 dollars.

2. A man gave 16 dollars for 8 barrels of apples; what was the cost of each barrel?

3. If 1 cord of wood cost 3 dollars, how many cords can be bought for 15 dollars?

4. At 6 shillings a bushel, how many bushels of corn can be bought for 24 shillings?

5. When flour is 6 dollars a barrel, how many barrels can be bought for 30 dollars?

6. If a man can dig 7 rods of ditch in a day, how many days will it take him to dig 28 rods?

7. If an orchard contain 56 trees, and 7 trees in a row, how many rows are there?

8. Bought 6 barrels of flour for 42 dollars; what was the cost of 1 barrel?

9. If a farmer divide 21 bushels of potatoes equally among 7 laborers, how many bushels will each receive?

10. How many oranges can be bought for 27 cents, at 3 cents each?

11. A farmer paid 35 dollars for sheep, at 5 dollars apiece; how many did he buy?

12. How many times 4 in 28? in 16? in 36?

13. How many times 8 in 40? in 56? in 64?

14. How many times 9 in 36? in 63? in 81?

15. How many times 7 in 49? in 70? in 84?

72. **Division** is the process of finding how many times one number is contained in another.

73. The **Dividend** is the number to be divided.

74. The **Divisor** is the number to divide by.

75. The **Quotient** is the result obtained by the process of division, and shows how many times the divisor is contained in the dividend.

NOTES. 1. When the dividend does not contain the divisor an exact number of times, the part of the dividend left is called the *remainder*, and it must be less than the divisor.

2. As the remainder is always a part of the dividend, it is always of the same name or kind.

3. When there is no remainder the division is said to be *complete*.

76. The sign, ÷, placed between two numbers, denotes division, and shows that the number on the *left* is to be divided by the number on the *right*. Thus, $20 \div 4 = 5$, is read, 20 divided by 4 is equal to 5.

Division is also indicated by writing the dividend *above*, and the divisor *below* a short horizontal line; thus, $\frac{12}{3} = 4$, shows that 12 divided by 3 equals 4.

CASE I.

77. When the divisor consists of one figure.

1. How many times is 4 contained in 848?

OPERATION.

	Dividend,
Divisor,	4) 848
Quotient,	212

ANALYSIS. After writing the divisor on the left of the dividend, with a line between them, we begin at the left hand and say: 4 is contained in 8 hundreds, 2 hundreds times, and write 2 in hundreds' place in the quotient; then 4 is contained in 4 tens 1 ten times, and write the 1 in tens' place in the quotient; then 4 is contained in 8 units 2 units times; and writing the 2 in units' place in the quotient, we have the entire quotient, 212.

Define division. Dividend. Divisor. Quotient. Remainder. What is complete division? What is the sign of division. Case I is what? Give first explanation.

2. How many times is 4 contained in 2884?

OPERATION.

$$4\overline{)2884}$$
$$721$$

ANALYSIS. As we cannot divide 2 thousands by 4, we take the 2 thousands and the 8 hundreds together, and say, 4 is contained in 28 hundreds 7 hundreds times, which we write in hundreds' place in the quotient; then 4 is contained in 8 tens 2 tens times, which we write in tens' place in the quotient; and 4 is contained in 4 units 1 unit time, which we write in units' place in the quotient, and we have the entire quotient, 721.

3. How many times is 6 contained in 1824?

OPERATION.

$$6\overline{)1824}$$
$$304$$

ANALYSIS. Beginning as in the last example, we say, 6 is contained in 18 hundreds 3 hundreds times, which we write in hundreds' place in the quotient; then 6 is contained in 2 tens no times, and we write a cipher in tens' place in the quotient: and taking the 2 tens and 4 units together, 6 is contained in 24 units 4 units times, which we write in units' place in the quotient, and we have 304 for the entire quotient.

4. How many times is 4 contained in 943?

OPERATION.

$$4\overline{)943}$$
$$235 \ldots 3 \text{ Rem.}$$

ANALYSIS. Here 4 is contained in 9 hundreds 2 hundreds times, and 1 hundred over, which, united to the 4 tens, makes 14 tens; 4 in 14 tens, 3 tens times and 2 tens over, which, united to the 3 units, make 23 units; 4 in 23 units 5 units times and 3 units over. The 3 which is left after performing the division, should be divided by 4; but the method of doing it cannot be explained until we reach Fractions; so we merely indicate the division by placing the divisor under the dividend, thus, $\frac{3}{4}$. The entire quotient is written $235\frac{3}{4}$, which may be read, two hundred thirty-five and *three divided by four*, or, two hundred thirty-five and a *remainder of three.*

From the foregoing examples and illustrations, we deduce the following

RULE. I. *Write the divisor at the left of the dividend, with a line between them.*

Second. Third. Rule, first step?

II. *Beginning at the left hand, divide each figure of the dividend by the divisor, and write the result under the dividend.*

III. *If there be a remainder after dividing any figure, regard it as prefixed to the figure of the next lower order in the dividend, and divide as before.*

IV. *Should any figure or part of the dividend be less than the divisor, write a cipher in the quotient, and prefix the number to the figure of the next lower order in the dividend, and divide as before.*

V. *If there be a remainder after dividing the last figure, place it over the divisor at the right hand of the quotient.*

PROOF. Multiply the divisor and quotient together, and to the product add the remainder, if any; if the result be equal to the dividend, the work is correct.

NOTES. 1. This method of proof depends on the fact that division is the reverse of multiplication. The *dividend* answers to the *product*, the *divisor* to one of the *factors*, and the *quotient* to the *other*.

2. In multiplication the two factors are given, to find the product: in division, the product and one of the factors are given to find the other factor.

EXAMPLES FOR PRACTICE.

1. Divide 7824 by 6.

OPERATION.			PROOF.	
Divisor.	6)7824	Dividend.	1304	Quotient.
	1304	Quotient.	6	Divisor.
			7824	Dividend.

(2.)	(3.)	(4.)
4)65432	5)89135	6)178932
(5.)	**(6.)**	**(7.)**
7)4708935	8)1462376	9)7468542

Second step? Third? Fourth? Fifth? Proof? How does division differ from multiplication?

	Quotients.
8. Divide 3102455 by 5.	620491.
9. Divide 1762891 by 4.	$440722\frac{3}{4}$.
10. Divide 546215747 by 11.	49655977.
11. Divide 30179624 by 12.	$2514968\frac{8}{12}$.
12. Divide 9254671 by 9.	$1028296\frac{7}{9}$.

	Quotients.	Rem.
13. Divide 7341568 by 7.		
14. Divide 3179632 by 5.		
15. Divide 19038716 by 8.		
16. Divide 84201763 by 9.		
17. Divide 2947691 by 12.		
18. Divide 42084796 by 6.		
Sums of quotients and remainders,	20680083.	28.

19. Divide 47645 dollars equally among 5 men; how much will each receive? *Ans.* 9529 dollars.

20. In one week are 7 days; how many weeks in 17675 days? *Ans.* 2525 weeks.

21. How many barrels of flour, at 6 dollars a barrel, can be bought for 6756 dollars? *Ans.* 1126 barrels.

22. Twelve things make a dozen; how many dozen in 46216464? *Ans.* 3851372 dozen.

23. How many barrels of flour can be made from 347560 bushels of wheat, if it take 5 bushels to make one barrel? *Ans.* 69512 barrels.

24. If there be 3240622 acres of land in 11 townships, how many acres in each township?

25. A gentleman left his estate, worth 38470 dollars, to be shared equally by his wife and 4 children; how much did each receive? *Ans.* 7694 dollars.

CASE II.

78. When the divisor consists of two or more figures.

NOTE. To illustrate more clearly the method of operation, we will first take an example usually performed by Short Division.

Case II is what?

1. How many times is 8 contained in 2528?

OPERATION.

```
8) 2528 (316
   24
   --
    12
     8
    --
     48
     48
     --
```

ANALYSIS. As 8 is not contained in 2 thousands, we take 2 and 5 as one number, and consider how many times 8 is contained in this *partial* dividend, 25 hundreds, and find that it is contained 3 hundreds times, and a remainder. To find this remainder, we multiply the divisor, 8, by the quotient figure, 3 hundreds, and subtract the product, 24 hundreds, from the partial dividend, 25 hundreds, and there remains 1 hundred. To this remainder we bring down the 2 tens of the dividend, and consider the 12 tens a *second* partial dividend. Then, 8 is contained in 12 tens 1 ten time and a remainder; 8 multiplied by 1 ten produces 8 tens, which, subtracted from 12 tens, leave 4 tens. To this remainder we bring down the 8 units, and consider the 48 units the *third* partial dividend. Then, 8 is contained in 48 units 6 units times. Multiplying and subtracting as before, we find that nothing remains, and we have for the entire quotient, 316.

2. How many times is 23 contained in 4807?

OPERATION.

```
Divisor. Divid'd. Quotient.
  23 ) 4807 ( 209
       46
       ---
        207
        207
        ---
```

ANALYSIS. We first find how many times 23 is contained in 48, the first partial dividend, and place the result in the quotient on the right of the dividend. We then multiply the divisor, 23, by the quotient figure, 2, and subtract the product, 46, from the part of the dividend used, and to the remainder bring down the next figure of the dividend, which is 0, making 20, for the second partial dividend. Then, since 23 is contained in 20 no times, we place a cipher in the quotient, and bring down the next figure of the dividend, making a third partial dividend, 207; 23 is contained in 207, 9 times; multiplying and subtracting as before, nothing remains, and we have for the entire quotient, 209.

NOTES. 1. When the process of dividing is performed mentally, and the results only are written, as in Case I, the operation is termed *Short Division.*

2. When the whole process of division is written, the operation is termed *Long Division.*

Give first explanation. Second. What is long division? What is short division? When is each used?

3. Short Division is generally used when the divisor is a number that will allow the process of dividing to be performed mentally.

From the preceding illustrations we derive the following general

RULE. I. *Write the divisor at the left of the dividend, as in short division.*

II. *Divide the least number of the left hand figures in the dividend that will contain the divisor one or more times, and place the quotient at the right of the dividend, with a line between them.*

III. *Multiply the divisor by this quotient figure, subtract the product from the partial dividend used, and to the remainder bring down the next figure of the dividend.*

IV. *Divide as before, until all the figures of the dividend have been brought down and divided.*

V. *If any partial dividend will not contain the divisor, place a cipher in the quotient, and bring down the next figure of the dividend, and divide as before.*

VI. *If there be a remainder after dividing all the figures of the dividend, it must be written in the quotient, with the divisor underneath.*

NOTES. 1. If any remainder be *equal to*, or *greater* than the divisor, the quotient figure is too *small*, and must be increased.

2. If the product of the divisor by the quotient figure be *greater* than the partial dividend, the quotient figure is too *large*, and must be diminished.

79. PROOF. 1. The same as in short division. Or,

2. Subtract the remainder, if any, from the dividend, and divide the difference by the quotient; if the result be the same as the given divisor, the work is correct.

80. The operations in long division consist of five principal steps, viz.:—

1st. Write down the numbers.

Rule, first step? Second? Third? Fourth? Fifth? Sixth? First direction? Second? Proof? Recapitulate the steps in their order.

2d. Find how many times.
3d. Multiply.
4th. Subtract.
5th. Bring down another figure.

EXAMPLES FOR PRACTICE.

3. Find how many times 36 is contained in 11798.

OPERATION.		PROOF BY MULTIPLICATION.	
Dividend.			
Divisor. 36) 11798 (327	Quotient.	327	Quotient.
108		36	Divisor.
99		1962	
72		981	
278		11772	
252		26	Remainder.
26	Remainder.	11798	Dividend.

4. Find how many times 82 is contained in 89634.

OPERATION.		PROOF BY DIVISION.	
82) 89634 (1093		89634	Dividend.
82		8	Remainder.
763	Quotient.	1093) 89626 (82	Divisor.
738		8744	
254		2186	
246		2186	
8			

5. Find how many times 154 is contained in 32740.

6. Divide 32572 by 34. *Ans.* 958.
7. Divide 1554768 by 216. *Ans.* 7198.
8. Divide 5497800 by 175. *Ans.* 31416.
9. Divide 3931476 by 556. *Ans.* 7071.
10. Divide 10983588 by 132. *Ans.* 83209.

11. Divide 73484248 by 19. *Ans.* 3867592.
12. Divide 8121918 by 21. *Ans.* 386758.
13. Divide 10557312 by 16. *Ans.* 659832.
14. Divide 93840 by 63. *Rem.* 33.
15. Divide 352417 by 29. *Rem.* 9.
16. Divide 51846734 by 102. *Rem.* 32.
17. Divide 1457924651 by 1204. *Rem.* 1051.
18. Divide 729386 by 731. *Rem.* 579.
19. Divide 4843167 by 3605. *Rem.* 1652.
20. Divide 49816657 by 9101. *Rem.* 6884.
21. Divide 75867308 by 10115. *Rem.* 4808.

	Quotients.	Rem.
22. Divide 28101418481 by 1107.	25385201.	974.
23. Divide 65358547823 by 2789.	23434402.	645.
24. Divide 102030405060 by 123456.	826451.	70404.
25. Divide 48659910 by 54001.	901.	5009.
26. Divide 2331883961 by 6739549.	346.	7.

27. A railroad cost one million eight hundred fifty thousand four hundred dollars, and was divided into eighteen thousand five hundred and four shares; what was the value of each share? *Ans.* 100 dollars.

28. If a tax of seventy-two million three hundred twenty thousand sixty dollars be equally assessed on ten thousand seven hundred thirty-five towns, what amount of tax must each town pay? *Ans.* $6736\frac{9100}{10735}$ dollars.

29. In 1850 there were in the United States 213 college libraries, containing 942321 volumes; what would be the average number of volumes to each library?

Ans. $4424\frac{9}{213}$ vols.

30. The number of post offices in the United States in 1853 was 22320, and the entire revenue of the post office department was 5937120 dollars; what was the average revenue of each office? *Ans.* 266 dollars.

CONTRACTIONS.

CASE I.

81. When the divisor is a composite number.

1. If 3270 dollars be divided equally among 30 men, how many dollars will each receive?

OPERATION.

$$\begin{array}{r} 5)\underline{3270} \\ 6)\underline{654} \\ 109 \end{array}$$ *Ans.*

ANALYSIS. If 3270 dollars be divided equally among 30 men, each man will receive as many dollars as 30 is contained times in 3270 dollars. 30 may be resolved into the factors 5 and 6; and we may suppose the 30 men divided into 5 groups of 6 men each; dividing the 3270 dollars by 5, the number of groups, we have 654, the number of dollars to be given to each group; and dividing the 654 dollars by 6, the number of men in each group, we have 109, the number of dollars that each man will receive. Hence,

RULE. *Divide the dividend by one of the factors, and the quotient thus obtained by another, and so on if there be more than two factors, until every factor has been made a divisor. The last quotient will be the quotient required.*

EXAMPLES FOR PRACTICE.

2. Divide 3690 by $15 = 3 \times 5$. *Ans.* 246.
3. Divide 3528 by $24 = 4 \times 6$. *Ans.* 147.
4. Divide 7280 by $35 = 5 \times 7$. *Ans.* 208.
5. Divide 6228 by $36 = 6 \times 6$. *Ans.* 173.
6. Divide 33642 by $27 = 3 \times 9$. *Ans.* 1246.
7. Divide 153160 by $56 = 7 \times 8$. *Ans.* 2735.
8. Divide 15625 by $125 = 5 \times 5 \times 5$. *Ans.* 125.

82. To find the true remainder.

1. Divide 1143 by 64, using the factors 2, 8, and 4, and find the true remainder.

What are contractions? Case I is what? Give explanation. Rule.

OPERATION.

```
2)1143
  8)571 -------------- 1 rem.
    4)71 ------ 3 × 2 =  6  "
      17 -- 3 × 8 × 2 = 48  "
                        ---
                        55 true rem.
```

ANALYSIS. Dividing 1143 by 2, we have a quotient of 571, and a remainder of 1 undivided, which, being a part of the given dividend, must also be a part of the true remainder. The 571 being a quotient arising from dividing by 2, its units are 2 times as great in value as the units of the given dividend, 1143. Dividing the 571 by 8, we have a quotient of 71, and a remainder of 3 undivided. As this 3 is a part of the 571, it must be multiplied by 2 to change it to the same kind of units as the 1. This makes a true remainder of 6 arising from dividing by 8. Dividing the 71 by 4, we have a quotient of 17, and a remainder of 3 undivided. This 3 is a part of the 71, the units of which are 8 times as great in value as those of the 571, and the units of the 571 are 2 times as great in value as those of the given dividend, 1143; therefore, to change this last remainder, 3, to units of the same value as the dividend, we multiply it by 8 and 2, and obtain a true remainder of 48 arising from dividing by 4. Adding the three partial remainders, we obtain 55, the true remainder. Hence,

RULE. I. *Multiply each partial remainder, except the first, by all the preceding divisors.*

II. *Add the several products with the first remainder, and the sum will be the true remainder.*

EXAMPLES FOR PRACTICE.

			Rem.
2. Divide	34712	by 42 = 6 × 7.	20.
3. Divide	401376	by 64 = 8 × 8.	32.
4. Divide	139074	by 72 = 3 × 4 × 6.	42.
5. Divide	9078126	by 90 = 3 × 5 × 6.	6.
6. Divide	18730627	by 120 = 4 × 5 × 6.	67.
7. Divide	7360479	by 96 = 2 × 6 × 8.	63.
8. Divide	24726300	by 70 = 2 × 5 × 7.	60.
9. Divide	5610207	by 84 = 7 × 2 × 6.	15.

Explain the process of finding the true remainder when dividing by the factors of a composite number.

CASE II.

83. When the divisor is 10, 100, 1000, &c.

1. Divide 374 acres of land equally among 10 men; how many acres will each have?

OPERATION.

1|0)37|4

Quotient. 37 - - - 4 Rem.

or, 37 $\frac{4}{10}$ acres.

ANALYSIS. Since we have shown, that to remove a figure one place toward the left by annexing a cipher increases its value tenfold, or multiplies it by 10, (**68**,) so, on the contrary, by cutting off or taking away the right hand figure of a number, each of the other figures is removed one place toward the right, and, consequently, the value of each is diminished tenfold, or divided by 10, (**32**.)

For similar reasons, if we cut off *two* figures, we divide by 100, if *three*, we divide by 1000, and so on. Hence the

RULE. *From the right hand of the dividend cut off as many figures as there are ciphers in the divisor. Under the figures so cut off, place the divisor, and the whole will form the quotient.*

EXAMPLES FOR PRACTICE.

2. Divide 4760 by 10.
3. Divide 362078 by 100.
4. Divide 1306321 by 1000.
5. Divide 9760347 by 10000.
6. Divide 2037160310 by 100000.

CASE III.

84. When there are ciphers on the right hand of the divisor.

1. Divide 437661 by 800.

OPERATION.

8|00)4376|61

547 - - - 61 Rem.

ANALYSIS. In this example we resolve 800 into the factors 8 and 100, and divide first by 100, by cutting off two right hand figures of the

---

Case II is what? Give explanation. Rule. Case III is what? Give explanation.

dividend, (**83**,) and we have a quotient of 4376, and a remainder of 61. We next divide by 8, and obtain 547 for a quotient; and the entire quotient is $547\frac{61}{800}$.

2. Divide 34716 by 900.

OPERATION.

$9|00)347|16$

38 Quotient. 5, 2d rem.

$5 \times 100 + 16 = 516$, true rem.

$38\frac{516}{900}$, *Ans.*

ANALYSIS. Dividing as in the last example, we have a quotient of 38, and two remainders, 16 and 5. Multiplying 5, the last remainder, by 100, the preceding divisor, and adding 16, the first remainder, (**82**,) we have 516 for the true remainder. But this remainder consists of the last remainder, 5, prefixed to the figures 16, cut off from the dividend. Hence,

85. When there is a remainder after dividing by the significant figures, it must be prefixed to the figures cut off from the dividend to give the true remainder; if there be no other remainder, the figures cut off from the dividend will be the true remainder.

EXAMPLES FOR PRACTICE.

		Quotients.	Rem.
3. Divide 34716	by 900.	38	516
4. Divide 1047634	by 2400.	436	1234
5. Divide 47321046	by 45000.	1051	26046
6. Divide 2037903176	by 140000.		63176
7. Divide 976031425	by 92000.		3425
8. Divide 80013176321	by 700000.		376321
9. Divide 19070367428	by 4160000.	4584	927428.
10. Divide 379025644319	by 554000000.		89644319

11. The circumference of the earth at the equator is 24898 miles. How many hours would a train of cars require to travel that distance, going at the rate of 50 miles an hour?

Ans. $497\frac{48}{50}$.

12. The sum of 350000 dollars is paid to an army of 14000 men; what does each man receive? *Ans.* 25 dollars.

How is the true remainder found?

EXAMPLES IN THE PRECEDING RULES.

1. George Washington was born in 1732, and lived 67 years; in what year did he die? *Ans.* in 1799.

2. How many dollars a day must a man spend, to use an income of 1095 dollars a year? *Ans.* 3 dollars.

3. If I give 141 dollars for a piece of cloth containing 47 yards, for how much must I sell it in order to gain one dollar a yard? *Ans.* 188 dollars.

4. A speculator who owned 500 acres, 17 acres, 98 acres, and 121 acres of land, sold 325 acres; how many acres had he left? *Ans.* 411 acres.

5. A dealer sold a cargo of salt for 2300 dollars, and gained 625 dollars; what did the cargo cost him? *Ans.* 1675 dollars.

6. If a man earn 60 dollars a month, and spend 45 dollars in the same time, how long will it take him to save 900 dollars from his earnings?

7. If 9 persons use a barrel of flour in 87 days, how many days will a barrel last 1 person at the same rate? *Ans.* 783 days.

8. The first of three numbers is 4, the second is 8 times the first, and the third is 9 times the second; what is their sum? *Ans.* 324.

9. If 2, 2, and 7 are three factors of 364, what is the other factor? *Ans.* 13.

10. A man has 3 farms; the first contains 78 acres, the second 104 acres, and the third as many acres as both the others; how many acres in the 3 farms?

11. If the expenses of a boy at school are 90 dollars for board, 30 dollars for clothes, 12 dollars for tuition, 5 dollars for books, and 7 dollars for pocket money, what would be the expenses of 27 boys at the same rate? *Ans.* 3888 dollars.

12. Four children inherited 2250 dollars each; but one dying, the remaining three inherited the whole; what was the share of each? *Ans.* 3000 dollars.

13. Two men travel in opposite directions, one at the rate of 35 miles a day, and the other at the rate of 40 miles a day; how far apart are they at the end of 6 days?

14. Two men travel in the same direction, one at the rate of 35 miles a day, and the other at the rate of 40 miles a day; how far apart are they at the end of 6 days?

15. A man was 45 years old, and he had been married 19 years; how old was he when married? *Ans.* 26 years.

16. Upon how many acres of ground can the entire population of the globe stand, supposing that 25000 persons can stand upon one acre, and that the population is 1000000000?

Ans. 40000 acres.

17. Add 384, 1562, 25, and 946; subtract 2723 from the sum; divide the remainder by 97; and multiply the quotient by 142; what is the result? *Ans.* 284.

18. How many steps of 3 feet each would a man take in walking a mile, or 5280 feet? *Ans.* 1760 steps.

19. A man purchased a house for 2375 dollars, and expended 340 dollars in repairs; he then sold it for railroad stock worth 867 dollars, and 235 acres of western land valued at 8 dollars an acre; how much did he gain by the trade?

Ans. 32 dollars.

20. The salary of a clergyman is 800 dollars a year, and his yearly expenses are 450 dollars; if he be worth 1350 dollars now, in how many years will he be worth 4500 dollars?

Ans. 9 years.

21. How many bushels of oats at 40 cents a bushel, must be given for 1600 bushels of wheat at 75 cents a bushel?

Ans. 3000 bushels.

22. Bought 325 loads of wheat, each load containing 50 bushels, at 2 dollars a bushel; what did the wheat cost?

23. If you deposit 225 cents each week in a savings bank, and take out 75 cents a week, how many cents will you have left at the end of the year? *Ans.* 7800 cents.

24. The product of two numbers is 31383450, and one of the numbers is 4050; what is the other number?

25. The Illinois Central Railroad is 700 miles long, and cost 31647000 dollars; what did it cost per mile?
Ans. 45210 dollars.

26. What number is that, which being divided by 7, the quotient multiplied by 3, the product divided by 5, and this quotient increased by 40, the sum will be 100? *Ans.* 700.

27. How many cows at 27 dollars apiece, must be given for 54 tons of hay at 17 dollars a ton?

28. A mechanic receives 56 dollars for 26 days' work, and spends 2 dollars a day for the whole time; how many dollars has he left? *Ans.* 4 dollars.

29. If 7 men can build a house in 98 days, how long would it take one man to build it? *Ans.* 686 days.

30. The number of school houses in the State of New York, in 1855, was 11,137; suppose their cash value to have been 5,301,212 dollars, what would be the average value?
Ans. 476 dollars.

31. A cistern whose capacity is 840 gallons has two pipes; through one pipe 60 gallons run into it in an hour, and through the other 39 gallons run out in the same time; in how many hours will the cistern be filled? *Ans.* 40 hours.

32. The average beat of the pulse of a man at middle age is about 4500 times in an hour; how many times does it beat in 24 hours? *Ans.* 108000 times.

33. How many years from the discovery of America, in 1492, to the year 1900?

34. According to the census, Maine has 31766 square miles; New Hampshire, 9280; Vermont, 10212; Massachusetts, 7800; Rhode Island, 1306; Connecticut, 4674; and New York, 47000; how many more square miles has all New England than New York?

35. What is the remainder after dividing 62530000 by 87900? *Ans.* 33100.

36. A pound of cotton has been spun into a thread 8 miles in length; allowing 235 pounds for waste, how many pounds will it take to spin a thread to reach round the earth, supposing the distance to be 25000 miles? *Ans.* 3360 pounds.

37. John has 8546 dollars, which is 342 dollars less than 4 times as much as Charles has; how many dollars has Charles? *Ans.* 2222 dollars.

38. The quotient of one number divided by another is 37, the divisor 245, and the remainder 230; what is the dividend? *Ans.* 9295.

39. What number multiplied by 72084 will produce 5190048? *Ans.* 72.

40. There are two numbers, the greater of which is 73 times 109, and their difference is 17 times 28; what is the less number? *Ans.* 7481.

41. The sum of two numbers is 360, and the less is 114; what is the product of the two numbers? *Ans.* 28044.

42. What number added to 2473248 makes 2568754? *Ans.* 95506.

43. A farmer sold 35 bushels of wheat at 2 dollars a bushel, and 18 cords of wood at 3 dollars a cord; he received 9 yards of cloth at 4 dollars a yard, and the balance in money; how many dollars did he receive? *Ans.* 88 dollars.

44. A farmer receives 684 dollars a year for produce from his farm, and his expenses are 375 dollars a year; how many dollars will he save in five years?

45. The salt manufacturer at Syracuse pays 58 cents for wood to boil one barrel of salt, 10 cents for boiling, 5 cents to the state for the brine, 28 cents for the packing barrel, and 3 cents for packing and weighing, and receives 125 cents from the purchaser; how many cents does he make on a barrel? *Ans.* 21 cents.

46. A company of 15 persons purchase a township of western land for 286000 dollars, of which sum one man pays 6000 dollars, and the others the remainder, in equal amounts; how much does each of the others pay? *Ans.* 20000 dollars.

47. If 256 be multiplied by 25, the product diminished by 625, and the remainder divided by 35, what will be the quotient? *Ans.* 165.

48. Two men start from different places, distant 189 miles, and travel toward each other; one goes 4 miles, and the other 5 miles an hour; in how many hours will they meet?

GENERAL PRINCIPLES OF DIVISION.

86. The quotient in Division depends upon the relative values of the dividend and divisor. Hence any change in the value of either dividend or divisor must produce a change in the value of the quotient. But some changes may be produced upon both dividend and divisor, at the same time, that will not affect the quotient. The laws which govern these changes are called *General Principles of Division*, which we will now examine.

I. $54 \div 9 = 6$.

If we multiply the dividend by 3, we have

$$54 \times 3 \div 9 = 162 \div 9 = 18,$$

and 18 equals the quotient, 6, multiplied by 3. Hence, *Multiplying the dividend by any number, multiplies the quotient by the same number.*

II. Using the same example, $54 \div 9 = 6$.

If we divide the dividend by 3 we have

$$\tfrac{54}{3} \div 9 = 18 \div 9 = 2,$$

and $2 =$ the quotient, 6, divided by 3. Hence, *Dividing the dividend by any number, divides the quotient by the same number.*

III. If we multiply the divisor by 3, we have

$$54 \div 9 \times 3 = 54 \div 27 = 2,$$

and $2 =$ the quotient, 6, divided by 3. Hence, *Multiplying the divisor by any number, divides the quotient by the same number.*

IV. If we divide the divisor by 3, we have

$$54 \div \tfrac{9}{3} = 54 \div 3 = 18,$$

Upon what does the value of the quotient depend? What is the first general principle of division? Second? Third? Fourth?

and 18 = the quotient, 6, multiplied by 3. Hence, *Dividing the divisor by any number, multiplies the quotient by the same number.*

V. If we multiply both dividend and divisor by 3, we have

$$54 \times 3 \div 9 \times 3 = 162 \div 27 = 6.$$

Hence, *Multiplying both dividend and divisor by the same number, does not alter the value of the quotient.*

VI. If we divide both dividend and divisor by 3, we have

$$\frac{54}{3} \div \frac{9}{3} = 18 \div 3 = 6.$$

Hence, *Dividing both dividend and divisor by the same number, does not alter the value of the quotient.*

87. These six examples illustrate all the different changes we ever have occasion to make upon the dividend and divisor in practical arithmetic. The principles upon which these changes are based may be stated as follows:

PRIN. I. *Multiplying the dividend multiplies the quotient; and dividing the dividend divides the quotient.* (**86.** I and II.)

PRIN. II. *Multiplying the divisor divides the quotient; and dividing the divisor multiplies the quotient.* (**86.** III and IV.)

PRIN. III. *Multiplying or dividing both dividend and divisor by the same number, does not alter the quotient.* (**86.** V and VI.)

88. These three principles may be embraced in one

GENERAL LAW.

A change in the dividend produces a LIKE *change in the quotient; but a change in the divisor produces an* OPPOSITE *change in the quotient.*

NOTE. If a number be multiplied and the product divided by the same number, the quotient will be equal to the number multiplied. Thus, 15 × 4 = 60, and 60 ÷ 4 = 15.

Fifth? Sixth? Into how many general principles can these be condensed? What is the first? Second? Third? In what general law are these embraced?

EXACT DIVISORS.

89. An **Exact Divisor** of a number is one that gives a whole number for a quotient.

As it is frequently desirable to know if a number has an exact divisor, we will present a few directions that will be of assistance, particularly in finding exact divisors of large numbers.

NOTE. A number whose unit figure is 0, 2, 4, 6, or 8 is called an *Even Number*. And a number whose unit figure is 1, 3, 5, 7, or 9, is called an *Odd Number*.

2 is an exact divisor of all even numbers.

4 is an exact divisor when it will exactly divide the tens and units of a number. Thus, 4 is an exact divisor of 268, 756, 1284.

5 is an exact divisor of every number whose unit figure is 0 or 5. Thus, 5 is an exact divisor of 20, 955, and 2840.

8 is an exact divisor when it will exactly divide the hundreds, tens, and units of a number. Thus, 8 is an exact divisor of 1728, 5280, and 213560.

9 is an exact divisor when it will exactly divide the sum of the digits of a number. Thus, in 2486790, the sum of the digits $2+4+8+6+7+9+0=36$, and $36 \div 9 = 4$.

10 is an exact divisor when 0 occupies units' place.

100 when 00 occupy the places of units and tens.

1000 when 000 occupy the places of units, tens, and hundreds, &c.

A composite number is an exact divisor of any number, when all its factors are exact divisors of the same number. Thus, 2, 2, and 3 are exact divisors of 12; and so also are 4 $(= 2 \times 2)$ and 6 $(= 2 \times 3)$.

An *even* number is not an exact divisor of an odd number.

If an *odd* number is an exact divisor of an even number,

What is an exact divisor? What is an even number? An odd number? When is 2 an exact divisor? 4? 5? 9? 10? 100? 1000? When is a composite number an exact divisor? An even number is not an exact divisor of what? An odd number is an exact divisor of what?

twice that odd number is also an exact divisor of the even number. Thus, 7 is an exact divisor of 42; so also is 7×2, or 14.

PRIME NUMBERS.

90. A **Prime Number** is one that can not be resolved or separated into two or more integral factors.

For reference, and to aid in determining the prime factors of composite numbers, we give the following:—

TABLE OF PRIME NUMBERS FROM 1 TO 1000.

1	59	139	233	337	439	557	653	769	883
2	61	149	239	347	443	563	659	773	887
3	67	151	241	349	449	569	661	787	907
5	71	157	251	353	457	571	673	797	911
7	73	163	257	359	461	577	677	809	919
11	79	167	263	367	463	587	683	811	929
13	83	173	269	373	467	593	691	821	937
17	89	179	271	379	479	599	701	823	941
19	97	181	277	383	487	601	709	827	947
23	101	191	281	389	491	607	719	829	953
29	103	193	283	397	499	613	727	839	967
31	107	197	293	401	503	617	733	853	971
37	109	199	307	409	509	619	739	857	977
41	113	211	311	419	521	631	743	859	983
43	127	223	313	421	523	641	751	863	991
47	131	227	317	431	541	643	757	877	997
53	137	229	331	433	547	647	761	881	

FACTORING NUMBERS.

CASE I.

91. To resolve any composite number into its prime factors.

What is a prime number? In factoring numbers, Case I is what?

1. What are the prime factors of 2772?

OPERATION.

2	2772
2	1386
3	693
3	231
7	77
11	11
	1

ANALYSIS. We divide the given number by 2, the least prime factor, and the result by 2; this gives an odd number for a quotient, divisible by the prime factor, 3, and the quotient resulting from this division is also divisible by 3. The next quotient, 77, we divide by its least prime factor, 7, and we obtain the quotient 11; this being a prime number, the division can not be carried further. The divisors and last quotient, 2, 2, 3, 3, 7, and 11 are all the prime factors of the given number, 2772. Hence the

RULE. *Divide the given number by any prime factor; divide the quotient in the same manner, and so continue the division until the quotient is a prime number. The several divisors and the last quotient will be the prime factors required.*

PROOF. The product of all the prime factors will be the given number.

EXAMPLES FOR PRACTICE.

2. What are the prime factors of 1140? *Ans.* 2, 2, 3, 5, 19.
3. What are the prime factors of 29925?
4. What are the prime factors of 2431?
5. Find the prime factors of 12673.
6. Find the prime factors of 2310.
7. Find the prime factors of 2205.
8. What are the prime factors of 13981?

CASE II.

92. To resolve a number into all the different sets of factors possible.

1. In 36 how many sets of factors, and what are they?

Give explanation. Rule. Proof. Case II is what?

OPERATION.

$$36=\begin{cases}2\times 18\\3\times 12\\4\times 9\\6\times 6\\2\times 2\times 9\\2\times 3\times 6\\3\times 3\times 4\\2\times 2\times 3\times 3\end{cases}$$

ANALYSIS. Writing the 36 at the left of the sign =, we arrange all the different sets of factors into which it can be resolved under each other, as shown in the operation, and we find that 36 can be resolved into 8 sets of factors.

EXAMPLES FOR PRACTICE.

2. How many sets of factors in the number 24? What are they? *Ans.* 6 sets.

3. In 125 how many sets of factors? What are they? *Ans.* 2 sets.

4. In 40 how many sets of factors, and what are they? *Ans.* 6 sets.

5. In 72 how many sets of factors, and what are they? *Ans.* 15 sets.

CANCELLATION.

93. **Cancellation** is the process of rejecting equal factors from numbers sustaining to each other the relation of dividend and divisor.

It has been shown (**77**) that the dividend is equal to the product of the divisor multiplied by the quotient. Hence, if the dividend can be resolved into two factors, one of which is the divisor, the other factor will be the quotient.

1. Divide 63 by 7.

OPERATION.

Divisor, $\not{7})\not{7}\times 9$ Dividend.

9 Quotient.

ANALYSIS. We see in this example that 63 is composed of the factors 7 and 9, and that the factor 7 is equal to the divisor. Therefore we reject the factor 7, and the remaining factor, 9, is the quotient.

Give explanation. What is cancellation? Upon what principle is it based? Give first explanation.

94. Whenever the dividend and divisor are each composite numbers, the factors common to both may first be rejected without altering the final result. (**87**, Prin. III.)

2. What is the quotient of 24 times 56 divided by 7 times 48?

OPERATION.

$$\frac{24 \times 56}{7 \times 48} = \frac{4 \times 6 \times 7 \times 8}{7 \times 6 \times 8} = 4, \textit{ Ans.}$$

ANALYSIS. We first *indicate* the operation to be performed by writing the numbers which constitute the dividend above a line, and those which constitute the divisor below it. Instead of multiplying 24 by 56, in the dividend, we resolve 24 into the factors 4 and 6, and 56 into the factors 7 and 8; and 48 in the divisor into the factors 6 and 8. We next cancel the factors 6, 7, and 8, which are common to the dividend and divisor, and we have left the factor 4 in the dividend, which is the quotient.

NOTE. When all the factors or numbers in the dividend are canceled, 1 should be retained.

95. If any two numbers, one in the dividend and one in the divisor, contain a common factor, we may reject that factor.

3. In 54 times 77, how many times 63?

OPERATION.

$$\frac{\overset{6}{54} \times \overset{11}{77}}{\underset{7}{63}}$$

ANALYSIS. In this example we see that 9 will divide 54 and 63; so we reject 9 as a factor of 54, and retain the factor 6, and also as a factor of 63, and retain the factor 7. Again, 7 will divide 7 in the divisor, and 77 in the dividend. Dividing both numbers by 7, 1 will be retained in the divisor, and 11 in the dividend. Finally, the product of $6 \times 11 = 66$, the quotient.

4. Divide $25 \times 16 \times 12$ by $10 \times 4 \times 6 \times 7$.

OPERATION.

$$\frac{\overset{5}{25} \times \overset{4}{16} \times \overset{2}{12}}{\underset{2}{10} \times 4 \times 6 \times 7} = \frac{5 \times 4}{7} = \tfrac{20}{7} = 2\tfrac{6}{7}.$$

ANALYSIS. In this, as in the preceding example, we reject all the factors that are common to both dividend and divisor,

---

Give second explanation.

and we have remaining the factor 7 in the divisor, and the factors 5 and 4 in the dividend. Completing the work, we have $\frac{20}{7} = 2\frac{6}{7}$, *Ans.*

From the preceding examples and illustrations we derive the following

RULE. I. *Write the numbers composing the dividend above a horizontal line, and the numbers composing the divisor below it.*

II. *Cancel all the factors common to both dividend and divisor.*

III. *Divide the product of the remaining factors of the dividend by the product of the remaining factors of the divisor, and the result will be the quotient.*

NOTES. 1. Rejecting a factor from any number is dividing the number by that factor.

2. When a factor is canceled, the unit, 1, is supposed to take its place.

3. *One* factor in the dividend will cancel only *one equal* factor in the divisor.

4. If all the factors or numbers of the divisor are canceled, the product of the remaining factors of the dividend will be the quotient.

5. By many it is thought more convenient to write the factors of the dividend on the right of a *vertical* line, and the factors of the divisor on the left.

EXAMPLES FOR PRACTICE.

1. What is the quotient of 16 × 5 × 4 divided by 20 × 8?

FIRST OPERATION.

$$\frac{\overset{2}{\not{16}} \times \not{5} \times \not{4}}{\underset{4}{\not{20}} \times \not{8}} = 2, \textit{ Ans.}$$

SECOND OPERATION.

$\overset{5}{\not{20}}$	$\not{16}^{2}$
$\not{8}$	$\not{5}$
	$\not{4}$
	2, *Ans.*

2. Divide the product of 120 × 44 × 6 × 7 by 72 × 33 × 14.

Rule, first step? Second? Third? What is the effect of rejecting a factor? What is the quotient when all the factors in the divisor are canceled?

FIRST OPERATION.

$$\frac{\overset{10}{\cancel{120}}\times\overset{\overset{2}{\cancel{4}}}{\cancel{44}}\times\cancel{6}\times\cancel{7}}{\underset{\cancel{6}}{\cancel{72}}\times\underset{3}{\cancel{33}}\times\underset{\cancel{2}}{\cancel{14}}}=\frac{10\times 2}{3}=\frac{20}{3}=6\tfrac{2}{3},\ \textit{Ans.}$$

SECOND OPERATION.

$$\begin{array}{r|l} {}^{\cancel{6}}\cancel{72} & \cancel{120}^{10} \\ {}^{3}\cancel{33} & \cancel{44}\quad 2 \\ {}^{\cancel{2}}\cancel{14} & \cancel{6} \\ & \cancel{7} \\ \hline 3 & 20 \\ \hline \end{array}$$

$6\frac{2}{3}$, *Ans.*

3. Divide the product of 33 × 35 × 28 by 11 × 15 × 14. *Ans.* 14.

4. What is the quotient of 21 × 11 × 26 divided by 14 × 13? *Ans.* 33.

5. Divide the product of the numbers 48, 72, 28, and 5, by the product of the numbers 84, 15, 7, and 6, and give the result. *Ans.* $9\frac{1}{7}$.

6. Divide 140 × 39 × 13 × 7 by 30 × 7 × 26 × 21. *Ans.* $4\frac{1}{3}$.

7. What is the quotient of 66 × 9 × 18 × 5 divided by 22 × 6 × 40? *Ans.* $10\frac{1}{8}$.

8. Divide the product of 200 × 36 × 30 × 21 by 270 × 40 × 15 × 14. *Ans.* 2.

9. Multiply 240 by 56, and divide the product by 60 multiplied by 28. *Ans.* 8.

10. The product of the numbers 18, 6, 4, and 42 is to be divided by the product of the numbers 4, 9, 3, 7, and 6; what is the result? *Ans.* 4.

11. How many tons of hay, at 12 dollars a ton, must be given for 30 cords of wood, at 4 dollars a cord? *Ans.* 10 tons.

12. How many firkins of butter, each containing 56 pounds, at 13 cents a pound, must be given for 4 barrels of sugar, each containing 182 pounds, at 6 cents a pound? *Ans.* 6 firkins.

13. A tailor bought 5 pieces of cloth, each piece containing 24 yards, at 3 dollars a yard. How many suits of clothes, at 18 dollars a suit, must be made from the cloth to pay for it?

Ans. 20 suits.

14. How many days' work, at 75 cents a day, will pay for 115 bushels of corn, at 50 cents a bushel? *Ans.* $76\frac{2}{3}$ days.

GREATEST COMMON DIVISOR.

96. A **Common Divisor** of two or more numbers is a number that will exactly divide each of them.

97. The **Greatest Common Divisor** of two or more numbers is the greatest number that will exactly divide each of them.

Numbers prime to each other are such as have no common divisor.

NOTE. A common divisor is sometimes called a Common Measure; and the greatest common divisor, the Greatest Common Measure.

CASE I.

98. When the numbers are readily factored.

1. What is the greatest common divisor of 6 and 10?

Ans. 2.

OPERATION.

```
2 | 6 .. 10
  |--------
  | 3 ..  5
```

ANALYSIS. We readily find by inspection that 2 will divide both the given numbers; hence 2 is a common divisor; and since the quotients 3 and 5 have no common factor, but are prime to each other, the common divisor, 2, must be the greatest common divisor.

2. What is the greatest common divisor of 42, 63, and 105?

What is a common divisor? The greatest common divisor? A common measure? The greatest common measure? What is Case I? Give analysis.

OPERATION.

3	42 .. 63 .. 105
7	14 .. 21 .. 35
	2 .. 3 .. 5

$3 \times 7 = 21$, *Ans.*

ANALYSIS. We observe that 3 will exactly divide each of the given numbers, and that 7 will exactly divide each of the resulting quotients. Hence, each of the given numbers can be exactly divided by 3 times 7; and these numbers must be *component factors* of the greatest common divisor. Now, if there were *any other* component factor of the greatest common divisor, the quotients, 2, 3, 5, would be exactly divisible by it. But these quotients are prime to each other. Hence 3 and 7 are *all* the component factors of the greatest common divisor sought.

3. What is the greatest common divisor of 28, 140, and 280?

OPERATION.

4	28 .. 140 .. 280
7	7 .. 35 .. 70
	1 .. 5 .. 10

$4 \times 7 = 28$, *Ans.*

ANALYSIS. We first divide by 4; then the quotients by 7. The resulting quotients, 1, 5, and 10, are prime to each other. Hence 4 and 7 are all the component factors of the greatest common divisor.

From these examples and analyses we derive the following

RULE. I. *Write the numbers in a line, with a vertical line at the left, and divide by any factor common to all the numbers.*

II. *Divide the quotients in like manner, and continue the division till a set of quotients is obtained that have no common factor.*

III. *Multiply all the divisors together, and the product will be the greatest common divisor sought.*

EXAMPLES FOR PRACTICE.

1. What is the greatest common divisor of 12, 36, 60, 72?
Ans. 12.

2. What is the greatest common divisor of 18, 24, 30, 36, 42?
Ans. 6.

Rule, first step? Second? Third?

3. What is the greatest common divisor of 72, 120, 240, 384? *Ans.* 24.

4. What is the greatest common divisor of 36, 126, 72, 216? *Ans.* 18.

5. What is the greatest common divisor of 42 and 112? *Ans.* 14.

6. What is the greatest common divisor of 32, 80, and 256? *Ans.* 16.

7. What is the greatest common divisor of 210, 280, 350, 630, and 840? *Ans.* 70.

8. What is the greatest common divisor of 300, 525, 225, and 375? *Ans.* 75.

9. What is the greatest common divisor of 252, 630, 1134, and 1386? *Ans.* 126.

10. What is the greatest common divisor of 96 and 544? *Ans.* 32.

11. What is the greatest common divisor of 468 and 1184? *Ans.* 4.

12. What is the greatest common divisor of 200, 625, and 150? *Ans.* 25.

CASE II.

99. When the numbers can not be readily factored.

As the analysis of the method under this case depends upon three properties of numbers which have not been introduced, we present them in this place.

I. An exact divisor divides any number of times its dividend.

II. A common divisor of two numbers is an exact divisor of their *sum*.

III. A common divisor of two numbers is an exact divisor of their *difference*.

What is Case II? What is the first principle upon which it is founded? Second? Third?

1. What is the greatest common divisor of 84 and 203?

OPERATION.

		203
84	2	168
70	2	35
14	2	28
14	2	7, *Ans.*
0		

ANALYSIS. We draw two vertical lines, and place the larger number on the right, and the smaller number on the left, one line lower down. We then divide 203, the larger number, by 84, the smaller, and write 2, the quotient, between the verticals, the product, 168, opposite, under the greater number, and the remainder, 35, below. We next divide 84 by this remainder, writing the quotient, 2, between the verticals, the product, 70, on the left, and the new remainder, 14, below the 70. We again divide the last divisor, 35, by 14, and obtain 2 for a quotient, 28 for a product, and 7 for a remainder, all of which we write in the same order as in the former steps. Finally, dividing the last divisor, 14, by the last remainder, 7, and we have no remainder. 7, the last divisor, is the greatest common divisor of the given numbers.

In order to show that the last divisor in such a process is the greatest common divisor, we will first trace the work in the reverse order, as indicated by the arrow line below.

OPERATION.

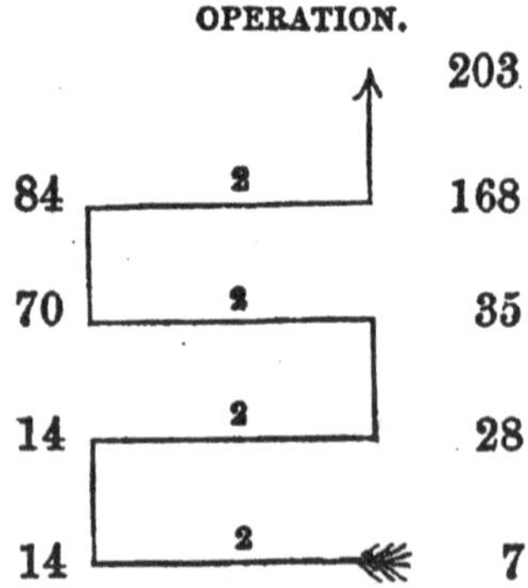

7 divides the 14, as proved by the last division; it will also divide two times 14, or 28, (I.) Now, as 7 divides both itself and 28, it will divide 35, their sum, (II.) It will also divide 2 times 35, or 70, (I;) and since it is a common divisor of 70 and 14, it must divide their sum, 84, which is one of the given numbers, (II.) It will also divide 2 times 84, or 168, (I;) and since it is a common divisor of 168 and 35, it must divide their sum, 203, the larger number, (II.) Hence 7 is a *common divisor* of the given numbers.

Again, tracing the work in the *direct* order, as indicated below, we

---

Give analysis.

know that the greatest common divisor, *whatever it be,* must divide 2 times 84, or 168, (I.) Then since it will divide both 168 and 203, it must divide their difference, 35, (III.) It will also divide 2 times 35, or 70, (I;) and as it will divide both 70 and 84, it must divide their difference, 14, (III.) It will also divide 2 times 14 or 28, (I;) and as it will divide both 28 and 35, it must divide their difference, 7, (III;) *hence, it cannot be greater than* 7.

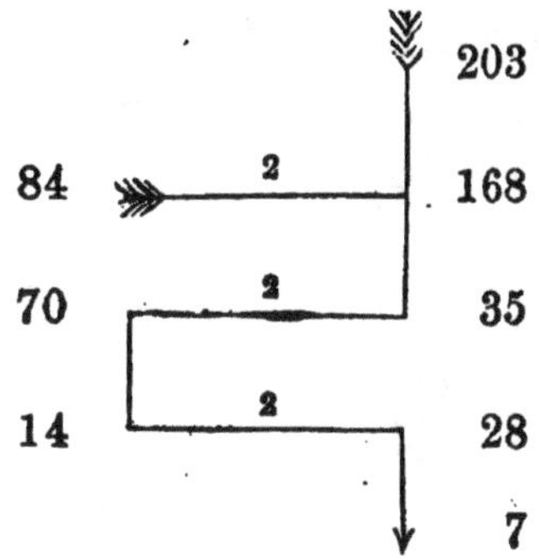

Thus we have shown,

1st. That 7 is a *common divisor* of the given numbers.

2d. That their greatest common divisor, whatever it be, cannot be *greater than* 7. Hence it must be 7.

From this example and analysis, we derive the following

RULE. I. *Draw two verticals, and write the two numbers, one on each side, the greater number one line above the less.*

II. *Divide the greater number by the less, writing the quotient between the verticals, the product under the dividend, and the remainder below.*

III. *Divide the less number by the remainder, the last divisor by the last remainder, and so on, till nothing remains. The last divisor will be the greatest common divisor sought.*

IV. *If more than two numbers be given, first find the greatest common divisor of two of them, and then of this divisor and one of the remaining numbers, and so on to the last; the last common divisor found will be the greatest common divisor of all the given numbers.*

NOTES. 1. When more than two numbers are given, it is better to begin with the least two.

2. If at any point in the operation a *prime* number occur as a remainder, it must be a common divisor or the given numbers have no common divisor.

Rule, first step? Second? Third? Fourth? What relation have numbers when their difference is a prime number?

EXAMPLES FOR PRACTICE.

1. What is the greatest common divisor of 221 and 5512?

OPERATION.

		5512
221	2	442
		1092
	4	884
208	1	208
Ans. 13	1	13
		78
	6	78
		0

2. Find the greatest common divisor of 154 and 210.
Ans. 14.

3. What is the greatest common divisor of 316 and 664?
Ans. 4.

4. What is the greatest common divisor of 679 and 1869?
Ans. 7.

5. What is the greatest common divisor of 917 and 1495?
Ans. 1.

6. What is the greatest common divisor of 1313 and 4108?
Ans. 13.

7. What is the greatest common divisor of 1649 and 5423?
Ans. 17.

The following examples may be solved by either of the foregoing methods.

8. John has 35 pennies, and Charles 50: how shall they arrange them in parcels, so that each boy shall have the same number in each parcel? *Ans.* 5 in each parcel.

9. A speculator has 3 fields, the first containing 18, the second 24, and the third 40 acres, which he wishes to divide into the largest possible lots having the same number of acres in each; how many acres in each lot? *Ans.* 2 acres.

10. A farmer had 231 bushels of wheat, and 273 bushels of oats, which he wished to put into the least number of bins containing the same number of bushels, without mixing the two kinds; what number of bushels must each bin hold?

Ans. 21.

11. A village street is 332 rods long; A owns 124 rods front, B 116 rods, and C 92 rods; they agree to divide their land into equal lots of the largest size that will allow each one to form an exact number of lots; what will be the width of the lots? *Ans.* 4 rods.

12. The Erie Railroad has 3 switches, or side tracks, of the following lengths: 3013, 2231, and 2047 feet; what is the length of the longest rail that will exactly lay the track on each switch? *Ans.* 23 feet.

13. A forwarding merchant has 2722 bushels of wheat, 1822 bushels of corn, and 1226 bushels of beans, which he wishes to forward, in the fewest bags of equal size that will exactly hold either kind of grain; how many bags will it take? *Ans.* 2885.

14. A has 120 dollars, B 240 dollars, and C 384 dollars; they agree to purchase cows, at the highest price per head that will allow each man to invest all his money; how many cows can each man purchase? *Ans.* A 5, B 10, and C 16.

MULTIPLES.

100. A **Multiple** is a number exactly divisible by a given number; thus, 20 is a multiple of 4.

101. A **Common Multiple** is a number exactly divisible by two or more given numbers; thus, 20 is a common multiple of 2, 4, 5, and 10.

102. The **Least Common Multiple** is the least number exactly divisible by two or more given numbers; thus, 24 is the least common multiple of 3, 4, 6, and 8.

What is a multiple? A common multiple? The least common multiple?

103. From the definition (**100**) it is evident that the product of two or more numbers, or any number of times their product, must be a common multiple of the numbers. Hence, *A common multiple of two or more numbers may be found by multiplying the given numbers together.*

104. To find the least common multiple.

FIRST METHOD.

From the nature of prime numbers we derive the following principles:—

I. If a number exactly contain another, it will contain all the prime factors of that number.

II. If a number exactly contain two or more numbers, it will also contain all the prime factors of those numbers.

III. The least number that will exactly contain all the prime factors of two or more numbers, is the least common multiple of those numbers.

1. Find the least common multiple of 30, 42, 66, and 78.

OPERATION.

$$30 = 2 \times 3 \times 5$$
$$42 = 2 \times 3 \times 7$$
$$66 = 2 \times 3 \times 11$$
$$78 = 2 \times 3 \times 13$$

$2 \times 3 \times 13 \times 11 \times 7 \times 5 = 30030$, *Ans.*

ANALYSIS. The number cannot be less than 78, since it must contain 78; hence it must contain the factors of 78, viz.: $2 \times 3 \times 13$. We here have all the prime factors of 78, and also all the factors of 66, except the factor 11. Annexing 11 to the series of factors,

$$2 \times 3 \times 13 \times 11,$$

and we have all the prime factors of 78 and 66, and also all the factors of 42 except the factor 7. Annexing 7 to the series of factors,

$$2 \times 3 \times 13 \times 11 \times 7,$$

and we have all the prime factors of 78, 66, and 42, and also all the

---

How can a common multiple of two or more numbers be found? First principle derived from prime numbers? Second? Third? Give analysis.

factors of 30 except the factor 5. Annexing 5 to the series of factors,

$$2 \times 3 \times 13 \times 11 \times 7 \times 5,$$

and we have all the prime factors of each of the given numbers; and hence the product of the series of factors is a common multiple of the given numbers, (II.) And as no factor of this series can be omitted without omitting a factor of one of the given numbers, the product of the series is the least common multiple of the given numbers, (III.)

From this example and analysis we deduce the following

RULE. I. *Resolve the given numbers into their prime factors.*

II. *Take all the prime factors of the largest number, and such prime factors of the other numbers as are not found in the largest number, and their product will be the least common multiple.*

NOTE. When a prime factor is repeated in any of the given numbers, it must be used as many times, as a factor of the multiple, as the greatest number of times it appears in any of the given numbers.

EXAMPLES FOR PRACTICE.

2. Find the least common multiple of 7, 35, and 98.
Ans. 490.

3. Find the least common multiple of 24, 42, and 17.
Ans. 2856.

4. What is the least common multiple of 4, 9, 6, 8?
Ans. 72.

5. What is the least common multiple of 8, 15, 77, 385?
Ans. 9240.

6. What is the least common multiple of 10, 45, 75, 90?
Ans. 450.

7. What is the least common multiple of 12, 15, 18, 35?
Ans. 1260.

Rule, first step? Second? What caution is given?

SECOND METHOD.

105. 1. What is the least common multiple of 4, 6, 9, and 12?

OPERATION.

2	4..6..9..12
2	2..3..9.. 6
3	3..9.. 3
3	3

$2 \times 2 \times 3 \times 3 = 36$, *Ans.*

ANALYSIS. We first write the given numbers in a series, with a vertical line at the left. Since 2 is a factor of some of the given numbers, it must be a factor of the least common multiple sought. Dividing as many of the numbers as are divisible by 2, we write the quotients and the undivided number, 9, in a line underneath. We now perceive that some of the numbers in the second line contain the factor 2; hence the least common multiple must contain another 2, and we again divide by 2, omitting to write down any quotient when it is 1. We next divide by 3 for a like reason, and still again by 3. By this process we have transferred all the factors of each of the numbers to the left of the vertical; and their product, 36, must be the least common multiple sought, (**104**, III.)

2. What is the least common multiple of 10, 12, 15, and 75?

OPERATION.

2, 5	10..12..15..75
2, 3	6.. 3..15
5	5

$2 \times 5 \times 2 \times 3 \times 5 = 300$, *Ans.*

ANALYSIS. We readily see that 2 and 5 are among the factors of the given numbers, and must be factors of the least common multiple; hence we divide every number that is divisible by *either* of these factors or by their *product*; thus, we divide 10 by both 2 and 5; 12 by 2; 15 by 5; and 75 by 5. We next divide the second line in like manner by 2 and 3; and afterwards the third line by 5. By this process we collect the factors of the given numbers into *groups*; and the product of the factors at the left of the vertical is the least common multiple sought.

3. What is the least common multiple of 6, 15, 35, 42, and 70?

Give explanation.

OPERATION.

3 , 7	15 . . 42 . . 70
2 , 5	5 . . 2 . . 10

$3 \times 7 \times 2 \times 5 = 210$, *Ans.*

ANALYSIS. In this operation we omit the 6 and 35, because they are exactly contained in some of the other given numbers; thus, 6 is contained in 42, and 35 in 70; and whatever will contain 42 and 70 must contain 6 and 35. Hence we have only to find the least common multiple of the remaining numbers, 15, 42, and 70.

From these examples we derive the following

RULE. I. *Write the numbers in a line, omitting any of the smaller numbers that are factors of the larger, and draw a vertical line at the left.*

II. *Divide by any prime factor, or factors, that may be contained in one or more of the given numbers, and write the quotients and undivided numbers in a line underneath, omitting the* 1's.

III. *In like manner divide the quotients and undivided numbers, and continue the process till all the factors of the given numbers have been transferred to the left of the vertical. Then multiply these factors together, and their product will be the least common multiple required.*

EXAMPLES FOR PRACTICE.

4. What is the least common multiple of 12, 15, 42, and 60? *Ans.* 420.

5. What is the least common multiple of 21, 35, and 42? *Ans.* 210.

6. What is the least common multiple of 25, 60, 100, and 125? *Ans.* 1500.

7. What is the least common multiple of 16, 40, 96, and 105? *Ans.* 3360.

8. What is the least common multiple of 4, 16, 20, 48, 60, and 72? *Ans.* 720.

9. What is the least common multiple of 84, 100, 224, and 300? *Ans.* 16800.

Rule, first step? Second? Third?

10. What is the least common multiple of 270, 189, 297, 243? *Ans.* 187110.

11. What is the least common multiple of 1, 2, 3, 4, 5, 6, 7, 8, 9? *Ans.* 2520.

12. What is the smallest sum of money for which I could purchase an exact number of books, at 5 dollars, or 3 dollars, or 4 dollars, or 6 dollars each? *Ans.* 60 dollars.

13. A farmer has 3 teams; the first can draw 12 barrels of flour, the second 15 barrels, and the third 18 barrels; what is the smallest number of barrels that will make full loads for any of the teams? *Ans.* 180.

14. What is the smallest sum of money with which I can purchase cows at $30 each, oxen at $55 each, or horses at $105 each? *Ans.* $2310.

15. A can shear 41 sheep in a day, B 63, and C 54; what is the number of sheep in the smallest flock that would furnish exact days' labor for each of them shearing alone?

Ans. 15498.

16. A servant being ordered to lay out equal sums in the purchase of chickens, ducks, and turkeys, and to expend as little money as possible, agreed to forfeit 5 cents for every fowl purchased more than was necessary to obey orders. In the market he found chickens at 12 cents, ducks at 30 cents, and turkeys at two prices, 75 cents and 90 cents, of which he imprudently took the cheaper; how much did he thereby forfeit? *Ans.* 80 cents.

CLASSIFICATION OF NUMBERS.

Numbers may be classified as follows:

106. I. As *Even* and *Odd.*

107. II. As *Prime* and *Composite.*

What is the first classification of numbers? What is an even number? An odd number? Second classification? A prime number? A composite number?

108. III. As *Integral* and *Fractional.*

An **Integral Number,** or **Integer,** expresses whole things. Thus, 281; 78 boys; 1000 books.

A **Fractional Number,** or **Fraction,** expresses equal parts of a thing. Thus, half a dollar; three-fourths of an hour; seven-eighths of a mile.

109. IV. As *Abstract* and *Concrete.*

110. V. As *Simple* and *Compound.*

A **Simple Number** is either an abstract number, or a concrete number of but one denomination. Thus, 48, 926; 48 dollars, 926 miles.

A **Compound Number** is a concrete number whose value is expressed in two or more different denominations. Thus, 32 dollars 15 cents; 15 days 4 hours 25 minutes; 7 miles 82 rods 9 feet 6 inches.

111. VI. As *Like* and *Unlike.*

Like Numbers are numbers of the same unit value.

If simple numbers, they must be all abstract, as 6, 62, 487; or all of one and the same denomination, as 5 apples, 62 apples, 487 apples; and, if compound numbers, they must be used to express the same kind of quantity, as time, distance, &c. Thus, 4 weeks 3 days 16 hours; 1 week 6 days 9 hours; 5 miles 40 rods; 2 miles 100 rods.

Unlike Numbers are numbers of different unit values. Thus, 75, 140 dollars, and 28 miles; 4 hours 30 minutes, and 5 bushels 1 peck.

What is the third classification? What is an integral number? A fractional number? What is the fourth classification? An abstract number? A concrete number? What is the fifth classification? A simple number? A compound number? Sixth classification? What are like numbers? Unlike numbers?

FRACTIONS.

DEFINITIONS, NOTATION, AND NUMERATION.

112. If a unit be divided into 2 equal parts, one of the parts is called *one half.*

If a unit be divided into 3 equal parts, one of the parts is called *one third,* two of the parts *two thirds.*

If a unit be divided into 4 equal parts, one of the parts is called *one fourth,* two of the parts *two fourths,* three of the parts *three fourths.*

If a unit be divided into 5 equal parts, one of the parts is called *one fifth,* two of the parts *two fifths,* three of the parts *three fifths,* &c.

The parts are expressed by figures; thus,

One half is written	$\frac{1}{2}$		One fifth is written		$\frac{1}{5}$
One third	"	$\frac{1}{3}$	Two fifths	"	$\frac{2}{5}$
Two thirds	"	$\frac{2}{3}$	One seventh	"	$\frac{1}{7}$
One fourth	"	$\frac{1}{4}$	Three eighths	"	$\frac{3}{8}$
Two fourths	"	$\frac{2}{4}$	Five ninths	"	$\frac{5}{9}$
Three fourths	"	$\frac{3}{4}$	Eight tenths	"	$\frac{8}{10}$

Hence we see that the parts into which a unit is divided take their *name,* and their *value,* from the *number* of equal parts into which the unit is divided. Thus, if we divide an orange into 2 equal parts, the parts are called *halves;* if into 3 equal parts, *thirds;* if into 4 equal parts, *fourths,* &c.; and each *third* is less in value than each *half,* and each *fourth* less than each *third;* and the greater the *number* of parts, the less their *value.*

When a unit is divided into any number of equal parts, one or more such parts is a fractional part of the whole number, and is called a *fraction.* Hence

113. A **Fraction** is one or more of the equal parts of a unit.

Define a fraction.

114. To write a fraction, two integers are required, one to express the number of parts into which the whole number is divided, and the other to express the number of these parts taken. Thus, if one dollar be divided into 4 equal parts, the parts are called *fourths*, and three of these parts are called three fourths of a dollar. This three fourths may be written

$\frac{3}{4}$ — 3 the number of parts taken.
4 the number of parts into which the dollar is divided.

115. The **Denominator** is the number below the line.

It denominates or names the parts; and

It shows how many parts are equal to a unit.

116. The **Numerator** is the number above the line.

It numerates or numbers the parts; and

It shows how many parts are taken or expressed by the fraction.

117. The **Terms** of a fraction are the numerator and denominator, taken together.

118. *Fractions indicate division*, the numerator answering to the dividend, and the denominator to the divisor. Hence,

119. The **Value** of a fraction is the quotient of the numerator divided by the denominator.

120. To analyze a fraction is to designate and describe its numerator and denominator. Thus, $\frac{3}{4}$ is analyzed as follows:—

4 is the *denominator*, and shows that the unit is divided into 4 equal parts; it is the divisor.

3 is the *numerator*, and shows that 3 parts are taken; it is the dividend, or integer divided.

3 and 4 are the *terms*, considered as dividend and divisor.

The *value* of the fraction is the quotient of $3 \div 4$, or $\frac{3}{4}$.

How many numbers are required to write a fraction? Why? Define the denominator. The numerator. What are the terms of a fraction? The value? What is the analysis of a fraction?

EXAMPLES FOR PRACTICE.

Express the following fractions by figures: —

1. Seven *eighths.*
2. Three *twenty-fifths.*
3. Nine *one hundredths.*
4. Sixteen *thirtieths.*
5. Thirty-one *one hundred eighteenths.*
6. Seventy-five *ninety-sixths.*
7. Two hundred fifty-four *four hundred forty-thirds.*
8. Eight *nine hundred twenty-firsts.*
9. One thousand two hundred thirty-two *seventy-five thousand six hundredths.*
10. Nine hundred six *two hundred forty-three thousand eighty-seconds.*

Read and analyze the following fractions:

11. $\frac{9}{10}$; $\frac{7}{12}$; $\frac{5}{20}$; $\frac{12}{28}$; $\frac{15}{75}$; $\frac{9}{112}$; $\frac{45}{220}$; $\frac{125}{428}$.
12. $\frac{90}{100}$; $\frac{325}{1000}$; $\frac{450}{1240}$; $\frac{25}{1500}$; $\frac{12}{2000}$; $\frac{726}{3475}$.
13. $\frac{17}{104}$; $\frac{1}{10110}$; $\frac{915}{84621}$; $\frac{38065}{4531429}$.

121. Fractions are distinguished as *Proper* and *Improper.*

A **Proper Fraction** is one whose numerator is less than its denominator; its value is less than the unit, 1. Thus, $\frac{7}{12}$, $\frac{5}{16}$, $\frac{9}{10}$, $\frac{72}{84}$ are proper fractions.

An **Improper Fraction** is one whose numerator equals or exceeds its denominator; its value is never less than the unit, 1. Thus, $\frac{7}{7}$, $\frac{3}{3}$, $\frac{15}{4}$, $\frac{35}{8}$, $\frac{50}{10}$, $\frac{180}{90}$ are improper fractions.

122. A **Mixed Number** is a number expressed by an integer and a fraction; thus, $4\frac{1}{4}$, $17\frac{18}{25}$, $9\frac{3}{10}$ are mixed numbers.

123. Since fractions indicate division, all changes in the *terms* of a fraction will affect the *value* of that fraction according to the laws of division; and we have only to modify the language of the General Principles of Division (**87**) by substituting the words *numerator, denominator,* and *fraction,* or *value*

What is a proper fraction? An improper fraction? A mixed number? What do fractions indicate?

of the fraction, for the words *dividend, divisor*, and *quotient*, respectively, and we shall have the following

GENERAL PRINCIPLES OF FRACTIONS.

124. PRIN. I. *Multiplying the numerator multiplies the fraction, and dividing the numerator divides the fraction.*

PRIN. II. *Multiplying the denominator divides the fraction, and dividing the denominator multiplies the fraction.*

PRIN. III. *Multiplying or dividing both terms of the fraction by the same number does not alter the value of the fraction.*

These three principles may be embraced in one

GENERAL LAW.

125. *A change in the* NUMERATOR *produces a* LIKE *change in the value of the fraction; but a change in the* DENOMINATOR *produces an* OPPOSITE *change in the value of the fraction.*

REDUCTION.

CASE I.

126. To reduce fractions to their lowest terms.

A fraction is in its *lowest terms* when its numerator and denominator are prime to each other; that is, when both terms have no common divisor.

1. Reduce the fraction $\frac{48}{60}$ to its lowest terms.

FIRST OPERATION.

$\frac{48}{60} = \frac{24}{30} = \frac{12}{15} = \frac{4}{5}$, *Ans.*

ANALYSIS. Dividing both terms of a fraction by the same number does not alter the value of the fraction or quotient, (**124**, III;) hence, we divide both terms of $\frac{48}{60}$, by 2, both terms of the result, $\frac{24}{30}$, by 2, and both terms of this result by 3. As the terms of $\frac{4}{5}$ are prime to each other, the lowest terms of $\frac{48}{60}$ are $\frac{4}{5}$. We have, in effect, canceled all the factors common to the numerator and denominator.

First general principle? Second? Third? General law? What is meant by reduction of fractions? Case I is what? What is meant by *lowest terms*? Give analysis.

SECOND OPERATION.

$12)\ \frac{48}{60} = \frac{4}{5}$, *Ans.*

In this operation we have divided both terms of the fraction by their greatest common divisor, (**97**,) and thus performed the reduction at a single division. Hence the

RULE. *Cancel or reject all factors common to both numerator and denominator.* Or,

Divide both terms by their greatest common divisor.

EXAMPLES FOR PRACTICE.

2. Reduce $\frac{144}{432}$ to its lowest terms. *Ans.* $\frac{1}{3}$.
3. Reduce $\frac{288}{360}$ to its lowest terms. *Ans.* $\frac{4}{5}$.
4. Reduce $\frac{441}{462}$ to its lowest terms. *Ans.* $\frac{21}{22}$.
5. Reduce $\frac{288}{504}$ to its lowest terms.
6. Reduce $\frac{1134}{21168}$ to its lowest terms.
7. Reduce $\frac{453}{1057}$ to its lowest terms.
8. Reduce $\frac{172}{1118}$ to its lowest terms.
9. Reduce $\frac{3060}{5940}$ to its lowest terms. *Ans.* $\frac{17}{33}$.
10. Reduce $\frac{5643}{5940}$ to its lowest terms. *Ans.* $\frac{19}{20}$.
11. Reduce $\frac{4680}{10600}$ to its lowest terms. *Ans.* $\frac{117}{265}$.
12. Express in its simplest form the quotient of 441 divided by 462. *Ans.* $\frac{21}{22}$.
13. Express in its simplest form the quotient of 189 divided by 273. *Ans.* $\frac{9}{13}$.
14. Express in its simplest form the quotient of 1344 divided by 1536. *Ans.* $\frac{7}{8}$.

CASE II.

127. To reduce an improper fraction to a whole or mixed number.

1. Reduce $\frac{324}{15}$ to a whole or mixed number.

OPERATION.

$\frac{324}{15} = 324 \div 15 = 21\frac{9}{15} = 21\frac{3}{5}$, *Ans.*

ANALYSIS. Since 15 fifteenths equal 1, 324 fifteenths are equal to as many times 1 as 15 is contained times in 324, which is $21\frac{9}{15}$ times. Or, since the numerator is a dividend and the denom-

---

Rule. Case II is what? Give explanation.

inator a divisor, (**118**,) we reduce the fraction to an equivalent whole or mixed number, by dividing the numerator, 324, by the denominator, 15. Hence the

RULE. *Divide the numerator by the denominator.*

NOTES. 1. When the denominator is an exact divisor of the numerator, the result will be a whole number.

2. In all answers containing fractions, reduce the fractions to their lowest terms.

EXAMPLES FOR PRACTICE.

2. In $\frac{13}{7}$ of a week, how many weeks? *Ans.* $1\frac{6}{7}$.
3. In $\frac{117}{5}$ of a bushel, how many bushels? *Ans.* $23\frac{2}{5}$.
4. In $\frac{461}{3}$ of a dollar, how many dollars?
5. In $\frac{872}{16}$ of a pound, how many pounds? *Ans.* $54\frac{1}{2}$.
6. Reduce $\frac{1258}{23}$ to a mixed number.
7. Reduce $\frac{738}{18}$ to a whole number.
8. Change $\frac{1512}{81}$ to a mixed number. *Ans.* $18\frac{2}{3}$.
9. Change $\frac{7321}{17}$ to a mixed number.
10. Change $\frac{237040}{225}$ to a mixed number. *Ans.* $1053\frac{23}{45}$.
11. Change $\frac{2531520}{360}$ to a whole number. *Ans.* 7032.

CASE III.

128. To reduce a whole number to a fraction having a given denominator.

1. Reduce 46 yards to fourths.

OPERATION.

$$\begin{array}{r} 46 \\ 4 \\ \hline \frac{184}{4}, \textit{Ans.} \end{array}$$

ANALYSIS. Since in 1 yard there are 4 fourths, in 46 yards there are 46 times 4 fourths, which are 184 fourths $= \frac{184}{4}$. In practice we multiply 46, the number of yards, by 4, the given denominator, and taking the product, 184, for the numerator of a fraction, and the given denominator, 4, for the denominator, we have $\frac{184}{4}$. Hence we have the

RULE. *Multiply the whole number by the given denominator; take the product for a numerator, under which write the given denominator.*

Rule. Case III is what? Give explanation. Rule.

NOTE. A whole number is reduced to a fractional form by writing 1 under it for a denominator; thus, $9 = \frac{9}{1}$.

EXAMPLES FOR PRACTICE.

2. Reduce 25 bushels to eighths of a bushel. *Ans.* $\frac{200}{8}$.
3. Reduce 63 gallons to fourths of a gallon. *Ans.* $\frac{252}{4}$.
4. Reduce 140 pounds to sixteenths of a pound.
5. In 56 dollars, how many tenths of a dollar? *Ans.* $\frac{560}{10}$.
6. Reduce 94 to a fraction whose denominator is 9.
7. Reduce 180 to seventy-fifths.
8. Change 42 to the form of a fraction. *Ans.* $\frac{42}{1}$.
9. Change 247 to the form of a fraction.
10. Change 347 to a fraction whose denominator shall be 14. *Ans.* $\frac{4858}{14}$.

CASE IV.

129. To reduce a mixed number to an improper fraction.

1. In $5\frac{3}{8}$ dollars, how many eighths of a dollar?

OPERATION.

$5\frac{3}{8}$
8
—
$\frac{43}{8}$, *Ans.*

ANALYSIS. Since in 1 dollar there are 8 eighths, in 5 dollars there are 5 times 8 eighths, or 40 eighths, and 40 eighths + 3 eighths = 43 eighths, or $\frac{43}{8}$. From this operation we derive the following

RULE. *Multiply the whole number by the denominator of the fraction; to the product add the numerator, and under the sum write the denominator.*

EXAMPLES FOR PRACTICE.

2. In $4\frac{1}{2}$ dollars, how many half dollars? *Ans.* $\frac{9}{2}$.
3. In $71\frac{6}{7}$ weeks, how many sevenths of a week?
4. In $341\frac{3}{4}$ acres, how many fourths? *Ans.* $\frac{1367}{4}$.
5. Change $12\frac{7}{12}$ years to twelfths.
6. Change $56\frac{9}{17}$ to an improper fraction. *Ans.* $\frac{961}{17}$.
7. Reduce $21\frac{7}{60}$ to an improper fraction. *Ans.* $\frac{1267}{60}$.
8. Reduce $225\frac{14}{25}$ to an improper fraction. *Ans.* $\frac{5639}{25}$.

Case IV is what? Give explanation. Rule.

9. In $96\frac{40}{120}$, how many one hundred twentieths?

10. In $1297\frac{3}{84}$, how many eighty-fourths? *Ans.* $\frac{108951}{84}$.

11. What improper fraction will express $400\frac{29}{37}$?

CASE V.

130. To reduce a fraction to a given denominator.

As fractions may be reduced to *lower terms* by division, they may also be reduced to *higher terms* by multiplication; and all higher terms must be multiples of the lowest terms. (**103.**)

1. Reduce $\frac{3}{4}$ to a fraction whose denominator is 20.

OPERATION.

$20 \div 4 = 5$

$\frac{3 \times 5}{4 \times 5} = \frac{15}{20}$, *Ans.*

ANALYSIS. We first divide 20, the required denominator, by 4, the denominator of the given fraction, to ascertain if it be a multiple of this term, 4. The division shows that it is a multiple, and that 5 is the factor which must be employed to produce this multiple of 4. We therefore multiply both terms of $\frac{3}{4}$ by 5, (**124,**) and obtain $\frac{15}{20}$, the desired result. Hence the

RULE. *Divide the required denominator by the denominator of the given fraction, and multiply both terms of the fraction by the quotient.*

EXAMPLES FOR PRACTICE.

2. Reduce $\frac{2}{5}$ to a fraction whose denominator is 15. *Ans.* $\frac{6}{15}$.

3. Reduce $\frac{5}{7}$ to a fraction whose denominator is 35.

4. Reduce $\frac{12}{17}$ to a fraction whose denominator is 51. *Ans.* $\frac{36}{51}$.

5. Reduce $\frac{28}{30}$ to a fraction whose denominator is 150.

6. Reduce $\frac{125}{436}$ to a fraction whose denominator is 3488. *Ans.* $\frac{1000}{3488}$.

7. Reduce $\frac{1}{125}$ to a fraction whose denominator is 1000.

Case V is what? How are fractions reduced to higher terms? What are all higher terms? Give analysis. Rule.

CASE VI.

131. To reduce two or more fractions to a common denominator.

A **Common Denominator** is a denominator common to two or more fractions.

1. Reduce $\frac{3}{4}$ and $\frac{2}{5}$ to a common denominator.

OPERATION.

$$\frac{3\times 5}{4\times 5}=\frac{15}{20}$$

$$\frac{2\times 4}{5\times 4}=\frac{8}{20}$$

ANALYSIS. We multiply the terms of the first fraction by the denominator of the second, and the terms of the second fraction by the denominator of the first, (**124.**) This must reduce each fraction to the same denominator, for each new denominator will be the product of the given denominators. Hence the

RULE. *Multiply the terms of each fraction by the denominators of all the other fractions.*

NOTE. Mixed numbers must first be reduced to improper fractions.

EXAMPLES FOR PRACTICE.

2. Reduce $\frac{2}{3}$, $\frac{1}{2}$, and $\frac{3}{4}$ to a common denominator.
Ans. $\frac{16}{24}$, $\frac{12}{24}$, $\frac{18}{24}$.

3. Reduce $\frac{3}{7}$ and $\frac{4}{9}$ to a common denominator.
Ans. $\frac{27}{63}$, $\frac{28}{63}$.

4. Reduce $\frac{4}{5}$, $\frac{7}{12}$, and $\frac{5}{6}$ to a common denominator.
Ans. $\frac{288}{360}$, $\frac{210}{360}$, $\frac{300}{360}$.

5. Reduce $\frac{3}{7}$, $\frac{5}{8}$, $\frac{2}{3}$, and $\frac{1}{2}$ to a common denominator.
Ans. $\frac{144}{336}$, $\frac{210}{336}$, $\frac{224}{336}$, $\frac{168}{336}$.

6. Reduce $\frac{9}{16}$, $\frac{1}{3}$, and $\frac{2}{9}$ to a common denominator.
Ans. $\frac{243}{432}$, $\frac{144}{432}$, $\frac{96}{432}$.

7. Reduce $\frac{5}{6}$, $2\frac{1}{2}$, $\frac{3}{4}$, and $\frac{1}{3}$ to a common denominator.
Ans. $\frac{120}{144}$, $\frac{360}{144}$, $\frac{108}{144}$, $\frac{48}{144}$.

8. Reduce $1\frac{7}{8}$, $\frac{3}{10}$, and 4 to a common denominator.
Ans. $\frac{150}{80}$, $\frac{24}{80}$, $\frac{320}{80}$.

Case VI is what? What is a common denominator? Give analysis. Rule.

CASE VII.

132. To reduce fractions to the least common denominator.

The **Least Common Denominator** of two or more fractions is the least denominator to which they can all be reduced, and it must be the least common multiple of the lowest denominators.

1. Reduce $\frac{1}{6}$, $\frac{3}{8}$, and $\frac{5}{12}$ to the least common denominator.

OPERATION.

$$\begin{array}{r|l} 2,3 & 6..8..12 \\ 2,2 & \quad 4..\ 2 \end{array}$$

$$2 \times 3 \times 2 \times 2 = 24$$

$$\left.\begin{array}{l} \frac{1}{6} = \frac{4}{24} \\ \frac{3}{8} = \frac{9}{24} \\ \frac{5}{12} = \frac{10}{24} \end{array}\right\} \textit{Ans.}$$

ANALYSIS. We first find the least common multiple of the given denominators, which is 24. This must be the least common denominator to which the fractions can be reduced. (III.) We then multiply the terms of each fraction by such a number as will reduce the fraction to the denominator, 24. Reducing each fraction to this denominator, by Case V, we have the answer.

Since the common denominator is already determined, it is only necessary to multiply the *numerators* by the multipliers. Hence the following

RULE. I. *Find the least common multiple of the given denominators, for the least common denominator.*

II. *Divide this common denominator by each of the given denominators, and multiply each numerator by the corresponding quotient. The products will be the new numerators.*

EXAMPLES FOR PRACTICE.

2. Reduce $\frac{2}{25}$, $\frac{3}{10}$, $\frac{47}{50}$, and $\frac{4}{75}$ to their least common denominator. *Ans.* $\frac{12}{150}$, $\frac{45}{150}$, $\frac{141}{150}$, $\frac{8}{150}$.

3. Reduce $\frac{1}{2}$, $\frac{4}{7}$, $\frac{3}{16}$, $\frac{2}{21}$ to their least common denominator. *Ans.* $\frac{168}{336}$, $\frac{192}{336}$, $\frac{63}{336}$, $\frac{32}{336}$.

What is Case VII? What must be the least common denominator? Give analysis. Rule, first step. Second.

4. Reduce $\frac{2}{9}$, $\frac{1}{21}$, $\frac{3}{4}$, and 6 to their least common denominator. *Ans.* $\frac{56}{252}$, $\frac{12}{252}$, $\frac{189}{252}$, $\frac{1512}{252}$.

5. Reduce $5\frac{1}{2}$, $2\frac{1}{4}$, and $1\frac{3}{8}$ to their least common denominator. *Ans.* $\frac{44}{8}$, $\frac{18}{8}$, $\frac{11}{8}$.

6. Reduce $\frac{9}{11}$, $\frac{3}{8}$, $\frac{4}{7}$, and $\frac{1}{4}$ to their least common denominator. *Ans.* $\frac{504}{616}$, $\frac{231}{616}$, $\frac{352}{616}$, $\frac{154}{616}$.

7. Reduce $\frac{3}{4}$, $\frac{1}{8}$, $\frac{2}{7}$, $2\frac{5}{6}$, and $\frac{5}{14}$ to their least common denominator. *Ans.* $\frac{126}{168}$, $\frac{21}{168}$, $\frac{48}{168}$, $\frac{476}{168}$, $\frac{60}{168}$.

8. Change $\frac{4}{5}$, $\frac{7}{15}$, $3\frac{2}{3}$, 9, and $\frac{7}{9}$ to equivalent fractions having the least common denominator.

9. Change $\frac{21}{28}$, $1\frac{6}{7}$, $\frac{7}{8}$, $\frac{11}{14}$, and 6 to equivalent fractions having the least common denominator.

10. Change $2\frac{7}{10}$, $\frac{37}{40}$, 4, $1\frac{2}{3}$, $\frac{11}{30}$, and $\frac{5}{8}$ to equivalent fractions having the least common denominator.

11. Reduce $\frac{4}{9}$, $\frac{2}{3}$, $\frac{1}{6}$, and $\frac{7}{12}$ to a common denominator.

12. Reduce $\frac{7}{8}$, $\frac{4}{7}$, $2\frac{3}{4}$, and $\frac{1}{2}$ to a common denominator.

13. Reduce $\frac{14}{15}$, $\frac{7}{10}$, $\frac{2}{3}$, and $3\frac{1}{5}$ to equivalent fractions having a common denominator. *Ans.* $\frac{28}{30}$, $\frac{21}{30}$, $\frac{20}{30}$, $\frac{96}{30}$.

14. Change $\frac{9}{27}$, $\frac{3}{8}$, and $\frac{4}{5}$ to equivalent fractions having a common denominator. *Ans.* $\frac{360}{1080}$, $\frac{405}{1080}$, $\frac{864}{1080}$.

15. Change $\frac{4}{11}$, $7\frac{1}{2}$, $\frac{20}{33}$, and 5 to equivalent fractions having a common denominator. *Ans.* $\frac{24}{66}$, $\frac{495}{66}$, $\frac{40}{66}$, $\frac{330}{66}$.

16. Change $\frac{7}{20}$, $6\frac{1}{4}$, $\frac{9}{10}$, 7, $\frac{3}{5}$, and $1\frac{1}{2}$ to equivalent fractions having a common denominator.

ADDITION.

133. 1. What is the sum of $\frac{1}{8}$, $\frac{3}{8}$, $\frac{5}{8}$, and $\frac{7}{8}$?

OPERATION.

$$\frac{1}{8}+\frac{3}{8}+\frac{5}{8}+\frac{7}{8}=\frac{16}{8}=2, \textit{ Ans.}$$

ANALYSIS. Since the given fractions have a common denominator, 8, their sum may be found by adding their numerators, 1, 3, 5, and 7, and placing the sum, 16, over the common denominator. We thus obtain $\frac{16}{8}=2$, the required sum.

2. Add $\frac{7}{10}$, $\frac{3}{10}$, $\frac{1}{10}$, $\frac{5}{10}$, and $\frac{9}{10}$. *Ans.* $2\frac{1}{2}$.

3. Add $\frac{4}{12}$, $\frac{5}{12}$, $\frac{7}{12}$, $\frac{1}{12}$, $\frac{3}{12}$, and $\frac{11}{12}$. *Ans.* $2\frac{7}{12}$.

Give first explanation.

4. What is the sum of $\frac{7}{25}$, $\frac{9}{25}$, $\frac{2}{25}$, $\frac{13}{25}$, $\frac{16}{25}$, and $\frac{21}{25}$?
5. What is the sum of $\frac{41}{120}$, $\frac{63}{120}$, $\frac{71}{120}$, $\frac{89}{120}$, and $\frac{109}{120}$?
6. What is the sum of $\frac{13}{225}$, $\frac{76}{225}$, $\frac{140}{225}$, $\frac{181}{225}$, and $\frac{223}{225}$?

Ans. $2\frac{61}{75}$.

134. 1. What is the sum of $\frac{3}{5}$ and $\frac{2}{9}$?

OPERATION.

$\frac{3}{5}+\frac{2}{9}=\frac{27}{45}+\frac{10}{45}=\frac{27+10}{45}=\frac{37}{45}$, *Ans.*

ANALYSIS. In whole numbers we can add like numbers only, or those having the same unit value; so in fractions we can add the numerators when they have a common denominator, but not otherwise. As $\frac{3}{5}$ and $\frac{2}{9}$ have not a common denominator, we first reduce them to a common denominator, and then add the numerators, $27+10=37$, the same as whole numbers, and place the sum over the common denominator. Hence the following

RULE. I. *When necessary, reduce the fractions to a common or to their least common denominator.*

II. *Add the numerators, and place the sum over the common denominator.*

NOTE. If the amount be an improper fraction, reduce it to a whole or a mixed number.

EXAMPLES FOR PRACTICE.

2. Add $\frac{3}{4}$ to $\frac{2}{9}$. *Ans.* $\frac{35}{36}$.
3. Add $\frac{4}{5}$ to $\frac{11}{14}$. *Ans.* $1\frac{41}{70}$.
4. Add $\frac{3}{4}$, $\frac{1}{8}$, $\frac{2}{7}$, and $\frac{5}{12}$. *Ans.* $1\frac{97}{168}$.
5. Add $\frac{14}{45}$, $\frac{27}{39}$, and $\frac{2}{21}$. *Ans.* $1\frac{404}{4095}$.
6. Add $\frac{42}{140}$, $\frac{9}{70}$, $\frac{7}{28}$, and $\frac{1}{14}$. *Ans.* $\frac{3}{4}$.
7. Add $\frac{51}{75}$, $\frac{131}{150}$, $\frac{24}{25}$, $\frac{1}{2}$, and $\frac{2}{3}$. *Ans.* $3\frac{17}{25}$.
8. Add $\frac{3}{4}$, $\frac{1}{2}$, $\frac{2}{3}$, $\frac{4}{5}$, $\frac{5}{6}$, $\frac{6}{7}$, $\frac{7}{8}$, $\frac{8}{9}$, and $\frac{9}{10}$. *Ans.* $7\frac{179}{2520}$.
9. Add $7\frac{1}{2}$, $5\frac{2}{3}$, and $10\frac{3}{4}$.

OPERATION.

$$\frac{1}{2}+\frac{2}{3}+\frac{3}{4}=1\frac{11}{12}$$
$$7+5+10=22$$

Ans. $23\frac{11}{12}$

ANALYSIS. The sum of the fractions $\frac{1}{2}$, $\frac{2}{3}$, and $\frac{3}{4}$ is $1\frac{11}{12}$; the sum of the integers, 7, 5, and 10, is 22; and the sum of both fractions and integers is $23\frac{11}{12}$. Hence,

---

Give second explanation? Rule, first step. Second.

To add mixed numbers, *add the fractions and integers separately, and then add their sums.*

NOTE. If the mixed numbers are small, they may be reduced to improper fractions, and then added after the usual method.

10. What is the sum of $14\frac{4}{5}$, $3\frac{9}{10}$, $1\frac{2}{3}$, and $\frac{19}{20}$? *Ans.* $21\frac{19}{60}$.

11. What is the sum of $\frac{7}{8}$, $1\frac{7}{12}$, $10\frac{5}{6}$, and 5? *Ans.* $18\frac{7}{24}$.

12. What is the sum of $17\frac{3}{4}$, $18\frac{5}{12}$, and $26\frac{1}{24}$?

13. What is the sum of $\frac{9}{48}$, $\frac{11}{16}$, $1\frac{1}{8}$, 3, and $\frac{17}{24}$?

14. What is the sum of $125\frac{4}{7}$, $327\frac{5}{12}$, and $25\frac{1}{4}$? *Ans.* $478\frac{5}{21}$.

15. What is the sum of $\frac{140}{320}$, $\frac{57}{80}$, $1\frac{1}{10}$, $\frac{19}{20}$, and $\frac{105}{160}$?

Ans. $3\frac{137}{160}$.

16. What is the sum of $3\frac{9}{70}$, $2\frac{12}{35}$, $40\frac{4}{7}$, and $10\frac{1}{10}$?

17. Bought 3 pieces of cloth containing $125\frac{7}{8}$, $96\frac{3}{4}$, and $48\frac{2}{3}$ yards; how many yards in the 3 pieces?

18. If it take $5\frac{1}{3}$ yards of cloth for a coat, $3\frac{1}{6}$ yards for a pair of pantaloons, and $\frac{5}{9}$ of a yard for a vest, how many yards will it take for all? *Ans.* $9\frac{1}{18}$.

19. A farmer divides his farm into 5 fields; the first contains $26\frac{7}{12}$ acres, the second $40\frac{16}{21}$ acres, the third $51\frac{6}{7}$ acres, the fourth $59\frac{3}{4}$ acres, and the fifth $62\frac{2}{3}$ acres; how many acres in the farm? *Ans.* $241\frac{13}{21}$.

20. A speculator bought $175\frac{3}{5}$ bushels of wheat for $205\frac{1}{3}$ dollars, $325\frac{4}{7}$ bushels of barley for $296\frac{3}{4}$ dollars, $270\frac{13}{21}$ bushels of corn for $200\frac{11}{12}$ dollars, and $437\frac{7}{15}$ bushels of oats for $156\frac{29}{42}$ dollars; how many bushels of grain did he buy, and how much did he pay for the whole?

Ans. $1209\frac{9}{35}$ bushels.
$859\frac{29}{42}$ dollars.

SUBTRACTION.

135. 1. From $\frac{7}{10}$ take $\frac{3}{10}$.

OPERATION.

$\frac{7}{10} - \frac{3}{10} = \frac{4}{10} = \frac{2}{5}$, *Ans.*

ANALYSIS. Since the given fractions have a common denominator, 10, we find the difference by subtracting 3, the less numerator, from 7, the greater, and write

How are mixed numbers added? Give note.

the remainder, 4, over the common denominator, 10. We thus obtain $\frac{4}{10}=\frac{2}{5}$, the required difference.

2. From $\frac{8}{9}$ take $\frac{5}{9}$. *Ans.* $\frac{1}{3}$.
3. From $\frac{14}{12}$ take $\frac{11}{12}$. *Ans.* $\frac{1}{4}$.
4. From $\frac{20}{27}$ take $\frac{6}{27}$. *Ans.* $\frac{14}{27}$.
5. From $\frac{48}{70}$ take $\frac{35}{70}$. *Ans.* $\frac{13}{70}$.
6. From $\frac{75}{128}$ take $\frac{11}{128}$. *Ans.* $\frac{1}{2}$.
7. From $\frac{182}{348}$ take $\frac{110}{348}$. *Ans.* $\frac{6}{29}$.

136. 1. From $\frac{8}{9}$ take $\frac{5}{6}$.

OPERATION.

$\frac{8}{9}-\frac{5}{6}=\frac{32}{36}-\frac{30}{36}=\frac{32-30}{36}=\frac{2}{36}=\frac{1}{18}$, *Ans.*

ANALYSIS. As in whole numbers, we can subtract *like* numbers only, or those having the same unit value, so, we can subtract fractions only when they have a common denominator. As $\frac{8}{9}$ and $\frac{5}{6}$ have not a common denominator, we first reduce them to a common denominator, and then subtract the less numerator, 30, from the greater, 32, and write the difference, 2, over the common denominator, 36. We thus obtain $\frac{2}{36}=\frac{1}{18}$, the required difference. Hence the following

RULE. I. *When necessary, reduce the fractions to a common denominator.*

II. *Subtract the numerator of the subtrahend from the numerator of the minuend, and place the difference over the common denominator.*

EXAMPLES FOR PRACTICE.

2. From $\frac{1}{2}$ take $\frac{2}{9}$. *Ans.* $\frac{5}{18}$.
3. From $\frac{15}{24}$ take $\frac{2}{5}$. *Ans.* $\frac{9}{40}$.
4. Subtract $\frac{4}{17}$ from $\frac{3}{8}$. *Ans.* $\frac{19}{136}$.
5. Subtract $\frac{4}{35}$ from $\frac{84}{120}$. *Ans.* $\frac{41}{70}$.
6. Subtract $\frac{50}{72}$ from $\frac{1500}{1728}$. *Ans.* $\frac{25}{144}$.
7. Subtract $\frac{332}{4272}$ from $\frac{60}{89}$. *Ans.* $\frac{637}{1068}$.
8. What is the difference between $9\frac{1}{3}$ and $2\frac{3}{4}$?

Give explanations. Rule, first step. Second.

OPERATION.
$9\frac{1}{3} = 9\frac{4}{12}$
$2\frac{3}{4} = 2\frac{9}{12}$
$6\frac{7}{12}$ *Ans.*

ANALYSIS. We first reduce the fractional parts, $\frac{1}{3}$ and $\frac{3}{4}$, to a common denominator, 12. Since we cannot take $\frac{9}{12}$ from $\frac{4}{12}$, we add $1 = \frac{12}{12}$ to $\frac{4}{12}$, which makes $\frac{16}{12}$, and $\frac{9}{12}$ from $\frac{16}{12}$ leaves $\frac{7}{12}$. We now add 1 to the 2 in the subtrahend, **(50,)** and say, 3 from 9 leaves 6. We thus obtain $6\frac{7}{12}$, the difference required.

Hence, to subtract mixed numbers, we may *reduce the fractional parts to a common denominator, and then subtract the fractional and integral parts separately.* Or,

We may reduce the mixed numbers to improper fractions, and subtract the less from the greater by the usual method.

9. From $8\frac{1}{2}$ take $3\frac{7}{9}$. *Ans.* $4\frac{13}{18}$.
10. From $25\frac{5}{6}$ take $9\frac{7}{10}$. *Ans.* $16\frac{2}{15}$.
11. From $4\frac{4}{5}$ take $\frac{14}{15}$.
12. Subtract $1\frac{1}{7}$ from 6.
13. Subtract $120\frac{9}{37}$ from $450\frac{1}{2}$. *Ans.* $330\frac{19}{74}$.
14. Subtract $\frac{43}{125}$ from $3\frac{7}{15}$. *Ans.* $3\frac{46}{375}$.
15. Find the difference between 49 and $75\frac{1}{4}$.
16. Find the difference between $227\frac{5}{8}$ and $196\frac{2}{3}$.
17. From a cask of wine containing $31\frac{1}{2}$ gallons, $17\frac{5}{8}$ gallons were drawn; how many gallons remained? *Ans.* $13\frac{7}{8}$.
18. A farmer, having $450\frac{7}{10}$ acres of land, sold $304\frac{3}{4}$ acres; how many acres had he left? *Ans.* $145\frac{19}{20}$.
19. If flour be bought for $6\frac{1}{4}$ dollars per barrel, and sold for $7\frac{2}{3}$ dollars, what will be the gain per barrel?
20. From the sum of $\frac{5}{7}$ and $3\frac{1}{2}$ take the difference of $4\frac{1}{3}$ and $5\frac{1}{4}$. *Ans.* $3\frac{25}{84}$.
21. A man, having $25\frac{7}{8}$ dollars, paid $6\frac{1}{2}$ dollars for coal, $2\frac{1}{5}$ dollars for dry goods, and $\frac{3}{4}$ of a dollar for a pound of tea; how much had he left? *Ans.* $\$16\frac{17}{40}$.
22. What number added to $2\frac{5}{9}$ will make $7\frac{1}{4}$? *Ans.* $4\frac{25}{36}$.
23. What fraction added to $\frac{11}{12}$ will make $\frac{19}{20}$? *Ans.* $\frac{1}{30}$.

In how many ways may mixed numbers be subtracted? What are they?

24. A gentleman, having 2000 dollars to divide among his three sons, gave to the first $912\frac{1}{4}$ dollars, to the second $545\frac{1}{3}$ dollars, and to the third the remainder; how much did the third receive? *Ans.* $\$542\frac{5}{12}$.

25. Bought a quantity of coal for $136\frac{9}{16}$ dollars, and of lumber for $350\frac{2}{3}$ dollars. I sold the coal for $184\frac{1}{3}$ dollars, and the lumber for $416\frac{3}{4}$ dollars. How much was my whole gain? *Ans.* $\$114\frac{1}{48}$.

MULTIPLICATION.

CASE I.

137. To multiply a fraction by an integer.

1. If 1 yard of cloth cost $\frac{3}{4}$ of a dollar, how much will 5 yards cost?

OPERATION.

$\frac{3}{4} \times 5 = \frac{15}{4} = 3\frac{3}{4}$, *Ans.*

ANALYSIS. Since 1 yard cost 3 *fourths* of a dollar, 5 yards will cost 5 times 3 *fourths* of a dollar, or 15 *fourths*, equal to $3\frac{3}{4}$ dollars. A fraction is multiplied by multiplying its numerator, (**124.**)

2. If 1 gallon of molasses cost $\frac{7}{20}$ of a dollar, how much will 5 gallons cost?

OPERATION.

$\frac{7}{20} \times 5 = \frac{7}{4} = 1\frac{3}{4}$, *Ans.*

ANALYSIS. Since 5, the multiplier, is a factor of 20, the denominator, of the multiplicand, we perform the multiplication by dividing the denominator, 20, by the multiplier, 5, and we have $\frac{7}{4}$, equal to $1\frac{3}{4}$ dollars. A fraction is multiplied by dividing its denominator, (**124.**) Hence,

Multiplying a fraction consists in multiplying its numerator, or dividing its denominator.

NOTE. Always divide the denominator when it is exactly divisible by the multiplier.

EXAMPLES FOR PRACTICE.

3. Multiply $\frac{3}{7}$ by 5. *Ans.* $\frac{15}{7} = 2\frac{1}{7}$.
4. Multiply $\frac{3}{11}$ by 7. *Ans.* $1\frac{10}{11}$.

Case I is what? Give explanations. Deduction.

5. Multiply $\frac{9}{14}$ by 12. *Ans.* $7\frac{5}{7}$.
6. Multiply $\frac{5}{21}$ by 63. *Ans.* 15.
7. Multiply $5\frac{1}{2}$ by 9.

OPERATION.

$$\begin{array}{r} 5\frac{1}{2} \\ 9 \\ \hline 4\frac{1}{2} \\ 45 \\ \hline 49\frac{1}{2} \end{array}$$

Or,

$$5\frac{1}{2} = \frac{11}{2}$$

$$\frac{11}{2} \times 9 = \frac{99}{2} = 49\frac{1}{2}.$$

ANALYSIS. In multiplying a mixed number, we first multiply the fractional part, and then the integer, and add the two products; or we reduce the mixed number to an improper fraction, and then multiply it.

8. Multiply $7\frac{3}{5}$ by 12. *Ans.* $91\frac{1}{5}$.
9. Multiply $\frac{81}{121}$ by 8. *Ans.* $5\frac{43}{121}$.
10. Multiply $\frac{4}{102}$ by 51. *Ans.* 2.
11. Multiply $15\frac{5}{8}$ by 16. *Ans.* 250.
12. Multiply $\frac{101}{132}$ by 22. *Ans.* $16\frac{5}{6}$.
13. If a man earn $8\frac{9}{10}$ dollars a week, how many dollars will he earn in 12 weeks?
14. What will 9 yards of silk cost at $\frac{11}{12}$ of a dollar per yard?
15. What will 27 bushels of barley cost at $\frac{7}{8}$ of a dollar per bushel? *Ans.* $23\frac{5}{8}$ dollars.

CASE II.

138. To multiply an integer by a fraction.

1. At 75 dollars an acre, how much will $\frac{3}{5}$ of an acre of land cost?

FIRST OPERATION.

5)	75	price of an acre.
	15	cost of $\frac{1}{5}$ of an acre.
	3	
Ans.	45	" " $\frac{3}{5}$ " " "

ANALYSIS. 3 fifths of an acre will cost three times as much as 1 fifth of an acre. Dividing 75 dollars by 5, we have 15 dollars, the cost of $\frac{1}{5}$ of an acre, which we multiply by 3, and obtain 45 dollars, the cost of $\frac{3}{5}$ of an acre.

Explain the process of multiplying mixed numbers. What is Case II? Give first explanation.

SECOND OPERATION.

$$\begin{array}{rl} & 75 \text{ price of 1 acre.} \\ & 3 \\ \hline 5\,) & 225 \text{ cost of 3 acres.} \\ \hline \textit{Ans.} & 45 \text{ " " } \tfrac{3}{5} \text{ of an acre.} \end{array}$$

Or, multiplying the price of 1 acre by 3, we have the cost of 3 acres; and as $\frac{1}{5}$ of 3 acres is the same as $\frac{3}{5}$ of 1 acre, we divide the cost of 3 acres by 5, and we have the cost of $\frac{3}{5}$ of an acre, the same as in the first operation. Hence,

Multiplying by a fraction consists in multiplying by the numerator and dividing by the denominator of the multiplier.

$$\begin{array}{r|l} & \overset{15}{\cancel{75}} \\ \cancel{5} & 3 \\ \hline & 45, \textit{ Ans.} \end{array}$$

NOTE. By using the vertical line and cancellation, we shall shorten, and combine both operations in one.

EXAMPLES FOR PRACTICE.

2. Multiply 3 by $\frac{4}{9}$. *Ans.* $1\frac{1}{3}$.
3. Multiply 100 by $\frac{9}{14}$. *Ans.* $64\frac{2}{7}$.
4. Multiply 105 by $\frac{17}{21}$. *Ans.* 85.
5. Multiply 19 by $\frac{13}{47}$. *Ans.* $5\frac{12}{47}$.
6. Multiply 24 by $6\frac{5}{8}$.

OPERATION.

$$\begin{array}{l} 24 \\ \underline{\;\;6\tfrac{5}{8}} \\ \;\;15 = \tfrac{5}{8} \text{ of } 24; \\ \underline{144} \\ 159, \textit{ Ans.} \end{array} \qquad \text{Or, } \begin{array}{r|l} & \overset{3}{\cancel{24}} \\ \cancel{8} & 53 \\ \hline & 159, \textit{ Ans.} \end{array}$$

ANALYSIS. We multiply by the integer and fraction separately, and add the products; or, reduce the mixed number to an improper fraction, and then multiply by it.

7. Multiply 42 by $9\frac{3}{4}$. *Ans.* $409\frac{1}{2}$.
8. Multiply 80 by $14\frac{9}{16}$. *Ans.* 1165.
9. Multiply 156 by $\frac{27}{39}$. *Ans.* 108.
10. At 8 dollars a bushel, what will $\frac{5}{6}$ of a bushel of clover seed cost?

Give second explanation. Note. Deduction.

11. If a man travel 36 miles a day, how many miles will he travel in $10\frac{2}{3}$ days? *Ans.* 384 miles.

12. If a village lot be worth 450 dollars, what is $\frac{7}{12}$ of it worth? *Ans.* $262\frac{1}{2}$ dollars.

13. At 16 dollars a ton, what is the cost of $2\frac{7}{9}$ tons of hay?

CASE III.

139. To multiply a fraction by a fraction.

1. At $\frac{2}{3}$ of a dollar per bushel, how much will $\frac{3}{4}$ of a bushel of corn cost?

OPERATION.

1st step,	$\frac{2}{3} \div 4 = \frac{2}{12}$,	cost of $\frac{1}{4}$ of a bushel.
2d step,	$\frac{2}{12} \times 3 = \frac{6}{12}$,	" " $\frac{3}{4}$ " " "
Whole work,	$\frac{2}{3} \times \frac{3}{4} = \frac{6}{12} = \frac{1}{2}$, *Ans.*	

Or,

$\not{3}$	$\not{2}$
2 $\not{4}$	$\not{3}$
2	$1 = \frac{1}{2}$, *Ans.*

ANALYSIS. Since 1 bushel cost $\frac{2}{3}$ of a dollar, $\frac{3}{4}$ of a bushel will cost $\frac{3}{4}$ times $\frac{2}{3}$ of a dollar, or 3 times $\frac{1}{4}$ of $\frac{2}{3}$ of a dollar. Dividing $\frac{2}{3}$ of a dollar by 4, we have $\frac{2}{12}$, the cost of $\frac{1}{4}$ of a bushel. A fraction is divided by multiplying its denominator, (**124.**) Multiplying the cost of $\frac{1}{4}$ of a bushel by 3, we have $\frac{6}{12}$ of a dollar, the cost of $\frac{3}{4}$ of a bushel. It will readily be seen that we have multiplied together the two numerators, 2 and 3, for a new numerator, and the two denominators, 3 and 4, for a new denominator, as shown in the whole work of the operation. Hence, for multiplication of fractions, we have this general

RULE. I. *Reduce all integers and mixed numbers to improper fractions.*

II. *Multiply together the numerators for a new numerator, and the denominators for a new denominator.*

NOTE. Cancel all factors common to numerators and denominators.

EXAMPLES FOR PRACTICE.

2. Multiply $\frac{3}{4}$ by $\frac{4}{9}$. *Ans.* $\frac{1}{3}$.
3 Multiply $\frac{7}{8}$ by $\frac{4}{5}$. *Ans.* $\frac{7}{10}$.
4. Multiply $\frac{11}{24}$ by $\frac{36}{55}$. *Ans.* $\frac{3}{10}$.
5. Multiply $4\frac{1}{5}$ by $\frac{6}{7}$. *Ans.* $3\frac{3}{5}$.

What is Case III? Give explanation. Rule, first step? Second? What shall be done with common factors?

6. What is the product of $\frac{9}{10}$, $\frac{2}{7}$, $\frac{5}{9}$, and $\frac{1}{4}$? *Ans.* $\frac{1}{28}$.

7. What is the product of $1\frac{5}{6}$, $\frac{3}{5}$, 2, and $5\frac{1}{3}$? *Ans.* $11\frac{11}{15}$.

8. What is the product of $\frac{3}{4}$ of $\frac{7}{10}$, $\frac{5}{6}$ of $\frac{2}{3}$ of $\frac{7}{8}$, and $\frac{4}{7}$ of $1\frac{3}{5}$?

OPERATION.

$$\frac{\cancel{3}}{\cancel{4}}\times\frac{7}{\underset{5}{\cancel{10}}}\times\frac{\cancel{5}}{6}\times\frac{\cancel{2}}{\cancel{3}}\times\frac{\cancel{7}}{\cancel{8}}\times\frac{\cancel{4}}{\cancel{7}}\times\frac{\cancel{8}}{\cancel{5}}=\frac{7}{30}, \textit{ Ans.}$$

Or,

$\cancel{4}$	$\cancel{3}$
$5\ \cancel{10}$	7
6	$\cancel{5}$
$\cancel{3}$	$\cancel{2}$
$\cancel{8}$	$\cancel{7}$
$\cancel{7}$	$\cancel{4}$
$\cancel{5}$	$\cancel{8}$
30	$7 = \frac{7}{30}$.

NOTE. Fractions with the word *of* between them are sometimes called *compound fractions*. The word *of* is simply an equivalent for the sign of multiplication, and signifies that the numbers between which it is placed are to be multiplied together.

9. Multiply $\frac{8}{15}$ of $2\frac{1}{4}$ by $\frac{1}{5}$ of $7\frac{1}{3}$. *Ans.* $1\frac{19}{25}$.

10. Multiply $\frac{2}{7}$ of 16 by $\frac{7}{10}$ of $26\frac{2}{3}$. *Ans.* $85\frac{1}{3}$.

11. What is the product of 3, $\frac{1}{2}$ of $\frac{4}{7}$, and $\frac{4}{5}$ of $3\frac{1}{4}$?

12. What is the value of $2\frac{1}{2}$ times $\frac{3}{4}$ of $\frac{4}{5}$ of $1\frac{1}{3}$? *Ans.* 2.

13. What is the value of $\frac{7}{8}$ of $\frac{1}{2}$ of $1\frac{2}{3}$ times $\frac{3}{2}$ of 8?

14. What is the product of $12\frac{1}{2}$ multiplied by $5\frac{1}{2}$ times $6\frac{3}{4}$? *Ans.* $464\frac{1}{16}$.

15. At $\frac{8}{9}$ of a dollar per yard, what will $\frac{3}{8}$ of a yard of cloth cost? *Ans.* $\frac{1}{3}$ of a dollar.

16. If a man own $\frac{6}{7}$ of a vessel, and sell $\frac{2}{3}$ of his share, what part of the whole vessel will he sell?

17. When oats are worth $\frac{1}{2}$ of a dollar per bushel, what is $\frac{3}{4}$ of a bushel worth?

18. What will $7\frac{3}{4}$ pounds of tea cost, at $\frac{3}{5}$ of a dollar per pound? *Ans.* $4\frac{13}{20}$ dollars.

19. What is the product of $9\frac{6}{7}$ by $4\frac{2}{3}$?

	$9\frac{6}{7}$	
	$4\frac{2}{3}$	
	$39\frac{3}{7}$	product by 4.
	$6\frac{4}{7}$	" " $\frac{2}{3}$.
Ans.	46	" " $4\frac{2}{3}$.

Or, $9\frac{6}{7}\times4\frac{2}{3}=\frac{\overset{23}{\cancel{69}}}{\cancel{7}}\times\frac{\overset{2}{\cancel{14}}}{\cancel{3}}=46.$

What does "*of*" signify when placed between two fractions? What is a compound fraction?

To multiply mixed numbers together we may either multiply by the integer and fractional part separately, and then add their products; or, we may reduce both numbers to improper fractions, and then multiply as in the foregoing rule.

20. Multiply $12\frac{3}{4}$ by $8\frac{1}{2}$. *Ans.* $108\frac{3}{8}$.

21. What cost $6\frac{3}{8}$ cords of wood, at $2\frac{4}{5}$ dollars a cord?

22. What cost $\frac{3}{4}$ of $2\frac{1}{2}$ tons of hay, at $11\frac{3}{10}$ dollars a ton? *Ans.* $\$21\frac{3}{16}$.

23. What will $8\frac{5}{8}$ cords of wood cost, at $2\frac{3}{5}$ dollars per cord? *Ans.* $22\frac{17}{40}$ dollars.

24. What must be paid for $\frac{4}{5}$ of $6\frac{1}{2}$ tons of coal, at $\frac{2}{3}$ of $7\frac{1}{4}$ dollars per ton?

25. A man owning $\frac{7}{9}$ of a farm, sold $\frac{1}{3}$ of his share; what part of the whole farm had he left? *Ans.* $\frac{14}{27}$.

26. Bought a horse for $125\frac{3}{4}$ dollars, and sold him for $\frac{4}{5}$ of what he cost; how much was the loss? *Ans.* $\$25\frac{3}{20}$.

27. A owned $\frac{2}{3}$ of $123\frac{5}{6}$ acres of land, and sold $\frac{3}{5}$ of his share; how many acres did he sell? *Ans.* $49\frac{8}{15}$.

28. If a family consume $1\frac{1}{4}$ barrels of flour a month, how many barrels will five such families consume in $4\frac{9}{10}$ months?

DIVISION.

CASE I.

140. To divide a fraction by an integer.

1. If my horse eat $\frac{9}{10}$ of a ton of hay in 3 months, what part of a ton will last him 1 month?

OPERATION.

$\frac{9}{10} \div 3 = \frac{3}{10}$, *Ans.*

ANALYSIS. If he eat $\frac{9}{10}$ of a ton in 3 months, in 1 month he will eat $\frac{1}{3}$ of $\frac{9}{10}$ of a ton, or $\frac{9}{10}$ divided by 3. Since a fraction is divided by dividing its numerator, (**124**,) we divide the numerator of the fraction, $\frac{9}{10}$, by 3, and we have $\frac{3}{10}$, the answer.

2. If 3 yards of ribbon cost $\frac{6}{8}$ of a dollar, what will 1 yard cost?

Case I is what? Give first explanation.

OPERATION.

$\frac{5}{6} \div 3 = \frac{5}{18}$, *Ans.*

ANALYSIS. Here we cannot exactly divide the numerator by 3; but, since a fraction is divided by multiplying the denominator, (**124**,) we multiply the denominator of the fraction, $\frac{5}{6}$, by 3, and we have $\frac{5}{18}$, the required result. Hence,

Dividing a fraction consists in dividing its numerator, or multiplying its denominator.

NOTE. We divide the numerator when it is exactly divisible by the divisor; otherwise we multiply the denominator.

EXAMPLES FOR PRACTICE.

3. Divide $\frac{6}{7}$ by 2. *Ans.* $\frac{3}{7}$.
4. Divide $\frac{9}{21}$ by 3. *Ans.* $\frac{1}{7}$.
5. Divide $\frac{14}{15}$ by 5. *Ans.* $\frac{14}{75}$.
6. Divide $\frac{75}{125}$ by 25.
7. Divide $\frac{13}{17}$ by 14. *Ans.* $\frac{13}{238}$.
8. Divide $\frac{51}{63}$ by 21. *Ans.* $\frac{17}{441}$.
9. If 6 pounds of sugar cost $\frac{2}{3}$ of a dollar, how much will 1 pound cost?
10. At 7 dollars a barrel, what part of a barrel of flour can be bought for $\frac{7}{8}$ of a dollar? *Ans.* $\frac{1}{8}$.
11. If a yard of cloth cost 5 dollars, what part of a yard can be bought for $\frac{6}{7}$ of a dollar? *Ans.* $\frac{6}{35}$.
12. If 9 bushels of barley cost $7\frac{1}{5}$ dollars, how much will 1 bushel cost?

OPERATION.

$7\frac{1}{5} = \frac{36}{5}$

$\frac{36}{5} \div 9 = \frac{4}{5}$, *Ans.*

NOTE. We reduce the mixed number to an improper fraction, and divide as before.

13. If 12 barrels of flour cost $76\frac{4}{5}$ dollars, how much will 1 barrel cost?

OPERATION.

$$\begin{array}{r} 12\,)\,\underline{76\frac{4}{5}} \\ 6\frac{2}{5}, \textit{Ans.} \end{array}$$

ANALYSIS. Here we first divide as in simple numbers, and we have a remainder of $4\frac{4}{5}$. We reduce this remainder to an improper fraction, $\frac{24}{5}$, which we divide (as in Ex. 1,) and annex the result, $\frac{2}{5}$, to the partial quotient, 6, and we have $6\frac{2}{5}$, the required result.

Give second explanation. Deduction.

14. How many times will $16\frac{3}{4}$ gallons of cider fill a vessel that holds 3 gallons? *Ans.* $5\frac{7}{12}$.

15. If 9 men consume $\frac{3}{4}$ of $9\frac{3}{5}$ pounds of meat in a day, how much does each man consume? *Ans.* $\frac{4}{5}$ of a pound.

16. A man paid $\$99\frac{21}{25}$ for 4 cows; how much was that apiece? *Ans.* $\$24\frac{24}{25}$.

CASE II.

141. To divide an integer by a fraction.

1. At $\frac{3}{4}$ of a dollar a yard, how many yards of cloth can be bought for 12 dollars?

FIRST OPERATION.

$$\begin{array}{r} 12 \\ 4 \\ \hline 3\,)\,48 \\ \hline 16 \text{ yards.} \end{array}$$

ANALYSIS. As many yards as $\frac{3}{4}$ of a dollar, the price of 1 yard, is contained times in 12 dollars. Integers cannot be divided by *fourths*, because they are not of the same denomination. Reducing 12 dollars to *fourths* by multiplying, we have 48 *fourths*; and 3 *fourths* is contained in 48 *fourths* 16 times, the required number of yards.

SECOND OPERATION.

$$\begin{array}{r} 3\,)\,12 \\ \hline 4 \\ 4 \\ \hline 16 \text{ yards.} \end{array}$$

ANALYSIS. Here we divide the integer by the numerator of the fraction, and multiply the quotient by the denominator, which produces the same result as in the first operation. Hence,

Dividing by a fraction consists in multiplying by the denominator; and dividing by the numerator of the divisor.

EXAMPLES FOR PRACTICE.

2. Divide 18 by $\frac{3}{8}$. *Ans.* 48.
3. Divide 63 by $\frac{7}{13}$. *Ans.* 117.
4. Divide 42 by $\frac{6}{7}$. *Ans.* 49.
5. Divide 120 by $\frac{7}{12}$. *Ans.* $205\frac{5}{7}$.
6. Divide 316 by $\frac{9}{25}$. *Ans.* $877\frac{7}{9}$.

Case II is what? Give first explanation. Second. Deduction.

7. How many bushels of oats, worth $\frac{2}{5}$ of a dollar per bushel, will pay for $\frac{2}{3}$ of a barrel of flour, worth 9 dollars a barrel? *Ans.* 15.

8. If $\frac{3}{7}$ of an acre of land sell for 21 dollars, what will an acre sell for at the same rate? *Ans.* \$49.

9. When potatoes are worth $\frac{4}{9}$ of a dollar a bushel, and corn $\frac{5}{8}$ of a dollar a bushel, how many bushels of potatoes are equal in value to 16 bushels of corn? *Ans.* $22\frac{1}{2}$.

10. If a man can chop $2\frac{3}{4}$ cords of wood in a day, in how many days can he chop 22 cords?

OPERATION.

$$2\frac{3}{4} = \frac{11}{4}$$

$$\begin{array}{r} 22 \\ 4 \\ \hline 11\,)\,88 \\ \hline \end{array}$$

Ans. 8 days.

ANALYSIS. We reduce the mixed number to an improper fraction, and then divide the integer in the same manner as by a proper fraction.

11. Divide 75 by $13\frac{4}{5}$. *Ans.* $5\frac{10}{23}$.

12. Divide 149 by $24\frac{1}{6}$. *Ans.* $6\frac{24}{145}$.

13. A farmer distributed 15 bushels of corn among some poor persons, giving them $1\frac{2}{3}$ bushels apiece; among how many persons did he divide it?

14. Divide $\frac{5}{8}$ of 320 by $\frac{5}{6}$ of $9\frac{1}{3}$. *Ans.* $25\frac{5}{7}$.

15. Bought $\frac{1}{3}$ of $7\frac{1}{2}$ cords of wood for $\frac{1}{4}$ of \$32; how much did 1 cord cost? *Ans.* $\$3\frac{1}{5}$.

16. A father divided 183 acres of land equally among his sons, giving them $45\frac{3}{4}$ acres apiece; how many sons had he? *Ans.* 4.

CASE III.

142. To divide a fraction by a fraction.

1. How many pounds of tea can be bought for $\frac{11}{12}$ of a dollar, at $\frac{3}{4}$ of a dollar a pound?

How divide by a mixed number? Case III is what?

OPERATION.

First step, $\frac{11}{12} \times 3 = \frac{33}{12}$

Second step, $\frac{33}{12} \div 2 = \frac{33}{24} = 1\frac{3}{8}$.

Whole work, $\frac{11}{12} \div \frac{2}{3} = \frac{11}{\not{12}_{4}} \times \frac{\not{3}}{2} = \frac{11}{8} = 1\frac{3}{8}$, *Ans.*

ANALYSIS. As many pounds as $\frac{2}{3}$ of a dollar is contained times in $\frac{11}{12}$ of a dollar. 1 is contained in $\frac{11}{12}$, $\frac{11}{12}$ times, and $\frac{1}{3}$ is contained in $\frac{11}{12}$ 3 times as many times as 1, or 3 times $\frac{11}{12}$, which is $\frac{33}{12}$ times, which is the number of pounds that could be bought at $\frac{1}{3}$ of a dollar per pound; but $\frac{2}{3}$ is contained but $\frac{1}{2}$ as many times as $\frac{1}{3}$, and $\frac{33}{12}$ divided by 2 gives $\frac{33}{24}$, equal to $1\frac{3}{8}$ times, or the number of pounds that can be bought at $\frac{2}{3}$ of a dollar per pound.

We see in the operation that we have multiplied the dividend by the denominator of the divisor, and divided the result by the numerator of the divisor, which is in accordance with **140** for dividing a fraction. Hence, by inverting the terms of the divisor, the two fractions will stand in such relation to each other that we can multiply together the two upper numbers for the numerator of the quotient, and the two lower numbers for the denominator, as shown in the operation. For division of fractions, we have this general

RULE. I. *Reduce integers and mixed numbers to improper fractions.*

II. *Invert the terms of the divisor, and proceed as in multiplication.*

NOTES. 1. The dividend and divisor may be reduced to a common denominator, and the numerator of the dividend be divided by the numerator of the divisor; this will give the same result as the rule.

2. Apply cancellation where practicable.

EXAMPLES FOR PRACTICE.

2. Divide $\frac{7}{8}$ by $\frac{3}{4}$. *Ans.* $1\frac{1}{6}$.
3. Divide $\frac{5}{9}$ by $\frac{1}{6}$. *Ans.* $3\frac{1}{3}$.
4. Divide $\frac{4}{7}$ by $\frac{9}{10}$. *Ans.* $\frac{40}{63}$.
5. Divide $\frac{1}{2}$ by $\frac{7}{13}$. *Ans.* $\frac{13}{14}$.
6. Divide $\frac{2}{3}$ by $\frac{27}{28}$. *Ans.* $\frac{56}{81}$.
7. How many times is $\frac{4}{5}$ contained in $\frac{5}{6}$? *Ans.* $1\frac{1}{24}$.
8. How many times is $\frac{3}{7}$ contained in $1\frac{2}{3}$? *Ans.* $3\frac{8}{9}$.

Rule, first step. Second. What other method is mentioned?

9. How many times is $\frac{7}{15}$ contained in $\frac{17}{15}$? *Ans.* $2\frac{3}{7}$.

10. How many times is $\frac{5}{16}$ contained in $\frac{13}{20}$?

11. How many times is $\frac{1}{2}$ of $\frac{3}{4}$ contained in $\frac{3}{7}$ of $2\frac{1}{2}$?

12. What is the quotient of $\frac{9}{10}$ of 4, divided by $\frac{5}{6}$ of $3\frac{1}{4}$?

13. What is the quotient of $\frac{1}{8}$ of $\frac{7}{9}$ of 36 divided by $1\frac{7}{8}$ times $\frac{3}{5}$? *Ans.* $3\frac{1}{9}$.

14. What is the value of $\dfrac{3\frac{1}{2}}{4\frac{3}{8}}$?

OPERATION.

$$\frac{3\frac{1}{2}}{4\frac{3}{8}} = \frac{\frac{7}{2}}{\frac{35}{8}} = \frac{7}{2} \div \frac{35}{8} = \frac{7}{2} \times \frac{8}{35} = \frac{4}{5}, \textit{ Ans.}$$

This example is only another form for expressing division of fractions; it is sometimes called a *complex fraction*, and the process of performing the division is called *reducing a complex fraction to a simple one.*

We simply reduce the upper number or dividend to an improper fraction, and the lower number, or divisor, to an improper fraction, and then divide as before.

15. What is the value of $\dfrac{6\frac{2}{9}}{8\frac{2}{3}}$? *Ans.* $\frac{28}{39}$.

16. What is the value of $\dfrac{11\frac{3}{7}}{\frac{4}{7}}$? *Ans.* 20.

17. What is the value of $\dfrac{\frac{5}{11}}{4\frac{2}{5}}$? *Ans.* $\frac{25}{242}$.

18. What is the value of $\dfrac{\frac{2}{3} \text{ of } \frac{3}{4}}{\frac{1}{2}}$? *Ans.* 1.

19. What is the value of $\dfrac{\frac{2}{5} \text{ of } \frac{5}{6}}{\frac{2}{9} \text{ of } 4\frac{1}{2}}$? *Ans.* $\frac{1}{3}$.

20. If a horse eat $\frac{3}{8}$ of a bushel of oats in a day, in how many days will he eat $5\frac{1}{4}$ bushels? *Ans.* 14.

21. If a man spend $1\frac{3}{5}$ dollars per month for tobacco, in what time will he spend $10\frac{2}{3}$ dollars? *Ans.* $6\frac{2}{3}$ months.

What is a complex fraction?

22. How many times will $4\frac{3}{8}$ gallons of camphene fill a vessel that holds $\frac{1}{2}$ of $\frac{5}{6}$ of 1 gallon? *Ans.* $10\frac{1}{2}$.

23. If 14 acres of meadow land produce $32\frac{2}{3}$ tons of hay, how many tons will 5 acres produce? *Ans.* $11\frac{2}{3}$.

24. If 2 yards of silk cost $\$3\frac{1}{4}$, how much less than \$17 will 9 yards cost? *Ans.* $\$2\frac{3}{8}$.

25. If $\frac{2}{3}$ of a yard of cloth cost $\frac{3}{10}$ of a dollar, how much will 1 yard cost?

26. A man, having \$10, gave $\frac{2}{3}$ of his money for clover seed at $\$3\frac{1}{3}$ a bushel; how much did he buy? *Ans.* 2 bush.

27. How many tons of hay can be purchased for $\$119\frac{1}{16}$, at $\$9\frac{3}{8}$ per ton? *Ans.* $12\frac{7}{10}$.

PROMISCUOUS EXAMPLES.

1. Reduce $\frac{1}{2}$, $\frac{5}{6}$, $\frac{3}{8}$, and $\frac{1}{4}$ to equivalent fractions whose denominators shall be 24. *Ans.* $\frac{12}{24}$, $\frac{20}{24}$, $\frac{9}{24}$, $\frac{6}{24}$.

2. Change $\frac{4}{7}$ to an equivalent fraction having 91 for its denominator *Ans.* $\frac{52}{91}$.

3. Find the least common denominator of $\frac{3}{4}$, $1\frac{2}{3}$, $\frac{1}{2}$ of $\frac{4}{5}$, 2, $\frac{1}{8}$ of $\frac{1}{4}$ of $1\frac{1}{10}$.

4. Add $4\frac{1}{3}$, $\frac{7}{9}$, $\frac{4}{5}$ of $1\frac{1}{8}$, 3, and $\frac{11}{12}$.

5. Find the difference between $\frac{2}{3}$ of $6\frac{7}{10}$ and $\frac{5}{9}$ of $4\frac{8}{15}$. *Ans.* $1\frac{128}{135}$.

6. The less of two numbers is $4756\frac{4}{9}$, and their difference is $128\frac{3}{4}$; what is the greater number? *Ans.* $4885\frac{7}{36}$.

7. What is the difference between the continued products of 3, $\frac{7}{8}$, $\frac{2}{3}$, $4\frac{2}{5}$, and $3\frac{7}{8}$, $\frac{2}{3}$, 4, $\frac{2}{5}$? *Ans.* $3\frac{17}{30}$.

8. Reduce the fractions $\dfrac{4}{\frac{1}{5}}$ and $\dfrac{2\frac{1}{2}}{1\frac{1}{3}}$ to their simplest form.

9. What number multiplied by $\frac{3}{5}$ will produce $1825\frac{7}{8}$? *Ans.* $3043\frac{1}{8}$.

10. A farmer had $\frac{1}{5}$ of his sheep in one pasture, $\frac{1}{4}$ in another, and the remainder, which were 77, in a third pasture; how many sheep had he? *Ans.* 140.

11. What will $7\frac{3}{4}$ cords of wood cost at $\frac{1}{3}$ of $9\frac{1}{2}$ dollars per cord? *Ans.* $\$24\frac{13}{24}$.

12. At $\frac{1}{4}$ of a dollar per bushel, how many bushels of apples can be bought for $5\frac{7}{8}$ dollars?

13. Paid $\$1837\frac{5}{8}$ for $7350\frac{1}{2}$ bushels of oats; how much was that per bushel? *Ans.* $\frac{1}{4}$ of a dollar.

14. If $235\frac{1}{2}$ acres of land cost $\$4725\frac{3}{8}$, how much will 628 acres cost? *Ans.* $12601.

15. A man, owning $\frac{2}{5}$ of an iron foundery, sold $\frac{1}{3}$ of his share for $\$540\frac{3}{4}$; what was the value of the foundery? *Ans.* $\$4055\frac{5}{8}$.

16. $14\frac{2}{7}$ less $\dfrac{\frac{1}{2} \text{ of } 8\frac{2}{5}}{14\frac{7}{10}}$ is $\frac{2}{3}$ of $\frac{7}{9}$ of what number? *Ans.* 27.

17. A merchant bought $4\frac{3}{4}$ cords of wood at $\$3\frac{1}{4}$ per cord, and paid for it in cloth at $\frac{5}{8}$ of a dollar per yard; how many yards were required to pay for the wood?

18. How many yards of cloth, $\frac{3}{4}$ of a yard wide, will line $20\frac{1}{2}$ yards, $1\frac{1}{4}$ yards wide? *Ans.* $34\frac{1}{6}$.

19. If the dividend be $\frac{7}{9}$, and the quotient $\frac{4}{39}$, what is the divisor?

20. If the sum of two fractions be $\frac{5}{8}$, and one of them be $\frac{9}{20}$, what is the other? *Ans.* $\frac{7}{40}$.

21. If the smaller of two fractions be $\frac{24}{31}$, and their difference $\frac{7}{93}$, what is the greater? *Ans.* $\frac{79}{93}$.

22. If $3\frac{2}{3}$ pounds of sugar cost 33 cents, how much must be paid for $65\frac{1}{2}$ pounds?

23. If 324 bushels of barley can be had for $259\frac{1}{5}$ bushels of corn, how much barley can be had for 2000 bushels of corn? *Ans.* 2500 bushels.

24. A certain sum of money is to be divided among 5 persons; A is to have $\frac{1}{4}$, B $\frac{1}{5}$, C $\frac{1}{10}$, D $\frac{1}{20}$, and E the remainder, which is 20 dollars; what is the whole sum to be divided? *Ans.* $50.

25. What number, diminished by the difference between $\frac{3}{4}$ and $\frac{3}{5}$ of itself, leaves a remainder of 34? *Ans.* 40.

26. If $\frac{3}{8}$ of a farm be valued at $1728, what is the value of the whole?

27. Bought 320 sheep at $\$2\frac{1}{4}$ per head; afterward bought 435 at $\$1\frac{7}{8}$ per head; then sold $\frac{3}{5}$ of the whole number at $\$1\frac{3}{4}$ per head, and the remainder at $\$2\frac{1}{8}$; did I gain or lose, and how much? *Ans.* Lost $\$44\frac{1}{2}$.

28. If 5 be added to both terms of the fraction $\frac{7}{8}$, will its value be increased or diminished? *Ans.* Increased $\frac{5}{104}$.

29. If 5 be added to both terms of the fraction $\frac{8}{7}$, will its value be increased or diminished? *Ans.* Diminished $\frac{5}{84}$.

30. How many times can a bottle holding $\frac{1}{4}$ of $\frac{2}{3}$ of a gallon, be filled from a demijohn containing $\frac{3}{4}$ of $1\frac{2}{3}$ gallons? *Ans.* $7\frac{1}{2}$.

31. Bought $\frac{1}{3}$ of $7\frac{1}{2}$ cords of wood for $\frac{1}{4}$ of $32; how much did 1 cord cost?

32. Purchased 728 pounds of candles at $16\frac{3}{8}$ cents a pound; had they been purchased for $3\frac{7}{8}$ cents less a pound, how many pounds could have been purchased for the same money? *Ans.* $953\frac{17}{25}$.

33. What number, divided by $1\frac{3}{8}$, will give a quotient of $9\frac{1}{8}$? *Ans.* $12\frac{35}{64}$.

34. The product of two numbers is 6, and one of them is 1846; what is the other? *Ans.* $\frac{3}{923}$.

35. A stone mason worked $11\frac{2}{3}$ days, and after paying his board and other expenses with $\frac{3}{7}$ of his earnings, he had $20 left; how much did he receive a day?

36. If $\frac{2}{5}$ of 4 tons of coal cost $\$5\frac{1}{3}$, what will $\frac{3}{4}$ of 2 tons cost? *Ans.* $5.

37. In an orchard $\frac{3}{4}$ of the trees are apple trees, $\frac{1}{10}$ peach trees, and the remainder are pear trees, which are 20 more than $\frac{1}{8}$ of the whole; how many trees in the orchard? *Ans.* 800.

38. A man gave $6\frac{2}{3}$ pounds of butter, at 12 cents a pound, for $\frac{4}{5}$ of a gallon of oil; how much was the oil worth a gallon? *Ans.* 100 cents.

39. A gentleman, having $271\frac{1}{2}$ acres of land, sold $\frac{1}{3}$ of it, and gave $\frac{3}{8}$ of it to his son; what was the value of the remainder, at $\$57\frac{4}{5}$ per acre? *Ans.* $\$4577\frac{3}{80}$.

40. A horse and wagon cost \$270; the horse cost $1\frac{1}{4}$ times as much as the wagon; what was the cost of the wagon?

41. What number taken from $2\frac{1}{2}$ times $12\frac{4}{5}$ will leave $20\frac{3}{4}$? *Ans.* $11\frac{1}{4}$.

42. A merchant bought a cargo of flour for \$$2173\frac{1}{2}$, and sold it for $\frac{22}{23}$ of the cost, thereby losing $\frac{3}{4}$ of a dollar per barrel; how many barrels did he purchase? *Ans.* 126.

43. A and B can do a piece of work in 14 days; A can do $\frac{3}{4}$ as much as B; in how many days can each do it?

Ans. A, $32\frac{2}{3}$ days; B, $24\frac{1}{2}$ days.

44. How many yards of cloth $\frac{4}{5}$ of a yard wide, are equal to 12 yards $\frac{3}{4}$ of a yard wide? *Ans.* $11\frac{1}{4}$.

45. A, B, and C can do a piece of work in 5 days; B and C can do it in 8 days; in what time can A do it?

46. A man put his money into 4 packages; in the first he put $\frac{2}{5}$, in the second $\frac{1}{3}$, in the third $\frac{1}{6}$, and in the fourth the remainder, which was \$24 more than $\frac{1}{15}$ of the whole; how much money had he? *Ans.* \$720.

47. If \$$7\frac{1}{4}$ will buy $3\frac{1}{4}$ cords of wood, how many cords can be bought for \$$10\frac{1}{2}$? *Ans.* $4\frac{41}{58}$.

48. How many times is $\frac{1}{6}$ of $\frac{4}{9}$ of 27 contained in $\frac{7}{8}$ of $\frac{1}{2}$ of $42\frac{2}{3}$?

49. A boy lost $\frac{1}{2}$ of his kite string, and then added 30 feet, when it was just $\frac{4}{5}$ of its original length; what was the length at first? *Ans.* 100 feet.

50. Bought $\frac{6}{7}$ of a box of candles, and having used $\frac{7}{8}$ of them, sold the remainder for $\frac{16}{25}$ of a dollar; how much would a box cost at the same rate? *Ans.* \$$5\frac{73}{75}$.

51. A post stands $\frac{1}{6}$ in the mud, $\frac{1}{4}$ in the water, and 21 feet above the water; what is its length?

52. A father left his eldest son $\frac{3}{7}$ of his estate, his youngest son $\frac{4}{7}$ of the remainder, and his daughter the remainder, who received \$$1723\frac{5}{8}$ less than the youngest son; what was the value of the estate? *Ans.* \$$21114\frac{13}{32}$.

DECIMAL FRACTIONS.

143. **Decimal Fractions** are fractions which have for their denominator 10, 100, 1000, or 1 with any number of ciphers annexed.

NOTES. 1. The word *decimal* is derived from the Latin *decem*, which signifies *ten*.

2. Decimal fractions are commonly called *decimals*.

3. Since $\frac{1}{10} = \frac{10}{100}$, $\frac{1}{100} = \frac{10}{1000}$, &c., the denominators of decimal fractions increase and decrease in a tenfold ratio, the same as simple numbers.

DECIMAL NOTATION AND NUMERATION.

144. Common Fractions are the common divisions of a unit into any number of equal parts, as into halves, fifths, twenty-fourths, &c.

Decimal Fractions are the decimal divisions of a unit, thus: A unit is divided into ten equal parts, called tenths; each of these tenths is divided into ten other equal parts called hundredths; each of these hundredths into ten other equal parts, called thousandths; and so on. Since the denominators of decimal fractions increase and decrease by the scale of 10, the same as simple numbers, in writing decimals the denominators may be omitted.

In simple numbers, the unit, 1, is the starting point of notation and numeration; and so also is it in decimals. We extend the scale of notation to the left of units' place in writing integers, and to the right of units' place in writing decimals. Thus, the first place at the left of units is tens, and the first place at the right of units is tenths; the second place at the left is hundreds, and the second place at the right is hundredths; the third place at the left is thousands, and the third place at the right is thousandths; and so on.

What are decimal fractions? How do they differ from common fractions? How are they written?

The Decimal Point is a period (.), which must always be placed before or at the left hand of the decimal. Thus,

$\frac{6}{10}$ is expressed .6
$\frac{54}{100}$ " " .54
$\frac{279}{1000}$ " " .279

NOTE. The decimal point is also called the *Separatrix.* This is a correct name for it only when it stands between the integral and decimal parts of the same number.

.5 is 5 tenths, which $= \frac{1}{10}$ of 5 units;
.05 is 5 hundredths, " $= \frac{1}{10}$ of 5 tenths;
.005 is 5 thousandths, " $= \frac{1}{10}$ of 5 hundredths.

And universally, the value of a figure in any decimal place is $\frac{1}{10}$ the value of the same figure in the next left hand place.

The relation of decimals and integers to each other is clearly shown by the following

NUMERATION TABLE.

Thousands.	Hundreds.	Tens.	Units.	Tenths.	Hundredths.	Thousandths.	Ten-thousandths.	Hundred-thousandths.	Millionths.	Ten-millionths.	Hundred-millionths.
4	7	5	3.	6	2	4	1	8	6	9	5
Integers.				Decimals.							

By examining this table we see that

Tenths	are expressed	by	one	figure.	
Hundredths	"	"	"	two	figures.
Thousandths	"	"	"	three	"
Ten thousandths	"	"	"	four	"

And any order of decimals by one figure less than the corresponding order of integers.

145. Since the denominator of tenths is 10, of hun-

What is the decimal point? What is it sometimes called? What is the value of a figure in any decimal place?

dredths 100, of thousands 1000, and so on, a decimal may be expressed by writing the numerator only; but in this case the numerator or decimal must always contain as many decimal places as are equal to the number of ciphers in the denominator; and the denominator of a decimal will always be the unit, 1, with as many ciphers annexed as are equal to the number of figures in the decimal or numerator.

The decimal point must never be omitted.

EXAMPLES FOR PRACTICE.

1. Express in figures thirty-eight hundredths.
2. Write seven tenths.
3. Write three hundred twenty-five thousandths.
4. Write four hundredths. *Ans.* .04.
5. Write sixteen thousandths.
6. Write seventy-four hundred-thousandths. *Ans.* .00074.
7. Write seven hundred forty-five millionths.
8. Write four thousand two hundred thirty-two ten-thousandths.
9. Write five hundred thousand millionths.
10. Read the following decimals:

.05	.681	.9034	.19248
.24	.024	.0005	.001385
.672	.8471	.100248	.1000087

NOTE. To read a decimal, we first numerate from left to right, and the name of the right hand figure is the name of the denominator. We then numerate from right to left, as in whole numbers, to read the numerator.

146. A mixed number is a number consisting of integers and decimals; thus, 71.406 consists of the integral part, 71, and the decimal part, .406; it is read the same as $71\frac{406}{1000}$, 71 and 406 thousandths.

EXAMPLES FOR PRACTICE.

1. Write eighteen, and twenty-seven thousandths.
2. Write four hundred, and nineteen ten-millionths.

How many decimal places must there be to express any decimal?

3. Write fifty-four, and fifty-four millionths.
4. Eighty-one, and 1 ten-thousandth.
5. One hundred, and 67 ten-thousandths.
6. Read the following numbers:

18.027	100.0067	400.0000019
81.0001	54.000054	3.03
75.075	9.2806	40.40404

147. From the foregoing explanations and illustrations we derive the following important

PRINCIPLES OF DECIMAL NOTATION AND NUMERATION.

1. The value of any decimal figure depends upon its *place* from the decimal point: thus .3 is ten times .03.

2. Prefixing a cipher to a decimal decreases its value the same as dividing it by ten; thus, .03 is $\frac{1}{10}$ the value of .3.

3. Annexing a cipher to a decimal does not alter its value, since it does not change the *place* of the significant figures of the decimal; thus, $\frac{6}{10}$, or .6, is the same as $\frac{60}{100}$, or .60.

4. Decimals increase from right to left, and decrease from left to right, in a tenfold ratio; and therefore they may be added, subtracted, multiplied, and divided the same as whole numbers.

5. The denominator of a decimal, though never expressed, is always the unit, 1, with as many ciphers annexed as there are figures in the decimal.

6. To read decimals requires two numerations; first, *from* units, to find the name of the denominator, and second, *towards* units, to find the value of the numerator.

148. Having analyzed all the principles upon which the writing and reading of decimals depend, we will now present these principles in the form of rules.

RULE FOR DECIMAL NOTATION.

I. *Write the decimal the same as a whole number, placing*

What is the first principle of decimal notation? Second? Third? Fourth? Fifth? Sixth? Rule for notation, first step?

ciphers where necessary to give each significant figure its true local value.

II. *Place the decimal point before the first figure.*

RULE FOR DECIMAL NUMERATION.

I. *Numerate from the decimal point, to determine the denominator.*

II. *Numerate towards the decimal point, to determine the numerator.*

III. *Read the decimal as a whole number, giving it the name or denomination of the right hand figure.*

EXAMPLES FOR PRACTICE.

1. Write 425 millionths.
2. Write six thousand ten-thousandths.
3. Write one thousand eight hundred fifty-nine hundred-thousandths.
4. Write 260 thousand 8 billionths.
5. Read the following decimals:

.6321	.748243	.2962999
.5400027	.60000000	.00000006

6. Write five hundred two, and one thousand six millionths.
7. Write thirty-one, and two ten-millionths.
8. Write eleven thousand, and eleven hundred-thousandths.
9. Write nine million, and nine billionths.
10. Write one hundred two tenths. *Ans.* 10.2.
11. Write one hundred twenty-four thousand three hundred fifteen thousandths.
12. Write seven hundred thousandths.
13. Write seven hundred-thousandths.
14. Read the following numbers:

12.36	9.052	62.9999
142.847	32.004	1858.4583
1.02	4.0005	27.00045

Second? Rule for numeration, first step? Second? Third?

REDUCTION.

CASE I.

149. To reduce decimals to a common denominator.

1. Reduce .5, .375, 3.25401, and 46.13 to their least common decimal denominator.

OPERATION.
.50000
.37500
3.25401
46.13000

ANALYSIS. The given decimals must contain as many places each, as are equal to the greatest number of decimal figures in any of the given decimals. We find that the third number contains five decimal places, and hence 100000 must be a common denominator. As annexing ciphers to decimals does not alter their value, (**144.**, 3) we give to each number five decimal places by annexing ciphers, and thus reduce the given decimals to a common denominator. Hence,

RULE. *Give to each number the same number of decimal places, by annexing ciphers.*

NOTES. 1. If the numbers be reduced to the denominator of that one of the given numbers having the greatest number of decimal places, they will have their least common decimal denominator.

2. A whole number may readily be reduced to decimals by placing the decimal point after units, and annexing ciphers; one cipher reducing it to tenths, two ciphers to hundredths, three ciphers to thousandths, and so on.

EXAMPLES FOR PRACTICE.

2. Reduce .17, 24.6, .0003, 84, and 721.8000271 to their least common denominator.

3. Reduce 7 tenths, 24 thousandths, 187 millionths, 5 hundred millionths, and 10845 hundredths to their least common denominator.

4. Reduce to their least common denominator the following decimals: 1000.001, 841.78, 2.6004, 90.000009, and 6000.

What is meant by the reduction of decimals? Case I is what? Give explanation. Rule.

CASE II.

150. To reduce a decimal to a common fraction.

1. Reduce .75 to its equivalent common fraction.

OPERATION.

$.75 = \frac{75}{100} = \frac{3}{4}.$

ANALYSIS. We omit the decimal point, supply the proper denominator to the decimal, and then reduce the common fraction thus formed to its lowest terms. Hence,

RULE. *Omit the decimal point, and supply the proper denominator.*

EXAMPLES FOR PRACTICE.

2. Reduce .125 to a common fraction. *Ans.* $\frac{1}{8}$.
3. Reduce .16 to a common fraction. *Ans.* $\frac{4}{25}$.
4. Reduce .655 to a common fraction. *Ans.* $\frac{131}{200}$.
5. Reduce .9375 to a common fraction. *Ans.* $\frac{15}{16}$.
6. Reduce .0008 to a common fraction. *Ans.* $\frac{1}{1250}$.

CASE III.

151. To reduce a common fraction to a decimal.

1. Reduce $\frac{3}{4}$ to its equivalent decimal.

FIRST OPERATION.

$\frac{3}{4} = \frac{300}{400} = \frac{75}{100} = .75$, *Ans.*

SECOND OPERATION.

$$4\,\underline{)\,3.00}$$
$$.75$$

ANALYSIS. We first annex the same number of ciphers to both terms of the fraction; this does not alter its value. We then divide both resulting terms by 4, the significant figure of the denominator, to obtain the *decimal* denominator, 100. Then the fraction is changed to the decimal form by omitting the denominator. If the intermediate steps be omitted, the true result may be obtained as in the second operation.

2. Reduce $\frac{1}{16}$ to its equivalent decimal.

Case II is what? Give explanation. Rule. Case III is what? Explain first operation. Second.

THIRD OPERATION.

16) 1.0000

.0625, *Ans.*

ANALYSIS. Dividing as in the former example, we obtain a quotient of 3 figures, 625. But since we annexed 4 ciphers, there must be 4 places in the required decimal; hence we prefix 1 cipher. This is made still plainer by the following operation; thus,

$$\frac{1}{16} = \frac{10000}{160000} = \frac{625}{10000} = .0625.$$

From these illustrations we derive the following

RULE. I. *Annex ciphers to the numerator, and divide by the denominator.*

II. *Point off as many decimal places in the result as are equal to the number of ciphers annexed.*

NOTE. A common fraction can be reduced to an exact decimal when its lowest denominator contains only the prime factors 2 and 5, and not otherwise.

EXAMPLES FOR PRACTICE.

3. Reduce $\frac{5}{8}$ to a decimal. *Ans.* .625.
4. Reduce $\frac{4}{5}$ to a decimal.
5. Reduce $\frac{15}{16}$ to a decimal. *Ans.* .9375.
6. Reduce $\frac{7}{8}$ to a decimal.
7. Reduce $\frac{2}{25}$ to a decimal. *Ans.* .08.
8. Reduce $\frac{3}{64}$ to a decimal. *Ans.* .046875.
9. Reduce $\frac{3}{8}$ to a decimal.
10. Reduce $\frac{3}{80}$ to a decimal.
11. Reduce $\frac{3}{800}$ to a decimal. *Ans.* .00375.
12. Reduce $\frac{1}{125}$ to a decimal. *Ans.* .008.
13. Reduce $\frac{1}{3}$ to a decimal. *Ans.* .33333+.

NOTE. The sign, +, in the answer indicates that there is still a remainder.

14. Reduce $\frac{19}{37}$ to a decimal. *Ans.* .513513+.

NOTE. The answers to the last two examples are called *repeating decimals;* and the figure 3 in the 13th example, and the figures 513 in the 14th, are called *repetends*, because they are repeated, or occur in regular order.

Third operation. Rule, first step? Second? When can a common fraction be reduced to an exact decimal?

ADDITION.

152. 1. What is the sum of 3.703, 621.57, .672, and 20.0074?

OPERATION.

```
  3.703
621.57
   .672
 20.0074
--------
645.9524
```

ANALYSIS. We write the numbers so that figures of like orders of units shall stand in the same columns; that is, units under units, tenths under tenths, hundredths under hundredths, &c. This brings the decimal points directly under each other. Commencing at the right hand, we add each column separately, and carry as in whole numbers, and in the result we place a decimal point between units and tenths, or directly under the decimal point in the numbers added. From this example we derive the following

RULE. I. *Write the numbers so that the decimal points shall stand directly under each other.*

II. *Add as in whole numbers, and place the decimal point, in the result, directly under the points in the numbers added.*

EXAMPLES FOR PRACTICE.

```
2. Add      .199           3. Add       4.015
           2.7569                       6.75
            .25                        27.38203
            .654                      375.01
          ------                        2.5
Sum,       3.8599                     ---------
                           Amount,    415.65703
```

4. Add 1152.01, 14.11018, 152348.21, 9.000083. *Ans.* 153523.330263.

5. Add 37.03, 0.521, .9, 1000, 4000.0004. *Ans.* 5038.4514.

6. What is the sum of twenty-six, and twenty-six hundredths; seven tenths; six, and eighty-three thousandths; four, and four thousandths? *Ans.* 37.047.

Explain the operation of addition of decimals. Give rule, first step. Second.

7. What is the sum of thirty-six, and fifteen thousandths; three hundred, and six hundred five ten-thousandths; five, and three millionths; sixty, and eighty-seven ten-millionths?

Ans. 401.0755117.

8. What is the sum of fifty-four, and thirty-four hundredths; one, and nine ten-thousandths; three, and two hundred seven millionths; twenty-three thousandths; eight, and nine tenths; four, and one hundred thirty-five thousandths?

Ans. 71.399107.

9. How many yards in three pieces of cloth, the first piece containing 18.375 yards, the second piece 41.625 yards, and the third piece 35.5 yards?

10. A's farm contains 61.843 acres, B's contains 143.75 acres, C's 218.4375 acres, and D's 21.9 acres; how many acres in the four farms?

11. My farm consists of 7 fields, containing $12\frac{3}{4}$ acres, $18\frac{3}{5}$ acres, 9 acres, $24\frac{1}{8}$ acres, $4\frac{13}{16}$ acres, $8\frac{9}{10}$ acres, and $15\frac{13}{20}$ acres respectively; how many acres in my farm?

NOTE. Reduce the common fractions to decimals before adding.

Ans. 93.6375.

12. A grocer has $2\frac{1}{2}$ barrels of A sugar, $5\frac{3}{4}$ barrels of B sugar, $3\frac{5}{8}$ barrels of C sugar, 3.0642 barrels of crushed sugar, and 8.925 barrels of pulverized sugar; how many barrels of sugar has he? *Ans.* 23.8642.

13. A tailor made 3 suits of clothes; for the first suit he used $2\frac{1}{8}$ yards of broadcloth, $3\frac{1}{16}$ yards of cassimere, and $\frac{7}{8}$ yards of satin; for the second suit 2.25 yards of broadcloth, 2.875 yards of cassimere, and 1 yard of satin; and for the third suit $5\frac{1}{16}$ yards of broadcloth, and $1\frac{1}{8}$ yards of satin. How many yards of each kind of goods did he use? How many yards of all? *Ans. to last,* 18.375.

SUBTRACTION.

153. 1. From 91.73 take 2.18.

OPERATION.

```
     91.73
      2.18
     -----
Ans. 89.55
```

2. From 2.9185 take 1.42.

OPERATION.

```
     2.9185
     1.42
     ------
Ans. 1.4985
```

3. From 124.65 take 95.58746.

OPERATION.

```
     124.65
      95.58746
     ---------
Ans.  29.06254
```

ANALYSIS. In each of these three examples, we write the subtrahend under the minuend, placing units under units, tenths under tenths, &c. Commencing at the right hand, we subtract as in whole numbers, and in the remainders we place the decimal points directly under those in the numbers above. In the second example, the number of decimal places in the minuend is greater than the number in the subtrahend, and in the third example the number is less. In both cases, we reduce both minuend and subtrahend to the same number of decimal places, by annexing ciphers; or we suppose the ciphers to be annexed, before performing the subtraction. Hence the

RULE. I. *Write the numbers so that the decimal points shall stand directly under each other.*

II. *Subtract as in whole numbers, and place the decimal point in the result directly under the points in the given numbers.*

4. Find the difference between 714 and .916. *Ans.* 713.084.
5. How much greater is 2 than .298? *Ans.* 1.702.
6. From 21.004 take 75 hundredths.
7. From 10.0302 take 2 ten-thousandths. *Ans.* 10.03.
8. From 900 take .009. *Ans.* 899.991.
9. From two thousand take two thousandths.
10. From one take one millionth. *Ans.* .999999.

Explain subtraction of fractions. Give the rule, first step. Second.

11. From four hundred twenty-seven thousandths take four hundred twenty-seven millionths. *Ans.* .426573.

12. A man owned thirty-four hundredths of a township of land, and sold thirty-four thousandths of the township; how much did he still own? *Ans.* .306.

MULTIPLICATION.

154. 1. What is the product of .35 multiplied by .5?

OPERATION.

$$\begin{array}{r} .35 \\ .5 \\ \hline .175 \end{array}$$ *Ans.*

ANALYSIS. We perform the multiplication the same as in whole numbers, and the only difficulty we meet with is in pointing off the decimal places in the product. To determine how many places to point off, we may reduce the decimals to common fractions; thus, $.35 = \frac{35}{100}$ and $.5 = \frac{5}{10}$. Performing the multiplication, and we have $\frac{35}{100} \times \frac{5}{10} = \frac{175}{1000}$, and this product, expressed decimally, is .175. Here we see that the product contains as many decimal places as are contained in both multiplicand and multiplier. Hence the following

RULE. *Multiply as in whole numbers, and from the right hand of the product point off as many figures for decimals as there are decimal places in both factors.*

NOTES. 1. If there be not as many figures in the product as there are decimals in both factors, supply the deficiency by prefixing ciphers.

2. To multiply a decimal by 10, 100, 1000, &c., remove the point as many places to the right as there are ciphers on the right of the multiplier.

EXAMPLES.

2. Multiply 1.245 by .27. *Ans.* .33615.
3. Multiply 79.347 by 23.15. *Ans.* 1836.88305.
4. Multiply 350 by .7853.
5. Multiply one tenth by one tenth. *Ans.* .01.
6. Multiply 25 by twenty-five hundredths. *Ans.* 6.25.

Explain multiplication of decimals. Give rule. If the product have less decimal places than both factors, how proceed? How multiply by 10, 100, 1000, &c.?

7. Multiply .132 by .241. *Ans.* .031812.

8. Multiply 24.35 by 10.

9. Multiply .006 by 1000. *Ans.* 6.

10. Multiply .23 by .009. *Ans.* .00207.

11. Multiply sixty-four thousandths by thirteen millionths. *Ans.* .000000832.

12. Multiply eighty-seven ten-thousandths by three hundred fifty-twc hundred-thousandths.

13. Multiply one million by one millionth. *Ans.* 1.

14. Multiply sixteen thousand by sixteen ten-thousandths. *Ans.* 25.6.

15. If a cord of wood be worth 2.37 bushels of wheat, how many bushels of wheat must be given for 9.58 cords of wood? *Ans.* 22.7046 bushels.

DIVISION.

155. 1. What is the quotient of .175 divided by .5?

OPERATION.

$.5\,)\,\underline{.175}$

Ans. .35

ANALYSIS. We perform the division the same as in whole numbers, and the only difficulty we meet with is in pointing off the decimal places in the quotient. To determine how many places to point off, we may reduce the decimals to common fractions; thus, $.175 = \frac{175}{1000}$, and $.5 = \frac{5}{10}$. Performing the division, and we have

$$\frac{175}{1000} \div \frac{5}{10} = \frac{\not{1}\not{7}\not{5}}{100\not{0}} \times \frac{1\not{0}}{\not{5}} = \frac{35}{100};$$

and this quotient, expressed decimally, is .35. Here we see that the dividend contains as many decimal places as are contained in both divisor and quotient. Hence the following

RULE. *Divide as in whole numbers, and from the right hand of the quotient point off as many places for decimals as the decimal places in the dividend exceed those in the divisor.*

Explain division of decimals. Give rule.

NOTES. 1. If the number of figures in the quotient be less than the excess of the decimal places in the dividend over those in the divisor, the deficiency must be supplied by prefixing ciphers.

2. If there be a remainder after dividing the dividend, annex ciphers, and continue the division: the ciphers annexed are decimals of the dividend.

3. The dividend must always contain at least as many decimal places as the divisor, before commencing the division.

4. In most business trañsactions, the division is considered sufficiently exact when the quotient is carried to 4 decimal places, unless great accuracy is required.

5. To divide by 10, 100, 1000, &c., remove the decimal point as many places to the left as there are ciphers on the right hand of the divisor.

EXAMPLES FOR PRACTICE.

2. Divide .675 by .15. *Ans.* 4.5.
3. Divide .288 by 3.6. *Ans.* .08.
4. Divide 81.6 by 2.5. *Ans.* 32.64
5. Divide 2.3421 by 21.1.
6. Divide 2.3421 by .211.
7. Divide 8.297496 by .153. *Ans.* 54.232.
8. Divide 12 by .7854.
9. Divide 3 by 3; divide 3 by .3; 3 by .03; 30 by .03.
10. Divide 15.34 by 2.7.
11. Divide .1 by .7. *Ans.* .142857+.
12. Divide 45.30 by .015. *Ans.* 3020.
13. Divide .003753 by 625.5. *Ans.* .000006.
14. Divide 9. by 450. *Ans.* .02.
15. Divide 2.39015 by .007. *Ans.* 341.45.
16. Divide fifteen, and eight hundred seventy-five thousandths, by twenty-five ten-thousandths. *Ans.* 6350.
17. Divide 365 by 100.
18. Divide 785.4 by 1000. *Ans.* .7854.
19. Divide one thousand by one thousandth. *Ans.* 1000000.

When are ciphers prefixed to the quotient? If there be a remainder, how proceed? If the dividend have less decimal places than the divisor, how proceed? How divide by 10, 100, 1000, &c.?

PROMISCUOUS EXAMPLES.

1. Add six hundred, and twenty-five thousandths; four tenths; seven, and sixty-two ten-thousandths; three, and fifty-eight millionths; ninety-two, and seven hundredths.

Ans. 702.501258.

2. What is the sum of $81.003 + 5000.4 + 5.0008 + 73.87563 + 1000 + 25 + 3.000548 + .0315$?

3. From eighty-seven take eighty-seven thousandths.

4. What is the difference between nine million and nine millionths? *Ans.* 8999999.999991.

5. Multiply .365 by .15. *Ans.* .05475.

6. Multiply three thousandths by four hundredths.

7. If one acre produce 42.57 bushels of corn, how many bushels will 18.73 acres produce? *Ans.* 797.3361.

8. Divide .125 by 8000. *Ans.* .000015625.

9. Divide .7744 by .1936.

10. Divide 27.1 by 100000. *Ans.* .000271.

11. If 6.35 acres produce 70.6755 bushels of wheat, what does one acre produce? *Ans.* 11.13 bushels.

12. Reduce .625 to a common fraction. *Ans.* $\frac{5}{8}$.

13. Express 26.875 by an integer and a common fraction.

Ans. $26\frac{7}{8}$.

14. Reduce $\frac{2}{125}$ to a decimal fraction. *Ans.* .016.

15. Reduce $\dfrac{8\frac{3}{4}}{17\frac{1}{2}}$ to a decimal fraction. *Ans.* .5.

16. How many times will .5 of 1.75 be contained in .25 of $17\frac{1}{2}$? *Ans.* 5.

17. What will be the cost of $3\frac{5}{8}$ bales of cloth, each bale containing 36.75 yards, at .85 dollars per yard?

18. Traveling at the rate of $4\frac{3}{5}$ miles an hour, how many hours will a man require to travel 56.925 miles.

Ans. $12\frac{3}{8}$ hours.

DECIMAL CURRENCY.

156. **Coin** is money stamped, and has a given value established by law.

157. **Currency** is coin, bank bills, treasury notes, &c., in circulation as a medium of trade.

158. **A Decimal Currency** is a currency whose denominations increase and decrease in a tenfold ratio.

NOTE. The currency of the United States is decimal currency, and is sometimes called *Federal Money*; it was adopted by Congress in 1786.

NOTATION AND NUMERATION.

The gold coins of the United States are the double eagle, eagle, half and quarter eagle, three dollar piece, and dollar.

The silver coins are the dollar, half and quarter dollar, dime and half dime, and three cent piece.

The nickel coin is the cent.

NOTES. 1. The following pieces of gold are in use, but are not legal coin, viz.; the fifty dollar piece, and the half and quarter dollar pieces.

2. The copper cent and half cent, though still in circulation, are no longer coined.

3. The mill is used only in computation; it is not a coin.

TABLE.

10 mills (*m.*)	make	1 cent,	... c.
10 cents	"	1 dime,	... d.
10 dimes	"	1 dollar,	... $.
10 dollars	"	1 eagle,	... E.

UNIT EQUIVALENTS.

Mills.		Cents.		Dimes.		Dollars.		Eagle.
10	=	1						
100	=	10	=	1				
1000	=	100	=	10	=	1		
10000	=	1000	=	100	=	10	=	1

NOTE. The character $ is supposed to be a contraction of U. S., (United States,) the U being placed upon the S.

What is coin? Currency? Decimal currency? Federal money? What are the gold coins of U. S.? Silver? Copper? What are the denominations of U. S. currency? What is the sign of dollars? From what derived?

159. The dollar is the *unit* of United States money; dimes, cents, and mills are fractions of a dollar, and are separated from the dollar by the decimal point; thus, two dollars one dime two cents five mills, are written $2.125.

By examining the *table*, we see that the *dime* is a *tenth* part of the unit, or dollar; the *cent* a tenth part of the dime or a *hundredth* part of the dollar; and the *mill* a tenth part of the cent, a hundredth part of the dime, or a *thousandth* part of the dollar. Hence the denominations of decimal currency increase and decrease the same as decimal fractions, and are expressed according to the same decimal system of notation; and they may be added, subtracted, multiplied, and divided in the same manner as decimals.

Dimes are not read *as dimes*, but the two places of dimes and cents are appropriated to cents; thus, 1 dollar 3 dimes 2 cents, or $1.32, are read one dollar thirty-two cents; hence,

When the number of cents is less than 10, we *write a cipher before it in the place of dimes.*

NOTE. The half cent is frequently written as 5 mills; thus, 24½ cents, written $.245.

160. Business men frequently write *cents* as common fractions of a dollar; thus, three dollars thirteen cents are written $3\frac{13}{100}$, and read, three and thirteen hundredths dollars. In business transactions, when the final result of a computation contains 5 mills or *more*, they are called one cent, and when *less* than 5, they are rejected.

EXAMPLES FOR PRACTICE.

1. Write four dollars five cents. *Ans.* $4.05.
2. Write two dollars nine cents.
3. Write ten dollars ten cents.
4. Write eight dollars seven mills. *Ans.* $8.007.

What is the unit of U. S. currency? What is the general law of increase and decrease? In practice, how many decimal places are given to cents? In business transactions, how are cents frequently written? What is done if the mills exceed 5? If less than 5?

5. Write sixty-four cents. *Ans.* $0.64.
6. Write three cents two mills.
7. Write one hundred dollars one cent one mill.
8. Read $7.93; $8.02; $6.542.
9. Read $5.272; $100.025; $17.005.
10. Read $16.205; $215.081; $1000.011; $4.002.

REDUCTION.

161. By examining the table of Decimal Currency, we see that 10 mills make one cent, and 100 cents, or 1000 mills, make one dollar; hence,

To change dollars to cents, multiply by 100; *that is, annex two ciphers.*

To change dollars to mills, annex three ciphers.

To change cents to mills, annex one cipher.

EXAMPLES FOR PRACTICE.

1. Change $792 to cents. *Ans.* 79200 cents.
2. Change $36 to cents.
3. Reduce $5248 to cents.
4. In 6.25 dollars how many cents? *Ans.* 625 cents.

NOTE. To change dollars and cents to cents, or dollars, cents, and mills to mills, remove the decimal point and the sign, $.

5. Change $63.045 to mills. *Ans.* 63045 mills.
6. Change 16 cents to mills.
7. Reduce $3.008 to mills.
8. In 89 cents how many mills?

162. Conversely,

To change cents to dollars, divide by 100; *that is, point off two figures from the right.*

To change mills to dollars, point off three figures.

To change mills to cents, point off one figure.

How are dollars changed to cents? to mills? How are cents changed to mills? How are cents changed to dollars? Mills to dollars? to cents?

EXAMPLES FOR PRACTICE.

1. Change 875 cents to dollars. *Ans.* $8.75.
2. Change 1504 cents to dollars.
3. In 13875 cents how many dollars?
4. In 16525 mills how many dollars?
5. Reduce 524 mills to cents.
6. Reduce 6524 mills to dollars.

ADDITION.

163. 1. A man bought a cow for 21 dollars 50 cents, a horse for 125 dollars 37½ cents, a harness for 46 dollars 75 cents, and a carriage for 210 dollars; how much did he pay for all?

OPERATION.

```
$  21.50
  125.375
   46.75
  210.00
 --------
Ans. $403.625
```

ANALYSIS. Writing dollars under dollars, cents under cents, &c., so that the decimal points shall stand under each other, we add and point off as in addition of decimals. Hence the following

RULE. I. *Write dollars under dollars, cents under cents, &c.*

II. *Add as in simple numbers, and place the point in the amount as in addition of decimals.*

EXAMPLES FOR PRACTICE.

2. What is the sum of 50 dollars 7 cents, 1000 dollars 75 cents, 60 dollars 3 mills, 18 cents 4 mills, 1 dollar 1 cent, and 25 dollars 45 cents 8 mills? *Ans.* $1137.475.

3. Add 364 dollars 54 cents 1 mill, 486 dollars 6 cents, 93 dollars 9 mills, 1742 dollars 80 cents, 3 dollars 27 cents 6 mills. *Ans.* $2689.686.

4. Add 92 cents, 10 cents 4 mills, 35 cents 7 mills, 18 cents 6 mills, 44 cents 4 mills, 12½ cents, and 99 cents. *Ans.* $3.126.

Explain the process of addition of decimal currency. Rule, first step. Second.

5. A farmer receives 89 dollars 74 cents for wheat, 13 dollars 3 cents for corn, 6 dollars $37\frac{1}{2}$ cents for potatoes, and 19 dollars $62\frac{1}{2}$ cents for oats; what does he receive for the whole? *Ans.* $128.77.

6. A lady bought a dress for 9 dollars 17 cents, trimmings for $87\frac{1}{2}$ cents, a paper of pins for $6\frac{1}{4}$ cents, some tape for 4 cents, some thread for 8 cents, and a comb for 11 cents; what did she pay for all? *Ans.* $10.3375.

7. Paid for building a house $2175.75, for painting the same 240.37\frac{1}{2}$, for furniture $605.40, for carpets 140.12\frac{1}{2}$; what was the cost of the house and furnishing?

8. Bought a ton of coal for $6.08, a barrel of sugar for $26.625, a box of tea for $16, and a barrel of flour for $7.40; what was the cost of all?

9. A merchant bought goods to the amount of $7425.50; he paid for duties on the same $253.96, and for freight $170.09; what was the entire cost of the goods?

10. I bought a hat for 3.62\frac{1}{2}$, a pair of shoes for 1\frac{3}{4}$, an umbrella for 1\frac{3}{8}$, a pair of gloves for $.62$\frac{1}{2}$, and a cane for $.87$\frac{1}{2}$; what was the cost of all my purchases? *Ans.* $8.25.

SUBTRACTION.

164. 1. A man, having $327.50, paid out $186.75 for a horse; how much had he left?

OPERATION.	
$327.50	
186.75	
Ans. $140.75	

ANALYSIS. Writing the less number under the greater, dollars under dollars, cents under cents, &c., we subtract and point off in the result as in subtraction of decimals. Hence the following

RULE. I. *Write the subtrahend under the minuend, dollars under dollars, cents under cents, &c.*

II. *Subtract as in simple numbers, and place the point in the remainder, as in subtraction of decimals.*

Explain the process of subtraction. Give rule, first step. Second.

EXAMPLES FOR PRACTICE.

2. From $365 dollars 5 mills take 267 dollars 1 cent 8 mills. *Ans.* $97.987.

3. From 50 dollars take 50 cents. *Ans.* $49.50.

4. From 100 dollars take 1 mill. *Ans.* $99.999.

5. From 1000 dollars take 3 cents 7 mills.

6. A man bought a farm for $1575.24, and sold it for $1834.16; what did he gain? *Ans.* $258.92.

7. Sold a horse for 145 dollars 27 cents, which is 37 dollars 69 cents more than he cost me; what did he cost me?

8. A merchant bought flour for $5.62½ a barrel, and sold it for $6.84 a barrel; how much did he gain on a barrel?

9. A gentleman, having $14725, gave $3560 for a store, and $7015.87½ for goods; how much money had he left?

10. A lady bought a silk dress for $13¾, a bonnet for $5¼, a pair of gaiters for $1⅜, and a fan for $⅞; she paid to the shopkeeper a twenty dollar bill and a five dollar bill; how much change should he return to her? *Ans.* $3.75.

NOTE. Reduce the fractions of a dollar to cents and mills.

11. A gentleman bought a pair of horses for $480, a harness for $80.50, and a carriage for $200 less than he paid for both horses and harness; what was the cost of the carriage? *Ans.* $360.50.

MULTIPLICATION.

165. 1. If a barrel of flour cost $6.375, what will 85 barrels cost?

OPERATION.

```
      $6.375
          85
      ------
       31875
      51000
      ------
Ans. $541.875
```

ANALYSIS. We multiply as in simple numbers, always regarding the multiplier as an *abstract* number, and point off from the right hand of the result, as in multiplication of decimals. Hence the following

---

Give analysis for multiplication in decimal currency.

Rule. ***Multiply as in simple numbers, and place the point in the product, as in multiplication of decimals.***

EXAMPLES FOR PRACTICE.

2. If a cord of wood be worth $4.275, what will 300 cords be worth? *Ans.* $1282.50.

3. What will 175 barrels of apples cost, at $2.45 per barrel? *Ans.* $428.75.

4. What will 800 barrels of salt cost, at $1.28 per barrel?

5. A grocer bought 372 pounds of cheese at $.15 a pound, 434 pounds of coffee at $.12½ a pound, and 16 bushels of potatoes at $.33 a bushel; what did the whole cost?

6. A boy, being sent to purchase groceries, bought 3 pounds of tea at 56 cents a pound, 15 pounds of rice at 7 cents a pound, 27 pounds of sugar at 8 cents a pound; he gave the grocer 5 dollars; how much change ought he to receive?

7. A farmer sold 125 bushels of oats at $.37½ a bushel, and received in payment 75 pounds of sugar at $.09 a pound, 12 pounds of tea at $.60 a pound, and the remainder in cash; how much cash did he receive? *Ans.* $32.92½.

8. A man bought 150 acres of land for $3975; he afterward sold 80 acres of it at $32.50 an acre, and the remainder at $34.25 an acre; how much did he gain by the transaction? *Ans.* $1022.50.

DIVISION.

166. 1. If 125 barrels of flour cost $850, how much will 1 barrel cost?

OPERATION.

```
125 ) $850.00 ( $6.80. Ans.
       750
       ----
       1000
       1000
       ----
          0
```

Analysis. We divide as in simple numbers, and as there is a remainder after dividing the dollars, we reduce the dividend to cents, by annexing two ciphers, and continue the division. Hence the following

Rule. Give rule for division in decimal currency.

RULE. *Divide as in simple numbers, and place the point in the quotient, as in division of decimals.*

NOTES. 1. In business transactions it is never necessary to carry the division further than to mills in the quotient.

2. If the dividend will not contain the divisor an exact number of times, ciphers may be annexed, and the division continued as in division of decimals. In this case it is always safe to reduce the dividend to mills, or to 3 more decimal places than the divisor contains, before commencing the division.

EXAMPLES FOR PRACTICE.

2. If 33 gallons of oil cost \$41.25, what is the cost per gallon? *Ans.* \$1.25.

3. If 27 yards of broadcloth cost \$94.50, what will 1 yard cost?

4. If 64 gallons of wine cost \$136, what will 1 gallon cost? *Ans.* \$2.125.

5. At 12 cents apiece, how many pine-apples can be bought for \$1.32? *Ans.* 11.

6. If 1 pound of tea cost 54 cents, how many pounds can be bought for \$405?

7. If a man earn \$180 in a year, how much does he earn a month?

8. If 100 acres of land cost \$2847.50, what will 1 acre cost? *Ans.* \$28.475.

9. What cost 1 pound of beef, if 894 pounds cost \$80.46? *Ans.* \$.09.

10. A farmer sells 120 bushels of wheat at \$1.12½ a bushel, for which he receives 27 barrels of flour; what does the flour cost him a barrel?

11. A man bought 4 yards of cloth at \$3.20 a yard, and 37 pounds of sugar at \$.08 a pound; he paid \$6.80 in cash, and the remainder in butter at \$.16 a pound; how many pounds of butter did it take? *Ans.* 56 pounds.

12. A man bought an equal number of calves and sheep, paying \$166.75 for them; for the calves he paid \$4.50 a head, and for the sheep \$2.75 a head; how many did he buy of each kind? *Ans.* 23.

13. If 154 pounds of sugar cost $18.48, what will 1 pound cost?

14. A merchant bought 14 boxes of tea for $560; it being damaged he was obliged to lose $106.75 on the cost of it; how much did he receive a box? *Ans.* $32.37½.

ADDITIONAL APPLICATIONS.

CASE I.

167. To find the cost of any number or quantity, when the price of a unit is an aliquot part of one dollar.

168. An **Aliquot Part** of a number is such a part as will exactly divide that number; thus, 3, 5, and 7½ are aliquot parts of 15.

NOTE. An *aliquot part* may be a whole or a mixed number, while a *factor* must be a whole number.

ALIQUOT PARTS OF ONE DOLLAR.

50 cents = ½ of 1 dollar.	12½ cents = ⅛ of 1 dollar.
33⅓ cents = ⅓ of 1 dollar.	10 cents = $\frac{1}{10}$ of 1 dollar.
25 cents = ¼ of 1 dollar.	8⅓ cents = $\frac{1}{12}$ of 1 dollar.
20 cents = ⅕ of 1 dollar.	6¼ cents = $\frac{1}{16}$ of 1 dollar.
16⅔ cents = ⅙ of 1 dollar.	5 cents = $\frac{1}{20}$ of 1 dollar.

1. What will be the cost of 3784 yards of flannel, at 25 cents a yard?

OPERATION.

4) 3784

Ans. $946

ANALYSIS. If the price were $1 a yard, the cost would be as many dollars as there are yards. But since the price is ¼ of a dollar a yard, the whole cost will be ¼ as many dollars as there are yards; or, ¼ of 3784 = 3784 ÷ 4 = $946. Hence the

RULE. *Take such a fractional part of the given number as the price is part of one dollar.*

EXAMPLES FOR PRACTICE.

2. What cost 963 bushels of oats, at 33⅓ cents per bushel? *Ans.* $321.

Case I is what? What is an aliquot part of a dollar? Give explanation. Rule.

3. What cost 478 yards of delaine, at 50 cents per yard?

4. What cost 4266 yards of sheeting, at $8\frac{1}{3}$ cents a yard? *Ans.* $355.50.

5. What cost 1250 bushels of apples, at $12\frac{1}{2}$ cents per bushel? *Ans.* $156.25.

6. What cost 3126 spools of thread, at $6\frac{1}{4}$ cents per spool? *Ans.* $195.375.

7. At $16\frac{2}{3}$ cents per dozen, what cost 1935 dozen of eggs? *Ans.* 322.50.

8. What cost 56480 yards of calico, at $12\frac{1}{2}$ per yard?

9. At 20 cents each what will be the cost of 1275 salt barrels? *Ans.* $255.

CASE II.

169. The price of one and the quantity being given, to find the cost.

1. How much will 9 barrels of flour cost, at $6.25 per barrel?

OPERATION.	
$6.25	
9	
Ans. $56.25	

ANALYSIS. Since one barrel cost $6.25, 9 barrels will cost 9 times $6.25, and $6.25 × 9 = $56.25. Hence

RULE. *Multiply the price of one by the quantity.*

EXAMPLES FOR PRACTICE.

2. If a pound of beef cost 9 cents, what will 864 pounds cost? *Ans.* $77.76.

3. What cost 87 acres of government land, at $1.25 per acre?

4. What cost 400 barrels of salt, at $1.45 per barrel? *Ans.* $580.

5 What cost 16 chests of tea, each chest containing 52 pounds, at 44 cents per pound?

Case II is what? Give explanation. Rule.

CASE III.

170. The cost and the quantity being given, to find the price of one.

1. If 30 bushels of corn cost $20.70, what will 1 bushel cost?

OPERATION.

3|0) $2|0.70
$.69

ANALYSIS. If 30 bushels cost $20.70, 1 bushel will cost $\frac{1}{30}$ of $20.70; and $20.70 ÷ 30 = $.69. Hence,

RULE. *Divide the cost by the quantity.*

EXAMPLES FOR PRACTICE.

2. If 25 acres of land cost $175, what will 1 acre cost?

3. If 48 yards of broadcloth cost $200, what will 1 yard cost? *Ans.* $4.16⅔.

4. If 96 tons of hay cost $1200, what will 1 ton cost?

5. If 10 Unabridged Dictionaries cost $56.25, what will 1 cost? *Ans.* $5.62½.

6. Bought 18 pounds of tea for $11.70; what was the price per pound? *Ans.* $.65.

7. If 53 pounds of butter cost $10.07, what will 1 pound cost?

8. A merchant bought 800 barrels of salt for $1016; what did it cost him per barrel?

9. If 343 sheep cost $874.65, what will 1 sheep cost? *Ans.* $2.55.

10. If board for a family be $684.37½ for 1 year, how much is it per day? *Ans.* $1.87½.

CASE IV.

171. The price of one and the cost of a quantity being given, to find the quantity.

1. At $6 a barrel for flour, how many barrels can be bought for $840?

Case III is what? Give explanation. Rule. Case IV is what?

OPERATION.

6) 840

Ans. 140 barrels.

ANALYSIS. Since $6 will buy 1 barrel of flour, $840 will buy $\frac{1}{6}$ as many barrels as there are dollars, or as many barrels as $6 is contained times in $840; 840 ÷ 6 = 140 barrels. Hence,

RULE. *Divide the cost of the quantity by the price of one.*

EXAMPLES FOR PRACTICE.

2. How many dozen of eggs can be bought for $5.55, if one dozen cost $.15? *Ans.* 37 dozen.

3. At $12 a ton, how many tons of hay can be bought for $216? *Ans.* 18 tons.

4. How many bushels of wheat can be bought for $2178.75, if 1 bushel cost $1.25? *Ans.* 1743 bushels.

5. A dairyman expends $643.50 in buying cows at $19½ apiece; how many cows does he buy? *Ans.* 33 cows.

6. At $.45 per gallon, how many gallons of molasses can be bought for $52.65?

7. A drover bought horses at $264 a pair; how many horses did he buy for $6336?

8. At $65 a ton, how many tons of railroad iron can be bought for $117715? *Ans.* 1811 tons.

CASE V.

172. To find the cost of articles sold by the 100, 1000, &c.

1. What cost 475 feet of timber, at $5.24 per 100 feet?

FIRST OPERATION.

```
        $5.24
          475
        -----
         2620
        3668
       2096
      -------
100 ) $2489.00
 Ans.  $24.89
```

ANALYSIS. If the price were $5.24 per *foot*, the cost of 475 feet would be 475 × $5.24 = $2489. But since $5.24 is the price of 100 feet, $2489 is 100 times the true value. Therefore, to obtain the true value, we divide $2489 by 100, which we may do by cutting off two figures from the right, and the result is $24.89. Or,

Give explanation. Rule. Case V is what? Give first explanation.

SECOND OPERATION.

```
    $5.24
     4.75
    -----
     2620
    3668
   2096
 --------
 $24.8900
```

ANALYSIS. Since 1 foot costs $\frac{1}{100}$, or .01, of \$5.24, 475 feet will cost $\frac{475}{100}$, or 4.75 times \$5.24, which is \$24.89.

NOTE. For the same reasons, when the price is per *thousand*, we divide the product by 1000, or, which is more convenient in practice, we reduce the given quantity to thousands and decimals of a thousand, by pointing off three figures from the right hand. Hence the

RULE. I. *Reduce the given quantity to hundreds and decimals of a hundred, or to thousands and decimals of a thousand.*

II. *Multiply the price by the quantity, and point off in the result as in multiplication of decimals.*

NOTE. The letter C is used to indicate hundreds, and M to indicate thousands.

EXAMPLES FOR PRACTICE.

2. What will 42650 bricks cost, at \$4.50 per M?
Ans. \$191.925.

3. What is the freight on 2489 pounds from Boston to New York, at \$.85 per 100 pounds? *Ans.* \$21.156+.

4. What will 7842 feet of pine boards cost, at \$17.25 per M? *Ans.* \$135.274+.

5. What cost 2348 pine-apples, at \$12½ per 100?

6. A broom maker bought 1728 broom-handles, at \$3 per 1000; how much did they cost him?

7. What is the cost of 2400 feet of boards, at \$7 per M; 865 feet of scantling, at \$5.40 per M; and 1256 feet of lath, at \$.80 per C? *Ans.* \$31.519.

8. What will be the cost of 1476 pounds of beef, at \$4.37½ per hundred pounds?

CASE VI.

173. To find the cost of articles sold by the ton of 2000 pounds.

1. How much will 2376 pounds of hay cost, at \$9.50 per ton?

Give second explanation. Rule, first step. Second. Case VI is what?

OPERATION.
2) \$9.50
\$4.75
2.376
\$11.28600

ANALYSIS. Since 1 ton, or 2000 pounds, cost \$9.50, 1000 pounds, or $\frac{1}{2}$ ton, will cost $\frac{1}{2}$ of \$9.50, or \$9.50 $\div$ 2 = \$4,75. One pound will cost $\frac{1}{1000}$, or .001, of \$4.75, and 2376 pounds will cost $\frac{2376}{1000}$, or 2.376 times \$4.75, which is \$11.286. Hence,

RULE. I. *Divide the price of* 1 *ton by* 2, *and the quotient will be the price of* 1000 *pounds.*

II. *Multiply this quotient by the given number of pounds expressed as thousandths, as in Case V.*

EXAMPLES FOR PRACTICE.

2. At \$7 a ton, what will 1495 pounds of hay cost? *Ans.* \$5.2325.

3. At \$8.75 a ton, what cost 325 pounds of hay? *Ans.* \$1.421+.

4. What is the cost of 3142 pounds of plaster, at \$3.84 per ton? *Ans.* \$6.032+.

5. What is the cost of 1848 pounds of coal, at \$5.60 per ton?

6. Bought 125 sacks of guano, each sack containing 148 pounds, at \$18 a ton; what was the cost?

7. What must be paid for transporting 31640 pounds of railroad iron from Philadelphia to Richmond, at \$3.05 per ton? *Ans.* \$48.251.

BILLS.

174. A **Bill**, in business transactions, is a written statement of articles bought or sold, together with the prices of each, and the whole cost.

Find the cost of the several articles, and the amount or footing of the following bills.

Give explanation. Rule. What is a bill? Explain the manner of making out a bill.

(1.)

NEW YORK, June 20, 1859.

MR. JOHN RICE,

Bo't. of BALDWIN & SHERWOOD,

7 yds.	Broadcloth,	@ $3.60	
9 "	Satinet,	" 1.12½	
12 "	Vesting,	" .90	
24 "	Cassimere,	" 1.37½	
32 "	Flannel,	" .65	
			$99.925

Rec'd Payment,

BALDWIN & SHERWOOD.

(2.)

BOSTON, Jan. 1, 1860.

DANIEL CHAPMAN & CO.,

Bo't. of PALMER & BROTHER.

67 pairs	Calf Boots,	@ $3.75	
108 "	Thick "	" 2.62	
75 "	Gaiters,	" 1.12	
27 "	Buskins,	" .86	
35 "	Slippers,	" .70	
50 "	Rubbers,	" 1.04	
			$717.93

Rec'd. Payment,

PALMER & BROTHER,
By GEO. BAKER.

(3.)

CHARLESTON, Sept. 6, 1859.

G. B. GRANNIS,

Bo't. of STEWART & HAMMOND,

325 lbs.	A. Sugar,	@ $.07	
148 "	B. "	" .06¼	
286 "	Rice,	" .05	
95 "	O. J. Coffee,	" .12½	
50 boxes	Oranges,	" 2.75	
75 "	Lemons,	" 3.62½	
12 "	Raisins,	" 2.85	
			$501.75

Rec'd. Payment, by note at 4 mo.

STEWART & HAMMOND.

(4.)

St. Louis, Oct. 15, 1858.

Messrs. Osborn & Eaton,

Bo't. of Rob't. H. Carter & Co.,

20000	feet	Pine Boards	@	$15	per M.
7500	"	Plank,	"	9.50	"
10750	"	Scantling,	"	6.25	"
3960	"	Timber,	"	2.62½	"
5287	"	"	"	3.00	"
					$464.6935

Rec'd. Payment,

Rob't. H. Carter & Co.

(5.)

Cincinnati, May 3, 1861.

Mr. J. C. Smith,

Bo't. of Silas Johnson,

25 lbs.	Coffee Sugar,	@	$.11	
5 "	Y. H. Tea,	"	.62½	
26 "	Mackerel,	"	.06¼	
4 gal.	Molasses,	"	.42	
46 yds.	Sheeting,	"	.09	
30 "	Bleached Shirting,	"	.14	
6 skeins	Sewing Silk,	"	.04	
4 doz.	Buttons,	"	.12	
				$18.24

Chgd. in a/c.

Silas Johnson,
Per John Wise.

PROMISCUOUS EXAMPLES.

1. What will 62.75 tons of potash cost, at $124.35 per ton? *Ans.* $7802.9625.

2. What cost 15 pounds of butter, at $.17 a pound? *Ans.* $2.55.

3. A cargo of corn, containing 2250 bushels, was sold for $1406.25; what did it sell for per bushel? *Ans.* $⅝.

4. If 12 yards of cloth cost $48.96, what will one yard cost?

5. A traveled 325 miles by railroad, and C traveled .45 of that distance; how far did C travel? *Ans.* 146.25 miles.

6. If 36.5 bushels of corn grow on one acre, how many acres will produce 657 bushels? *Ans.* 18 acres.

7. Bought a horse for $105, a yoke of oxen for $125, 4 cows at $35 apiece, and sold them all for $400; how much was gained or lost in the transaction?

8. A man bought 28 tons of hay at $19 a ton, and sold it at $15 a ton; how much did he lose? *Ans.* $112.

9. If a man travel $4\frac{3}{5}$ miles an hour, in how many hours can he travel $34\frac{1}{2}$ miles? *Ans.* 7.5 hours.

10. At $.31$\frac{1}{4}$ per bushel, how many bushels of potatoes can be bought for $9? *Ans.* 28.8 bushels.

11. If a man's income be $2000 a year, and his expenses $3.50 a day, what will he save at the end of a year, or 365 days?

12. A merchant deposits in a bank, at one time, $687.25, and at another, $943.64; if he draw out $875.29, how much will remain in the bank?

13. Bought 288 barrels of flour for $1728, and sold one half the quantity for the same price I gave for it, and the other half for $8 per barrel; how much did I receive for the whole? *Ans.* $2016.

14. What will eight hundred seventy-five thousandths of a cord of wood cost, at $3.75 per cord? *Ans.* $3.281+.

15. A drover bought cattle at $46.56 per head, and sold them at $65.42 per head, and thereby gained $3526.82; how many cattle did he buy? *Ans.* 187.

16. If 36.48 yards of cloth cost $54.72, what will 14.25 yards cost? *Ans.* $21.375.

17. A house cost $3548, which is 4 times as much as the furniture cost; what did the furniture cost? *Ans.* $887.

18. How many bushels of onions at $.82 per bushel, can be bought for $112.34?

19. If 46 tons of iron cost \$3461.50, what will 5 tons cost?

20. A gentleman left his widow one third of his property, worth \$24000, and the remainder was to be divided equally among 5 children; how much was the portion of each child?
Ans. \$3200.

21. A man purchased one lot, containing 160 acres of land, at \$1.25 per acre; and another lot, containing 80 acres, at \$5 per acre; he sold them both at \$2.50 per acre; what did he gain or lose in the transaction?

22. A druggist bought 54 gallons of oil for \$72.90, and lost 6 gallons of it by leakage. He sold the remainder at \$1.70 per gallon; how much did he gain? *Ans.* \$8.70.

23. A miller bought 122½ bushels of wheat of one man, and 75¼ bushels of another, at \$.93¾ per bushel. He sold 60 bushels at a profit of \$12.50; if he sell the remainder at \$.81¼ per bushel, what will be his entire gain or loss?
Ans. \$4.718+ loss.

24. A laborer receives \$1.40 per day, and spends \$.75 for his support; how much does he save in a week?

25. How many pounds of butter, at \$.16 per pound, must be given for 39 yards of sheeting, at \$.08 a yard?
Ans. 19½ pounds.

26. What cost 23487 feet of hemlock boards, at \$4.50 per 1000 feet? *Ans.* \$105.6915.

27. A man has an income of \$1200 a year; how much must he spend per day to use it all?

28. Bought 28 firkins of butter, each containing 56 pounds, at \$.17 per pound; what was the whole cost?

29. A merchant bought 16 bales of cotton cloth, each bale containing 13 pieces, and each piece 26 yards, at \$.07 per yard; what did the whole cost? *Ans.* \$378.56.

30. What cost 4868 bricks, at \$4.75 per M?

31. A farmer sold 27 bushels of potatoes, at \$.33⅓ per bushel; 28 bushels of oats, at \$.25 per bushel; and 19 bushels of corn, at \$.50 per bushel; what did he receive for the whole? *Ans.* \$25.50.

32. John runs 32 rods in a minute, and Henry pursues him at the rate of 44 rods in a minute; how long will it take Henry to overtake John, if John have 8 minutes the start?
Ans. $21\frac{1}{3}$ minutes.

33. If $4\frac{3}{4}$ barrels of flour cost $32.3, what will $7\frac{1}{2}$ barrels cost? *Ans.* $51.

34. If .875 of a ton of coal cost $5.635, what will $9\frac{1}{4}$ tons cost? *Ans.* $59.57.

35. For the first three years of business, a trader gained $1200.25 a year; for the next three, he gained $1800.62 a year, and for the next two he lost $950.87 a year; supposing his capital at the beginning of trade to have been $5000, what was he worth at the end of the eighth year? *Ans.* $12100.87.

36. What will be the cost of 18640 feet of timber, at $4.50 per 100? *Ans.* $838.80.

37. Reduce $\frac{2\frac{1}{2}}{3\frac{1}{5}}$ to a decimal fraction. *Ans.* .78125.

38. What will 1375 pounds of potash cost, at $96.40 per ton? *Ans.* $66.275.

39. Reduce .5625 to a common fraction. *Ans.* $\frac{9}{16}$.

40. Reduce $\frac{3}{32}$, $.62\frac{1}{2}$, $.37\frac{1}{16}$, $\frac{3}{8}$, to decimals, and find their sum. *Ans.* 1.464375.

41. A man's account at a store stands thus:

Dr.	Cr.
$4.745	$2.76½
2.62½	1.245
1.27	.62½
.45	3.45
5.28½	1.87½

What is due the merchant? *Ans.* $4.41½.

42. A gardener sold, from his garden, 120 bunches of onions at $.12½ a bunch, 18 bushels of potatoes at $.62½ per bushel, 47 heads of cabbage at $.07 a head, 6 dozen cucumbers at $.18 a dozen; he expended $1.50 in spading, $1.27 for fertilizers, $1.87 for seeds, $2.30 in planting and hoeing; what were the profits of his garden? *Ans.* $23.68.

REDUCTION.

175. A **Compound Number** is a concrete number whose value is expressed in two or more different denominations.

176. **Reduction** is the process of changing a number from one denomination to another without altering its value.

Reduction is of two kinds, Descending and Ascending.

177. **Reduction Descending** is changing a number of one denomination to another denomination of *less unit value;* thus, $1 = 10 dimes = 100 cents = 1000 mills.

178. **Reduction Ascending** is changing a number of one denomination to another denomination of *greater unit value;* thus, 1000 mills = 100 cents = 10 dimes = $1.

179. A **Scale** is a series of numbers, descending or ascending, used in operations upon compound numbers.

CURRENCY.

180. I. United States Money.

TABLE.

10 mills (m.)	make	1 cent,	......ct.
10 cents	"	1 dime,	...... d.
10 dimes	"	1 dollar,	.....$.
10 dollars	"	1 eagle,	.....E.

UNIT EQUIVALENTS.

E.	$	d.	ct.	m.
			1 =	10
		1 =	10 =	100
	1 =	10 =	100 =	1000
1 =	10 =	100 =	1000 =	10000

Scale — uniformly 10.

Canada Money.

The currency of Canada is decimal, and the table and denominations are the same as those of the United States money.

Note. The decimal currency was adopted by the Canadian Parliament in 1858, and the Act took effect in 1859. Previously the money of Canada was reckoned in pounds, shillings, and pence, the same as in England.

Coins. The *silver coins* are the shilling, or 20-cent piece, the dime, and half dime. The *copper coin* is the cent.

Note. The 20-cent piece represents the value of the shilling of the old Canada Currency.

II. English Money.

181. **English Currency** is the currency of Great Britain.

TABLE.

4 farthings (far. or qr.)	make	1 penny,	d.
12 pence	"	1 shilling,	s.
20 shillings	"	1 pound or sovereign,	£, or sov.

UNIT EQUIVALENTS.

	s.	d.	far.
		1 =	4
£, or sov.	1 =	12 =	48
1 =	20 =	240 =	960

Scale ascending, 4, 12, 20; descending, 20, 12, 4.

Note. 1. Farthings are generally expressed as fractions of a penny; thus, 1 far., sometimes called 1 quarter, (qr.), = $\frac{1}{4}$d; 3 far. = $\frac{3}{4}$d.

2. The *gold coins* are the sovereign (= £1), and the half sovereign, (= 10s.)

3. The *silver coins* are the crown (= 5s.), the half-crown (= 2s. 6d.), the shilling, and the six-penny piece.

4. The *copper coins* are the penny, halfpenny, and farthing.

5. The guinea (= 21s.) and the half-guinea (= 10s. 6d. sterling), are old gold coins, that are still in circulation, but are no longer coined.

6. In France accounts are kept in francs and decimes. A franc is equal to 18.6 cents U. S. money.

CASE I.

182. To perform reduction descending.

1. Reduce 21£ 18 s. 10 d. 2 far. to farthings.

OPERATION.

```
21 £ 18 s. 10 d. 2 far.
  20
 438 s
  12
5266 d.
   4
21066 far. Ans.
```

Analysis. Since in £1 there are 20 s., in 21 £ there are 20 s. × 21 = 420 s., and 18 s. in the given number added, makes 438 s. in 21£ 18 s. Since in 1 s. there are 12 d., in 438 s. there are 12 d. × 438 = 5256 d., and 10 d. in the given number added, makes 5266 d. in 21£ 18 s. 10 d. Since in 1 d. there are 4 far., in 5266 d. there are 4 far. × 5266 = 21064 far., and 2 far. in the given number added, makes 21066 far. in the given number. Hence,

RULE. I. MULTIPLY *the highest denomination of the given number by that number of the scale which will reduce it to the next lower denomination, and add to the product the given number, if any, of that lower denomination.*

II. *Proceed in the same manner with the results obtained in each lower denomination, until the reduction is brought to the denomination required.*

CASE II.

183. To perform reduction ascending.

1. Reduce 21066 farthings to pounds.

OPERATION.

4) 21066 far.
12) 5266 d. + 2 far.
2|0) 43|8 s. + 10 d.
21 £ + 18 s.

Ans. 21 £ 18 s. 10 d. 2 far.

ANALYSIS. We first divide the 21066 far. by 4, because there are $\frac{1}{4}$ as many pence as farthings, and we find that 21066 far. = 5266 d. + a remainder of 2 far. We next divide 5266 d. by 12, because there are $\frac{1}{12}$ as many shillings as pence, and we find that 5266 d. = 438 s. + 10 d. Lastly we divide the 438 s. by 20, because there are $\frac{1}{20}$ as many pounds as shillings, and we find that 438 s. = 21 £ + 18 s. The last quotient with the several remainders annexed in the order of the succeeding denominations, gives the answer 21 £ 18 s. 10 d. 2 far. Hence,

RULE. I. DIVIDE *the given number by that number of the scale which will reduce it to the next higher denomination.*

II. *Divide the quotient by the next higher number in the scale; and so proceed to the highest denomination required. The last quotient, with the several remainders annexed in a reversed order, will be the answer.*

NOTE. Reduction descending and reduction ascending mutually prove each other.

EXAMPLES FOR PRACTICE.

1. In 14194 farthings how many pounds?
2. In 14 £ 15 s. 8 d. 2 far. how many farthings?
3. In 15359 farthings how many pounds?
4. In 46 sov. 12 s. 2 d. how many pence?
5. In 11186 pence how many sovereigns?

WEIGHTS.

184. Weight is a measure of the quantity of matter a body contains, determined according to some fixed standard. Three scales of weight are used in the United States and Great Britain, namely, Troy, Apothecaries', and Avoirdupois.

I. Troy Weight.

185. Troy Weight is used in weighing gold, silver, and jewels; in philosophical experiments, &c.

TABLE.

24 grains (gr.)	make	1 pennyweight, . . pwt. or dwt.
20 pennyweights	"	1 ounce, ... oz.
12 ounces	"	1 pound, ... lb.

UNIT EQUIVALENTS.

lb.		oz.		pwt.		gr.
				1	=	24
		1	=	20	=	480
1	=	12	=	240	=	5760

SCALE — ascending, 24, 20, 12; descending, 12, 20, 24.

EXAMPLES FOR PRACTICE.

1. How many grains in 14 lb. 10 oz. 18 pwt. 22 gr.?

OPERATION.

14 lb. 10 oz. 18 pwt. 22 gr.
12
178 oz.
20
3578 pwt.
24
14334
7156
85894 gr., *Ans.*

2. How many pounds in 85894 grains?

OPERATION.

24) 85894 gr.
20) 3578 pwt. + 22 gr.
12) 178 oz. + 18 pwt.
14 lb. + 10 oz.

Ans. 14 lb. 10 oz. 18 pwt. 22 gr.

3. In 5 lb. 7 oz. 12 pwt. 9 gr., how many grains?

4. In 32457 grains how many pounds?

Define weight. Troy weight. Repeat the table. Give the scale.

5. Reduce 41760 grains to pounds. *Ans.* 7 lb. 3 oz.

6. A miner had 14 lb. 10 oz. 18 pwt. of gold dust; how much was it worth at $.75 a pwt.? *Ans.* $2683.50.

7. How many spoons, each weighing 2 oz. 15 pwt., can be made from 5 lb. 6 oz. of silver? *Ans.* 24.

8. A goldsmith manufactured 1 lb. 1 pwt. 16 grs. of gold into rings, each weighing 4 pwt. 20 gr.; he sold the rings for $1.25 apiece; how much did he receive for them? *Ans.* $62.50.

II. Apothecaries' Weight.

186. Apothecaries' Weight is used by apothecaries and physicians in compounding medicines; but medicines are bought and sold by avoirdupois weight.

TABLE.

20 grains (gr.)	make	1 scruple,	......sc. or ℈.
3 scruples	"	1 dram,	........dr. or ʒ.
8 drams	"	1 ounce,	.......oz. or ℥.
12 ounces	"	1 pound,	.......lb. or ℔.

UNIT EQUIVALENTS.

lb.	oz.	dr.	sc.	gr.
			1 =	20
		1 =	3 =	60
	1 =	8 =	24 =	480
1 =	12 =	96 =	288 =	5760

SCALE — ascending, 20, 3, 8, 12; descending, 12, 8, 3, 20.

EXAMPLES FOR PRACTICE.

1. How many gr. in 12 ℔ 8 ℥ 3 ʒ 1 ℈ 15 gr.?

OPERATION.

12 ℔ 8 ℥ 3 ʒ 1 ℈ 15 gr.
12
152 ℥
8
1219 ʒ
3
3658 ℈
20
73175 gr., *Ans.*

2. How many ℔ in 73175 gr.?

OPERATION.

2|0) 7317|5 gr.
3) 3658 ℈ + 15 gr.
8) 1219 ʒ + 1 ℈
12) 152 ℥ + 3 ʒ
12 ℔ + 8 ℥

Ans. 12 ℔ 8 ℥ 3 ʒ 1 ℈ 15 gr.

Define apothecaries' weight. Repeat the table. Give the scale.

3. In 16 lb. 11 oz. 7 dr. 2 sc. 19 gr., how many grains?

4. Reduce 47 ℔ 6 ℥ 4 ʒ to scruples. *Ans.* 13692 sc.

5. How many pounds of medicine would a physician use in one year, or 365 days, if he averaged daily 5 prescriptions of 20 grains each? *Ans.* 6 ℔. 4 ℥ 1 ℈.

III. Avoirdupois Weight.

187. Avoirdupois Weight is used for all the ordinary purposes of weighing.

TABLE.

16 drams (dr.)	make	1 ounce, ... oz.
16 ounces	"	1 pound, ... lb.
100 lb.	"	1 hundred weight, . cwt.
20 cwt., or 2000 lbs.,	"	1 ton, ... T.

UNIT EQUIVALENTS.

T.	cwt.	lb.	oz.	dr.
			1 =	16
		1 =	16 =	256
	1 =	100 =	1600 =	25600
1 =	20 =	2000 =	32000 =	512000

Scale—ascending, 16, 16, 100, 20; descending, 20, 100, 16, 16.

Note. The *long* or *gross ton*, hundred weight, and quarter were formerly in common use; but they are now seldom used except in estimating English goods at the U. S. custom-houses, and in freighting and wholesaling coal from the Pennsylvania mines.

LONG TON TABLE.

28 lb.	make	1 quarter,	marked	qr.
4 qr. = 112 lb.	"	1 hundred weight,	"	cwt.
20 cwt. = 2240 lb.	"	1 ton,	"	T.

Scale—ascending, 28, 4, 20; descending, 20, 4, 28.

The following denominations are also in use.

56	pounds	make	1 firkin of butter.
100	"	"	1 quintal of dried salt fish.
100	"	"	1 cask of raisins.
196	"	"	1 barrel of flour.
200	"	"	1 " " beef, pork, or fish.
280	"	"	1 " " salt at the N. Y. State salt works.
56	"	"	1 bushel " " " " " " "
32	"	"	1 " " oats.
48	"	"	1 " " barley.
56	"	"	1 " " corn or rye.
60	"	"	1 " " wheat.

Define avoirdupois weight. Repeat the table. Give the scale. The long ton table. What other denominations are in use? What is the value of each?

EXAMPLES FOR PRACTICE.

1. In 25 T. 15 cwt. 70 lb. how many pounds?

OPERATION.

25 T. 15 cwt. 70 lb.
20
515 cwt.
100
51570 lb., *Ans.*

2. In 51570 pounds how many tons?

OPERATION.

100) 51570 lb.
2|0) 51|5 cwt. + 70 lb.
25 T. + 15 cwt.
Ans. 25 T. 15 cwt. 70 lb.

3. Reduce 3 T. 14 cwt. 74 lb. 12 oz. 15 dr. to drams.

4. Reduce 1913551 drams to tons.

5. A tobacconist bought 3 T. 15 cwt. 20 lb. of tobacco, at 22 cents a pound; how much did it cost him? *Ans.* $1654.40.

6. How much will 115 pounds of hay cost, at $10 per ton?

7. A grocer bought 10 barrels of sugar, each weighing 2 cwt. 17 lb., at 6 cents a pound; 5 barrels, each weighing 3 cwt. 6 lb., at 7½ cents a pound; he sold the whole at an average price of 8 cents a pound; how much was his whole gain? *Ans.* $51.05.

8. Paid $360 for 2 tons of cheese, and retailed it for 12½ cents a pound; how much was my whole gain? *Ans.* $140.

9. If a person buy 10 T. 6 cwt. 3 qr. 14 lb. of English iron, by the long ton weight, at 6 cents a pound, and sell the same at $130 per short ton, how much will he gain? *Ans.* $115.85.

10. A farmer sold 2 loads of corn, weighing 2352 lbs. each, at $.90 per bu.; what did he receive? *Ans.* $75.60.

11. How many pounds in 300 barrels of flour?

12. A grocer bought 3 barrels of salt at $1.25 per barrel, and retailed it at ¾ of a cent per pound? what did he gain? *Ans.* $2.55.

STANDARD OF WEIGHT.

188. In the year 1834 the U. S. government adopted a uniform standard of weights and measures, for the use of the custom houses, and the other branches of business connected with the general government. Most of the States which have adopted any standards have taken those of the general government.

189. *The United States standard unit of weight* is the Troy pound of the mint, which is the same as the imperial standard pound of Great Britain, and is determined as follows: A cubic inch of distilled water in a vacuum, weighed by brass weights, also in a vacuum, at a temperature of 62° Fahrenheit's thermometer, is equal to 252.458 grains, of which the standard Troy pound contains 5760.

190. *The U. S. Avoirdupois pound* is determined from the standard Troy pound, and contains 7000 Troy grains. Hence, the Troy pound is $\frac{5760}{7000} = \frac{144}{175}$ of an avoirdupois pound. But the Troy ounce contains $\frac{5760}{12} = 480$ grains, and the avoirdupois ounce $\frac{7000}{16} = 437.5$ grains; and an ounce Troy is $480 - 437.5 = 42.5$ grains greater than an ounce avoirdupois. The pound, ounce, and grain, Apothecaries' weight, are the same as the like denominations in Troy weight, the only difference in the two tables being in the divisions of the ounce.

191. COMPARATIVE TABLE OF WEIGHTS.

	Troy.		Apothecaries'.		Avoirdupois.
1 pound =	5760 grains,	=	5760 grains,	=	7000 grains.
1 ounce =	480 "	=	480 "	=	437.5 "
	175 pounds,	=	175 pounds,	=	144 pounds.

EXAMPLES FOR PRACTICE.

1. An apothecary bought 5 lb. 10 oz. of rhubarb, by avoirdupois weight, at 50 cents an ounce, and retailed it at 12 cents a dram apothecaries' weight; how much did he gain?
Ans. $33.75.

2. Change 424 drams apothecaries' weight to Troy weight.
Ans. 4 lb. 5 oz.

3. Change 20 lb. 8 oz. 12 pwt. Troy weight to avoirdupois weight. *Ans.* $17\frac{41}{875}$ lb.

4. Bought by avoirdupois weight 20 lb. of opium, at 40 cents an ounce, and sold the same by Troy weight at 50 cents an ounce; how much was gained or lost? *Ans.* $$17.83\frac{1}{3}$.

What is the U. S. standard of weight? How obtained? How is the avoirdupois pound determined? How is the apothecaries' pound determined? What are the values of the denominations of Troy, avoirdupois, and apothecaries' weight?

MEASURES OF EXTENSION.

192. Extension has three dimensions — length, breadth, and thickness.

A **Line** has only one dimension — length.

A **Surface** or **Area** has two dimensions — length and breadth.

A **Solid** or **Body** has three dimensions — length, breadth, and thickness.

I. Long Measure.

193. Long Measure, also called Linear Measure, is used in measuring lines or distances.

TABLE.

12	inches (in.)	make	1 foot, ... ft.
3	feet	"	1 yard, ... yd.
5½	yd., or 16½ ft.,	"	1 rod, ... rd.
40	rods	"	1 furlong, ... fur.
8	furlongs, or 320 rd.,	"	1 statute mile, . . mi.

UNIT EQUIVALENTS.

mi.		fur.		rd.		yd.		ft.		in.
								1	=	12
						1	=	3	=	36
				1	=	5½	=	16½	=	198
		1	=	40	=	220	=	660	=	7920
1	=	8	=	320	=	1760	=	5280	=	63360

Scale — ascending, 12, 3, 5½, 40, 8; descending, 8, 40, 5½, 3, 12.

The following denominations are also in use: —

3 barleycorns make 1 inch, { used by shoemakers in measuring the length of the foot.

4 inches " 1 hand, { used in measuring the height of horses directly over the fore feet.

6 feet " 1 fathom, used in measuring depths at sea.

1.15 statute miles " 1 geographic mile, { used in measuring distances at sea.

3 geographic " " 1 league.

60 " " " } 1 degree { of latitude on a meridian or of longitude on the equator.
69.16 statute " " }

360 degrees " the circumference of the earth.

How many dimensions has extension? Define a line. Surface or area. A solid or body. Define long measure. What are the denominations? The value of each. What other denominations are used?

NOTES. 1. For the purpose of measuring cloth and other goods sold by the yard, the yard is divided into halves, fourths, eighths, and sixteenths. The old table of cloth measure is practically obsolete.

2. The geographic mile is $\frac{1}{60}$ of $\frac{1}{360}$ or $\frac{1}{21600}$ of the distance round the center of the earth. It is a small fraction more than 1.15 statute miles.

3. The length of a degree of latitude varies, being 68.72 miles at the equator, 68.9 to 69.05 miles in middle latitudes, and 69.30 to 69.34 miles in the polar regions. The mean or average length is as stated in the table. A degree of longitude is greatest at the equator, where it is 69.16 miles, and it gradually decreases toward the poles, where it is 0.

EXAMPLES FOR PRACTICE.

1. In 2 mi. 4 fur. 32 rd. 2 yd. how many inches?

OPERATION.

2 mi. 4 fur. 32 rd. 2 yd.
8
20 fur.
40
832 rd.
$5\frac{1}{2}$
416
4162
4578 yd.
3
13734 ft.
12
164808 in., *Ans.*

2. In 164808 inches how many miles?

OPERATION.

12) 164808 in.
3) 13734 ft.
$5\frac{1}{2}$ / 2) 4578 yd. / 2
11) 9156
4|0) 83|2 rd. + $\frac{4}{2}$ yd. = 2 yd.
8) 20 fur. + 32 rd.
2 mi. + 4 fur.

Ans. 2 mi. 4 fur. 32 rd. 2 yd.

3. The diameter of the earth being 7912 miles, how many inches is it? *Ans.* 501304320 inches.

4. In 168474 feet how many miles?

5. In 31 mi. 7 fur. 10 rd. 3 yd., how many feet?

6. If the greatest depth of the Atlantic telegraphic cable from Newfoundland to Ireland be 2500 fathoms, how many miles is it? *Ans.* 2 mi. 6 fur. 29 rd. $1\frac{1}{2}$ ft.

7. If this cable be 2200 miles in length, and cost 10 cents a foot, what was its whole cost? *Ans.* $1161600.

8. A pond of water measures 4 fathoms 3 feet 8 inches in depth; how many inches deep is it? *Ans.* 332.

9. How many times will the driving wheels of a locomotive turn round in going from Albany to Boston, a distance of 200 miles, supposing the wheels to be 18 ft. 4 inches in circumference? *Ans.* 57600 times.

10. If a vessel sail 120 leagues in a day, how many statute miles does she sail? *Ans.* 414.

11. How many inches high is a horse that measures 14½ hands? *Ans.* 58.

SURVEYORS' LONG MEASURE.

194. **A Gunter's Chain**, used by land surveyors, is 4 rods or 66 feet long, and consists of 100 links.

TABLE.

7.92	inches	(in.) make	1 link, ...	l.
25	links	"	1 rod, ...	rd.
4	rods, or 66 feet,	"	1 chain ..	ch.
80	chains	"	1 mile, ..	mi.

UNIT EQUIVALENTS.

mi.		ch.		rd.		l.		in.
						1	=	7.92
				1	=	25	=	198
		1	=	4	=	100	=	792
1	=	80	=	320	=	8000	=	63360

SCALE — ascending, 7.92, 25, 4, 80; descending, 80, 4, 25, 7.92.

NOTE. Rods are seldom used in chain measure, distances being taken in chains and links.

EXAMPLES FOR PRACTICE.

1. In 3 mi. 51 ch. 73 l. how many links?

2. Reduce 29173 l. to miles.

3. A certain field, enclosed by a board fence, is 17 ch. 31 l. long, and 12 ch. 87 l. wide; how many feet long is the fence which encloses it? *Ans.* 3983.76 ft.

Repeat the table of surveyors' long measure. Give the scale.

II. Square Measure.

195. A **Square** is a figure having four equal sides, and four equal angles or corners.

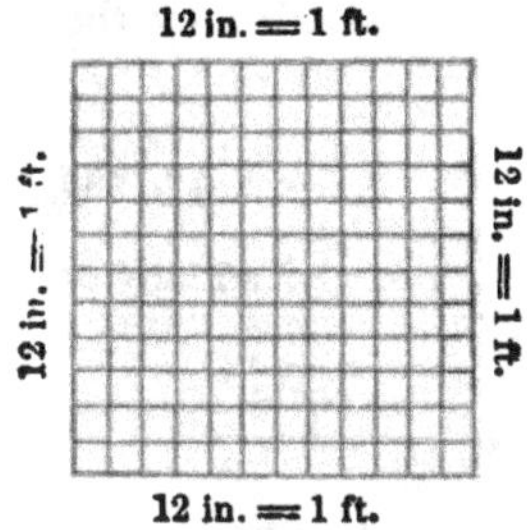

1 square foot is a figure having four sides of 1 ft. or 12 in. each, as shown in the diagram. Its contents are 12 × 12 = 144 square inches. Hence

The contents or area of a square, or of any other figure having a uniform length and a uniform breadth, is found by multiplying the length by the breadth. Thus, a square foot is 12 in. long and 12 in. wide, and the contents are 12 × 12 = 144 square inches. A board 20 in. long and 10 in. wide, is a rectangle, containing 20 × 10 = 200 square inches.

196. **Square Measure** is used in computing areas or surfaces; as of land, boards, painting, plastering, paving, &c.

TABLE.

144	square inches (sq. in.)	make	1 square foot,	marked	sq. ft.
9	square feet	"	1 square yard,	"	sq. yd.
30¼	square yards	"	1 square rod,	"	sq. rd.
40	square rods	"	1 rood,	"	R.
4	roods	"	1 acre,	"	A.
640	acres	"	1 square mile,	"	sq. mi.

UNIT EQUIVALENTS

sq. mi.	A.	R.	sq. rd.	sq. yd.	sq. ft.	sq. in.
					1 =	144
				1 =	9 =	1296
			1 =	30¼ =	272¼ =	39204
		1 =	40 =	1210 =	10890 =	1568160
	1 =	4 =	160 =	4840 =	43560 =	6272640
1 =	640 =	2560 =	102400 =	3097600 =	27878400 =	4014489600

Scale — ascending, 144, 9, 30¼, 40, 4, 640; descending, 640, 4, 40, 30¼, 9, 144.

Define a square. How is the area of a square or any rectangular figure found? For what is square measure used? Repeat the table. Give the scale.

Artificers estimate their work as follows:

By the square foot: glazing and stone-cutting.

By the square yard: painting, plastering, paving, ceiling, and paper-hanging.

By the square of 100 feet: flooring, partitioning, roofing, slating, and tiling.

Brick-laying is estimated by the thousand bricks; also by the square yard, and the square of 100 feet.

NOTES. 1. In estimating the painting of moldings, cornices, &c., the measuring-line is carried into all the moldings and cornices.

2. In estimating brick-laying by the square yard or the square of 100 feet, the work is understood to be $1\frac{1}{2}$ bricks, or 12 inches, thick.

EXAMPLES FOR PRACTICE.

1. In 10 A. 1 R. 25 sq. rd. 16 sq. yd. 4 sq. ft. 136 sq. in. how many square inches?

OPERATION.

```
10 A. 1 R. 25 sq. rd. 16 sq. yd. 4 sq. ft. 136 sq. in.
 4
 ――
 41 R.
 40
 ――――
 1665 sq. rd.
   30¼
 ――――――
 416¼
49966
――――――
50382¼ sq. yd.
     9
――――――――
453444¼ sq. ft.
    144
――――――――――
     36 = ¼ sq. ft.
 1813912 with 136 sq. in.
1813776
453444
――――――――
65296108 sq. in., Ans.
```

2. In 65296108 sq. in. how many acres?

How do artisans estimate work?

OPERATION.

144) 65296108 sq. in.

9) 453445 sq. ft. + 28 sq. in.

$30\frac{1}{4}$) 50382 sq. yd. + 7 sq. ft.
4   4

121) 201528 fourths sq. yd.

4|0) 166|5 sq. rd. + $\frac{63}{4} = 15\frac{3}{4}$ sq. yd.

4) 41 R. + 25 sq. rd.

10 A. + 1 R.

Ans. 10 A. 1 R. 25 sq. rd. $15\frac{3}{4}$ sq. yd. 7 sq. ft. 28 sq. in.

Or { 10 A. 1 R. 25 sq. rd. 15 sq. yd. 7 sq. ft. 28 sq. in.
                                         6 sq. ft. 108 sq. in.

Or 10 A. 1 R. 25 sq. rd. 16 sq. yd. 4 sq. ft. 136 sq. in.

ANALYSIS. Dividing by the numbers in the ascending scale, and arranging the remainders according to their order in a line below, we find the square yards a mixed number, $15\frac{3}{4}$. But $\frac{3}{4}$ of a sq. yd. $= \frac{3}{4}$ of 9 sq. ft. $= 6\frac{3}{4}$ sq. ft.; and $\frac{3}{4}$ of a sq. ft. $= \frac{3}{4}$ of 144 sq. in. $=$ 108 sq. in. Therefore $\frac{3}{4}$ sq. yd. $=$ 6 sq. ft. 108 sq. in.; and adding 108 sq. in. to 28 sq. in. we have 136 sq. in., and 6 sq. ft. to 7 sq. ft. we have 13 sq. ft. $=$ 1 sq. yd. 4 sq. ft., and writing the 4 sq. ft. in the result, and adding 1 sq. yd. to 15 sq. yd. we have for the reduced result, 10 A. 1 R. 25 sq. rd. 16 sq. yd. 4 sq. ft. 136 sq. in.

3. Reduce 87 A. 2 R. 38 sq. rd. 7 sq. yd. 1 sq. ft. 100 sq. in. to square inches. *Ans.* 550355068 sq. in.

4. Reduce 550355068 square inches to acres.

5. A field 100 rods long and 30 rods wide contains how many acres? *Ans.* 18 A. 3 R.

6. How many rods of fence will enclose a farm a mile square? *Ans.* 1280 rods.

7. How much additional fence will divide it into four equal square fields? *Ans.* 640 rods.

8. How many acres of land in Boston, at $1 a square foot, will $100000 purchase?

Ans. 2 A. 1 R. 7 sq. rd. 9 sq. yd. $3\frac{1}{4}$ sq. ft.

9. How many yards of carpeting, 1 yd. wide, will be required to carpet a room $18\frac{1}{2}$ ft. long and 16 ft. wide? *Ans.* $32\frac{8}{9}$ yd.

10. What would be the cost of plastering a room 18 ft. long, 16½ ft. wide, and 9 ft. high, at 22 cts. a sq. yd.? *Ans.* $22.44.

11. What will be the expense of slating a roof 40 feet long and each of the two sides 20 feet wide, at $10 per square? *Ans.* $160.

SURVEYORS' SQUARE MEASURE.

197. This measure is used by surveyors in computing the area or contents of land.

TABLE.

625 square links (sq. l.)	make	1 pole, ... P.
16 poles	"	1 square chain, . . sq. ch.
10 square chains	"	1 acre, ... A.
640 acres	"	1 square mile, . . . sq. mi.
36 square miles (6 miles square)	"	1 township, ... Tp.

UNIT EQUIVALENTS.

Tp.	sq. mi.	A.	sq. ch.	P.	sq. l.
				1 =	625
			1 =	16 =	1000
		1 =	10 =	160 =	100000
	1 =	640 =	6400 =	102400 =	64000000
1 =	36 =	23040 =	230400 =	3686400 =	2304000000

SCALE — ascending, 625, 16, 10, 640, 36; descending, 36, 640, 10, 16, 625.

NOTES. 1. A square mile of land is also called a *section*.

2. Canal and railroad engineers commonly use an engineers' chain, which consists of 100 links, each 1 foot long.

3. The contents of land are commonly estimated in square miles, acres, and hundredths; the denomination, *rood*, is fast going into disuse.

EXAMPLES FOR PRACTICE.

1. How many poles in a township of land?

2. Reduce 3686400 P. to sq. mi.

3. In 94 A. 7 sq. ch. 12 P. 118 sq. l. how many square links?

4. What will be the cost of a farm containing 4550000 square links, at $50 per acre? *Ans.* $22750.

Repeat the table of surveyors' square measure. Give the scale.

III. Cubic Measure.

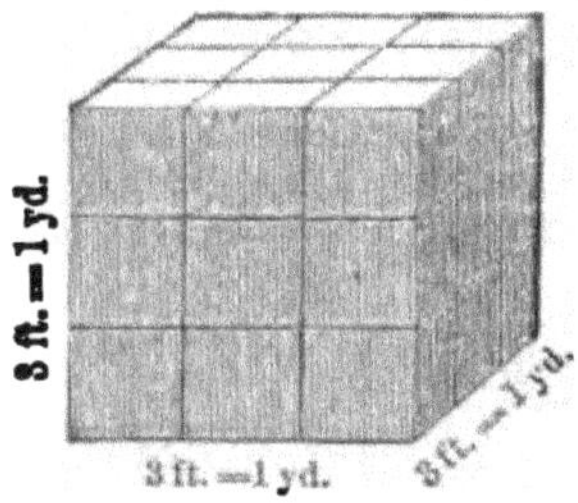

198. A **Cube** is a solid, or body, having six equal square sides, or faces. If each side of a cube be 1 yard, or 3 feet, 1 foot in thickness of this cube will contain $3 \times 3 \times 1 = 9$ cubic feet, and the whole cube will contain $3 \times 3 \times 3 = 27$ cubic feet.

A solid, or body, may have the three dimensions all alike or all different. A body 4 ft. long, 3 ft. wide, and 2 ft. thick contains $4 \times 3 \times 2 = 24$ cubic or solid feet. Hence we see that

The cubic or solid contents of a body are found by multiplying the length, breadth, and thickness together.

199. Cubic Measure, also called Solid Measure, is used in estimating the contents of solids, or bodies; as timber, wood, stone, &c.

TABLE.

1728 cubic inches (cu. in.)	make	1 cubic foot,......cu. ft.
27 cubic feet	"	1 cubic yard,....cu. yd.
16 cubic feet	"	1 cord foot,......cd. ft.
8 cord feet, or 128 cubic feet,	"	1 cord of wood,....Cd.
$24\frac{3}{4}$ cubic feet	"	1 perch of stone or masonry, Pch.

Scale — ascending, 1728, 27. The other numbers are not in a regular scale, but are merely so many times 1 foot. The unit equivalents, being fractional, are consequently omitted.

Notes. 1. A cubic yard of earth is called a load.

2. Railroad and transportation companies estimate light freight by the space it occupies in cubic feet, and heavy freight by weight.

3. A pile of wood 8 feet long, 4 feet wide, and 4 feet high, contains 1 cord; and a cord foot is 1 foot in length of such a pile.

4. A perch of stone or of masonry is $16\frac{1}{2}$ feet long, $1\frac{1}{2}$ feet wide, and 1 foot high.

Define a cube. How are the contents of a cube or rectangular solid found? For what is cubic measure used? Repeat the table. Give the scale. How is railroad freight estimated? What is understood by a cord foot? By a perch of stone or masonry?

5. Joiners, bricklayers, and masons make no allowance for windows, doors, &c. Bricklayers and masons, in estimating their work by cubic measure, make no allowance for the corners of the walls of houses, cellars, &c., but estimate their work by the girt, that is, the entire length of the wall on the outside.

6. Engineers, in making estimates for excavations and embankments, take the dimensions with a line or measure divided into feet and decimals of a foot. The estimates are made in feet and decimals, and the results are reduced to cubic yards.

EXAMPLES FOR PRACTICE.

1. In 125 cu. ft. 840 cu. in. how many cu. in.? *Ans.* 216840.

2. Reduce 5224 cubic feet to cords. *Ans.* $40\frac{13}{16}$.

3. In a solid, 3 ft. 2 in. long, 2 ft. 2 in. wide, and 1 ft. 8 in. thick, how many cubic inches? *Ans.* 19760.

4. How many small cubes, 1 inch on each edge, can be sawed from a cube 6 feet on each edge, allowing no waste for sawing? *Ans.* 373248.

5. In a pile of wood 60 feet long, 20 feet wide, and 15 feet high, how many cords? *Ans.* $140\frac{5}{8}$.

6. How many cubic feet in a load of wood 10 feet long, $3\frac{1}{4}$ feet wide, and $3\frac{1}{2}$ feet high? *Ans.* $113\frac{3}{4}$ cu. ft.

7. If a load of wood be 12 feet long and 3 feet wide, how high must it be to make a cord? *Ans.* $3\frac{5}{9}$ ft. high.

8. The gray limestone of Central New York weighs 175 pounds a cubic foot. What is the weight of one solid yard? *Ans.* 2 T. 7 cwt. 25 lb.

9. A cellar wall, 32 ft. by 24 ft., is 6 ft. high and $1\frac{1}{2}$ ft. thick. How much did it cost at $1.25 a perch? *Ans.* $50.909+

10. How much did it cost to dig the same cellar, at 15 cents a cubic yard? *Ans.* $25.60.

11. My sleeping room is 10 ft. long, 9 ft. wide, and 8 ft. high. If I breathe 10 cu. ft. of air in one minute, in how long a time will I breathe as much air as the room contains? *Ans.* 72 min.

12. In a school room 30 ft. long, 20 ft. wide, and 10 ft. high, with 50 persons breathing each 10 cu. ft. of air in one minute, in how long a time will they breathe as much as the room contains? *Ans.* 12 min.

How are excavations and embankments measured?

MEASURES OF CAPACITY.

I. LIQUID MEASURE.

200. **Liquid Measure,** also called Wine Measure, is used in measuring liquids; as liquors, molasses, water, &c.

TABLE.

4	gills (gi.)	make	1 pint,........pt.
2	pints	"	1 quart,.......qt.
4	quarts	"	1 gallon, ...gal.
$31\frac{1}{2}$	gallons	"	1 barrel, ...bbl.
2	barrels, or 63 gal.	"	1 hogshead,..hhd.

UNIT EQUIVALENTS.

hhd.		bbl.		gal.		qt.		pt.		gi.
								1	=	4
						1	=	2	=	8
				1	=	4	=	8	=	32
		1	=	$31\frac{1}{2}$	=	126	=	252	=	1008
1	=	2	=	63	=	252	=	504	=	2016

SCALE — ascending, 4, 2, 4, $31\frac{1}{2}$, 2; descending, 2, $31\frac{1}{2}$, 4, 2, 4.

The following denominations are also in use:

36 gallons	make	1 barrel of beer.
54 " or $1\frac{1}{2}$ barrels	"	1 hogshead " "
42 "	"	1 tierce.
2 hogsheads, or 120 gallons,	"	1 pipe or butt.
2 pipes or 4 hogsheads,	"	1 tun.

NOTES. 1. The denominations, barrel and hogshead, are used in estimating the capacity of cisterns, reservoirs, vats, &c.

2. The tierce, hogshead, pipe, butt, and tun are the names of casks, and do not express any fixed or definite measures. They are usually gauged, and have their capacities in gallons marked on them.

3. Ale or beer measure, formerly used in measuring beer, ale, and milk, is almost entirely discarded.

What is liquid measure? Repeat the table. Give the scale. What other denominations are sometimes used? How are the capacities of cisterns, reservoirs, &c., reckoned? Of large casks?

EXAMPLES FOR PRACTICE.

1. In 2 hhd. 1 bar. 30 gal. 2 qt. 1 pt. 3 gi. how many gills?

OPERATION.

2 hhd. 1 bar. 30 gal. 2 qt. [1 pt. 3 gi.
2
5 bbl.
31½
2½
185
187½ gal.
4
752 qt.
2
1505 pt.
4
6023 gi., *Ans.*

2. In 6023 gi. how many hhds.?

OPERATION.

4) 6023 gi.
2) 1505 pt. + 3 gi.
4) 752 qt. + 1 pt.
31½) 188 gal.
2   2
63) 376
2) 5 bbl. + 61/2 gal. = 30½ [gal.
2 hhd. + 1 bar.

Ans. 2 hhd. 1 bar. 30½ gal. 1 pt. 3 gi.

But ½ gal. = 2 qt., making the *Ans.* 2 hhd. 1 bar. 30 gal. 2 qt. 1 pt. 3 gi.

3. Reduce 3 hogsheads to gills.
4. Reduce 6048 gills to hogsheads.
5. In 13 hhd. 15 gal. 1 qt. how many pints?
6. In 6674 pints how many hogsheads?
7. What will be the cost of a hogshead of wine, at 6 cents a gill? *Ans.* $120.96.
8. A grocer bought 10 barrels of cider, at $2 a barrel; after converting it into vinegar, he retailed it all at 5 cents a quart; how much was his whole gain? *Ans.* $43.
9. At 6 cents a pint, how much molasses can be bought for $3.84? *Ans.* 8 gal.
10. How many demijohns, that will contain 2 gal. 2 qt. 1 pt. each, can be filled from a hogshead of wine? *Ans.* 24.

II. Dry Measure.

201. **Dry Measure** is used in measuring articles not liquid, as grain, fruit, salt, roots, ashes, &c.

What is dry measure?

TABLE.

2 pints (pt.)	make	1 quart, ... qt.
8 quarts	"	1 peck, ... pk.
4 pecks	"	1 bushel, . bu. or bush.

UNIT EQUIVALENTS.

bu.	pk.	qt.	pt.
		1 =	2
	1 =	8 =	16
1 =	4 =	32 =	64

SCALE — ascending, 2, 8, 4; descending, 4, 8, 2.

NOTE. In England, 8 bu. of 70 lbs. each are called a *quarter*, used in measuring grain. The weight of the English quarter is $\frac{1}{4}$ of a long ton.

EXAMPLES FOR PRACTICE.

1. In 49 bu. 3 pk. 7 qt. 1 pt. how many pints?
2. In 3199 pt. how many bushels?
3. Reduce 1 bu. 1 pk. 1 qt. 1 pt. to pints.
4. Reduce 83 pints to bushels.
5. An innkeeper bought a load of 50 bushels of oats at 65 cents a bushel, and retailed them at 25 cents a peck; how much did he make on the load? *Ans.* $17.50.

STANDARD OF EXTENSION.

202. *The U. S. standard unit of measures of extension*, whether linear, superficial, or solid, is the yard of 3 feet, or 36 inches, and is the same as the imperial standard yard of Great Britain. It is determined as follows: The rod of a pendulum vibrating seconds of mean time, in the latitude of London, in a vacuum, at the level of the sea, is divided into 391393 equal parts, and 360000 of these parts are 36 inches, or 1 standard yard. Hence, such a pendulum rod is 39.1393 inches long, and the standard yard is $\frac{360000}{391393}$ of the length of the pendulum rod.

203. *The U. S. standard unit of liquid measure* is the old English wine gallon, of 231 cubic inches, which is equal to 8.33888 pounds avoirdupois of distilled water at its maximum density, that is, at the temperature of 39.83° Fahrenheit, the barometer at 30 inches.

Repeat the table. What is a quarter? What is the U. S. standard unit of measurement of extension? How is it determined? What is the U. S. standard unit of liquid measure?

204. *The U. S. standard unit of dry measure* is the British Winchester bushel, which is $18\frac{1}{2}$ inches in diameter and 8 inches deep, and contains 2150.42 cubic inches, equal to 77.6274 pounds avoirdupois of distilled water, at its maximum density. A gallon, dry measure, contains 268.8 cubic inches.

NOTE. 1. The wine and dry measures of the same denomination are of different capacities. The exact and the relative size of each may be readily seen by the following

205. COMPARATIVE TABLE OF MEASURES OF CAPACITY.

	Cu. in. in one gallon.	Cu. in. in one quart.	Cu. in. in one pint.	Cu. in. in one gill.
Wine measure,	231	$57\frac{3}{4}$	$28\frac{7}{8}$	$7\frac{7}{32}$
Dry measure, ($\frac{1}{2}$ pk.,)	$268\frac{4}{5}$	$67\frac{1}{5}$	$33\frac{3}{5}$	$8\frac{2}{5}$

2. The beer gallon of 282 inches is retained in use only by custom A bushel is commonly estimated at 2150.4 cubic inches.

EXAMPLES FOR PRACTICE.

1. A fruit dealer bought a bushel of strawberries, dry measure, and sold them by wine measure; how many quarts did he gain? *Ans.* $5\frac{13}{55}$ quarts.

2. A grocer bought 40 quarts of milk by beer measure, and sold it by wine measure; how many quarts did he gain? *Ans.* $8\frac{64}{77}$ quarts.

3. A bushel, or 32 quarts, dry measure, contains how many more cubic inches than 32 quarts wine measure? *Ans.* $302\frac{2}{5}$ cu. in.

TIME.

206. Time is used in measuring periods of duration, as years, days, minutes, &c.

TABLE.

60 seconds (sec.)	make	1 minute,	min.
60 minutes	"	1 hour,	h.
24 hours	"	1 day,	da.
7 days	"	1 week,	wk.
365 days	"	1 common year,	yr.
366 days	"	1 leap year,	yr.
12 calendar months	"	1 year,	yr.
100 years	"	1 century,	C.

What is the U. S. standard unit of dry measure? How is it obtained? What is the relative size of the wine and the dry gallon? What is the size of a beer gallon? What is time? Repeat the table.

UNIT EQUIVALENTS.

yr	mo.	da.	h.	min.	sec.
				1 =	60
			1 =	60 =	3600
		wk. 1 =	24 =	1440 =	86400
		1 = 7 =	168 =	10080 =	604800
1 =	12 =	365 =	8760 =	525600 =	31536000
		366 =	8784 =	527040 =	31622400

SCALE — ascending, 60, 60, 24, 7; descending, 7, 24, 60, 60.

The calendar year is divided as follows: —

No. of mo.	Season.	Names.	Abbreviations.	No. of days.
1	Winter,	January,	Jan.	31
2	"	February,	Feb.	28 or 29
3	Spring,	March,	Mar.	31
4	"	April,	Apr.	30
5	"	May,	——	31
6	Summer,	June,	Jun.	30
7	"	July,	——	31
8	"	August,	Aug.	31
9	Autumn,	September,	Sept.	30
10	"	October,	Oct.	31
11	"	November,	Nov.	30
12	Winter,	December,	Dec.	31
				365 or 366

NOTES. 1. The exact length of a solar year is 365 da. 5 h. 48 min. 46 sec.; but for convenience it is reckoned 11 min. 14 sec. more than this, or 365 da. 6 h. = 365¼ da. This ¼ day in 4 years makes one day, which, every fourth, bissextile, or leap year, is added to the shortest month, giving it 29 days. The leap years are exactly divisible by 4, as 1856, 1860, 1864. The number of days in each calendar month may be easily remembered by committing the following lines: —

"Thirty days hath September,
April, June, and November;
All the rest have thirty-one,
Save February, which alone
Hath twenty-eight; and one day more
We add to it one year in four."

2. In most business transactions 30 days are called 1 month.

EXAMPLES FOR PRACTICE.

1. Reduce 365 da. 5 h. 48 min. 46 sec. to seconds.

2. Reduce 31556926 seconds to days.

Give the scale. What is the length of each of the calendar months? What is the exact length of a solar year? Explain the use of bissextile or leap year. What is the length of a month in business transactions?

3. In 5 wk. 1 da. 1 h. 1 min. 1 sec. how many seconds?

4. In 3114061 seconds how many weeks?

5. How many times does a clock pendulum, 3 ft. 3 in. long, beating seconds, vibrate in one day? *Ans.* 86400.

6. If a man take 1 step a yard long in a second, in how long a time will he walk 10 miles? *Ans.* 4 h. 53 min. 20 sec.

7. In a lunar month of 29 da. 12 h. 44 min. 3 sec. how many seconds? *Ans.* 2551443.

8. How much time will a person gain in 40 years, by rising 45 minutes earlier every day? *Ans.* 456 da. 13 h. 30 min.

Circular Measure.

207. Circular Measure, or Circular Motion, is used principally in surveying, navigation, astronomy, and geography, for reckoning latitude and longitude, determining locations of places and vessels, and computing difference of time.

Every circle, great or small, is divisible into the same number of equal parts, as quarters, called quadrants, twelfths, called signs, 360ths, called degrees, &c. Consequently the parts of different circles, although having the same names, are of different lengths.

TABLE.

60 seconds (″)	make	1 minute,... ′.
60 minutes	"	1 degree,... °.
30 degrees	"	1 sign,.....S.
12 signs, or 360°,	"	1 circle,....C.

UNIT EQUIVALENTS.

C.		S.		°		′		″
						1	=	60
				1	=	60	=	3600
		1	=	30	=	1800	=	108000
1	=	12	=	360	=	21600	=	1296000

Scale — ascending, 60, 60, 30, 12; descending, 12, 30, 60, 60.

Notes. 1. Minutes of the earth's circumference are called geographic or nautical miles.

2. The denomination, *signs*, is confined exclusively to Astronomy.

Define circular measure. How are circles divided? Repeat the table. Give the scale. What is a geographic mile? What is a sign?

3. Degrees are not strictly divisions of a circle, but of the space about a point in any plane.

4. 90° make a quadrant, or right angle, and 60° a sextant, or $\frac{1}{6}$ of a circle.

EXAMPLES FOR PRACTICE.

1. Reduce 10 S. 10° 10′ 10″ to seconds.

2. Reduce 1116610″ to signs.

3. How many degrees in 11400 geographic or nautical miles? *Ans.* 190°.

4. If 1 degree of the earth's circumference is 69$\frac{1}{5}$ statute miles, how many statute miles in 11400 geographic miles, or 190 degrees? *Ans.* 13148.

5. How many minutes, or nautical miles, in the circumference of the earth? *Ans.* 21600′ or mi.

6. A ship during 4 days' storm at sea changed her longitude 397 geographical miles; how many degrees and minutes did she change? *Ans.* 6° 37′.

208. IN COUNTING.

12 units or things....make....1 dozen.
12 dozen " 1 gross.
12 gross " 1 great gross.
20 units " 1 score.

209. PAPER.

24 sheets........make........1 quire.
20 quires " 1 ream.
2 reams " 1 bundle.
5 bundles " 1 bale.

210. BOOKS.

The terms *folio, quarto, octavo, duodecimo,* &c., indicate the number of leaves into which a sheet of paper is folded.

A sheet folded in 2 leaves is called a folio.
A sheet folded in 4 leaves " a quarto, or 4to.
A sheet folded in 8 leaves " an octavo, or 8vo.
A sheet folded in 12 leaves " a 12mo.
A sheet folded in 16 leaves " a 16mo.
A sheet folded in 18 leaves " an 18mo.
A sheet folded in 24 leaves " a 24mo.
A sheet folded in 32 leaves " a 32mo.

What is a degree? Repeat the table for counting. For reckoning paper. For indicating the size of books.

EXAMPLES FOR PRACTICE.

1. If in Birmingham, England, 150 million Gillott pens are manufactured annually, how many great gross will they make?

Ans. 86805 great gross 6 gross 8 dozen.

2. In 100000 sheets of paper, how many bales?

Ans. 20 bales 4 bundles 6 quires 16 sheets.

3. What is the age of a man 4 score and 10 years old?

4. How many printed pages, 2 pages to each leaf, will there be in an octavo book, having 8 fully printed sheets?

Ans. 128 pages.

5. How large a book will ten 32mo. sheets make, if every page be printed? *Ans.* 640 pages.

PROMISCUOUS EXAMPLES IN REDUCTION.

1. How many suits of clothes, each containing 6 yd. $3\frac{3}{4}$ qr., can be cut from 333 yards of cloth? *Ans.* 48.

2. A man bought a gold chain, weighing 1 oz. 15 pwt., at seven dimes a pennyweight; what did it cost? *Ans.* $24.50.

3. A physician, having 2 ℔ 3℥ 5ʒ 1℈ 10 gr. of medicine, dealt it out in prescriptions averaging 15 grains each; how many prescriptions did it make? *Ans.* 886.

4. A man bought 1 T. 11 cwt. 12 lbs. of hay, at $1\frac{1}{4}$ cents a pound; what did it cost? *Ans.* $38.90.

5. What will be the cost of a load of oats weighing 1456 pounds, at $37\frac{1}{2}$ cents per bushel? *Ans.* $17.0625.

6. If one bushel of wheat will make 45 pounds of flour, how many barrels will 1000 bushels make? *Ans.* 229 bbl. 116 lb.

7. A load of wheat weighing 2430 pounds is worth how much, at $1.20 a bushel? *Ans.* $48.60.

8. Paid $12.50 for a barrel of beef; how much was that per pound? *Ans.* $6\frac{1}{4}$ cents.

9. If a silver dollar measure one inch in diameter, how many dollars, laid side by side on the equator, would reach round the earth? *Ans.* 1573862400.

10. In 10 mi. 7 ch. 4 rd, 20 l., how many links?

Ans. 80820 links.

11. What is the value of a city lot, 25 feet wide and 100 feet long, if every square inch is worth one cent? *Ans.* $3600.

12. How many cords of wood can be piled in a shed 50 ft. long, 25 ft. wide, and 10 ft. high? *Ans.* 97 Cd. 5 cd. ft. 4 cu. ft.

13. A cistern 10 feet square and 10 feet deep, will hold how many hogsheads of water? *Ans.* 118 hhd. 46$\frac{49}{77}$ gal.

14. A bin 8 feet long, 5 feet wide, and 4$\frac{1}{2}$ feet high, will hold how many bushels of grain? *Ans.* 144$\frac{8}{14}$ bu.

15. How many seconds less in every Autumn than in either Spring or Summer? *Ans.* 86400 sec.

16. If a person could travel at the rate of a second of distance in a second of time, how much time would he require to travel round the earth? *Ans.* 15 days.

17. How many yards of carpeting, 1 yd. wide, will be required to carpet a room 20 ft. long and 18 ft. wide? *Ans.* 40.

18. A printer calls for 4 reams 10 quires and 10 sheets of paper to print a book; how many sheets does he call for? *Ans.* 2170.

19. How many times will a wheel, 16 ft. 6 in. in circumference, turn round in running 42 miles? *Ans.* 13440.

20. How many days, working 10 hours a day, will it require for a person to count $10000, at the rate of one cent each second? *Ans.* 27 da. 7h. 46 min. 40 sec.

21. A town, 6 miles long and 4$\frac{1}{2}$ miles wide, is equal to how many farms of 80 acres each? *Ans.* 216.

22. At $21.75 per rod, what will be the cost of grading 10 mi. 176 rds. of road? *Ans.* $73428.

REDUCTION OF DENOMINATE FRACTIONS.

CASE I.

211. To reduce a denominate fraction from a greater to a less unit.

1. Reduce $\frac{1}{80}$ of a bushel to the fraction of a pint.

Case I is what?

OPERATION.

$$\overset{\text{bu.}}{\tfrac{1}{80}} \times \tfrac{4}{1} \times \tfrac{8}{1} \times \tfrac{2}{1} = \overset{\text{pt.}}{\tfrac{4}{5}}, \textit{ Ans.}$$

Or,

$$\begin{array}{r|l} {}^{5}\not{8}\not{0} & 1 \\ & 4 \\ & \not{8} \\ & \not{2} \\ \hline 5 & 4 = \tfrac{4}{5} \text{ pt., } \textit{Ans.} \end{array}$$

ANALYSIS. To reduce bushels to pints, we must multiply by 4, 8, and 2, the numbers in the scale. And since the given number is a fraction of a bushel, we indicate the process as in multiplication of fractions, and after canceling, obtain $\frac{4}{5}$, the Answer. Hence,

RULE. *Multiply the fraction of the higher denomination by the numbers in the scale successively, between the given and the required denominations.*

NOTE. Cancellation may be applied wherever practicable.

EXAMPLES FOR PRACTICE.

2. Reduce $\frac{1}{1000}$ of a £ to the fraction of a penny.
Ans. $\frac{6}{25}$ d.
3. Reduce $\frac{1}{14400}$ of a week to the fraction of a minute.
Ans. $\frac{7}{10}$ min.
4. What part of a gill is $\frac{1}{4032}$ of a hosghead? *Ans.* $\frac{1}{2}$ gi.
5. What fraction of a grain is $\frac{1}{960}$ of an ounce? *Ans.* $\frac{1}{2}$ gr.
6. Reduce $\frac{1}{1000000}$ of a mile to the fraction of an inch.
Ans. $\frac{198}{3125}$ in.
7. Reduce $\frac{2}{9}$ of $\frac{1}{6}$ of 2 pounds to the fraction of an ounce Troy. *Ans.* $\frac{8}{9}$ oz.
8. Reduce $\frac{1}{680}$ of a hogshead to the fraction of a pint.
Ans. $\frac{63}{85}$ pt.
9. Reduce $\frac{7}{1440}$ of an acre to the fraction of a rod.
Ans. $\frac{7}{9}$ rd.

CASE II.

212. To reduce a denominate fraction from a less to a greater unit.

1. Reduce $\frac{4}{5}$ of a pint to the fraction of a bushel.

Give explanation. Rule. Case II is what?

OPERATION.

$$\frac{\not 4}{5} \times \frac{1}{2} \times \frac{1}{8} \times \frac{1}{\not 4} = \frac{1}{80}, \textit{ Ans.}$$

Or,

$$\begin{array}{r|l} 5 & \not 4 \\ 2 & \\ 8 & \\ \not 4 & \\ \hline 80 & 1 = \frac{1}{80} \text{ bu., } \textit{Ans.} \end{array}$$

ANALYSIS. To reduce pints to bushels, we must divide by 2, 8, and 4, the numbers of the scale. And since the given number of pints is a fraction, we indicate the process, as in division of fractions, and cancelling, obtain $\frac{1}{80}$, the Answer.

RULE. *Divide the fraction of the lower denomination by the numbers in the scale, successively, between the given and the required denomination.*

NOTE. The operation will frequently be shortened by cancellation.

EXAMPLES FOR PRACTICE.

2. What part of a rod is $\frac{1}{8}$ of a foot? *Ans.* $\frac{1}{132}$ rd.
3. What part of a pound is $\frac{3}{5}$ of a dram? *Ans.* $\frac{3}{1280}$ lb.
4. Reduce $\frac{1}{2}$ of a cent to the fraction of an eagle. *Ans.* $\frac{1}{2000}$ E.
5. A hand is $\frac{1}{3}$ of a foot; what fraction is that of a mile? *Ans.* $\frac{1}{15840}$ mi.
6. Reduce $\frac{3}{7}$ of 2 pwt. to the fraction of a pound. *Ans.* $\frac{1}{280}$ lb.
7. How much less is $\frac{3}{5}$ of a pint than $\frac{1}{2}$ of a hogshead? *Ans.* $\frac{419}{840}$ hhd.
8. In $\frac{3}{5}$ of an inch what fraction of a mile? *Ans.* $\frac{1}{105600}$ mi.
9. $\frac{8}{9}$ of an ounce Troy is $\frac{2}{9}$ of what fraction of 2 pounds?
10. $\frac{8}{9}$ of an ounce is $\frac{1}{6}$ of what fraction of 2 pounds Troy?

CASE III.

213. To reduce a denominate fraction to integers of lower denominations.

1. What is the value of $\frac{5}{8}$ of a hogshead of wine?

Give explanation. Rule. Case III is what?

OPERATION.

$$\tfrac{5}{8}\text{ hhd.}\times 63=\tfrac{315}{8}\text{ gal.}=39\tfrac{3}{8}\text{ gal.}$$

$$\tfrac{3}{8}\text{ gal.}\times 4=\tfrac{12}{8}\text{ qt.}=1\tfrac{4}{8}\text{ qt.};\ \tfrac{4}{8}\text{ qt.}\times 2=\tfrac{8}{8}\text{ pt.}=1\text{ pt.}$$

Ans. 39 gal. 1 qt. 1 pint.

ANALYSIS. $\frac{5}{8}$ hhd. = $\frac{5}{8}$ of 63 gal., or $39\frac{3}{8}$ gal.; and $\frac{3}{8}$ gal. = $\frac{3}{8}$ of 4 qt., or $1\frac{4}{8}$ qt.; and $\frac{4}{8}$ qt. = $\frac{4}{8}$ of 2 pt., or 1 pt. Hence,

RULE. I. *Multiply the fraction by that number in the scale which will reduce it to the next lower denomination, and if the result be an improper fraction, reduce it to a whole or mixed number.*

II. *Proceed with the fractional part, if any, as before, until reduced to the denominations required.*

III. *The units of the several denominations, arranged in their order, will be the required result.*

EXAMPLES FOR PRACTICE.

2. Reduce $\frac{4}{7}$ of a month to lower denominations.
   Ans. 17 da. 3 h. 25 min. $42\frac{6}{7}$ sec.
3. What is the value of $\frac{3}{7}$ of a £? *Ans.* 8 s. 6 d. $3\frac{3}{7}$ far.
4. What is the value of $\frac{2}{5}$ of a bushel?
5. Reduce $\frac{6}{7}$ of 15 cwt. to its equivalent value.
   Ans. 12 cwt. 85 lbs. 11 oz. $6\frac{6}{7}$ dr.
6. Reduce $\frac{2}{3}$ of $\frac{4}{9}$ of a pound avoirdupois to integers.
   Ans. 4 oz. $11\frac{23}{27}$ dr.
7. What is the value of $\frac{5}{6}$ of an acre? *Ans.* 3 R. $13\frac{1}{3}$ P.
8. Reduce $\frac{18}{26}$ of a day to its value in integers.
   Ans. 16 h. 36 min. $55\frac{5}{13}$ sec.
9. What is the value of $\frac{3}{5}$ of a pound Troy?
10. What is the value of $\frac{7}{9}$ of $5\frac{1}{2}$ tons? *Ans.* 4 T. 5 cwt. $55\frac{5}{9}$ lb.
11. What is the value of $\frac{3}{8}$ of $3\frac{2}{3}$ acres? *Ans.* 1 A. 1 R. 20 P.

CASE IV.

214. To reduce a compound number to a fraction of a higher denomination.

1. What part of a week is 5 da. 14 h. 24 min.?

Give explanation. Rule. Case IV is what?

OPERATION.

5 da. 14 h. 24 min. = 8064 min.

1 wk. = 10080 min.

$\frac{8064}{10080} = \frac{4}{5}$ wk., *Ans.*

ANALYSIS. To find what part one compound number is of another, they must be reduced to the same denomination. In 5 da. 14 h. 24 min. there are 8064 minutes, and in 1 week there are 10080 minutes. Since 1 minute is $\frac{1}{10080}$ of a week, 8064 minutes is $\frac{8064}{10080} = \frac{4}{5}$ of a week. Hence,

RULE. *Reduce the given number to its lowest denomination for the numerator, and a unit of the required denomination to the same denomination for the denominator of the required fraction.*

NOTE. If the given number contain a fraction, the denominator of this fraction must be regarded as the lowest denomination.

EXAMPLES FOR PRACTICE.

2. What part of a mi. is 6 fur. 26 rd. 3 yd. 2 ft.? *Ans.* $\frac{5}{6}$ mi.
3. What fraction of a £ is 13 s. 7 d. 3 far.?
4. Reduce 10 oz. 10 pwt. 10 gr. to the fraction of a pound Troy. *Ans.* $\frac{505}{576}$ lb.
5. Reduce 2 cd. ft. 8 cu. ft. to the fraction of a cord. *Ans.* $\frac{5}{16}$ Cd.
6. Reduce 1 bbl. 1 gal. 1 qt. 1 pt. 1 gi. to the fraction of a hogshead. *Ans.* $\frac{117}{224}$ hhd.
7. What part of 2 rods is 4 yards $1\frac{1}{2}$ feet? *Ans.* $\frac{9}{22}$.
8. Reduce $1\frac{3}{5}$ pecks to the fraction of a bushel. *Ans.* $\frac{2}{5}$ bu.
9. What part of 9 feet square are 9 square feet?
10. From a piece of cloth containing 8 yd. 3 qr. a tailor cut 2 yd. 2 qr.; what part of the whole piece did he take? *Ans.* $\frac{2}{7}$.

CASE V.

215. To reduce a denominate decimal to integers of lower denominations.

1. Reduce .78125 of a pound Troy to integers of lower denominations.

Give explanation. Rule. Case V is what?

OPERATION.

```
.78125 lb.
     12
----------
9.37500 oz.
     20
----------
7.50000 pwt.
     24
----------
12.0000 gr.
```

9 oz. 7 pwt. 12 gr., *Ans.*

ANALYSIS. We first multiply by 12 to reduce the given number from pounds to ounces, and the result is 9 ounces and the decimal .375 of an oz. We then multiply this decimal by 20 to reduce it to pennyweights, and get 7 pwt. and .5 of a pwt. This last decimal we multiply by 24, to reduce it to grains, and the result is 12 gr. Hence the answer is 9 oz. 7 pwt. 12 gr.

RULE. I. *Multiply the given decimal by that number in the scale which will reduce it to the next lower denomination, and point off as in multiplication of decimals.*

II. *Proceed with the decimal part of the product in the same manner until reduced to the required denominations. The integers at the left will be the answer required.*

EXAMPLES FOR PRACTICE.

2. What is the value of .217°? *Ans.* 13′ 1.2″.
3. What is the value of .659 of a week? *Ans.* 4 da. 14 h. 42 min. 43.2 sec.
4. Reduce .578125 of a bushel to integers of lower denominations. *Ans.* 2 pk. 2 qt. 1 pt.
5. Reduce .125 bbl. to integers of lower denominations. *Ans.* 3 gal. 3 qt. 1 pt. 2 gi.
6. What is the value of .628125 £?
7. What is the value of .22 of a hogshead of molasses? *Ans.* 13 gal. 3 qts. 3.52 gi.
8. What is the value of .67 of a league? *Ans.* 2 mi. 3 rd. 1 yd. 3$\frac{3}{5}$ in.
9. What is the value of .42857 of a month? *Ans.* 12 da. 20 h. 34 min. 13$\frac{11}{25}$ sec.
10. What is the value of .78875 of a long ton? *Ans.* 15 cwt. 3 qr. 2 lb. 12.8 oz.

Give explanation. Rule.

11. What is the value of 5.88125 acres? *Ans.* 5 A. 3 R. 21 P.

12. Reduce .0055 T. to pounds. *Ans.* 11 lb.

13. Reduce .034375 of a bundle of paper to its value in lower denominations. *Ans.* 1 quire 9 sheets.

CASE VI.

216. To reduce a compound number to a decimal of a higher denomination.

1. Reduce 3 pk. 2 qt. to the decimal of a bushel.

OPERATION.

8	2.00 qt.
4	3.2500 pk.
	.8125 bu., *Ans.*

Or, 3 pk. 2 qt. = 26 qt.
1 bu. = 32 qt.
$\frac{26}{32}$ = .8125 bu., *Ans.*

ANALYSIS. Since 8 quarts make 1 peck, and 4 pecks 1 bushel, there will be $\frac{1}{8}$ as many pecks as quarts (**183**), and $\frac{1}{4}$ as many bushels as pecks.

Or we may reduce 3 pk. 2 qt. to the fraction of a bushel (as in **214**), and we have $\frac{26}{32}$ of a bushel, which, reduced to a decimal, equals .8125. Hence the

RULE. *Divide the lowest denomination given by that number in the scale which will reduce it to the next higher, and annex the quotient as a decimal to that higher. Proceed in the same manner until the whole is reduced to the denomination required.* Or,

Reduce the given number to a fraction of the required denomination, and reduce this fraction to a decimal.

EXAMPLES FOR PRACTICE.

2. Reduce 3 qt. 1 pt. 1 gi. to the decimal of a gallon. *Ans.* .90625 gal.

3. Reduce 10 oz. 13 pwt. 9 gr. to the decimal of a pound Troy. *Ans.* .8890625 lb.

4. Reduce 1.2 pints to the decimal of a hogshead. *Ans.* .00238 + hhd.

5. What part of a bushel is 3 pk. 1.12 qt.? *Ans.* .785 bu.

Case VI is what? Give explanations. Rule.

6. What part of an acre is 3 R. 12.56 P.?
7. Reduce 17 yd. 1 ft. 6 in. to the decimal of a mile.
Ans. .00994318 + mi.
8. Reduce .32 of a pint to the decimal of a bushel.
Ans. .005 bu.
9. Reduce $4\frac{7}{8}$ feet to the decimal of a fathom.
Ans. .8125 fathom.
10. Reduce 150 sheets of paper to the decimal of a ream.
Ans. .3125 Rm.
11. Reduce 47.04 lb. of flour to the decimal of a barrel.
12. Reduce .33 of a foot to the decimal of a mile.
13. Reduce 5 h. 36 min. $57\frac{6}{10}$ sec. to the decimal of a day.

ADDITION.

217. 1. A miner sold at one time 10 lb. 4 oz. 16 pwt. 8 gr. of gold; at another time, 2 lb. 9 oz. 3 pwt.; at another, 11 oz. 20 gr.; and at another, 25 lb. 16 pwt. 23 gr.; how much did he sell in all?

OPERATION.

	lb.	oz.	pwt.	gr.
	10	4	16	8
	2	9	3	0
	0	11	0	20
	25	0	16	23
Ans.	39	1	17	3

ANALYSIS. Arranging the numbers in columns, placing units of the *same* denomination under each other, we first add the units in the right hand column, or lowest denomination, and find the amount to be 51 grains, which is equal to 2 pwt. 3 gr. We write the 3 gr. under the column of grains, and add the 2 pwt. to the column of pwt. We find the amount of the second column to be 37 pwt., which is equal to 1 oz. 17 pwt. Writing the 17 pwt. under the column of pwt., we add the 1 oz. to the next column. Adding this column in the same manner as the preceding ones, we find the amount to be 25 oz., equal to 2 lb. 1 oz. Placing the 1 oz. under the column of oz., we add the 2 lb. to the column of lb. Adding the last column, we find the amount to be 39 lb. Hence the following

---

What is addition of compound numbers? Give explanation.

RULE. I. *Write the numbers so that those of the same unit value will stand in the same column.*

II. *Beginning at the right hand, add each denomination as in simple numbers, carrying to each succeeding denomination one for as many units as it takes of the denomination added, to make one of the next higher denomination.*

EXAMPLES FOR PRACTICE.

(2.)

£.	s.	d.
43	13	8
51	6	4
67	11	3
76	18	10
244	10	1

(3.)

lb.	℥.	ʒ.	℈.	gr.
12	8	7	2	15
	10	4	1	10
15	00	2	1	19
	11	6	0	12
13	4	4	2	00

(4.)

T.	cwt.	lb.	oz.	dr.
4	7	18	4	10
	15	98	15	5
3	9	10	6	15
1	0	15	0	4
9	12	42	11	2

(5.)

bu.	pk.	qt.	pt.
1	3	7	1
3	2	2	0
	1	6	1
17	0	5	1
45	2	4	0

6. What is the sum of 4 mi. 3 fur. 30 rd. 2 yd. 1 ft. 10 in., 5 mi. 6 fur. 18 rd. 1 yd. 2 ft. 6 in., 10 mi. 4 fur. 25 rd. 2 yd. 2 ft. 11 in., and 6 fur. 28 rd. 4 yd. 2 ft. 1 in.?

7. Find the sum of 197 sq. yd. 4 sq. ft. $104\frac{1}{2}$ sq. in., 122 sq. yd. 2 sq. ft. $27\frac{3}{4}$ sq. in., 5 sq. yd. 8 sq. ft. $2\frac{3}{8}$ sq. in., and 237 sq. yd. 7 sq. ft. $128\frac{1}{5}$ sq. in.?

Ans. 563 sq. yd. 4 sq. ft. 118.825 sq. in.

NOTE. When common fractions occur, they should be reduced to a common denominator, to decimals, or to integers of a lower denomination, and added according to the usual method.

Give the Rule.

(8.)

A.	R.	P.	sq. yd.	sq. ft.	sq. in.
26	3	28	25	8	125
19	2	38	30	7	150
456	2	20	16	6	98
503	1	8	12($\frac{1}{2}$)	5	85
			($\frac{1}{2}$) =	4($\frac{1}{2}$)	
				($\frac{1}{2}$) =	72
503	1	8	13	1	13

(9.)

mi.	fur.	rd.	yd.	ft.	in.
1	7	30	4	2	11
3	4	00	2	1	10
10	7	25	1	2	11
16	3	16	$3\frac{1}{2}$	1	8

(10.)

hhd.	gal.	qt.	pt.
27	65	3	2
112	60	2	3
50	29	0	1
421	00	2	3
14	39	1	2

(11.)

bu.	pk.	qt.	pt.
23	3	7	1
34	2	0	1
42	3	5	0
51	1	4	1
23	0	3	0
11	3	4	0

(12.)

yr.	da.	h.	min.	sec.
25	300	19	54	35
21	40	12	40	24
3	112	14	15	17
6	19	11	45	59
1	1	1	1	1
57	109	11	37	16

13. If a printer one day use 4 bundles 1 ream 15 quires 20 sheets of paper, the next day 3 bundles 1 ream 10 quires 10 sheets, and the next 2 bundles 13 sheets, how much does he use in the three days?

Ans. 2 bales 1 ream 6 quires 19 sheets.

14. A tailor used, in one year, 2 gross 5 doz. 10 buttons, another year 3 gross 7 doz. 9, and another year 4 gross 6 doz. 11; how many did he use in the three years?

Ans. 10 gross 8 doz. 6.

15. A ship, leaving New York, sailed east the first day 3° 45′ 50″; the second day, 4° 50′ 10″; the third, 2° 10′ 55″; the fourth, 2° 39″; how far was she then east from the place of starting? *Ans.* 12° 47′ 34″.

16. A man, in digging a cellar, removed 127 cu. yd. 20 cu. ft. of earth; in digging a drain, 6 cu. yd. 25 cu. ft.; and in digging a cistern, 17 cu. yds. 18 cu. ft.; what was the amount of earth removed, and what the cost at 16 cents a cu. yd.?

Ans. $152\frac{1}{3}$ cu. yds.; \$$24.37\frac{1}{3}$.

17. A farmer received 80 cents a bushel for 4 loads of corn, weighing as follows: 2564, 2713, 3000, and 3109 lbs.; how much did he receive for the whole? *Ans.* $162.657+

18. A druggist sold for medicine, in three years, at an average price of 9 cents a gill, the following amounts of brandy, viz.: 1 bbl. 4 gal. 1 pt.; 30 gal. 2 qt. 1 gi.; 2 bbl. 15 gal.; how much did he receive for the whole? *Ans.* $415.17.

218. To add denominate fractions.

1. Add $\frac{5}{6}$ of a mile to $\frac{1}{3}$ of a furlong.

OPERATION.

$\frac{5}{6}$ mi. =	6 fur.	26 rd.	11 ft.
$\frac{1}{3}$ fur. =		13 rd.	$5\frac{1}{2}$ ft.
Ans.	7 fur.	00	0

Or, $\frac{1}{3}$ fur. ÷ 8 = $\frac{1}{24}$ mi.

$\frac{1}{24}$ mi. + $\frac{5}{6}$ mi. = $\frac{21}{24}$ mi. = 7 fur.

ANALYSIS. We find the value of each fraction in integers of less denominations (**213**), and then add their values as in compound numbers (**217**).

Or, we may reduce the given fractions to fractions of the same denomination (**212**), then add them, and find the value of their sum in lower denominations (**213**).

2. Add $\frac{3}{4}$ of a rod to $\frac{3}{4}$ of a foot. *Ans.* 13 ft. $1\frac{1}{2}$ in.

3. What is the sum of $\frac{7}{8}$ of a mile, $\frac{2}{3}$ of a furlong, and $\frac{5}{6}$ of a rod? *Ans.* 7 fur. 27 rd. 8 ft. 3 in.

4. What is the sum of $\frac{2}{3}$ of a pound and $\frac{5}{9}$ of a shilling?

Ans. 13 s. 10 d. $2\frac{2}{3}$ qr.

5. What is the sum of $\frac{3}{5}$ of a ton and $\frac{3}{7}$ of 1 cwt.?

Ans. 12 cwt. 42 lb. $13\frac{5}{7}$ oz.

Give explanation of the process of adding denominate fractions.

6. What is the sum of $\frac{3}{8}$ of a day added to $\frac{1}{2}$ an hour?

Ans. 9 h. 30 min.

7. What is the sum of $\frac{1}{6}$ of a week, $\frac{3}{4}$ of a day, and $\frac{1}{4}$ of an hour? *Ans.* 1 da. 22 h. 15 min.

8. Add $\frac{6}{7}$ of a hhd. to $\frac{3}{4}$ of a gal.

9. What is the sum of $\frac{4}{7}$ of a cwt., $8\frac{5}{6}$ lb., and $3\frac{9}{10}$ oz. by long ton table? *Ans.* 73 lb. 1 oz. $3\frac{11}{15}$ dr.

10. What is the sum of $\frac{3}{8}$ of a mile, $\frac{2}{3}$ of a yard, and $\frac{3}{4}$ of a foot?

11. Sold 4 village lots; the first contained $\frac{1}{2}$ of $\frac{1}{3}$ of an acre; the second, $60\frac{3}{4}$ rods; the third, $\frac{4}{7}$ of an acre; and the fourth, $\frac{3}{8}$ of $\frac{2}{9}$ of an acre; how much land in the four lots?

Ans. 3 R. 26 P. $126\frac{45}{112}$ sq. ft.

12. A farmer sold three loads of hay; the first weighed $1\frac{1}{6}$ T., the second, $1\frac{3}{16}$ T., and the third, $18\frac{5}{6}$ cwt.; what was the aggregate weight of the three loads?

Ans. 3 T. 5 cwt. 91 lb. $10\frac{2}{3}$ oz.

SUBTRACTION.

219. 1. If a druggist buy 25 gal. 2 qt. 1 pt. 1 gi. of wine, and sell 18 gal. 3 qt. 1 pt. 2 gi., how much has he left?

OPERATION.

	gal.	qt.	pt.	gi.
	25	2	1	1
	18	3	0	2
Ans.	6	3	0	3

ANALYSIS. Writing the subtrahend under the minuend, placing units of the same denomination under each other, we begin at the right hand, or lowest denomination; since we cannot take 2 gi. from 1 gi., we add 1 pt. or 4 gi. to 1 gi., making 5 gi.; and taking 2 gi. from 5 gi., we write the remainder, 3 gi., underneath the column of gills. Having added 1 pt. or 4 gi. to the minuend, we now add 1 pt. to the 0 pt. in the subtrahend, making 1 pt.; and 1 pt. from 1 pt. leaves 0 pt., which we write in the remainder. Next, as we cannot take 3 qt. from 2 qt., we add 1 gal. or 4 qt. to 2 qt., making 6 qt., and taking 3 qt. from 6 qt., we write the remainder, 3 qt., under the denomination of quarts. Adding 1 gal. to 18 gal., we subtract 19 gal. from 25 gal., as in simple

What is subtraction of compound numbers? Give explanation.

numbers, and write the remainder, 6 gal., under the column of gallons. Hence the following

RULE. I. *Write the subtrahend under the minuend, so that units of the same denomination shall stand under each other.*

II. *Beginning at the right hand, subtract each denomination separately, as in simple numbers.*

III. *If the number of any denomination in the subtrahend exceed that of the same denomination in the minuend, add to the number in the minuend as many units as make one of the next higher denomination, and then subtract; in this case add 1 to the next higher denomination of the subtrahend before subtracting. Proceed in the same manner with each denomination.*

EXAMPLES FOR PRACTICE.

(2.)

	lb.	oz.	pwt.	gr.
From	18	6	10	14
Take	10	5	4	6
Rem.	8	1	6	8

(3.)

A.	R.	P.
25	2	16.9
19	3	25.14
5	2	31.76

(4.)

T.	cwt.	lb.
14	11	69¾
10	12	98⅛

(5.)

yr.	da.	h.	min.	sec.
38	187	16	45	50
17	190	20	50	40
20	361	19	55	10

6. A Boston merchant bought English goods to the amount of 4327 £ 13 s. 7½ d., and he paid 1374 £ 10 s. 11¾ d.; how much did he then owe?

7. From 300 miles take 198 mi. 7 fur. 25 rd. 2 yd. 1 ft. 10 in. *Ans.* 101 mi. 14 rd. 2 yd. 2 ft. 8 in.

8. What is the difference in the longitude of two places, one 75° 20′ 30″ west, and the other 71° 19′ 35″ west?

Ans. 4° 55″.

9. From 10 ℔ 7 ℥ 4 ʒ 1 ℈ 15 gr. take 3 ℔ 8 ℥ 2 ʒ 2 ℈ 18 gr. *Ans.* 6 ℔ 11 ℥ 1 ʒ 1 ℈ 17 gr.

Give the Rule.

10. The apparent periodic revolution of the sun is made in 365 da. 6 h. 9 min. 9 sec., and that of the moon in 29 da. 12 h. 44 min. 3 sec.; what is the difference?

Ans. 335 da. 15 h. 25 min. 6 sec.

11. A man, having a hogshead of wine, drank, on an average, for five years, including two leap years, one gill of wine a day; how much remained? *Ans.* 5 gal. 3 qt. 1 pt. 1 gi.

12. A section of land containing 640 acres is owned by four men; the first owns 196 A. 2 R. 16¼ P.; the second, 200 A. 1½ R.; the third, 177 A. 36 P.; how much does the fourth own? *Ans.* 65 A. 3 R. 7.75 P.

13. From a pile of wood containing 75¾ Cd. was sold at one time 16 Cd. 5 cd. ft.; at another, 24 Cd. 6 cd. ft. 12 cu. ft.; at another, 27 Cd. 112 cu. ft.; how much remained in the pile? *Ans.* 6 Cd. 3 cd. ft. 4 cu. ft.

14. If from a hogshead of molasses 10 gal. 1 qt. 1 pt. be drawn at one time, 15 gal. 1 pt. at another, and 14 gal. 3 qt. at another, how much will remain?

220. To find the difference in dates.

1. What length of time elapsed from the discovery of America by Columbus, Oct. 14, 1492, to the Declaration of Independence, July 4, 1776?

FIRST OPERATION.

yr.	mo.	da.
1776	7	4
1492	10	14
283	8	20

ANALYSIS. We place the earlier date under the later, writing first on the left the number of the year from the Christian era, next the number of the month, counting January as the first month, and next the number of the day from the first day of the month. Instead of the number of the year, month, and day, some use the number of years, months, and days that *have elapsed* since the Christian era, thus: instead of saying July is the 7th month, we say 6 months and 3 days have elapsed, and instead of saying October is the 10th month, we say 9 months and 13 days have elapsed.

SECOND OPERATION.

yr.	mo.	da.
1775	6	3
1491	9	13
283	8	20

How is the difference of dates found?

Both methods will obtain the same result; the former is generally used.

NOTES. 1. When hours are to be obtained, we reckon from 12 at night, and if minutes and seconds, we write them still at the right of hours.

2. In finding the time between two dates, or in computing interest, 12 months are considered a year, and 30 days a month.

When the *exact number of days* is required for any period not exceeding one ordinary year, it may be readily found by the following

TABLE,

Showing the number of days from any day of one month to the same day of any other month within one year.

FROM ANY DAY OF	TO THE SAME DAY OF THE NEXT.											
	Jan.	Feb.	Mar.	Apr.	May.	June	July	Aug.	Sept.	Oct.	Nov.	Dec.
January . . .	365	31	59	90	120	151	181	212	243	273	304	334
February . .	334	365	28	59	89	120	150	181	212	242	273	303
March	306	337	365	31	61	92	122	153	184	214	245	275
April	275	306	334	365	30	61	91	122	153	183	214	244
May.	245	276	304	335	365	31	61	92	123	153	184	214
June	214	245	273	304	334	365	30	61	92	122	153	183
July.	184	215	243	274	304	335	365	31	62	92	123	153
August . . .	153	184	212	243	273	304	334	365	31	61	92	122
September .	122	153	181	212	242	273	303	334	365	30	61	91
October. . . .	92	123	151	182	212	243	273	304	335	365	31	61
November .	61	92	120	151	181	212	242	273	304	334	365	30
December. .	31	62	90	121	151	182	212	243	274	304	335	365

If the days of the different months are not the same, the number of days of difference should be *added* when the earlier day belongs to the month *from* which we reckon, and *subtracted* when it belongs to the month *to* which we find the time. If the 29th of February is to be included in the time computed, one day must be added to the result.

EXAMPLES FOR PRACTICE.

2. George Washington was born Feb. 22, 1732, and died Dec. 14 1799; what was his age? *Ans.* 67 yr. 9 mo. 22 da.

How can the number of days, if less than a year, be obtained?

3. How much time has elapsed since the declaration of independence of the United States?

4. How many years, months, and days from your birthday to this date; or what is your age?

5. How long from the battle of Bunker Hill, June 17, 1775, to the battle of Waterloo, June 18, 1815? *Ans.* 40 yr. 1 da.

6. What length of time will elapse from 20 minutes past 2 o'clock, P. M., June 24, 1856, to 10 minutes before 9 o'clock, A. M., January 3, 1861? *Ans.* 4 yr. 6 mo. 8 da. 18 h. 30 min.

7. How many days from any day of April to the same day of August? of December? of February?

8. How many days from the 6th of November to the 15th of April? *Ans.* 160 days.

9. How many days from the 20th of August to the 15th of the following June? *Ans.* 299 days.

221. To subtract denominate fractions.

1. From $\frac{3}{8}$ of an oz. take $\frac{7}{8}$ of a pwt.

OPERATION.

$\frac{3}{8}$ oz. = 7 pwt. 12 gr.
$\frac{7}{8}$ pwt. = 21 gr.

6 pwt. 15 gr., *Ans.*

Or, $\frac{3}{8}$ oz. $\times$ 20 = $\frac{60}{8}$ pwt.
$\frac{60}{8} - \frac{7}{8} = \frac{53}{8}$ pwt. = 6 pwt. 15 gr.

ANALYSIS. We perform the same reductions as in addition of denominate fractions, (**218**), and then subtract the less value from the greater.

2. What is the difference between $\frac{1}{2}$ rod and $\frac{3}{4}$ of a foot? *Ans.* 7ft. 6 in.

3. From $\frac{5}{8}$ £ take $\frac{2}{3}$ of $\frac{3}{4}$ of a shilling.

4. From $\frac{2}{3}$ of a league take $\frac{7}{10}$ of a mile. *Ans.* 1 mi. 2 fur. 16 rd.

5. From $8\frac{9}{10}$ cwt. take 1 qr. $2\frac{2}{7}$ lb. *Ans.* 8 cwt. 2 qr. 14 lb. 5 oz. $15\frac{3}{35}$ dr.

6. From $\frac{1}{5}$ of a week take $\frac{1}{5}$ of a day. *Ans.* 1 da. 4 h. 48 min.

Give explanation of the process of subtracting denominate fractions.

7. Two persons, A and B, start from two places 120 miles apart, and travel toward each other; after A travels $\frac{2}{5}$, and B $\frac{3}{7}$, of the distance, how far are they apart?

Ans. 41. mi. 7 fur. 9 rd. 8 ft. $7\frac{5}{7}$ in.

8. From a cask of brandy containing 96 gallons, $\frac{1}{5}$ leaked out, and $\frac{2}{3}$ of the remainder was sold; how much still remained in the cask? *Ans.* 25 gal. 2 qt. $3\frac{1}{5}$ gi.

MULTIPLICATION.

222. 1. A farmer has 8 fields, each containing 4 A. 2 R. 27 P.; how much land in all?

OPERATION.

A.	R.	P.
4	2	27
		8
37	1	16

ANALYSIS. In 8 fields are 8 times as much land as in 1 field. We write the multiplier under the lowest denomination of the multiplicand, and proceed thus; 8 times 27 P. are 216 P., equal to 5 R. 16 P.; and we write the 16 P. under the number multiplied. Then 8 times 2 R. are 16 R., and 5 R. added make 21 R., equal to 4 A. 1 R.; and we write the 1 R. under the number multiplied. Again, 8 times 4 A are 32 A., and 4 A. added make 36 A., which we write under the same denomination in the multiplicand, and the work is done. Hence,

RULE. I. *Write the multiplier under the lowest denomination of the multiplicand.*

II. *Multiply as in simple numbers, and carry as in addition of compound numbers.*

EXAMPLES FOR PRACTICE.

(2.)

bu.	pk.	qt.	pt.
4	2	5	1
			2
9	1	3	0

(3.)

mi.	fur.	rd.	ft.
9	4	20	13
			6
57	3	4	12

Multiplication of compound numbers, how performed? Rule.

(4.)

£.	s.	d.
5	18	4
		4

(5.)

lb.	oz.	pwt.	gr.
3	4	0	22
			7

(6.)

T.	cwt.	lb.	oz.
14	16	48	12
			11

(7.)

13°	10′	35″
		9

8. In 6 barrels of grain, each containing 2 bu. 3 pk. 5 qt., how many bushels? *Ans.* 17 bu. 1 pk. 6 qt.

9. If a druggist deal out 3 ℔ 4 ℥ 1 ʒ 2 ℈ 16 gr. of medicine a day, how much will he deal out in 6 days?

10. If a man travel 29 mi. 3 fur. 30 rd. 15 ft. in 1 day, how far will he travel in 8 days?

11. If a woodchopper can cut 3 Cd. 48 cu. ft. of wood in 1 day, how many cords can he cut in 12 days? *Ans.* 40½ Cd.

12. What is the weight of 48 loads of hay, each weighing 1 T. 3 cwt. 50 lb.?

OPERATION.

T.	cwt.	lb.	
1	3	50	
		6	
7	1	00	weight of 6 loads.
		8	
56	8	00	weight of 48 loads.

ANALYSIS. When the multiplier is large, and a composite number, we may multiply by one of the factors, and that product by the other. Multiplying the weight of 1 load by 6, we obtain the weight of 6 loads, and the weight of 6 loads multiplied by 8, gives the weight of 48 loads.

13. If 1 acre of land produce 45 bu. 3 pk. 6 qt. 1 pt. of corn, how much will 64 acres produce? *Ans.* 2941 bu.

14. How much will 120 yards of cloth cost, at 1 £ 9 s. 8½ d. per yard?

15. If $80 will buy 4 A. 3 R. 26 P. 20 sq. yd. 3 sq. ft. of land, how much will $4800 buy? *Ans.* 295 A. 10 sq. yd.

16. If a load of coal by the long ton weigh 1 T. 6 cwt. 2 qr. 26 lb. 10 oz., what will be the weight of 73 loads?

Ans. 97 T. 11 cwt. 3 qr. 11 lb. 10 oz.

17. The sun, on an average, changes his longitude 59′ 8.33″ per day; how much will be the change in 365 days?

18. If 1 pt. 3 gi. of wine fill 1 bottle, how much will be required to fill a great gross of bottles of the same capacity?

DIVISION.

223. 1. If 4 acres of land produce 102 bu. 3 pk. 2 qt. of wheat, how much will 1 acre produce?

OPERATION.

	bu.	pk.	qt.	pts.
4)	102	3	2	
	25	2	6	1

ANALYSIS. One acre will produce ¼ as much as 4 acres. Writing the divisor on the left of the dividend, we divide 102 bu. by 4, and we obtain a quotient of 25 bu., and a remainder of 2 bu. We write the 25 bu. under the denomination of bushels, and reduce the 2 bu. to pecks, making 8 pk., and the 3 pk. of the dividend added makes 11 pk. Dividing 11 pk. by 4, we obtain a quotient of 2 pk. and a remainder of 3 pk.; writing the 2 pk. under the order of pecks, we next reduce 3 pk. to quarts, adding the 2 qt. of the dividend, making 26 qt., which divided by 4 gives a quotient of 6 qt. and a remainder of 2 qt. Writing the 6 qt. under the order of quarts, and reducing the remainder, 2 qt., to pints, we have 4 pt., which divided by 4 gives a quotient of 1 pt., which we write under the order of pints, and the work is done.

2. A farmer put 132 bu. 1 pk. of apples into 46 barrels; how many bu. did he put into a barrel?

OPERATION.

```
       bu.  pk.
46 )  132   1 ( 2 bu.
       92
      ---
       40
        4
      ---
      161 ( 3 pk.
      138
      ---
       23
        8
      ---
      184 ( 4 qt.
      184
      ---      Ans. 2 bu. 3 pk. 4 qt.
```

When the divisor is large, and not a composite number, we divide by long division, as shown in the operation. From these examples we derive the

---

R.P. Explain the process of dividing compound numbers.

RULE. I. *Divide the highest denomination as in simple numbers, and each succeeding denomination in the same manner, if there be no remainder.*

II. *If there be a remainder after dividing any denomination, reduce it to the next lower denomination, adding in the given number of that denomination, if any, and divide as before.*

III. *The several partial quotients will be the quotient required.*

NOTES. 1. When the divisor is large and is a *composite* number, we may shorten the work by dividing by the factors.

2. When the divisor and dividend are both compound numbers, they must both be reduced to the same denomination before dividing, and then the process is the same as in simple numbers.

EXAMPLES FOR PRACTICE.

(3.)

	£.	s.	d.
5)	25	8	4
	5	1	8

(4.)

	T.	cwt.	lb.
7)	45	15	25
	6	10	75

(5.)

	wk.	da.	h.	min.
4)	3	5	22	00
		6	17	30

(6.)

10)	25°	42′	40″
	2	34	16

7. Bought 6 large silver spoons, which weighed 11 oz. 3 pwt.; what was the weight of each spoon?

8. A man traveled by railroad 1000 miles in one day; what was the average rate per hour?

Ans. 41 mi. 5 fur. 13 rd. 5 ft. 6 in.

9. If a family use 10 bbl. of flour in a year, what is the average amount each day? *Ans.* 5 lb. 5 oz. $14\frac{59}{73}$ dr.

10. The aggregate weight of 123 hogsheads of sugar is 57 T. 19 cwt. 42 lb. 14 oz.; what is the average weight per hogshead? *Ans.* 9 cwt. 42 lb. 10 oz.

11. How many times are 5 £ 10 s. 10 d. contained in 537 £ 10 s. 10 d.? *Ans.* 97.

Give the rule. When the divisor is a composite number, how may we proceed? When the divisor and dividend are both compound numbers, how proceed?

12. A cellar 50 ft. long, 30 ft. wide, and 6 ft. deep was excavated by 5 men in 6 days; how many cubic yards did each man excavate daily? *Ans.* 11 cu. yd. 3 cu. ft.

13. If a town 5 miles square be divided equally into 150 farms, what will be the size of each farm?

Ans. 106 A. 2 R. 26 P. 20 sq. yd. 1 sq. ft. 72 sq. in.

14. How many times are 4 bu. 3 pk. 2 qt. contained in 336 bu. 3 pk. 4 qt.? *Ans.* 70.

15. A merchant tailor bought 4 pieces of cloth, each containing 60 yd. 2.25 qr.; after selling $\frac{1}{3}$ of the whole, he made up the remainder into suits containing 9 yd. 2 qr. each; how many suits did he make? *Ans.* 17.

LONGITUDE AND TIME.

224. Every circle is supposed to be divided into 360 equal parts, called *degrees.*

Since the sun appears to pass from east to west round the earth, or through 360°, once in every 24 hours, it will pass through $\frac{1}{24}$ of 360°, or 15° of the distance, in 1 hour; and 1° of distance in $\frac{1}{15}$ of 1 hour, or 4 minutes; and 1′ of distance in $\frac{1}{60}$ of 4 minutes, or 4 seconds.

TABLE OF LONGITUDE AND TIME.

360° of longitude	=	24 hours, or 1 day of time.
15° " "	=	1 hour " "
1° " "	=	4 minutes " "
1′ " "	=	4 seconds " "

CASE I.

225. To find the difference of time between two places, when their longitudes are given.

1. The longitude of Boston is 71° 3′, and of Chicago 87° 30′; what is the difference of time between these two places?

Explain how distance is measured by time. Repeat the table of longitude and time. Case I is what?

OPERATION.

87°	30′
71	3′
16°	27′
	4

1 h. 5 min. 48 sec., *Ans.*

ANALYSIS. By subtraction of compound numbers we first find the difference of longitude between the two places, which is 16° 27′. Since 1° of longitude makes a difference of 4 minutes of time, and 1′ of longitude a difference of 4 seconds of time, we multiply 16° 27′, the difference in longitude, by 4, and we obtain the difference of time in minutes and seconds, which, reduced to higher denominations, gives 1 h. 5 min. 48 sec., the difference in time. Hence the

RULE. *Multiply the difference of longitude in degrees and minutes by 4, and the product will be the difference of time in minutes and seconds, which may be reduced to hours.*

NOTE. If one place be in east, and the other in west longitude, the difference of longitude is found by *adding* them, and if the sum be greater than 180°, it must be subtracted from 360°.

EXAMPLES FOR PRACTICE.

2. New York is 74° 1′ and Cincinnati 84° 24′ west longitude; what is the difference of time? *Ans.* 41 min. 32 sec.

3. The Cape of Good Hope is 18° 28′ east, and the Sandwich Islands 155° west longitude; what is the difference of time? *Ans.* 11 h. 33 min. 52 sec.

4. Washington is 77° 1′ west, and St. Petersburg 30° 19′ east longitude; what is their difference of time?

Ans. 7 h. 9 min. 20 sec.

5. If Pekin is 118° east, and San Francisco 122° west longitude, what is their difference of time?

6. If a message be sent by telegraph without any loss of time, at 12 M. from London, 0° 0′ longitude, to Washington, 77° 1′ west, what is the time of its receipt at Washington?

NOTE. Since the sun appears to move from east to west, when it is exactly 12 o'clock at one place, it will be *past* 12 o'clock at all places east, and *before* 12 at all places west. Hence, knowing the difference of time between two places, and the exact time at one of them, the exact time at the other will be found by *adding* their difference to the given time, if it be *east*, and by *subtracting* if it be *west*.

Ans. 6 h. 51 min. 56 sec., A. M.

Give explanation. Rule.

7. A steamer arrives at Halifax, 63° 36′ west, at 4 o'clock, P. M.; the fact is telegraphed to St. Louis, 90° 15′ west, without loss of time; what is the time of its receipt at St. Louis? *Ans.* 2 h. 13 min. 24 sec., P. M.

8. If, at a presidential election, the voting begin at sunrise and end at sunset, how much sooner will the polls open and close at Eastport, Me., 67° west, than at Astoria, Oregon, 124° west? *Ans.* 3 h. 48 min.

9. When it was 1 o'clock, A. M., on the first day of January, 1859, at Bangor, Me., 68° 47′ west, what was the time at the city of Mexico, 99° 5′ west?

Ans. Dec. 31, 1858, 58 min. 48 sec. past 10, P. M.

CASE II.

226. To find the difference of longitude between two places, when the difference of time is known.

1. If the difference of time between New York and Cincinnati be 41 min. 32 sec., what is the difference of longitude?

OPERATION.

	min.	sec.
4)	41	32
	10°	23′, *Ans.*

ANALYSIS. Since 4 minutes of time make a difference of 1° of longitude, and 4 seconds of time, a difference of 1′ of longitude, there will be $\frac{1}{4}$ as many degrees of longitude as there are minutes of time, and $\frac{1}{4}$ as many minutes of longitude as there are seconds of time. Hence,

RULE. *Reduce the difference of time to minutes and seconds, and then divide by* 4; *the quotient will be the difference in longitude, in degrees and minutes.*

2. What is the difference of longitude between the Cape of Good Hope and the Sandwich Islands, if the difference of time be 11 h. 33 min. 52 sec.? *Ans.* 173° 28′.

3. What is the difference of longitude between Washington and St. Petersburg, if their difference of time be 7 h. 9 min. 20 sec.? *Ans.* 107° 20′.

Case II is what? Give explanation. Rule.

4. When it is half past 4, P. M., at St. Petersburg, 30° 19′ east, it is 32 min. 36 sec. past 8, A. M., at New Orleans, west; what is the difference of longitude? *Ans.* 119° 21′

5. The longitude of New York is 74° 1′ west. A sea captain leaving that port for Canton, with New York time, finds that his chronometer constantly loses time. What is his longitude when it has lost 4 hours? 8 h. 40 min.? 13 h. 25 min.?

Ans. 14° 1′ west; 55° 59′ east; 127° 14′ east.

6. When the days are of equal length, and it is noon on the 1st meridian, on what meridian is it then sunrise? sunset? midnight? *Ans.* 90° west; 90° east; 180° east or west.

DUODECIMALS.

227. **Duodecimals** are the divisions and subdivisions of a unit, resulting from continually dividing by 12, as 1, $\frac{1}{12}$, $\frac{1}{144}$, $\frac{1}{1728}$, &c. In practice, duodecimals are applied to the measurement of extension, the foot being taken as the unit.

If the foot be divided into 12 equal parts, the parts are called inches, or primes; the inches divided by 12 give seconds; the seconds divided by 12 give thirds; the thirds divided by 12 give fourths; and so on.

From these divisions of a foot it follows that

1′ (inch or prime) . . . . is $\frac{1}{12}$ of a foot.
1″ (second) or $\frac{1}{12}$ of $\frac{1}{12}$, ... " $\frac{1}{144}$ of a foot.
1‴ (third) or $\frac{1}{12}$ of $\frac{1}{12}$ of $\frac{1}{12}$, . . " $\frac{1}{1728}$ of a foot, &c.

TABLE.

12 fourths, marked (⁗),	make	1 third	marked	1‴
12 thirds	"	1 second,	"	1″
12 seconds	"	1 prime, or inch,	"	1′
12 primes, or inches,	"	1 foot,	"	ft.

SCALE — uniformly 12.

The marks ′, ″, ‴, ⁗, are called indices.

What are duodecimals? To what applied? Explain the divisions of the foot. Repeat the table.

NOTE. Duodecimals are really common fractions, and can always be treated as such; but usually their denominators are not expressed, and they are treated as compound numbers.

ADDITION AND SUBTRACTION OF DUODECIMALS.

228. We add and subtract duodecimals the same as other compound numbers.

EXAMPLES.

1. Add 13 ft. 4′ 8″, 10 ft. 6′ 7″, 145 ft. 9′ 11″.
Ans. 169 ft. 9′ 2″.

2. Add 179 ft. 11′ 4″, 245 ft. 1′ 4″, 3 ft. 9′ 9″.
Ans. 428 ft. 10′ 5″.

3. From 25 ft. 6′ 3″ take 14 ft. 9′ 8″. *Ans.* 10 ft. 8′ 7″.

4. From a board 15 ft. 7′ 6″ in length, 3 ft. 8′ 11″ were sawed off; what was the length of the piece left?
Ans. 11 ft. 10′ 7″.

MULTIPLICATION OF DUODECIMALS.

229. Length multiplied by breadth gives surface, and surface multiplied by thickness gives solid contents (**198**).

1. How many square feet in a board 11 feet 8 inches long and 2 feet 7 inches wide?

OPERATION.

11 ft.	8′	
2	7′	
6 ft.	9′	8″
23	4′	
30 ft.	1′	8″

ANALYSIS. We first multiply by the 7′. 7 twelfths times 8 twelfths equals 56 one hundred forty-fourths, which equals 4 twelfths and 8 one hundred forty-fourths. We write the 8 144ths — marked with two indices — to the right, and add the 4 12ths to the next product. 7′ times 11 equals 77′, which added to 4′ equals 81′, equal to 6 feet and 9′. We write the 9′ under the inches, or 12ths, and the 6 under the feet, or units. 2 times 8′ equals 16′, or 1 foot and 4′. We write the 4′ under the 9′, and add the 1 foot to the next product. 2 times 11 feet are 22 feet, and 1 foot added make 23 feet, which we write under the 6 feet. Add-

How are duodecimals added and subtracted? Give analysis of example 1.

ing these partial products, and we have 30 ft. 1′ and 8″ for the entire product.

It will be seen from the above that the number of indices to every product of any two factors is equal to the sum of the indices of those factors; thus $7' \times 8' = 56''$; $4'' \times 5''' = 20'''''$. Hence the

RULE. I. *Write the several terms of the multiplier under the corresponding terms of the multiplicand.*

II. *Multiply each term of the multiplicand by each term of the multiplier, beginning with the lowest term in each, and call the product of any two denominations the denomination denoted by the sum of their indices, carrying* 1 *for every* 12.

III. *Add the partial products, carrying* 1 *for every* 12; *their sum will be the required answer.*

EXAMPLES FOR PRACTICE.

2. How many square feet in a board 13 ft. 9′ long and 11′ wide? *Ans.* 12 ft. 7′ 3″.

3. How many square feet in a stock of 4 boards, each 11 ft. 9′ long and 1 ft. 3′ wide? *Ans.* 58 ft. 9′.

4. How many square yards of plastering on the walls of a room 12 ft. 11′ square, and 9 ft. 3′ high, allowing for two windows and one door, each 6 ft. 2′ high and 2 ft. 4′ wide? *Ans.* 48 sq. yd. 2 ft. 9′.

5. How many solid feet in a mow of hay 30 ft. 4′ long, 25 ft. 6′ wide, and 12 ft. 5′ high? *Ans.* 9604 ft. 3′ 6″.

6. How many cords in a pile of wood 18 ft. 6′ long, 12 ft. wide, and 5 ft. 6′ high? *Ans.* 9 cords 69 ft.

7. How many cubic yards of earth must be removed in digging a cellar 36 ft. 10′ long, 22 ft. 3′ wide, and 5 ft. 2′ deep? *Ans.* 156 cu. yd. 22 ft. 3′ 7″.

8. What would it cost to plaster a wall 32 ft. 8′ long and 9 ft. high, at 17 cents per square yard? *Ans.* \$5.55$\frac{1}{3}$.

9. How many yards of carpeting, 27′ wide, will be required to cover a floor 48 ft. long and 33 ft. 9′ wide? *Ans.* 240 yards.

Give the rule.

Division of Duodecimals.

230. 1. A flagstone, 3 ft. 9′ wide, has a surface of 20 ft 11′ 3″; what is its length?

OPERATION.

```
3 ft. 9′ ) 20 ft. 11′  3″ ( 5 ft. 7′.
           18     9′
           --------------
            2     2′  3″
            2     2′  3″
           --------------
```

Analysis. We divide the surface by the width to obtain the length. The divisor is something more than 3 ft., and to obtain the first quotient figure, we consider how many times 3 ft. and something more is contained in nearly 21 ft. (20 ft. 11′); we estimate it to be 5 times, and multiplying the divisor by this quotient figure, we have 18 ft. 9′, which, subtracted from 20 ft. 11′, leaves 2 ft. 2′, to which we bring down 3″, the last term of the dividend. We next seek how many times the divisor is contained in this remainder, and find by trial the quotient 7′; multiplying the divisor by this figure, we obtain 2 ft. 2′ 3″, and there is no remainder. Hence the

Rule. I. *Write the divisor on the left hand of the dividend, as in simple numbers.*

II. *Find the first term of the quotient either by dividing the first term of the dividend by the first term of the divisor, or by dividing the first two terms of the dividend by the first two terms of the divisor; multiply the divisor by this term of the quotient, subtract the product from the corresponding terms of the dividend, and to the remainder bring down another term of the dividend.*

III. *Proceed in like manner till there is no remainder, or till a quotient has been obtained sufficiently exact.*

EXAMPLES FOR PRACTICE.

2. Divide 44 ft. 5′ 4″ by 16 ft. 8′. *Ans.* 2 ft. 8′.

3. The square contents of a walk are 184 ft. 3′, and the length is 40 ft. 11′ 4″; what is the width? *Ans.* 4 ft. 6′.

4. A blanket whose square contents are 14 ft. 6′, is to be lined with cloth 2 ft. 7′ wide; how much in length will be required?

Give analysis of example 1. Rule.

5. A block of granite contains 64 ft. 2′ 5″; its width is 2 ft. 6′, and its thickness 3 ft. 7′; what is its length?

NOTE. Since the solid contents are the product of the *three* dimensions, we divide the solid contents by any two dimensions or by their product, to obtain the other dimension.

Ans. 7 ft. 2′.

PROMISCUOUS EXAMPLES.

1. In 115200 grains Troy, how many pounds?

2. In 365 da. 5 h. 48 min. 46 sec., how many seconds? *Ans.* 31556926.

3. A man wishes to ship 1560 bushels of potatoes in barrels containing 3 bu. 1 pk. each; how many barrels will be required? *Ans.* 480.

4. Reduce 295218 inches to miles.

5. Reduce 456575 grains to pounds, apothecaries' weight. *Ans.* 79 ℔ 3 ℥ 13 1 ℈ 15 gr.

6. How many sheets in 3 reams of paper?

7. What is the value of 4 piles of wood, each 20 ft. long, 6 ft. wide, and 10 ft. high, at $3.25 per cord? *Ans.* $121.87½.

8. How many bottles, each holding 1 qt. 1 gi., can be filled from a barrel of cider? *Ans.* 112.

9. At $26.40 per sq. rd. for land, what will be the cost of a village lot 8¼ rd. long, and 4½ rd. wide? *Ans.* $980.10.

10. Divide 259 A. 1 R. 10 P. of land into 36 equal lots. *Ans.* 7 A. 32½ P.

11. How many times can a box holding 4 bu. 3 pk. 2 qt. be filled from 336 bu. 3 pk. 4 qt.? *Ans.* 70.

12. What is the value of .875 of a gallon?

13. What part of a mile is 2 fur. 36 rd. 2 yd.? *Ans.* $\frac{4}{11}$.

14. What part of 2 days is 13 h. 26 min. 24 sec.?

15. From 26 A. 2 R. of land, 5 A. 3 R. were sold; what part of the whole piece remained unsold? *Ans.* $\frac{83}{106}$.

16. What is the difference between ⅗ of a pound sterling and 5¼ pence? *Ans.* 11 s. 6¾ d.

17. What is the sum of ¼ of a yard, ¼ of a foot, and ¼ of an inch? *Ans.* 7 inches.

18. Reduce 3 cwt. 1qr. 7 lb. of coal to the decimal of a long ton. *Ans.* .165625.

19. Benjamin Franklin was born Jan. 18, 1706, and George Washington Feb. 22, 1732; how much older was Franklin than Washington? *Ans.* 26 yr. 1 mo. 4 da.

20. The longitude of Boston is 71° 4′ west, and that of Chicago 87° 30′ west; when it is 12 M. at Boston, what is the time in Chicago? *Ans.* 10 h. 54 min. 16 sec. A. M.

21. If the difference of time between New York and New Orleans be 1 h. 4 sec., what is the difference in longitude? *Ans.* 15° 1′.

22. Add $\frac{2}{3}$ of a mile, $\frac{1}{2}$ of a furlong, and $\frac{3}{18}$ of a rod together. *Ans.* 5 fur. 33 rd. 8 ft. 3 in.

23. If a bushel of barley cost $.80, what will 20 bu. 3 pk. 6 qt. cost? *Ans.* $16.75.

24. What is the value of .875 of a gross? *Ans.* $10\frac{1}{2}$ doz.

25. How many acres in a field $56\frac{1}{4}$ rods long, and 24.6 rods wide? *Ans.* 8 A. 2 R. 29.9 P.

26. How many perches of masonry in the wall of a cellar which is 20 feet square on the inside, 8 feet high, and $1\frac{1}{2}$ feet in thickness? *Ans.* 44.6+.

27. A, B, and C rent a farm, and agree to work it upon shares; they raise 640 bu. 3 pk. of grain, which they divide as follows: one fourth is given for the rent; of the remainder A takes $10\frac{1}{2}$ bu. more than one third, after which B takes one half of the remainder less 7 bushels, and C has what is left; how much is C's share? *Ans.* 161 bu. 3 pk. 6 qt.

28. What is the value in Troy weight of 13 lb. 8 oz. 11.4 dr. avoirdupois weight? *Ans.* 16 lb. 5 oz. 10 pwt. 11.7 + gr.

29. If 154 bu. 1 pk. 6 qt. cost $173.74, how much will 1.5 bushels cost? *Ans.* $1.687+.

30. What is the value of .0125 of a ton? *Ans.* 25 lbs.

31. What fraction of 3 bushels is $\frac{7}{12}$ of 2 bu. 3 pk.? *Ans.* $\frac{77}{144}$.

32. How many wine gallons in a water tank 4 feet long, $3\frac{1}{2}$ feet wide, and 1 ft. 8 in. deep? *Ans.* $174\frac{6}{11}$.

33. How many bushels will a bin contain that is $7\frac{1}{2}$ feet square, and 6 ft. 8 in. deep? *Ans.* 301.339 + bu.

34. How much must be paid for lathing and plastering overhead a room 36 feet long and 20 feet wide, at 26 cents a square yard?

35. How many shingles will it take to cover the roof of a building 46 feet long, each of the two sides of the roof being 20 feet wide, allowing each shingle to be 4 inches wide, and to lie 5 inches to the weather? *Ans.* 13248.

36. John Young was born at a quarter before 4 o'clock, A. M., Sept. 4, 1836; what will be his age at half past 6 o'clock, P. M., April 20, 1864? *Ans.* 27 yr. 7 mo. 16 da. 14 h. 45 min.

37. How many cubic yards of earth were removed in digging a cellar 28 ft. 9′ long, 22 ft. 8′ wide, and 7 ft. 6′ deep? *Ans.* $181\frac{1}{54}$ cu. yd.

38. What will 30 bu. 54 lb. of wheat cost, at $\$1.37\frac{1}{2}$ per bushel? *Ans.* $42.4875.

39. How many square yards of carpeting will it take to cover a floor 24 ft. 8′ long and 18 ft. 6′ wide? *Ans.* $50\frac{19}{27}$.

40. What is the cost of 54 bu. 8 lb. of barley, at 84 cents per bushel? *Ans.* $45.50.

41. What is the depth of a lot that has 120 feet front, and contains 18720 square feet?

42. How many steps of 30 inches each must a person take in walking 21 miles?

43. How long will it require one of the heavenly bodies to move through a quadrant, if it move at the rate of 3′ 12″ per minute? *Ans.* 1 da. 4 h. 7 min. 30 sec.

44. How many times will a wheel, 9 ft. 2 in. in circumference, turn round in going 65 miles?

45. If a man buy 10 bushels of chestnuts, at $5.00 per bushel, dry measure, and sell the same at 22 cents per quart, liquid measure, how much is his gain? *Ans.* $31.92.

46. What will it cost to build a wall 240 feet long, 6 feet high, and 3 feet thick, at $3.25 per 1000 bricks, each brick being 8 inches long, 4 inches wide, and 2 inches thick?

Ans. $379.08.

PERCENTAGE.

231. Per cent. is a term derived from the Latin words *per centum*, and signifies *by the hundred*, or *hundredths*, that is, a certain number of parts of each *one hundred* parts, of whatever denomination. Thus, by 5 per cent. is meant 5 cents of every 100 cents, $5 of every $100, 5 bushels of every 100 bushels, &c. Therefore, 5 per cent. equals 5 hundredths $= .05 = \frac{5}{100} = \frac{1}{20}$. 8 per cent. equals 8 hundredths $= .08 = \frac{8}{100} = \frac{2}{25}$.

232. Percentage is such a part of a number as is indicated by the per cent.

233. The **Base** of percentage is the number on which the percentage is computed.

234. Since per cent. is any number of hundredths, it is usually expressed in the form of a *decimal;* but it may be expressed either as a *decimal* or *a common fraction*, as in the following

TABLE.

			Decimals.		Common Fractions.		Lowest Terms.
1	per cent.	=	.01	=	$\frac{1}{100}$	=	$\frac{1}{100}$
2	per cent.	"	.02	"	$\frac{2}{100}$	"	$\frac{1}{50}$
4	per cent.	"	.04	"	$\frac{4}{100}$	"	$\frac{1}{25}$
5	per cent.	"	.05	"	$\frac{5}{100}$	"	$\frac{1}{20}$
6	per cent.	"	.06	"	$\frac{6}{100}$	"	$\frac{3}{50}$
7	per cent.	"	.07	"	$\frac{7}{100}$	"	$\frac{7}{100}$
8	per cent.	"	.08	"	$\frac{8}{100}$	"	$\frac{2}{25}$
10	per cent.	"	.10	"	$\frac{10}{100}$	"	$\frac{1}{10}$
16	per cent.	"	.16	"	$\frac{16}{100}$	"	$\frac{4}{25}$
20	per cent.	"	.20	"	$\frac{20}{100}$	"	$\frac{1}{5}$
25	per cent.	"	.25	"	$\frac{25}{100}$	"	$\frac{1}{4}$
50	per cent.	"	.50	"	$\frac{50}{100}$	"	$\frac{1}{2}$
100	per cent.	"	1.00	"	$\frac{100}{100}$	"	1
125	per cent.	"	1.25	"	$\frac{125}{100}$	"	$\frac{5}{4}$
$\frac{1}{2}$	per cent.	"	.005	"	$\frac{5}{1000}$	"	$\frac{1}{200}$
$\frac{3}{4}$	per cent.	"	.0075	"	$\frac{75}{10000}$	"	$\frac{3}{400}$
$12\frac{1}{2}$	per cent.	"	.125	"	$\frac{125}{1000}$	"	$\frac{1}{8}$
$16\frac{1}{4}$	per cent.	"	.1625	"	$\frac{1625}{10000}$	"	$\frac{13}{80}$

What is meant by per cent.? From what is the term derived? What is percentage? What is the base of percentage? How is per cent. expressed?

EXAMPLES FOR PRACTICE.

1. Express decimally 3 per cent.; 6 per cent.; 9 per cent.; 14 per cent.; 24 per cent.; 40 per cent.; $112\frac{1}{2}$ per cent.; 150 per cent.

2. Express decimally $6\frac{1}{4}$ per cent.; $8\frac{3}{4}$ per cent.; $33\frac{1}{3}$ per cent.; $7\frac{1}{2}$ per cent.; $10\frac{2}{5}$ per cent.; $9\frac{5}{8}$ per cent.; $103\frac{1}{2}$ per cent.; 225 per cent.

3. Express decimally $\frac{1}{4}$ per cent.; $\frac{3}{4}$ per cent.; $\frac{2}{3}$ per cent.; $\frac{4}{5}$ per cent.; $\frac{5}{8}$ per cent.; $1\frac{1}{4}$ per cent.; $2\frac{4}{5}$ per cent.; $4\frac{1}{3}$ per cent.; $5\frac{3}{4}$ per cent.; $7\frac{1}{8}$ per cent.; $12\frac{1}{5}$ per cent.; $25\frac{3}{8}$ per cent.

4. Express in the form of common fractions, in their lowest terms, 6 per cent.; 8 per cent.; 12 per cent.; $14\frac{1}{2}$ per cent.; $18\frac{3}{8}$ per cent.; $21\frac{4}{5}$ per cent.; $31\frac{1}{4}$ per cent.; $37\frac{1}{2}$ per cent.; $40\frac{3}{4}$ per cent.; 112 per cent.; 225 per cent.

CASE I.

235. To find the percentage of any number.

1. A man, having $125, lost 4 per cent. of it; how many dollars did he lose?

OPERATION.

$$\begin{array}{r} \$125 \\ .04 \\ \hline \$5.00 \end{array}$$

ANALYSIS. Since 4 per cent. is $\frac{4}{100} = .04$, he lost .04 of $125, or $\$125 \times .04 = \$5$. Or, 4 per cent. is $\frac{4}{100} = \frac{1}{25}$, and $\frac{1}{25}$ of $\$125 = \$5$. Hence the

RULE. *Multiply the given number or quantity by the rate per cent. expressed decimally, and point off as in decimals.* Or, *Take such a part of the given number as the number expressing the rate is part of* 100.

EXAMPLES FOR PRACTICE.

2. What is 6 per cent. of $320? *Ans.* $19.20.
3. What is 8 per cent. of $327.25? *Ans.* $26.18.

Case I is what? Give explanation. Rule.

4. What is $7\frac{1}{4}$ per cent. of \$56.75? *Ans.* \$4.11$\frac{7}{16}$.

5. What is $12\frac{1}{2}$ per cent. of 2450 pounds? *Ans.* 306.25 pounds.

6. What is $6\frac{3}{4}$ per cent. of 19072 bushels? *Ans.* 1287.36 bushels.

7. What is $33\frac{1}{3}$ per cent. of 846 gallons? *Ans.* 282 gallons.

8. What is $9\frac{4}{5}$ per cent. of 275 miles? *Ans.* 26.95 miles.

9. What is 14 per cent. of 450 sheep?

10. What is 50 per cent. of 1240 men?

11. What is 105 per cent. of \$5760? *Ans.* \$6048.

12. What is 175 per cent. of \$12967?

13. What is 25 per cent. of $\frac{7}{8}$?

25 per cent. equals $\frac{25}{100} = \frac{1}{4}$, and $\frac{7}{8} \times \frac{1}{4} = \frac{7}{32}$, *Ans.*

14. What is 15 per cent. of $\frac{5}{9}$? *Ans.* $\frac{1}{12}$.

15. What is $2\frac{1}{2}$ per cent. of $6\frac{2}{3}$? *Ans.* $\frac{1}{6}$.

16. What is $33\frac{1}{3}$ per cent. of $\frac{9}{10}$? *Ans.* $\frac{3}{10}$.

17. What is 84 per cent. of $7\frac{1}{2}$? *Ans.* $6\frac{3}{10}$.

18. Find $\frac{3}{4}$ per cent. of \$40.80 *Ans.* \$.306.

19. Find $1\frac{2}{3}$ per cent. of \$15.60 *Ans.* \$.26.

20. A farmer, having 760 sheep, kept 25 per cent. of them, and sold the remainder; how many did he sell?

21. A man has a capital of \$24500; he invests 18 per cent. of it in bank stock, 30 per cent. of it in railroad stocks, and the remainder in bonds and mortgages; how much does he invest in bonds and mortgages? *Ans.* \$12740.

22. A speculator bought 1576 barrels of apples, and upon opening them he found $12\frac{1}{2}$ per cent. of them spoiled; how many barrels did he lose?

23. Two men engaged in trade, each with \$2760. One of them gained $33\frac{1}{3}$ per cent. of his capital, and the other gained 75 per cent.; how much more did the one gain than the other? *Ans.* \$1150.

24. A man, owning $\frac{4}{5}$ of an iron foundery, sold 35 per cent. of his share; what part of the whole did he sell, and what part did he still own? *Ans.* He still owned $\frac{13}{25}$

25. A owed B $575.40; he paid at one time 40 per cent. of the debt; afterward he paid 25 per cent. of the remainder; and at another time $12\frac{1}{2}$ per cent. of what he owed after the second payment; how much of the debt did he still owe?

Ans. 226.56\frac{3}{8}$.

CASE II.

236. To find what per cent. one number is of another.

1. A man, having $125, lost $5; what per cent. of his money did he lose?

OPERATION.

$5 \div 125 = .04 = 4$ per cent.

Or,

$\frac{5}{125} = \frac{1}{25} = .04 = 4$ per cent.

ANALYSIS. We multiply the base by the rate per cent. to obtain the percentage (**235**); conversely, we divide the percentage by the base to obtain the rate per cent. Or, since $125 is 100 per cent. of his money, $5 is $\frac{5}{125}$, equal to $\frac{1}{25}$ of 100 per cent. which is 4 per cent. Hence the

RULE. *Divide the percentage by the base, and the quotient will be the rate per cent. expressed decimally.* Or,

Take such a part of 100 *as the percentage is part of the base.*

EXAMPLES FOR PRACTICE.

2. What per cent. of $450 is $90? *Ans.* 20.
3. What per cent. of $1400 is $175? *Ans.* $12\frac{1}{2}$.
4. What per cent. of $750 is $165?
5. What per cent. of $240 is $13.20? *Ans.* $5\frac{1}{2}$.
6. What per cent. of $2 is 15 cents?
7. What per cent. of 6 bushels 1 peck is 4 bushels 2 pecks 6 quarts? *Ans.* 75 per cent.
8. What per cent. of 15 pounds is 5 pounds 10 ounces avoirdupois weight? *Ans.* $37\frac{1}{2}$ per cent.
9. What per cent. of 250 head of cattle is 40 head?

Case II is what? Give explanation. Rule.

10. From a hogshead of sugar containing 760 pounds, 100 pounds were sold at one time, and 90 pounds at another; what per cent. of the whole was sold?

11. A man, having 600 acres of land, sold $\frac{1}{4}$ of it at one time, and $\frac{1}{3}$ of the remainder at another time; what per cent. remained unsold? *Ans.* 50 per cent.

CASE III.

237. To find a number when a certain per cent. of it is given.

1. A man lost $5, which was 4 per cent. of all the money he had; how much had he at first?

OPERATION.

$\$5 \div .04 = \$125.$

Or,

$\frac{5}{4} \times 100 = \$125.$

ANALYSIS. We are here required to find the base, of which $5 is the percentage. Now, percentage equals base multiplied by the rate per cent.; conversely, base equals percentage divided by rate per cent. Or, $5 is 4 per cent. of all he had; $\frac{1}{4}$ of $5, or $\frac{5}{4}$, equals 1 per cent. of all he had, and 100 times $\frac{5}{4}$ equals 100 per cent., or all he had. Hence the

RULE. *Divide the percentage by the rate per cent., expressed decimally, and the quotient will be the base, or number required.* Or,

Take as many times 100 *as the percentage is times the rate per cent.*

EXAMPLES FOR PRACTICE.

2. 16 is 8 per cent. of what number? *Ans.* 200.
3. 42 is 7 per cent. of what number?
4. 75 is $12\frac{1}{2}$ per cent. of what number? *Ans.* 600.
5. 33 is $2\frac{3}{4}$ per cent. of what number? *Ans.* 1200.
6. $281.25 is $37\frac{1}{2}$ per cent. of what sum of money? *Ans.* $750.
7. A farmer sold 50 sheep, which was 20 per cent. of his whole flock; how many sheep had he at first?

Case III is what? Give explanation. Rule.

8. I loaned a man a certain sum of money; at one time he paid me $59.75, which was 12½ per cent. of the whole sum loaned to him; how much did I loan him?

9. A merchant invested $975 in dry goods, which was 15 per cent. of his entire capital; what was the amount of his capital? *Ans.* $6500.

10. If a man, owning 40 per cent. of an iron foundery, sell 25 per cent. of his share for $1246.50, what is the value of the whole foundery? *Ans.* $12465.

11. A merchant pays $75 a month for clerk hire, which is 25 per cent. of his entire profits; how much are his profits for one year, after paying his clerk hire? *Ans.* $2700.

12. A produce buyer, having a quantity of corn, bought 2000 bushels more, and he found that this purchase was 40 per cent. of his whole stock; how much had he before he bought this last lot? *Ans.* 3000 bushels.

COMMISSION AND BROKERAGE.

238. An **Agent, Factor, or Broker,** is a person who transacts business for another, or buys and sells money, stocks, notes, &c.

239. **Commission** is the percentage, or compensation allowed an agent, factor, or commission merchant, for buying and selling goods or produce, collecting money, and transacting other business.

240. **Brokerage** is the fee, or allowance paid to a broker or dealer in money, stocks, or bills of exchange, for making exchanges of money, buying and selling stocks, negotiating bills of exchange, or transacting other like business.

NOTE. The rates of commission and brokerage are not regulated by law, but are usually reckoned at a certain per cent. upon the money employed in the transaction.

Define an agent, factor, or broker. What is meant by commission? Brokerage?

CASE I.

241. To find the commission or brokerage on any sum of money.

1. A commission merchant sells butter and cheese to the amount of $1540; what is his commission at 5 per cent.?

OPERATION.

$1540 \times .05 = \$77$, *Ans.*

Or, $\frac{5}{100} = \frac{1}{20}$, and $\frac{1}{20} \times 1540 = \$77$.

ANALYSIS. Since the commission on $1 is 5 cents or .05 of a dollar, on $1540 it is $\$1540 \times .05 = \$77$. Or, since 5 per cent is $\frac{5}{100} = \frac{1}{20}$ of the sum received, the commission is $\frac{1}{20}$ of $\$1540 = \$77$. Hence the

RULE. *Multiply the given sum by the rate per cent. expressed decimally, and the result will be the commission or brokerage.* Or,

Take such a part of the given sum as the number expressing the per cent. is part of 100.

EXAMPLES FOR PRACTICE.

2. A commission merchant sells goods to the amount of $6756; what is his commission at 2 per cent.? *Ans.* $135.12.

3. What commission must be paid for collecting $17380, at $3\frac{1}{2}$ per cent.? *Ans.* $608.30.

4. An agent in Chicago purchased 4700 bushels of wheat, at 75 cents a bushel; what was his commission at $1\frac{1}{2}$ per cent. on the purchase money?

5. A broker in New York exchanged $25875 on the Suffolk Bank, Boston, at $\frac{1}{4}$ per cent.; how much brokerage did he receive? *Ans.* $64.6875.

6. An auctioneer sold at auction a house for $3284, and the furniture for $2176.50; what did his fees amount to at $2\frac{1}{4}$ per cent.?

7. A broker negotiates a bill of exchange of $2890 for $\frac{4}{5}$ per cent. commission; how much is his brokerage? *Ans.* $23.12.

Case I is what? Give explanation. Rule.

8. An agent buys for a manufacturing company 26750 pounds of wool, at 32 cents a pound, and receives a commission of $2\frac{3}{4}$ per cent.; what amount does he receive?

Ans. $235.40.

9. If I sell 400 bales of cotton, each weighing 570 pounds, at 9 cents a pound, and receive a commission of $2\frac{1}{4}$ per cent., how much do I make by the transaction? *Ans.* $461.70.

10. A commission merchant in New Orleans sells 450 barrels of flour at $7.60 a barrel; 38 firkins of butter, each containing 56 pounds, at 25 cents a pound; and 105 cheeses, each weighing 48 pounds, at 9 cents a pound; how much is his commission for selling, at $5\frac{1}{2}$ per cent.? *Ans.* $242.308.

11. A lawyer collected a note of $950, and charged $6\frac{1}{2}$ per cent. commission; what was his fee, and what the sum to be remitted? *Ans.* Fee, $61.75; remitted, $888.25.

12. An insurance agent's fees are 6 per cent. on all sums received for the company, and 4 per cent. additional on all sums remaining, at the end of the year, after the losses are paid; he receives, during the year, $30456.50, and pays losses to the amount of $19814.15; how much commission does he receive during the year? *Ans.* $2253.084.

CASE II.

242. To find the commission or brokerage, when it is to be deducted from the given sum, and the balance invested.

1. A merchant sends his agent $1260 with which to buy merchandise, after deducting his commission of 5 per cent.; what is the sum invested, and how much is the commission?

OPERATION.

$1260 ÷ 1.05 = $1200, invested.
$1260 — $1200 = $60, commission.

Or, $\frac{100}{100} + \frac{5}{100} = \frac{21}{20}$; $1260 ÷ $\frac{21}{20}$ = $1200, invested;
And $1260 — $1200 = $60, commission.

Case II is what? Give explanation. Rule.

ANALYSIS. Since the commission is 5 per cent., the agent must receive $1.05 for every $1 he expends; he can invest as many dollars as $1.05 is contained times in $1260, which is $1200; and the difference between the given sum and the sum invested is his commission.

Or, the money expended is $\frac{100}{100}$ of itself, the commission is $\frac{5}{100}$ of this sum, and the commission added to the sum expended is $\frac{105}{100}$ of the whole sum. Since $1260 is $\frac{105}{100} = \frac{21}{20}$, $1260 $\div \frac{21}{20}$ = $1200, the sum expended; and $1260 — $1200 = $60 the commission. Hence the

RULE. I. *Divide the given amount by* 1 *increased by the rate per cent. of commission, and the quotient is the sum invested.*

II. *Subtract the investment from the given amount, and the remainder is the commission.*

EXAMPLES FOR PRACTICE.

2. A man sends $3246.20 to his agent in Boston, requesting him to lay it out in shoes, after deducting his commission of 2 per cent; how much is his commission? *Ans.* $63.65.

3. What amount of stock can be bought for $9682, and allow 3 per cent. brokerage? *Ans.* $9400.

4. A flour merchant sent $10246.50 to his agent at Chicago, to invest in flour, after deducting his commission of $3\frac{1}{2}$ per cent.; how many barrels of flour could he buy at $5.50 per barrel? *Ans.* 1800 barrels.

5. An agent receives a remittance of $4908, with which to purchase grain, at a commission of $4\frac{1}{2}$ per cent.; what will be the amount of the purchase?

6. Remitted $603.75 to my agent in New York, for the purchase of merchandise, agent's commission being 5 per cent.; what amount of broadcloth at $5 per yard should I receive? *Ans.* 115 yds.

7. A commission merchant receives $9376.158, with orders to purchase grain; his commission is 3 per cent., and he charges $1\frac{1}{2}$ per cent. additional for guaranteeing its delivery at a specified time; how much will he pay out, and what are his fees? *Ans.* Fees, $403.758.

8. A real estate broker, whose stated commission is $1\frac{3}{4}$ per cent., receives $13842.07, to be used in the purchase of city lots; how much does he invest, and what is his commission? *Ans.* $13604 invested; $238.07 commission.

9. A broker received $10650, to be invested in stocks after deducting $\frac{1}{4}$ per cent. for brokerage; what amount of stock did he purchase?

STOCKS.

243. A **Corporation** is a body authorized by a general law, or by a special charter, to transact business as a single individual.

244. A **Charter** is the legal act of incorporation, and defines the powers and obligations of the incorporated body.

245. A **Firm** is the name under which an unincorporated company transacts business.

246. **Capital** or **Stock** is the property or labor of an individual, corporation, company, or firm; it receives different names, as Bank Stock, Railroad Stock, Government Stock, &c.

247. A **Share** is one of the equal parts into which the stock is divided.

248. **Stockholders** are the owners of the shares.

249. The **Nominal** or **Par Value** of stock is its first cost, or original valuation.

NOTE. The original value of a share varies in different companies. A share of bank, insurance, railroad, or like stock is usually $100.

250. Stock is **At Par** when it sells for its first cost, or original valuation;

251. **Above Par**, at a premium, or in advance, when it sells for more than its original cost; and

252. **Below Par**, or at a discount, when it sells for less than its original cost.

Define a corporation. A charter. A firm. Capital or stock. Shares. Stockholders. Par value. At par. Above par. Below par.

253. The **Market** or **Real Value** of stock is what it will bring per share in money.

254. A **Dividend** is a sum paid to stockholders from the profits of the business of the company.

255. An **Assessment** is a sum required of stockholders to meet the losses or expenses of the business of the company.

256. Premium or advance, and discount on stock, dividends, and assessments, are computed at a certain per cent. upon the original value of the shares of the stock.

CASE I.

257. To find the value of stock when at an advance, or at a discount.

1. What will $3240 of bank stock cost, at 8 per cent. advance?

OPERATION.

$$\$1 + .08 = \$1.08$$

$$\$3240 \times \$1.08 = \$3499.20, \textit{ Ans.}$$

ANALYSIS. Since $1 of the stock at par value will cost $1 *plus* the premium, or $1.08, $3240 of the same stock will cost 3240 × $1.08 = $3499.20. If the stock were 8 per cent. *below* par, $1 *minus* the discount, or $1.00 — $.08 = $.92, would show what $1 of the stock would cost. Hence the

RULE. *Multiply the par value of the stock by the number indicating the price of* $1 *of the same stock, and the product will be the real value.*

NOTE. In all examples relating to stocks, $100 is considered the par value of a share of stock, unless otherwise stated.

EXAMPLES FOR PRACTICE.

2. If the stock of an insurance company sell at 5 per cent. below par, what will $1200 of the stock cost? *Ans.* $1140.

3. What is the market value of 35 shares of New York Central Railroad stock, at 15 per cent. below par?

Market value. A dividend. An assessment. Case I is what? Give explanation. Rule.

4. What must be paid for 48 shares of Panama Railroad stock, at a premium of $5\frac{1}{2}$ per cent., if the par value be $150 per share? *Ans.* $7596.

5. What costs $5364 stock in the Minnesota copper mines, at 9 per cent. above par?

6. A man purchased $6275 stock in the Pennsylvania Coal Company, and sold the same at a discount of 12 per cent.; what was his loss? *Ans.* $753.

7. What must be paid for 125 shares of United States stock, at $4\frac{3}{4}$ per cent. premium, the par value being $1000 per share? *Ans.* $130937.50.

8. Bought 42 shares of Illinois Central Railroad stock, at 14 per cent. discount, and sold the same at an advance of $12\frac{1}{2}$ per cent.; how much did I gain? *Ans.* $1113.

9. What is the market value of 175 shares of stock in the Suffolk Bank, at $\frac{3}{4}$ per cent. advance? *Ans.* $17631.25.

10. Bought 75 shares of stock in the Bank of New Orleans, of $50 each, at 3 per cent. discount, and sold it at $2\frac{1}{4}$ per cent. advance; what was my gain? *Ans.* $196.875.

11. B exchanged 28 shares of bank stock, of $50 each, worth 7 per cent. premium, for 25 shares of railroad stock, of $100 each, at $12\frac{1}{2}$ per cent. discount, and paid the difference in cash; how much cash did he pay? *Ans.* $689.50.

CASE II.

258. To find how much stock may be purchased for a given sum.

1. How many shares of bank stock, at 3 per cent. advance, may be bought for $5150?

OPERATION.

$5150 ÷ 1.03 = $5000 = 50 shares, *Ans.*

ANALYSIS. Since the stock is at 3 per cent. advance, $1 of stock at par will cost $1.03; and if we divide $5150, the whole sum to be expended, by $1.03, the cost of $1 of stock, the quotient must be the amount of stock purchased. Hence the

Case II is what? Give explanation.

RULE. *Divide the given sum by the cost of $1 of stock, and the quotient will be the nominal amount of stock purchased.*

2. How many shares of railroad stock, at 5 per cent. advance, can be purchased for $6300? *Ans.* 60 shares.

3. I invested $6187.50, in Ocean Telegraph stock, at 10 per cent. discount; how much stock did I purchase?

Ans. $6875.

4. I sent my agent $53500 to be invested in Illinois Central Railroad stock, which sold at 7 per cent. advance; what amount did he purchase? *Ans.* $50000.

5. Sold 50 shares of stock in a Pittsburg ferry company, at 8 per cent. discount, and received $1150; what is the par value of 1 share? *Ans.* $25.

PROFIT AND LOSS.

259. Profit and Loss are commercial terms, used to express the gain or loss in business transactions, which is usually reckoned at a certain per cent. on the prime or first cost of articles.

CASE I.

260. To find the amount of profit or loss, when the cost and the gain or loss per cent. are given.

1. A man bought a horse for $135, and afterward sold him for 20 per cent. more than he gave; how much did he gain?

OPERATION.

$\$135 \times .20 = \$27$, *Ans.*

Or, $\frac{20}{100} = \frac{1}{5}$; $\$135 \times \frac{1}{5} = \$27$.

ANALYSIS. Since $1 gains 20 cents, or 20 per cent., $135 will gain $\$135 \times .20 = \$27$. Or, since 20 per cent. equals $\frac{20}{100} = \frac{1}{5}$, the whole gain will be $\frac{1}{5}$ of the cost. Hence the following

RULE. *Multiply the cost by the rate per cent. expressed decimally.* Or,

Take such part of the cost as the rate per cent. is part of 100.

Rule. What is meant by profit and loss? Case I is what? Give explanation. Rule.

EXAMPLES FOR PRACTICE.

2. A grocer bought a hogshead of sugar for $84.80, and sold it at $12\frac{1}{2}$ per cent. profit; what was his gain?

3. A miller bought 500 bushels of wheat at $1.15 a bushel, and he sold the flour at $16\frac{2}{3}$ per cent. advance on the cost of the wheat; what was his gain? *Ans.* 95.83\frac{1}{3}$.

4. Bought 76 cords of wood at 3.62\frac{1}{2}$ a cord, and sold it so as to gain 26 per cent.; what did I make?

5. A hatter bought 40 hats at $1.75 apiece, and sold them at a loss of $14\frac{2}{7}$ per cent.; what was his whole loss?

6. A grocer bought 3 barrels of sugar, each containing 230 pounds, at $8\frac{1}{4}$ cents a pound, and sold it at $18\frac{2}{11}$ per cent. profit; what was his whole gain, and what the selling price per pound?
Ans. Whole gain, $10.35; price per pound, $9\frac{3}{4}$ cents.

7. A sloop, freighted with 3840 bushels of corn, encountered a storm, when it was found necessary to throw $37\frac{1}{2}$ per cent. of her cargo overboard; what was the loss, at $62\frac{1}{2}$ cents a bushel? *Ans.* $900 loss.

8. A gentleman bought a store and contents for $4720; he sold the same for $12\frac{1}{2}$ per cent. less than he gave, and then lost 15 per cent. of the selling price in bad debts; what was his entire loss? *Ans.* $1209.50.

9. A man commenced business with $3000 capital; the first year he gained $22\frac{1}{2}$ per cent., which he added to his capital; the second year he gained 30 per cent. on the whole sum, which gain he also put into his business; the third year he lost $16\frac{2}{3}$ per cent. of his entire capital; how much did he make in the 3 years? *Ans.* $981.25.

CASE II.

261. To find the gain or loss per cent., when the cost and selling price are given.

1. Bought wool at 32 cents a pound, and sold it for 40 cents a pound; what per cent. was gained?

Case II is what? Give explanation. Rule.

OPERATION.

$$40 - 32 = 8;\ 8 \div 32 = \tfrac{8}{32} = .25,\ \textit{Ans.}$$

Or, $40 - 32 = 8;\ 8 \div 32 = \frac{8}{32} = \frac{1}{4};\ \frac{1}{4} \times 100 = 25$ per cent.

ANALYSIS. Since the gain on 32 cents is $40 - 32 = 8$ cents, the whole gain is $\frac{8}{32} = \frac{1}{4}$ of the purchase money; and $\frac{1}{4}$ reduced to a decimal is 25 *hundredths*, equal to 25 per cent. Or, if the gain were equal to the purchase money, it would be 100 per cent.; but since the gain is $\frac{8}{32} = \frac{1}{4}$ of the purchase money, it will be $\frac{1}{4}$ of 100 per cent., equal to 25 per cent. Hence the following

RULE. *Make the difference between the purchase and selling prices the numerator, and the purchase price the denominator; reduce to a decimal, and the result will be the per cent.* Or,

Take such a part of 100 *as the gain or loss is part of the purchase price.*

EXAMPLES FOR PRACTICE.

2. A man bought a pair of horses for $275, and sold them for $330; what per cent. did he gain? *Ans.* 20 per cent.

3. If a merchant buy cloth at $.60 a yard, and sell it for $.75 a yard, what does he gain per cent.?

4. A speculator bought 108 barrels of flour at $4.62½ a barrel, and sold it so as to gain $114.88½; what per cent. profit did he make? *Ans.* 23 per cent.

5. Bought sugar at 8 cents a pound, and sold it for 9½ cents a pound; what per cent. was gained?

6. A drover bought 150 head of cattle for $42 per head, and sold them for $5400; what was his loss per cent.?

Ans. 14$\frac{2}{7}$ per cent.

7. If I sell for $15 what cost me $25, what do I lose per cent.? *Ans.* 40 per cent.

8. Bought paper at $2 per ream, and sold it at 25 cents a quire; what was the gain per cent.? *Ans.* 150 per cent.

9. If I sell ½ of an article for ¾ of its cost, what is gained per cent.? *Ans.* 50 per cent.

10. If $\frac{4}{5}$ of an article be sold for what ½ of it cost, what is the loss per cent.? *Ans.* 37½ per cent.

11. If I sell 3 pecks of clover-seed for what one bushel cost me, what per cent. do I gain? *Ans.* $33\frac{1}{3}$ per cent.

12. A, having a debt against B, agreed to take \$.87½ on the dollar; what per cent. did A lose?

13. A grocer bought 7 cwt. 20 lb. of sugar, at 7 cents a pound, and sold 3 cwt. 42 lb. at 8 cents, and the remainder at 8½ cents; what was his gain per cent.? *Ans.* $18\frac{1}{28}$ per cent.

14. Bought 2 hogsheads of wine, at \$1.25 a gallon, and sold the same at \$1.60; what was the whole gain, and what the gain per cent.? *Ans.* Gain 28 per cent.

15. A grain dealer bought corn at \$.55 a bushel and sold it at \$.66, and wheat for \$1.10, and sold it for \$1.37½; upon which did he make the greater per cent.?

Ans. 5 per cent., upon the wheat.

CASE III.

262. To find the selling price, when the cost and the gain or loss per cent. are given.

1. Bought a horse for \$136; for how much must he be sold to gain 25 per cent.?

OPERATION.

$\$1 + .25 = \$1.25.$

$\$1.25 \times 136 = \$170$, *Ans.*

Or, $\frac{100}{100} + \frac{25}{100} = \frac{125}{100} = \frac{5}{4}.$

$\$136 \times \frac{5}{4} = \$170$, *Ans.*

ANALYSIS. Since \$1 of cost sells for \$1.25, \$136 of cost will sell for 136 times \$1.25, which equals \$170, the selling price. Or, since the cost is $\frac{100}{100}$, and the gain $\frac{25}{100}$, the selling price will be $\frac{125}{100} = \frac{5}{4}$ of the cost, or $\frac{5}{4}$ of \$136 = \$170. If the horse had been sold at a loss of 25 per cent., then \$1 of cost would have sold for \$1 minus .25, or \$.75, &c. Hence,

RULE. *Multiply* \$1 *increased by the gain or diminished by the loss per cent. by the number denoting the cost.* Or,

Take such a part of the cost as is equal to $\frac{100}{100}$ *increased or diminished by the gain or loss per cent.*

Case III is what? Give explanation. Rule.

EXAMPLES FOR PRACTICE.

2. If $12\frac{1}{2}$ hundred weight of sugar cost \$140, how must it be sold per pound to gain 25 per cent.? *Ans.* 14 cents.

3. Bought a hogshead of molasses for 30 cents a gallon, and paid $16\frac{2}{3}$ per cent. on the prime cost, for freight and cartage; how much must it sell for, per gallon, to gain $33\frac{1}{3}$ per cent. on the whole cost? *Ans.* \$.$46\frac{2}{3}$.

4. For what price must I sell coffee that cost $10\frac{1}{2}$ cents a pound, to gain $17\frac{1}{3}$ per cent.?

5. If I am compelled to sell damaged goods at a loss of 15 per cent., how should I mark goods that cost me \$.$62\frac{1}{2}$? \$1.20? \$3.$87\frac{1}{2}$? *Ans.* \$.$53\frac{1}{8}$; \$1.02; \$3.$29\frac{3}{8}$.

6. A man, wishing to raise some money, offers his house and lot, which cost him \$3240, for 18 per cent. less than cost; what is the price?

7. C bought a farm of 120 acres, at \$28 an acre, paid \$480 for fencing, and then sold it for $12\frac{1}{2}$ per cent. advance on the whole cost; what was his whole gain, and what did he receive an acre? *Ans.* \$480 gain; \$36 an acre.

8. Bought a cask of brandy, containing 52 gallons, at \$2.60 per gallon; if 7 gallons leak out, how must the remainder be sold per gallon, to gain $37\frac{1}{2}$ per cent. on the cost of the whole? *Ans.* \$4.$13\frac{1}{3}$.

9. A merchant bought 15 pieces of broadcloth, each piece containing $23\frac{1}{3}$ yards, for \$840, and sold it so as to gain $18\frac{3}{4}$ per cent.; how much did he receive a yard?

CASE IV.

263. To find the cost, when the selling price and the gain or loss per cent. are given.

1. A merchant sold cloth for \$4.80 a yard, and by so doing made $33\frac{1}{3}$ per cent.; how much did it cost?

OPERATION.

$1 + .33\frac{1}{3} = 1.33\frac{1}{3}$; $\$4.80 \div 1.33\frac{1}{3} = \$3.60$, *Ans.*

Or, $\$4.80 = \frac{4}{3}$ of the cost; $\$4.80 \div \frac{4}{3} = \$3.60$.

Case IV is what?

ANALYSIS. Since the gain is $33\frac{1}{3}$ per cent. of the cost, $1 of the cost, increased by $33\frac{1}{3}$ per cent., will be what $1 of cost sold for: therefore there will be as many dollars of cost, as $1.33\frac{1}{3}$ is contained times in $4.80, or $3.60. Or, since he gained $33\frac{1}{3}$ per cent. $= \frac{1}{3}$ of the cost, $4.80 is $\frac{4}{3}$ of the cost; $\$4.80 \div \frac{4}{3} = \$3.60$.

NOTE. If the rate per cent. be loss, we subtract it from 1, instead of adding it. Hence the following

RULE. *Divide the selling price by* 1 *increased by the gain or diminished by the loss per cent., expressed decimally, or in the form of a common fraction, and the quotient will be the cost.*

EXAMPLES FOR PRACTICE.

2. By selling sugar at 8 cents a pound, a merchant lost 20 per cent.; what did the sugar cost him? *Ans.* 10 cents.

3. Sold flour for $$6.12\frac{1}{2}$ per barrel, and lost $12\frac{1}{2}$ per cent.; what was the cost? *Ans.* $7.00.

4. A grocer, by selling tea at $.96 a pound, gains 28 per cent.; how much did it cost him? *Ans.* $.75.

5. Sold a quantity of flour for $1881, which was $18\frac{3}{4}$ per cent. more than it cost; how much did it cost?

6. Sold 25 barrels of apples for $69.75, and made 24 per cent.; how much did they cost per barrel?

7. Sold $9\frac{1}{5}$ cwt. of sugar at $$8\frac{1}{4}$ per cwt., and thereby lost 12 per cent.; how much was the whole cost?

8. Having used a carriage six months, I sold it for $96, which was 20 per cent. below cost; what would I have received had I sold it for 15 per cent. above cost? *Ans.* $138.

9. B sells a pair of horses to C, and gains $12\frac{1}{2}$ per cent.; C sells them to D for $570, and by so doing gains $18\frac{3}{4}$ per cent.; how much did the horses cost B? *Ans.* $$426.66\frac{2}{3}$.

10. A grocer sold 4 barrels of sugar for $24 each; on 2 barrels he gained 20 per cent., and on the other 2 he lost 20 per cent.; did he gain or lose on the whole? *Ans.* Lost $4.

11. A person sold out his interest in business for $4900, which was 40 per cent. more than 3 times as much as he began with; how much did he begin with? *Ans.* $$1166.66\frac{2}{3}$.

Give explanation. Rule.

INSURANCE.

264. **Insurance** on property is security guaranteed by one party to another, for a stipulated sum, against the loss of that property by fire, navigation, or any other casualty.

265. The **Insurer** or **Underwriter** is the party taking the risk.

266. The **Insured** is the party protected.

267. The **Policy** is the written contract between the parties.

268. The **Premium** is the sum paid by the *insured* to the *insurer*, and is estimated at a certain rate per cent. of the amount insured, which rate varies according to the degree of hazard, or class of risk.

NOTE. As a security against fraud, most insurance companies take risks at not more than two thirds the full value of the property insured.

269. To find the premium when the rate of insurance and the amount insured are given.

1. What must I pay annually for insuring my house to the amount of \$3250, at $1\frac{1}{4}$ per cent. premium?

OPERATION.

$\$3250 \times .01\frac{1}{4}$ or $.0125 = \$40.625$.

Or, $1\frac{1}{4}$ per ct. $= \frac{5}{400} = \frac{1}{80}$;

$\$3250 \times \frac{1}{80} = \$40.62\frac{1}{2}$.

ANALYSIS. We multiply the amount insured, \$3250, by the rate, $1\frac{1}{4}$ per cent., and the result, \$40.625, is the premium. Or, the rate, $1\frac{1}{4}$ per cent., is $\frac{5}{400} = \frac{1}{80}$ of the amount insured, and $\frac{1}{80}$ of \$3250 is $\$40.62\frac{1}{2}$. Hence the

RULE. *Multiply the amount insured by the rate per cent., and the product will be the premium.* Or,

Take such a part of the amount insured as the rate is part of 100.

Define insurance. Insurer, or underwriter. Policy. Premium. To what amount can property usually be insured? Give analysis of example 1. Rule.

EXAMPLES FOR PRACTICE.

2. What is the premium on a policy for $750, at 4 per cent.? *Ans.* $30.

3. What premium must be paid for $4572.80 insurance, at $2\frac{1}{2}$ per cent.? *Ans.* $114.32.

4. A house and furniture, valued at $5700, are insured at $1\frac{3}{4}$ per cent.; what is the premium? *Ans.* $99.75.

5. A vessel and cargo, valued at $28400, are insured at $3\frac{1}{2}$ per cent.; what is the premium? *Ans.* $994.

6. A woolen factory and contents, valued at $55800, are insured at $2\frac{4}{5}$ per cent.; if destroyed by fire, what would be the actual loss of the company? *Ans.* $54237.60.

7. What must be paid to insure a steamboat and cargo from Pittsburg to New Orleans, valued at $47500, at $\frac{3}{4}$ of 1 per cent.? *Ans.* $356.25.

8. A gentleman has a house, insured for $8000, and the furniture for $4000, at $2\frac{3}{8}$ per cent.; what premium must he pay? *Ans.* $285.

9. A cargo of 4000 bushels of wheat, worth $1.20 a bushel, is insured at $\frac{3}{4}$ of $1\frac{1}{2}$ per cent. on $\frac{2}{3}$ of its value; if the cargo be lost, how much will the owner of the wheat lose? *Ans.* $1636.

10. What will it cost to insure a factory valued at $21000, at $\frac{4}{5}$ per cent.; and the machinery valued at $15400, at $\frac{5}{8}$ per cent.? *Ans.* $264.25.

TAXES.

270. A **Tax** is a sum of money assessed on the person or property of an individual, for public purposes.

271. When a tax is assessed on *property*, it is apportioned at a certain *per cent.* on the estimated value.

When assessed on the *person*, it is apportioned *equally* among the male citizens liable to assessment, and is called a *poll tax.* Each person so assessed is called a *poll.*

What is a tax? How is a tax on property apportioned? On the person, how?

272. Property is of two kinds — real estate, and personal property.

273. **Real Estate** consists of *immovable* property, such as lands, houses, &c.

274. **Personal Property** consists of *movable* property, such as money, notes, furniture, cattle, tools, &c.

275. An **Inventory** is a written list of articles of property, with their value.

276. Before taxes are assessed, a complete inventory of all the taxable property upon which the tax is to be levied must be made. If the assessment include a poll tax, then a complete list of taxable polls must also be made out.

1. A tax of \$3165 is to be assessed on a certain town; the valuation of the taxable property, as shown by the assessment roll, is \$600,000, and there are 220 polls to be assessed 75 cents each; what will be the tax on a dollar, and how much will be A's tax, whose property is valued at \$3750, and who pays for 3 polls?

OPERATION.

$\$.75 \times 220 = \$165$, amount assessed on the polls.
$\$3165 - \$165 = \$3000$, amount to be assessed on the property.
$\$3000 \div \$600{,}000 = .005$, tax on \$1.
$\$3750 \times .005 = \$18.75$, A's tax on property.
$\$.75 \times 3 = \$2.25$, A's tax on 3 polls.
$\$18.75 + \$2.25 = \$21$, amount of A's tax.

Hence the following

RULE. I. *Find the amount of poll tax, if any, and subtract this sum from the whole amount of tax to be assessed.*

II. *Divide the sum to be raised on property, by the whole amount of taxable property, and the quotient will be the per cent., or the tax on one dollar.*

III. *Multiply each man's taxable property by the per cent., or the tax on \$1, and to the product add his poll tax, if any; the result will be the whole amount of his tax.*

What is real estate? Personal property? An inventory? Explain the process of levying a state or other tax. Rule.

NOTE. Having found the tax on $1, or the per cent., which in the preceding example we find to be 5 mills, or ½ per cent., the operation of assessing taxes may be greatly facilitated by finding the tax on $2, $3, &c., to $10, and then on $20, $30, &c., to $100, and arranging the numbers as in the following

TABLE.

Prop.	Tax.	Prop.	Tax.	Prop.	Tax.	Prop.	Tax.
$1 gives	$.005	$10	$.05	$100	$ .50	$1000	$5.00
2 "	.01	20	.10	200	1.00	2000	10.
3 "	.015	30	.15	300	1.50	3000	15.
4 "	.02	40	.20	400	2.00	4000	20.
5 "	.025	50	.25	500	2.50	5000	25.
6 "	.03	60	.30	600	3.00	6000	30.
7 "	.035	70	.35	700	3.50	7000	35.
8 "	.04	80	.40	800	4.00	8000	40.
9 "	.045	90	.45	900	4.50	9000	45.

EXAMPLES FOR PRACTICE.

2. According to the conditions of the last example, how much would be a person's tax whose property was assessed at $3845, and who paid for 2 polls?

Finding the amount from the table,

The tax on $3000 . . . . is $15.00
" " " 800 . . . . " 4.00
" " " 40 . . . . " .20
" " " 5 . . . . " .025
" " " 2 polls " 1.50

Total tax is $20.725

3. How much would be W's tax, who was assessed for 1 poll, and on property valued at $5390? *Ans.* $27.70.

4. A tax of $9190.50 is to be assessed on a certain village; the property is valued at $1400000, and there are 2981 polls, to be taxed 50 cents each; what is the assessment on a dollar? what is C's tax, his property being assessed at $12450, and he paying for 2 polls? *Ans.* $.005½ on $1; $69.47½, C's tax.

5. What is the tax of a non-resident, having property in the same village valued at $5375? *Ans.* $29.5625.

Explain the table and its use.

6. A mining corporation, consisting of 30 persons, are taxed $4342.75; their property is assessed for $188000, and each poll is assessed $62\frac{1}{2}$ cents; what per cent. is their tax, and how much must he pay whose share is assessed for $2500, and who pays for 1 poll? *Ans.* $2\frac{3}{10}$ per cent.; $58.125.

7. In a certain county, containing 25482 taxable inhabitants, a tax of $103294.60 is assessed for town, county, and state purposes; a part of this sum is raised by a tax of 30 cents on each poll; the entire valuation of property on the assessment roll is $38260000; what per cent. is the tax, and how much will a person's tax be who pays for 3 polls, and whose property is valued at $9470? *Ans. to last,* $24.575.

8. The number of polls in a certain school district is 225, and the taxable property $1246093.75; it is proposed to build a union school house at an expense of $10000; if the poll tax be $1.25 a poll, and the cost of collecting be $2\frac{1}{2}$ per cent., what will be the tax on a dollar, and how much will be E's tax, who pays for 1 poll, and has property to the amount of $11500?
Ans. $.008, tax on $1; $93.25, E's tax.

9. In a certain district the school was supported by a rate-bill; the teacher's wages amounted to $200, the fuel and other expenses to $75.57; the public money received was $98, and the whole number of days' attendance was 3946; A sent 2 pupils 118 days each; how much was his rate-bill? *Ans.* $10.62

CUSTOM HOUSE BUSINESS.

277. **Duties,** or **Customs,** are taxes levied on imported goods, for the support of government and the protection of home industry.

278. A **Custom House** is an office established by government for the transaction of business relating to duties.

279. A **Port of Entry** is a seaport town having a custom house.

Define duties. A custom house.

280. Tonnage is a tax levied upon a vessel, independent of its cargo, for the privilege of coming into a port of entry.

281. Revenue is the income to government from duties and tonnage.

Duties are of two kinds — ad valorem and specific.

282. Ad Valorem Duty is a sum computed on the cost of goods in the country from which they were imported.

283. Specific Duty is a sum computed on the weight or measure of goods, without regard to their cost.

284. An **Invoice** is a bill of goods imported, showing the quantity and price of each kind.

285. By the New Tariff Act, approved March 2, 1857, all duties taken at the U. S. custom houses, are *ad valorem.*

In collecting customs, it is the design of government to tax only so much of the merchandise as will be available to the importer in the market. The goods are weighed, measured, gauged, or imported, in order to ascertain the actual quantity and value received in port; and an allowance is made in every case of waste, loss, or damage.

286. Tare is an allowance of the weight of the package or covering that contains the goods. It is ascertained by actually weighing one or more of the empty boxes, casks, or coverings. In common articles of importation, it is sometimes computed at a certain per cent. previously ascertained by frequent trials.

287. Leakage is an allowance on liquors imported in casks or barrels.

288. Breakage is an allowance on liquors imported in bottles.

NOTE. Actual leakage or breakage is allowed, there being no fixed or legal rate.

289. Gross Weight or **Value** is the weight or value of the goods before any allowance has been made.

290. Net Weight or **Value** is the weight or value after all allowances have been deducted.

Define Tonnage. Revenue. Ad valorem duty. Specific duty. An invoice. Tare. Leakage. Breakage. Gross weight or value. Net weight or value.

NOTE. Draft is an allowance for the waste of certain articles, and is made only for *statistical purposes*; it does not affect the amount of duty. The rates of this allowance are as follows:

On 112 lb.	....	1 lb.
Above 112 lb.	and not exceeding 224 lb.,	2 lb.
" 224 lb.	" " " 336 lb.,	3 lb.
" 336 lb.	" " " 1120 lb.,	4 lb.
" 1120 lb.	" " " 2016 lb.,	7 lb.
" 2016 lb.	....	9 lb.

1. What is the duty, at 24 per cent., on 50 gross of London ale, invoiced at \$1.20 per dozen, $2\frac{1}{2}$ per cent. being allowed for breakage?

OPERATION.

\$1.20 × 12 × 50 = \$720, gross value.
\$720 × .025 = \$18, leakage.
\$720 — \$18 = \$702, net value.
\$702 × .24 = \$168.48, duty.

ANALYSIS. We first find the cost of the ale, at the invoice price, which is \$720. From this sum we deduct the allowance for breakage, \$18, and compute the duty on the remainder. Hence the following

RULE.. *Deduct allowances, if necessary, and compute the duty, at the given rate, on the net value.*

NOTE.—In the following examples, the legal rate of duty will be given, according to the Tariff of 1851.

EXAMPLES FOR PRACTICE.

2. What is the duty at 19 per cent. on 224 yards of plaid silk, invoiced at \$.95 per yard? *Ans.* \$40.43+.

3. What is the duty at 24 per cent. on 50 barrels of sperm oil, each containing originally $31\frac{1}{2}$ gallons, invoiced at \$.54 per gallon, allowing 2 per cent. for leakage? *Ans.* \$200.03+.

4. What is the duty at 15 per cent. on 175 bags of Java coffee, each containing 115 lbs., valued at 15 cents per pound? *Ans.* $\$452.81\frac{1}{4}$.

5. John Jones imported from Havana 25 hhds. of W. I. molasses, which was invoiced at 36 cents per gallon; allowing $\frac{1}{2}$ per cent. for leakage, what was the duty at 24 per cent.? *Ans.* \$135.399+.

Define draft. Give analysis. Rule.

SIMPLE INTEREST.

291. **Interest** is a sum paid for the use of money.

292. **Principal** is the sum for the use of which interest is paid.

293. **Rate per cent. per annum** is the sum per cent. paid for the use of $100 annually.

NOTE. The rate per cent. is commonly expressed decimally, as hundredths (**231**).

294. **Amount** is the sum of the principal and interest.

295. **Simple Interest** is the sum paid for the use of the principal only, during the whole time of the loan or credit.

296. **Legal Interest** is the rate per cent. established by law. It varies in different States, as follows:

Alabama,	8	per	cent.	Mississippi,	8	per	cent.
Arkansas,	6	"	"	Missouri,	6	"	"
Connecticut,	6	"	"	New Hampshire,	6	"	"
Delaware,	6	"	"	New Jersey,	6	"	"
Dist. of Columbia,	6	"	"	New York,	7	"	"
Florida,	8	"	"	North Carolina,	6	"	"
Georgia,	7	"	"	Ohio,	6	"	"
Illinois,	6	"	"	Pennsylvania,	6	"	"
Indiana,	6	"	"	Rhode Island,	6	"	"
Iowa,	7	"	"	South Carolina,	7	"	"
Kentucky,	6	"	"	Tennessee,	6	"	"
Louisiana,	5	"	"	Texas,	8	"	"
Maine,	6	"	"	United States (debts),	6	"	"
Maryland,	6	"	"	Vermont,	6	"	"
Massachusetts,	6	"	"	Virginia,	6	"	"
Michigan,	7	"	"	Wisconsin,	7	"	"

NOTE. When the rate per cent. is not specified, in accounts, notes, mortgages, contracts, &c., the legal rate is always understood.

297. **Usury** is illegal interest, or a greater per cent. than the legal rate.

CASE I.

298. To find the interest on any sum, at any rate per cent., for years and months.

Define interest. Principal. Rate per cent. per annum. Amount. What is simple interest? Legal interest? Usury? Case I?

In *percentage*, any per cent. of any given number is so many hundredths of that number; but in *interest*, any rate per cent. is confined to 1 year, and the per cent. to be obtained of any given number is *greater* than the rate per cent. per annum if the time be *more* than 1 year, and *less* than the rate per cent. per annum if the time be *less* than 1 year. Thus, the interest on any sum, at any rate per cent., for 3 years 6 months, is $3\frac{1}{2}$ times the interest on the same sum for 1 year; and the interest for 3 months is $\frac{1}{4}$ of the interest for 1 year.

1. What is the interest on $75.19 for 3 years 6 months, at 6 per cent.?

OPERATION.

$$\begin{array}{r} \$75.19 \\ .06 \\ \hline \$4.5114 \\ 3\frac{1}{2} \\ \hline 22557 \\ 135342 \\ \hline \$15.7899, \textit{Ans.} \end{array}$$

ANALYSIS. The interest on $75.19, for 1 yr., at 6 per cent., is .06 of the principal, or $4.5114, and the interest for 3 yr. 6 mo. is $3\frac{6}{12} = 3\frac{1}{2}$ times the interest for 1 yr., or $\$4.5114 \times 3\frac{1}{2}$, which is $15.789 +, the *Ans.* Hence, the following

RULE. I. *Multiply the principal by the rate per cent., and the product will be the interest for 1 year.*

II. *Multiply this product by the time in years and fractions of a year, and the result will be the required interest.*

EXAMPLES FOR PRACTICE.

2. What is the interest of $150 for 3 years, at 4 per cent.? *Ans.* $18.

3. What is the interest of $328 for 2 years, at 7 per cent.?

4. What is the interest of $125 for 1 year 6 months, at 6 per cent.? *Ans.* $11.25.

5. What is the interest of $200 for 3 years 10 months, at 7 per cent? *Ans.* $53.66 +.

6. What is the interest of $76.50 for 2 years 2 months, at 5 per cent.? *Ans.* $8.287 +.

Explain the difference between percentage and interest. Give analysis. Rule.

7. What is the interest of $1276.25 for 11 months, at 7 per cent.? *Ans.* $81.89 +.

8. What is the interest of $2569.75 for 4 years 6 months, at 6 per cent.?

9. What is the interest of $1500.60 for 2 years 4 months, at 6¼ per cent.? *Ans.* $218.8375.

10. What is the amount of $26.84 for 2 years 6 months, at 5 per cent.? *Ans.* $30.195.

11. What is the amount of $450 for 5 years, at 7 per cent.?

12. What is the interest of $4562.09 for 3 years 3 months, at 3 per cent.? *Ans.* $444.80 +.

13. What is the amount of $3050 for 4 years 8 months, at 5¼ per cent.? *Ans.* $3797.25 +.

14. What is the interest of $5000 for 9 months, at 8 per cent.? *Ans.* $300.

15. If a person borrow $375 at 7 per cent., how much will be due the lender at the end of 2 yr. 6 mo.?

16. What is the interest paid on a loan of $1374.74, at 6 per cent., made January 1, 1856, and called in January 1, 1860? *Ans.* $329.937 +.

17. If a note of $605.70 given May 20, 1858, on interest at 8 per cent., be taken up May 20, 1861, what amount will then be due if no interest has been paid? *Ans.* $751.068.

CASE II.

299. To find the interest on any sum, for any time, at any rate per cent.

The analysis of our rule is based upon the following

Obvious Relations between Time and Interest.

I. The interest on any sum, for 1 year, at 1 per cent., is .01 of that sum, and is equal to the principal with the separatrix removed two places to the left.

II. A month being $\frac{1}{12}$ of a year, $\frac{1}{12}$ of the interest on any sum for 1 year is the interest for 1 month.

What is Case II? Give the first relation between time and interest. Second.

III. The interest on any sum for 3 days is $\frac{3}{30} = \frac{1}{10} = .1$ of the interest for 1 month, and any number of days may readily be reduced to *tenths* of a month by dividing by 3.

IV. The interest on any sum, for 1 month, multiplied by any given time expressed in months and tenths of a month, will produce the required interest.

1. What is the interest on $724.68 for 2 yr. 5 mo. 19 da., at 7 per cent.?

OPERATION.

2 yr. 5 mo. 19 da. = 29.6⅓ mo.

```
12 ) $7.2468
     $.6039
      29.6⅓
      2013
     36234
    54351
   12078
  $17.89557
          7
  $125.26899, Ans.
```

ANALYSIS. We remove the separatrix in the given principal two places to the left, and we have $7.2468, the interest on the given sum for 1 year at 1 per cent. (**300** I.). Dividing this by 12, we have $.6039, the interest for 1 month, at 1 per cent. (II.) Multiplying this quotient by 29.6⅓, the time expressed in months and decimals of a month, (III. IV.,) we have $17.89557, the interest on the given sum for the given time, at 1 per cent. (IV.). And multiplying this product by 7 (7 times 1 per cent.), we have $125.268+, the interest on the given principal, for the given time, at the given rate per cent. Hence,

RULE. I. *Remove the separatrix in the given principal two places to the left; the result will be the interest for* 1 *year, at* 1 *per cent.*

II. *Divide this interest by* 12; *the result will be the interest for* 1 *month, at* 1 *per cent.*

III. *Multiply this interest by the given time expressed in months and tenths of a month; the result will be the interest for the given time, at* 1 *per cent.*

IV. *Multiply this interest by the given rate; the product will be the interest required.*

Give the third. Fourth. Give analysis. Rule.

CONTRACTIONS. After removing the separatrix in the principal two places to the left, the result may be regarded either as the interest on the given principal for 12 months at 1 per cent., or for 1 month at 12 per cent. If we regard it as for 1 month at 12 per cent., and if the given rate be an aliquot part of 12 per cent., the interest on the given principal for 1 month may readily be found by taking such an aliquot part of the interest for 1 month as the given rate is part of 12 per cent. Thus,

To find the interest for 1 month at 6 per cent., remove the separatrix two places to the left, and divide by 2.

To find it at 3 per cent., proceed as before, and divide by 4; at 4 per cent., divide by 3; at 2 per cent., divide by 6, &c.

SIX PER CENT. METHOD.

300. By referring to **296** it will be seen that the legal rate of interest in 21 States is 6 per cent. This is a sufficient reason for introducing the following brief method into this work:

ANALYSIS. At 6 per cent. per annum the interest on $1

For 12 months .... is $.06.
" 2 months ($\frac{2}{12}=\frac{1}{6}$ of 12 mo.)..... " .01.
" 1 month, or 30 days($\frac{1}{12}$ of 12 mo.) " .00½=$.005 ($\frac{1}{12}$ of $.06).
" 6 days ($\frac{1}{5}$ of 30 days).......... " .001.
" 1 " ($\frac{1}{6}$ of 6 da.=$\frac{1}{30}$ of 30 days) " .000$\frac{1}{6}$.

Hence we conclude that,

1st. The interest on $1 is $.005 per month, or $.01 for every 2 months;

2d. The interest on $1 is $.000⅙ per day, or $.001 for every 6 days.

From these principles we deduce the

RULE. I. To find the rate:— *Call every year* $.06, *every* 2 *months* $.01, *every* 6 *days* $.001, *and any less number of days sixths of* 1 *mill.*

II. To find the interest:—*Multiply the principal by the rate.*

NOTES.—1. To find the interest at any other rate per cent. by this method, first find it at 6 per cent., and then increase or diminish the result by as many times itself as the given rate is greater or less than 6 per cent. Thus, for 7 per cent. add ⅙, for 4 per cent. subtract ⅓, &c.

What contractions are given? Give analysis of the 6 per cent. method. Rule. Its application to any other rate per cent.

2. The interest of $10 for 6 days, or of $1 for 60 days, is $.01. Therefore, if the principal be less than $10 and the time less than 6 days, or the principal less than $1 and the time less than 60 days, the interest will be less than $.01, and may be disregarded.

3. Since the interest of $1 for 60 days is $.01, the interest of $1 for any number of days is as many cents as 60 is contained times in the number of days. Therefore, if any principal be multiplied by the number of days in any given number of months and days, and the product divided by 60, the result will be the interest in cents. That is, *Multiply the principal by the number of days, divide the product by 60, and point off two decimal places in the quotient. The result will be the interest in the same denomination as the principal.*

EXAMPLES FOR PRACTICE.

2. What is the interest of $100 for 7 years 7 months, at 6 per cent.? *Ans.* $45.50.

3. What is the amount of $47.50 for 4 years 1 month, at 9 per cent.? *Ans.* $64.956 +.

4. What is the amount of $2000 for 3 months, at 7 per cent.? *Ans.* $2035.

5. What is the interest of $250 for 1 year 10 months and 15 days, at 6 per cent.? *Ans.* $28.12½.

6. What is the interest of $36.75 for 2 years 4 months and 12 days, at 7 per cent.? *Ans.* $6.088 +.

7. What is the amount of $84 for 5 years 5 months and 9 days, at 5 per cent.?

8. What is the interest of $51.10 for 10 months and 3 days, at 4 per cent.?

9. What is the interest of $175.40 for 15 months and 8 days, at 10 per cent.? *Ans.* $22.31 +.

10. What is the amount of $1500 for 6 months and 24 days, at 7½ per cent.? *Ans.* $1563.75.

11. What is the amount of $84.25 for 1 year 5 months and 10 days, at 6¼ per cent.?

12. What is the interest of $25 for 3 years 6 months and 20 days, at 6 per cent.? *Ans.* $5.33⅓.

13. What is the interest of $112.50 for 3 months and 1 day, at 9½ per cent.? *Ans.* $2.70 +.

What contractions are given?

14. What is the interest of $408 for 20 days, at 6 per cent.? *Ans.* $1.36.

15. What is the interest of $500 for 22 days, at 7 per cent.?

16. What is the amount of $4500 for 10 days, at 10 per cent.? *Ans.* $4512.50.

17. What is the amount of $1000 for 1 month 5 days, at $6\frac{3}{4}$ per cent.? *Ans.* 1006.56\frac{1}{4}$.

18. Find the interest of $973.68 for 7 months 9 days, at $4\frac{1}{5}$ per cent.

19. If I borrow $275 at 7 per cent., how much will I owe at the end of 4 months 25 days?

20. A person bought a piece of property for $2870, and agreed to pay for it in 1 year and 6 months, with $6\frac{1}{2}$ per cent. interest; what amount did he pay? *Ans.* $3149.825.

21. In settling with a merchant, I gave my note for $97.75, due in 11 months, at 5 per cent.; what must be paid when the note falls due? *Ans.* $102.23 +.

22. How much is the interest on a note cf $384.50 in 2 years 8 months and 4 days, at 8 per cent.?

23. What is the interest of $97.86 from May 17, 1850, to December 19, 1857, at 7 per cent.? *Ans.* $51.98 +.

24. Find the interest of $35.61, from Nov. 11, 1857, to Dec. 15, 1859, at 6 per cent. *Ans.* $4.474.

25. Required the interest of $50 from Sept. 4, 1848, to Jan. 1, 1860, at $3\frac{1}{2}$ per cent.

26. Required the amount of $387.20, from Jan. 1 to Oct. 20, 1859, at 7 per cent. *Ans.* $408.957 +.

27. A man, owning a furnace, sold it for $6000; the terms were, $2000 in cash on delivery, $3000 in 9 months, and the remainder in 1 year 6 months, with 7 per cent. interest; what was the whole amount paid? *Ans.* $6262.50.

28. Wm. Gallup bought bills of dry goods of Geo. Bliss & Co., of New York, as follows, viz.: Jan. 10, 1858, $350; April 15, 1858, $150; and Sept. 20, 1858, $550.50; he bought on time, paying legal interest; what was the whole amount of his indebtedness Jan. 1, 1859? *Ans.* $1092.66 +.

PARTIAL PAYMENTS OR INDORSEMENTS.

301. A **Partial Payment** is payment in part of a note, bond, or other obligation; when the amount of a payment is written on the back of the obligation, it becomes a receipt, and is called an *Indorsement.*

$2000. SPRINGFIELD, MASS., Jan. 4, 1857.

1. For value received I promise to pay James Parish, or order, two thousand dollars, one year after date, with interest.

GEORGE JONES.

On this note were indorsed the following payments:

Feb. 19, 1858, ... $400
June 29, 1859, ... $1000
Nov. 14, 1859, ... $520

What remained due Dec. 24, 1860?

OPERATION.

Principal on interest from Jan. 4, 1857, ...	$2000
Interest to Feb. 19, 1858, 1 yr. 1 mo. 15 da., ...	135
Amount, ...	$2135
Payment Feb. 19, 1858, ...	400
Remainder for a new principal, ...	$1735
Interest from Feb. 19, 1858, to June 29, 1859, 1 yr. 4 mo. 10 da., ...	141.69
Amount, ...	$1876.69
Payment June 29, 1859, ...	1000.
Remainder for a new principal, ...	$876.69
Interest from June 29, 1859, to Nov. 14, 1859, 4 mo. 15 da., ...	19.725
Amount, ...	$896.415
Payment Nov. 14, 1859, ...	520.
Remainder for a new principal, ...	$376.415
Interest from Nov. 14, 1859, to Dec. 24, 1860, 1 yr. 1 mo. 10 da., ...	25.09
Remains due Dec. 24, 1860, ...	$401.505+

What is meant by partial payment? By an indorsement?

$475.50. NEW YORK, May 1, 1855.

2. For value received, we jointly and severally promise to pay Mason & Bro., or order, four hundred seventy-five dollars fifty cents, nine months after date, with interest.

JONES, SMITH & Co.

The following indorsements were made on this note:

Dec. 25, 1855,	received, ...	$50
July 10, 1856,	"	15.75
Sept. 1, 1857,	"	25.50
June 14, 1858,	"	104

How much was due April 15, 1859?

OPERATION.

Principal on interest from May 1, 1855, ...		$475.50
Interest to Dec. 25, 1855, 7 mo. 24 da., ...		21.63
Amount, ...		$497.13
Payment Dec. 25, 1855, ...		50.
Remainder for a new principal, ...		$447.13
Interest from Dec. 25, 1855, to June 14, 1858, 2 yr. 5 mo. 19 da., ...		77.29
Amount, ...		$524.42
Payment July 10, 1856, less than interest then due, ...	$15.75	
Payment Sept. 1, 1857, ...	25.50	
Their sum less than interest then due, ...	$41.25	
Payment June 14, 1858, ...	104.	
Their sum exceeds the interest then due, ...		$145.25
Remainder for a new principal, ...		$379.17
Interest from June 14, 1858, to April 15, 1859, 10 mo. 1 da., ...		22.19
Balance due April 15, 1859, ...		$401.36 +

These examples have been wrought according to the method prescribed by the Supreme Court of the U. S., and are sufficient to illustrate the following

UNITED STATES RULE.

I. *Find the amount of the given principal to the time of the first payment, and if this payment exceed the interest then due subtract it from the amount obtained, and treat the remainder as a new principal.*

II. *But if the interest be greater than any payment, cast the interest on the same principal to a time when the sum of the payments shall equal or exceed the interest due; subtracting the sum of the payments from the amount of the principal, the remainder will form a new principal, on which interest is to be computed as before.*

$514.96. SAN FRANCISCO, June 20, 1858.

3. Three years after date we promise to pay Ross & Wade, or order, five hundred fourteen and $\frac{96}{100}$ dollars, for value received, with 10 per cent. interest. WILDER & BRO.

On this note were indorsed the following payments: Nov. 12, 1858, $105.50; March 20, 1860, $200; July 10, 1860, $75.60. How much remains due on the note at the time of its maturity? *Ans.* $242.12 +.

$3000. CHARLESTON, May 7, 1859.

4. For value received, I promise to pay George Babcock three thousand dollars, on demand, with 7 per cent. interest.

JOHN MAY.

On this note were indorsed the following payments:—

Sept. 10, 1859,	received	$25
Jan. 1, 1860,	"	500
Oct. 25, 1860,	"	75
April 4, 1861,	"	1500

How much was due Feb. 20, 1862? *Ans.* $1344.35 +.

Give the United States Court rule for computing interest where partial payments have been made.

912\frac{75}{100}$. NEW ORLEANS, Aug. 3, 1850.

5. One year after date I promise to pay George Bailey, or order, nine hundred twelve $\frac{75}{100}$ dollars, with 5 per cent. interest, for value received. JAMES POWELL.

The note was not paid when due, but was settled Sept. 15, 1853, one payment of $250 having been made Jan. 1, 1852, and another of $316.75, May 4, 1853. How much was due at the time of settlement? *Ans.* $467.53 +.

$184.56. CINCINNATI, April 2, 1860.

6. Four months after date I promise to pay J. Ernst & Co. one hundred eighty-four dollars fifty-six cents, for value received. S. ANDERSON.

The note was settled Aug. 26, 1862, one payment of $50 having been made May 6, 1861. How much was due, legal interest being 6 per cent.? *Ans.* $154.188 +.

NOTE. A note is on interest after it becomes due, if it contain no mention of interest.

7. Mr. B. gave a mortgage on his farm for $6000, dated Oct. 1, 1851, to be paid in 6 years, with 8 per cent. interest. Three months from date he paid $500; Sept. 10, 1852, $1126; March 31, 1854, $2000; and Aug. 10, 1854, $876.50. How much was due at the expiration of the time? *Ans.* $3284.84 +.

302. The United States rule for partial payments has been adopted by nearly all the States of the Union; the only prominent exceptions are Connecticut, Vermont, and New Hampshire.

CONNECTICUT RULE.

I. *Payments made one year or more from the time the interest commenced, or from another payment, and payments less than the interest due, are treated according to the United States rule.*

Give Connecticut rule for partial payments.

II. *Payments exceeding the interest due, and made within one year from the time interest commenced, or from a former payment, shall draw interest for the balance of the year, provided the interval does not extend beyond the settlement, and the amount must be subtracted from the amount of the principal for one year; the remainder will be the new principal.*

III. *If the year extend beyond the settlement, then find the amount of the payment to the day of settlement, and subtract it from the amount of the principal to that day; the remainder will be the sum due.*

$460. WOODSTOCK, CT., Jan. 1, 1858.

1. For value received, I promise to pay Henry Bowen, or order, four hundred sixty dollars, on demand, with interest.

JAMES MARSHALL.

On this note are indorsed the following payments: April 16, 1858, $148; March 11, 1860, $75; Sept. 21, 1860, $56. How much was due Dec. 11, 1860? *Ans.* $238.15+.

303. A note containing a promise to pay interest *annually* is not considered in law a contract for any thing more than simple interest on the principal. For partial payments on such notes, the following is the

VERMONT RULE.

I. *Find the amount of the principal from the time interest commenced to the time of settlement.*

II. *Find the amount of each payment from the time it was made to the time of settlement.*

III. *Subtract the sum of the amounts of the payments from the amount of the principal, and the remainder will be the sum due.*

$600. RUTLAND, April 11, 1856.

1. For value received, I promise to pay Amos Cotting, or order, six hundred dollars on demand, with interest annually.

JOHN BROWN.

Give the Connecticut rule for partial payments. The Vermont rule.

On this note were indorsed the following payments: Aug. 10, 1856, $156; Feb. 12, 1857, $200; June 1, 1858, $185. What was due Jan. 1, 1859? *Ans.* $105.50+.

304. In New Hampshire interest is allowed on the annual interest if not paid when due, in the nature of damages for its detention; and if payments are made *before* one year's interest has occurred, interest must be allowed on such payments for the balance of the year. Hence the following

New Hampshire Rule.

I. *Find the amount of the principal for one year, and deduct from it the amount of each payment of that year, from the time it was made up to the end of the year; the remainder will be a new principal, with which proceed as before.*

II. *If the settlement occur less than a year from the last annual term of interest, make the last term of interest a part of a year, accordingly.*

$575. KEENE, N. H., Aug. 4, 1858.

1. For value received, I promise to pay George Cooper, or order, five hundred seventy-five dollars, on demand, with interest annually. DAVID GREENMAN.

On this note were indorsed the following payments: Nov. 4, 1858, $64; Dec. 13, 1859, $48; March 16, 1860, $248; Sept. 28, 1860, $60. What was due on the note Nov. 4, 1860? *Ans.* $215.33.

305. When no payment whatever is made, upon a note promising annual interest, till the day of settlement, in New Hampshire the following is the

Court Rule.

Compute separately the interest on the principal from the time the note is given to the time of settlement, and the interest on each year's interest from the time it should be paid to the time of settlement. The sum of the interests thus obtained, added to the principal, will be the sum due.

The New Hampshire rule. The New Hampshire court rule.

$500.

KEENE, N. H., Feb. 2, 1855.

1. Three years after date, I promise to pay James Clark, or order, five hundred dollars, for value received, with interest annually till paid. JOHN S. BRIGGS.

What is due on the above note, Aug. 2, 1859? *Ans.* $649.40.

PROBLEMS IN INTEREST.

306. In examples of interest there are five parts involved, the Principal, the Rate, the Time, the Interest, and the Amount.

CASE I.

307. The time, rate per cent., and interest being given, to find the principal.

1. What principal in 2 years, at 6 per cent., will gain $31.80 interest?

OPERATION.

$.12, interest of $1 in 2 years at 6 per cent.

$31.80 ÷ .12 = $265, *Ans.*

ANALYSIS. Since $1, in 2 years, at 6 per cent., will gain $.12 interest, the principal that will gain $31.80, at the same rate and time, must be as many dollars as $.12 is contained times in $31.80; dividing, we obtain $265, the required principal. Hence,

RULE. *Divide the given interest by the interest of* $1 *for the given time and rate, and the quotient will be the principal.*

EXAMPLES FOR PRACTICE.

2. What principal, at 6 per cent., will gain $28.12½ in 6 years 3 months? *Ans.* $75.

3. What sum, put at interest for 4 months 18 days, at 4 per cent., will gain $9.20? *Ans.* $600.

4. What sum of money, invested at 7 per cent., will pay me an annual income of $1260? *Ans.* $18000.

5. What sum must be invested in real estate, yielding 10 per cent. profit in rents, to produce an income of $3370? *Ans.* $33700.

How many parts are considered in examples in interest? What are they? What is Case I? Give analysis. Rule.

CASE II.

308. The time, rate per cent., and amount being given, to find the principal.

1. What principal in 2 years 6 months, at 7 per cent., will amount to $88.125?

OPERATION.

$1.175 Amt. of $1 in 2 years 6 months, at 7 per cent.

$88.125 ÷ 1.175 = $75, *Ans.*

ANALYSIS. Since $1, in 2 years 6 months, at 7 per cent., will amount to $1.175, the principal that will amount to $88.125, at the same rate and time, must be as many dollars as $1.175 is contained times in $88.125; dividing, we obtain $75, the required principal. Hence the

RULE. *Divide the given amount by the amount of* $1 *for the given time and rate, and the quotient will be the principal required.*

EXAMPLES FOR PRACTICE.

2. What principal, at 6 per cent., will amount to $655.20 in 8 months? *Ans.* $630.

3. What principal, at 5 per cent., will amount to $106.855 in 5 years 5 months and 9 days? *Ans.* $84.

4. What sum, put at interest, at $5\frac{1}{2}$ per cent., for 8 years 5 months, will amount to $1897.545? *Ans.* $1297.09+.

5. What sum, at 7 per cent., will amount to $221.075 in 3 years 4 months? *Ans.* $179.25.

6. What is the interest of that sum, for 11 years 8 days, at $10\frac{1}{2}$ per cent., which will at the given rate and time amount to $857.54? *Ans.* $460.04.

CASE III.

309. The principal, time, and interest being given, to find the rate per cent.

1. I lent $450 for 3 years, and received for interest $67.50; what was the rate per cent.?

Give case II. Analysis. Rule. Case III.

OPERATION.

$ 4.50
3
$13.50, int. of $450 for 3 years at 1 per cent.
$67.50 ÷ 13.50 = 5 per cent., *Ans.*

ANALYSIS. Since at 1 per cent. $450, in 3 years, will gain $13.50 interest, the rate per cent. at which the same principal, in the same time, will gain $67.50, must be equal to the number of times $13.50 is contained in $67.50; dividing, we obtain 5, the required rate per cent. Hence the

RULE. *Divide the given interest by the interest on the principal for the given time at 1 per cent., and the quotient will be the rate per cent. required.*

EXAMPLES FOR PRACTICE.

2. If I pay $45 interest for the use of $500 3 years, what is the rate per cent.? *Ans.* 3.

3. The interest of $180 for 1 year 2 months 6 days is $12.78; what is the rate per cent.? *Ans.* 6.

4. A man invests $2000 in bank stock, and receives a semi-annual dividend of $75; what is the rate per cent.?

5. At what per cent. must $1000 be loaned for 3 years 3 months and 29 days, to gain $183.18? *Ans.* 5½.

6. A man builds a block of stores at a cost of $21640, and receives for them an annual rent of $2596.80; what per cent. does he receive on the investment? *Ans.* 12.

CASE IV.

310. Principal, interest, and rate per cent. being given, to find the time.

1. In what time will $360 gain $86.40 interest, at 6 per cent.?

OPERATION.

$ 360
.06
$21.60 Interest of $360 in 1 year at 6 per cent.
$86.40 ÷ 21.60 = 4 years, *Ans.*

ANALYSIS. Since in 1 year $360, at 6 per cent., will gain $21.60, the number of years in which the same principal, at the same rate, will gain $86.40, will be

---

Analysis. Rule. Case IV. Analysis.

as many as $21.60 is contained times in $86.40; dividing, we obtain 4 years, the required time. Hence the

RULE. *Divide the given interest by the interest on the principal for 1 year, and the quotient will be the time required in years and decimals.*

NOTE. The decimal part of the quotient, if any, may be reduced to months and days (by **209**).

EXAMPLES FOR PRACTICE.

2. The interest of $325 at 6 per cent. is $58.50; what is the time? *Ans.* 3 years.

3. B loaned $1600 at 6 per cent. until it amounted to $2000; what was the time? *Ans.* 4 years 2 months.

4. How long must $204 be on interest at 7 per cent., to amount to $217.09? *Ans.* 11 months.

5. Engaging in business, I borrowed $750 of a friend at 6 per cent., and kept it until it amounted to $942; how long did I retain it? *Ans.* 4 years 3 months 6 days.

6. How long will it take $200 to double itself at 6 per cent. simple interest? *Ans.* 16 years 8 months.

7. In what time will $675 double itself at 5 per cent.?

NOTE. The time in years in which any sum will double itself may be found by dividing 100 by the rate per cent.

COMPOUND INTEREST.

311. Compound Interest is interest on both principal and interest, when the interest is not paid when due.

NOTE. The simple interest may be added to the principal annually, semi-annually, or quarterly, as the parties may agree; but the taking of compound interest is not *legal.*

1. What is the compound interest of $200, for 3 years, at 6 per cent.?

Rule. In what time will any sum double itself at interest? What is compound interest?

OPERATION.

	\$200	Principal for 1st year.
$\$200 \times .06 =$	12	Interest for 1st year.
	\$212	Principal for 2d year.
$\$212 \times .06 =$	12.72	Interest for 2d year.
	\$224.72	Principal for 3d year.
$\$224.72 \times .06 =$	13.483	Interest for 3d year.
	\$238.203	Amount for 3 years.
	200.000	Given principal.
	\$38.203	Compound interest.

RULE. I. *Find the amount of the given principal at the given rate for one year, and make it the principal for the second year.*

II. *Find the amount of this new principal, and make it the principal for the third year, and so continue to do for the given number of years.*

III. *Subtract the given principal from the last amount, and the remainder will be the compound interest.*

NOTES. 1. When the interest is payable semi-annually or quarterly, find the amount of the given principal for the first interval, and make it the principal for the second interval, proceeding in all respects as when the interest is payable yearly.

2. When the time contains years, months, and days, find the amount for the years, upon which compute the interest for the months and days, and add it to the last amount, before subtracting.

EXAMPLES FOR PRACTICE.

2. What is the compound interest of \$500 for 2 years at 7 per cent.? *Ans.* \$72.45.

3. What is the amount of \$312 for 3 years, at 6 per cent. compound interest? *Ans.* \$371.59+.

4. What is the compound interest of \$250 for 2 years, payable semi-annually, at 6 per cent.? *Ans.* \$31.37+.

5. What will \$450 amount to in 1 year, at 7 per cent. compound interest, payable quarterly? *Ans.* \$482.33.

6. What is the compound interest of \$236 for 4 years 7 months and 6 days, at 6 per cent.? *Ans.* \$72.66+.

Explain operation. Give rule.

7. What is the amount of $700 for 3 years 9 months and 24 days, at 7 per cent. compound interest? *Ans.* $906.55+.

A more expeditious method of computing compound interest than the preceding, is by means of the following

TABLE,

Showing the amount of $1, *or* £1, *at* 3, 4, 5, 6, *and* 7 *per cent., compound interest, for any number of years, from* 1 *to* 20.

Yrs.	3 per cent.	4 per cent.	5 per cent.	6 per cent.	7 per cent.
1	1.030,000	1.040,000	1.050,000	1.060,000	1.07,000
2	1.060,900	1.081,600	1.102,500	1.123,600	1.14,490
3	1.092,727	1.124,864	1.157,625	1.191,016	1.22,504
4	1.125,509	1.169,859	1.215,506	1.262,477	1.31,079
5	1.159,274	1.216,653	1.276,282	1.338,226	1.40,255
6	1.194,052	1.265,319	1.340,096	1.418,519	1.50,073
7	1.229,874	1.315,932	1.407,100	1.503,630	1.60,578
8	1.266,770	1.368,569	1.477,455	1.593,848	1.71,818
9	1.304,773	1.423,312	1.551,328	1.689,479	1.83,845
10	1.343,916	1.480,244	1.628,895	1.790,848	1.96,715
11	1.384,234	1.539,454	1.710,339	1.898,299	2.10,485
12	1.425,761	1.601,032	1.795,856	2.012,196	2.25,219
13	1.468,534	1.665,074	1.885,649	2.132,928	2.40,984
14	1.512.590	1.731,676	1.979,932	2.260,904	2.57,853
15	1.557,967	1.800,944	2.078,928	2.396,558	2.75,903
16	1.604,706	1.872,981	2.182,875	2.540,352	2.95,216
17	1.652,848	1.947,900	2.292,018	2.692,773	3.15,881
18	1.702,433	2.025,817	2.406,619	2.854,339	3.37,293
19	1.753,506	2.106,849	2.526,950	3.025,600	3.61,652
20	1.806,111	2.191,123	2.653,298	3.207,135	3.86,968

8. What is the amount of $800 for 6 years, at 7 per cent.

OPERATION.

From the table $1.50073 Amount of $1 for the time.
800 Principal.

$1200.58400, *Ans.*

9. What is the compound interest of $120 for 15 years, at 5 per cent.? *Ans.* $129.47+.

Of what use is the table in computing compound interest?

10. What is the amount of $.10 for 20 years, at 7 per cent.? *Ans.* $.38696.

DISCOUNT.

312. **Discount** is an abatement or allowance made for the payment of a debt before it is due.

313. The **Present Worth** of a debt, payable at a future time without interest, is such a sum as, being put at legal interest, will amount to the given debt when it becomes due.

1. A owes B $321, payable in 1 year; what is the present worth of the debt, the use of money being worth 7 per cent.?

OPERATION.

Am't of $1, 1.07) $321 ($300, Present value.
321

$321 Given sum or debt.
300 Present worth.
$21 Discount.

ANALYSIS. The amount of $1 for 1 year is $1.07; therefore the present worth of every $1.07 of the given debt is $1; and the present worth of $321 will be as many dollars as $1.07 is contained times in $321. $321 ÷ 1.07 = $300, *Ans.* Hence the following

RULE. I. *Divide the given sum or debt by the amount of* $1 *for the given rate and time, and the quotient will be the present worth of the debt.*

II. *Subtract the present worth from the given sum or debt, and the remainder will be the discount.*

NOTE. The terms *present worth, discount,* and *debt,* are equivalent to *principal, interest,* and amount. Hence, when the time, rate per cent., and amount are given, the principal may be found by (**308**); and the interest by subtracting the principal from the amount.

EXAMPLES FOR PRACTICE.

2. What is the present worth of $180, payable in 3 years 4 months, discounting at 6 per cent.? *Ans.* $150.

Define discount. Present worth. Give analysis. Rule.

3. What is the present worth of a note for $1315.389, due in 2 years 6 months, at 7 per cent.? *Ans.* $1119.48.

4. What is the present worth of a note for $866.038, due in 3 years 6 months and 6 days, when money is worth 8 per cent.? What the discount? *Ans.* $190.15+, discount.

5. What is the present worth of a debt for $1005, on which $475 is to be paid in 10 months, and the remainder in 1 year 3 months, the rate of interest being 6 per cent.?

NOTE. When payments are to be made at different times without interest, find the present worth of each payment separately, and take their sum.

Ans. $945.40+.

6. I hold a note against C for $529.925, due Sept. 1, 1859; what must I discount for the payment of it to-day, Feb. 7, 1859, money being worth 6 per cent.? *Ans.* $17.425.

7. A man was offered $3675 in cash for his house, or $4235 in 3 years, without interest; he accepted the latter offer; how much did he lose, money being worth 7 per cent.? *Ans.* $175.

8. A man, having a span of horses for sale, offered them for $480 cash in hand, or a note of $550 due in 1 year 8 months, without interest; the buyer accepted the latter offer; did the seller gain or lose thereby, and how much, interest being 6 per cent.? *Ans.* Seller gained $20.

9. What must be discounted for the present payment of a debt of $2637:72, of which $517.50 is to be paid in 6 months, $793.75 in 10 months, and the remainder in 1 year 6 months, the use of money being worth 7 per cent.? *Ans.* $187.29+.

10. What is the difference between the interest and discount of $130, due 10 months hence, at 10 per cent.? *Ans.* $.83$\frac{1}{3}$.

PROMISCUOUS EXAMPLES IN PERCENTAGE.

1. A merchant bought sugar in New York at 6$\frac{1}{4}$ cents per pound; the wastage by transportation and retailing was 5 per cent., and the interest on the first cost to the time of sale was 2 per cent.; how much must he ask per pound to gain 25 per cent.? *Ans.* 8$\frac{1}{3}$+ cents.

2. A person purchased 2 lots of land for $200 each, and sold one at 40 per cent. more than cost, and the other at 20 per cent. less; how much did he gain? *Ans.* $40.

3. Sold goods to the amount of $425, on 6 months' credit, which was $25 more than the goods cost; what was the true profit, money being worth 6 per cent.? *Ans.* $12.62 +.

4. Bought cotton cloth at 13 cents a yard, on 8 months' credit, and sold it the same day at 12 cents *cash;* how much did I gain or lose per cent., money being worth 6 per cent.?

Ans. Lost 4 per cent.

5. A farmer sold a pair of horses for $150 each; on one he gained 25 per cent., on the other he lost 25 per cent.; did he gain or lose on both, and how much? *Ans.* Lost $20.

6. A man invested $\frac{2}{3}$ of all he was worth in the coal trade, and at the end of 2 years 8 months sold out his entire interest for $3100, which was a yearly gain of 9 per cent. on the money invested; how much was he worth when he commenced trade? *Ans.* $3750.

7. In how many years will a man, paying interest at 7 per cent. on a debt for land, pay the face of the debt in interest?

Ans. $14\frac{2}{7}$ years.

8. Two persons engaged in trade; A furnished $\frac{5}{8}$ of the capital, and B $\frac{3}{8}$; and at the end of 3 years 4 months they found they had made a clear profit of $5000, which was $12\frac{1}{2}$ per cent. per annum on the money invested; how much capital did each furnish? *Ans.* A, $7500; B, $4500.

9. Bought $500 worth of dry goods, and $800 worth of groceries; on the dry goods I lost 20 per cent., but on the groceries I gained 15 per cent.; did I gain or lose on the whole investment, and how much? *Ans.* Gained $20.

10. What amount of accounts must an attorney collect, in order to pay over $1100, and retain $8\frac{1}{3}$ per cent. for collecting? *Ans.* $1200.

11. A merchant sold goods to the amount of $667, to be paid in 8 months; the same goods cost him $600 one year previous to the sale of them; money being worth 6 per cent., what was his true gain? *Ans.* $5.346 +.

12. A nurseryman sold trees at $18 per hundred, and cleared $\frac{1}{3}$ of his receipts; what per cent. profit did he make? *Ans.* 50 per cent.

13. If $\frac{4}{9}$ of an article be sold for what $\frac{5}{8}$ of it cost, what is the gain per cent.? *Ans.* $40\frac{5}{8}$.

14. A lumber merchant sells a lot of lumber, which he has had on hand 6 months, on 10 months' credit, at an advance of 30 per cent. on the first cost; if he is paying 5 per cent. interest on capital, what are his profits per cent.? *Ans.* $21\frac{7}{8}$.

15. A person, owning $\frac{5}{8}$ of a piece of property, sold 20 per cent. of his share; what part did he then own? *Ans.* $\frac{1}{2}$.

16. A speculator, having money in the bank, drew 60 per cent. of it, and expended 30 per cent. of 50 per cent. of this for 728 bushels of wheat, at 1.12\frac{1}{2}$ per bushel; how much was left in the bank? *Ans.* $3640.

17. I wish to line the carpet of a room, that is 6 yards long and 5 yards wide, with duck $\frac{3}{4}$ yard wide; how many yards of lining must I purchase, if it will shrink 4 per cent. in length, and 5 per cent. in width? *Ans.* $43\frac{49}{57}$.

18. A's money is 28 per cent. more than B's; how many per cent. is B's less than A's? *Ans.* $21\frac{7}{8}$.

19. A capitalist invested $\frac{3}{5}$ of his money in railroad stock, which depreciated 5 per cent. in value; the remaining $\frac{2}{5}$ he invested in bank stock, which, at the end of 1 year, had gained $1200, which was 12 per cent. of the investment; what was the whole amount of his capital, and what was his entire loss or gain? *Ans.* $25000, capital; $450, gain.

20. C's money is to D's as 2 to 3; if $\frac{1}{2}$ of C's money be put at interest for 3 years 9 months, at 10 per cent., it will amount to $1933.25; how much money has each?
Ans. C, $2812; D, $4218.

BANKING.

314. A **Bank** is a corporation chartered by law for the purpose of receiving and loaning money, and furnishing a paper circulation.

What is a bank?

315. A **Promissory Note** is a written or printed engagement to pay a certain sum, either on demand or at a specified time.

316. **Bank Notes,** or **Bank Bills,** are the notes made and issued by banks to circulate as money. They are payable in specie at the banks.

317. The **Face** of a note is the sum made payable by the note.

318. **Days of Grace** are the three days usually allowed by law for the payment of a note after the expiration of the time specified in the note.

319. The **Maturity** of a note is the expiration of the days of grace; a note is *due* at maturity.

320. Notes may contain a promise of interest, which will be reckoned from the date of the note, unless some other time be specified.

The transaction of borrowing money at banks is conducted in accordance with the following custom: the borrower presents a note, either made or indorsed by himself, payable at a specified time, and receives for it a sum equal to the face, less the interest for the time the note has to run. The amount thus withheld by the bank is in consideration of advancing money on the note prior to its maturity.

321. **Bank Discount** is an allowance made to a bank for the payment of a note before it becomes due.

322. The **Proceeds** of a note is the sum received for it when discounted, and is equal to the face of the note less the discount.

CASE I.

323. Given the face of a note to find the proceeds.

The law of custom at banks makes the discount of a note

Define a promissory note. Bank notes. The face of a note. Days of grace. The maturity of a note. Explain the process of discounting a note at a bank. Define bank discount. The proceeds of a note. What is Case I?

equal to the simple interest at the legal rate for the time specified in the note. Hence the

RULE. I. *Compute the interest on the face of the note for three days more than the specified time; the result will be the discount.*

II. *Subtract the discount from the face of the note, and the remainder will be the proceeds.*

EXAMPLES FOR PRACTICE.

1. What is the discount, and what the proceeds, of a note for $450, at 60 days, discounted at a bank at 6 per cent.?
Ans. Discount, $4.725; proceeds, $445.275.

2. What are the proceeds of a note for $368, at 90 days, discounted at the Bank of New York? *Ans.* $361.345 +.

3. What shall I receive on my note for $475.50, at 60 days, if discounted at the Crescent City Bank, New Orleans? *Ans.* $471.33+.

4. What are the proceeds of a note for $10000, at 90 days, discounted at the Philadelphia Bank? *Ans.* $9845.

5. Paid, in cash, $240 for a lot of merchandise. Sold it the same day, receiving a note for $250 at 60 days, which I got discounted at the Hartford Bank. What did I make by this speculation? *Ans.* $7.37½.

6. A note for $360.76, drawn at 90 days, is discounted at the Vermont Bank. Find the proceeds. *Ans.* $355.168 +.

7. Wishing to borrow $530 of a western bank which is discounting paper at 8 per cent., I give my note for $536.75, payable in 60 days. How much do I need to make up the required amount? *Ans.* $.7645.

NOTES. 1. To indicate the maturity of a note or draft, a vertical line (|) is used, with the day at which the note is nominally due on the left, and the date of maturity on the right; thus, Jan. 7|10.

2. When a note is *on interest*, payable at a future specified time, the *amount* is the face of the note, or the sum made payable, and must be made the basis of discount.

Give rule.

Find the maturity, term of discount, and proceeds of the following notes: —

$500. BOSTON, Jan. 4, 1859.

8. Three months after date, I promise to pay to the order of John Brown & Co. five hundred dollars, at the Suffolk Bank, value received.

JAMES BARKER.

Discounted March 2.

Ans. Due, April $^{4}|_{7}$. Term of discount, 36 da. Proceeds, $497.

$750. ST. LOUIS, June 12, 1859.

9. Six months after date, I promise to pay Thomas Lee, or order, seven hundred fifty dollars, with interest, value received.

BYRON QUINBY.

Discounted at a broker's, Nov. 15, at 10 per cent.

Ans. Due, Dec. $^{12}|_{15}$. Term of discount, 30 da. Proceeds, $766.434 +.

CASE II.

324. Given the proceeds of a note, to find the face.

1. I wish to borrow $400 at a bank. For what sum must I draw my note, payable in 60 days, so that when discounted at 6 per cent. I shall receive the desired amount?

OPERATION.

$1.0000
.0105 = disc. on $1 for 63 da.
$ .9895 = proceeds of $1.
$400 ÷ .9895 = $404.244 = face of the required note.

ANALYSIS. $400 is the proceeds of a certain note, the face of which we are required to find. We first obtain the proceeds of $1 by the last case, and then divide the given proceeds, $400, by this sum; for, as many times as the proceeds of $1 is contained in the given proceeds, so many dollars must be the face of the required note. Hence the

Give Case II. Analysis.

RULE. *Divide the proceeds by the proceeds of* $1 *for the time and rate mentioned, and the quotient will be the face of the note.*

EXAMPLES FOR PRACTICE.

2. What is the face of a note at 60 days, which yields $680 when discounted at a New Haven bank?

Ans. $687.215 +.

3. What is the face of a note at 90 days, of which the proceeds are $1000 when discounted at a Louisiana bank?

Ans. $1013.085 +.

4. Wishing to borrow $500 at a bank, for what sum must my note be drawn, at 30 days, to obtain the required amount, discount being at 7 per cent.? *Ans.* $503.22 +.

5. James Hopkins buys merchandise of me in New York, at cash price, to the amount of $1256. Not having money, he gives his note in payment, drawn at 6 months. What must be the face of the note? *Ans.* $1302.341 +.

EXCHANGE.

325. **Exchange** is a method of remitting money from one place to another, or of making payments by written orders.

326. A **Bill of Exchange** is a written request or order upon one person to pay a certain sum to another person, or to his order, at a specified time.

327. A **Sight Draft** or **Bill** is one requiring payment to be made "at sight," which means, at the time of its presentation to the person ordered to pay. In other bills, the time specified is usually a certain number of days "after sight."

There are always three parties, and usually four, to a transaction in exchange:

328. The **Drawer** or **Maker** is the person who signs the order or bill.

Give the rule. Define exchange. A bill of exchange. A sight draft. The drawer.

329. The **Drawee** is the person to whom the order is addressed.

330. The **Payee** is the person to whom the money is ordered to be paid.

331. The **Buyer** or **Remitter** is the person who purchases the bill. He may be himself the *payee*, or the bill may be drawn in favor of any other person.

332. The **Indorsement** of a bill is the *writing* upon its back, by which the *payee* relinquishes his title, and transfers the payment to another. The payee may indorse *in blank* by writing his name only, which makes the bill payable to the *bearer*, and consequently transferable like a bank note; or he may accompany his signature by a special order to pay to another person, who in his turn may transfer the title in like manner. *Indorsers* become separately responsible for the amount of the bill, in case the *drawee* fails to make payment. A bill made payable to the *bearer* is transferable without indorsement.

333. The **Acceptance** of a bill is the promise which the *drawee* makes when the bill is presented to him to pay it at maturity; this obligation is usually acknowledged by writing the word "Accepted," with his signature, across the face of the bill.

NOTE. Three days of grace are usually allowed for the payment of a bill of exchange after the time specified has expired. But in New York State no grace is allowed on sight drafts.

From these definitions, the use of a bill of exchange in monetary transactions is readily perceived. If a man wishes to make a remittance to a creditor, agent, or any other person residing at a distance, instead of transporting specie, which is attended with expense and risk, or sending bank notes, which are liable to be uncurrent at a distance from the banks that issued them, he remits a bill of exchange, purchased at a bank or elsewhere, and made payable to the proper person in or

---

The drawee. The payee. The buyer. An indorsement. An acceptance. What of grace on bills of exchange?

near the place where he resides. Thus a man by paying Boston funds in Boston, may put New York funds into the hands of his New York agent.

334. The **Course of Exchange** is the variation of the cost of *sight bills* from their par value, as affected by the relative conditions of trade and commercial credit at the two places between which exchange is made. It may be either at a *premium* or *discount*, and is rated at a certain per cent. on the face of the bill. Bills payable a specified time *after sight* are subject to *discount*, like notes of hand, for the term of credit given. Hence their value in the money market is affected by both the course of exchange and the discount for time.

335. **Foreign Exchange** relates to remittances made between different countries.

336. **Domestic** or **Inland Exchange** relates to remittances made between different places in the same country.

An inland bill of exchange is commonly called a **Draft.** In this work we shall treat only of *Inland Exchange.*

CASE I.

337. To find the cost of a draft.

$500. SYRACUSE, May 7, 1859.

1. At sight, pay to James Clark, or order, five hundred dollars, value received, and charge the same to our account.

To M. SMITH & Co.

Messrs. BROWN & FOSTER, Baltimore.

What is the cost of the above draft, the rate of exchange being $1\frac{1}{2}$ per cent. premium?

OPERATION.

$\$500 \times 1.015 = \$507.50$, *Ans.*

ANALYSIS. Since exchange is at $1\frac{1}{2}$ per cent. premium, each dollar of the draft will cost \$1.015; and to find the whole cost of the draft,

---

How is exchange conducted? Explain course of exchange. Foreign exchange. Inland exchange. Define a draft. What is Case I? Give analysis.

we multiply its face, $500, by 1.015, and obtain $507.50, the required *Ans.*

$480. BOSTON, June 12, 1859.

2. Thirty days after sight, pay to John Otis, or bearer, four hundred eighty dollars, value received, and charge the same to account of AMOS TRENCHARD.

To JOHN STILES & Co., New York.

What is the cost of the above draft, exchange being at a premium of 3 per cent.?

OPERATION.

$1.0000
.0055 = discount for 33 days.
$ .9945 = proceeds of $1.
.03 = rate of exchange.
$1.0245 = cost of $1 of the draft.
$480 × 1.0245 = $491.76, *Ans.*

ANALYSIS. Since time is allowed, the draft must suffer discount in the sale. The discount of $1, at the legal rate in Boston, for the specified time, allowing grace, is $.0055, which, subtracted from $1, gives $.9945, the cost of $1 of the draft, provided sight exchange were at *par*; but sight exchange being at *premium*, we add the rate, .03, to .9945, and obtain $1.0245, the *actual* cost of $1. Then, multiplying $480 by 1.0245, we obtain $491.76, the *Ans.* From these examples we derive the following

RULE. I. For sight drafts. — *Multiply the face of the draft by* 1 *plus the rate when exchange is at a premium, and by* 1 *minus the rate when exchange is at a discount.*

II. For drafts payable after sight. — *Find the proceeds of* $1 *at bank discount for the specified time, at the legal rate where the draft is purchased; then add the rate of exchange when at a premium, or subtract it when at a discount, and multiply the face of the draft by this result.*

EXAMPLES FOR PRACTICE.

3. A merchant in Cincinnati wishes to remit $1000 by

Give analysis. Rule I; II.

draft to his agent in New York; what will the bill cost, exchange being at 3 per cent. premium? *Ans.* $1030.

4. What will be the cost in Rochester of a draft on Albany for $400, payable at sight, exchange being at $\frac{3}{4}$ per cent. premium? *Ans.* $403.

5. A merchant in St. Louis orders goods from New York, to the amount of $530, which amount he remits by draft, exchange being at $2\frac{3}{4}$ per cent. premium. If he pays $20 for transportation, what will the goods cost him in St. Louis? *Ans.* $564.575.

6. What will be the cost, in Detroit, of a draft on Boston for $800, payable 60 days after sight, exchange being at a premium of 2 per cent.? *Ans.* $806.20.

7. A man in Philadelphia purchased a draft on Chicago for $420, payable 30 days after sight; what did it cost him, the rate of exchange being $1\frac{1}{2}$ per cent. discount? *Ans.* $411.39.

8. A merchant in Portland receives from his agent 320 barrels of flour, purchased in Chicago at $10 per barrel; in payment for which he remits a draft on Chicago, at $2\frac{1}{4}$ per cent. discount. The transportation of his flour cost $312. What must he sell it for per barrel to gain $400? *Ans.* $12.

CASE II.

338. To find the face of a draft which a given sum will purchase.

1. A man in Indiana paid $369.72 for a draft on Boston, drawn at 30 days; what was the face of the draft, exchange being at $3\frac{1}{4}$ per cent. premium?

OPERATION.

$369.72 ÷ 1.027 = $360, *Ans.*

ANALYSIS. We find, by Case I, that a draft for $1 will cost $1.027; hence the draft that will cost $369.72 must be for as many dollars as 1.027 is contained times in $369.72; dividing, we obtain $360, the *Ans.* From this example and analysis we derive the following

What is Case II? Give analysis.

RULE. *Divide the given cost by the cost of a draft for $1, at the given rate of exchange; the quotient will be the face of the required draft.*

EXAMPLES FOR PRACTICE.

2. What draft may be purchased for $243.60, exchange being at 1½ per cent. premium? *Ans.* $240.

3. What draft may be purchased for $79.20, exchange being at 1 per cent. discount? *Ans.* $80.

4. An agent in Pittsburg holding $282.66, due his employer in New Haven, is directed to make the remittance by draft, drawn at 60 days. What will be the face of the draft, exchange being at 2 per cent. premium? *Ans.* $280.

5. An emigrant from Bangor takes $240 in bank bills to St. Paul, Min., and there pays ½ per cent. brokerage in exchange for current money. What would he have saved by purchasing in Bangor a draft on St. Paul, drawn at 30 days, exchange being at 1¼ per cent. discount? *Ans.* $5.599+.

6. A Philadelphia manufacturer is informed by his agent in Buffalo that $3600 is due him on the sale of some property. He instructs the agent to remit by a draft payable in 60 days after sight, exchange being at ¾ per cent. premium. The agent, by mistake, remits a sight draft, which, when received in Philadelphia, is *accepted*, and paid after the expiration of the three days of grace. If the manufacturer immediately puts this money at interest at the legal rate, will he gain or lose by the blunder of his agent? *Ans.* He will lose $8.24+.

EQUATION OF PAYMENTS.

339. **Equation of Payments** is the process of finding the mean or equitable time of payment of several sums, due at different times without interest.

340. The **Term of Credit** is the time to elapse before a debt becomes due.

Rule. Define equation of payments. Term of credit.

341. The **Average Term of Credit** is the time to elapse before several debts, due at different times, may all be paid at once, without loss to debtor or creditor.

342. The **Equated Time** is the date at which the several debts may be canceled by one payment.

CASE I.

343. When all the terms of credit begin at the same date.

1. On the first day of January I find that I owe Mr. Smith 8 dollars, to be paid in 5 months, 10 dollars to be paid in 2 months, and 12 dollars to be paid in 10 months; at what time may I pay the whole amount?

OPERATION.

$$\begin{array}{rl} \$\,8 \times 5 = & 40 \\ 10 \times 2 = & 20 \\ 12 \times 10 = & 120 \\ \hline 30 & 180 \div 30 = 6 \text{ mo., average time of credit.} \end{array}$$

Jan. 1. + 6 mo. = July 1, equated time of payment.

ANALYSIS. The whole amount to be paid, as seen above, is \$30: and we are to find how long it shall be withheld, or what term of credit it shall have, as an equivalent for the various terms of credit on the different items. Now, the value of credit on any sum is measured by the product of the money and time. And we say, the credit on \$8 for 5 mo. = the credit on \$40 for 1 mo., because $8 \times 5 = 40 \times 1$. In the same manner, we have, the credit on \$10 for 2 mo. = the credit on \$20 for 1 mo.; and the credit on \$12 for 10 mo. = the credit on \$120 for 1 mo. Hence, by addition, the value of the several terms of credit on their respective sums equals a credit of 1 month on \$180; and this equals a credit of 6 months on \$30, because

$$30 \times 6 = 180 \times 1.$$

RULE. I. *Multiply each payment by its term of credit, and divide the sum of the products by the sum of the payments; the quotient will be the average term of credit.*

Average term of credit. Equated time. Give Case I. Analysis. Rule.

II. *Add the average term of credit to the date at which all the credits begin, and the result will be the equated time of payment.*

NOTES. 1. The periods of time used as multipliers must all be of the same denomination, and the quotient will be of the same denomination as the terms of credit; if these be months, and there be a remainder after the division, continue the division to days by reduction, always taking the nearest unit in the last result.

2. The several rules in equation of payments are based upon the principle of bank discount; for they imply that the *discount* of a sum paid before it is due equals the *interest* of the same amount paid after it is due.

EXAMPLES FOR PRACTICE.

2. On the 25th of September a trader bought merchandise, as follows: $700 on 20 days' credit; $400 on 30 days' credit; $700 on 40 days' credit: what was the average term of credit, and what the equated time of payment?

Ans. { Average credit, 30 days.
Equated time of payment, Oct. 25.

3. On July 1 a merchant gave notes, as follows: the first for $250, due in 4 months; the second for $750, due in 2 months; the third for $500, due in 7 months: at what time may they all be paid in one sum? *Ans.* Nov. 1.

4. A farmer bought a cow, and agreed to pay $1 on Monday, $2 on Tuesday, $3 on Wednesday, and so on for a week; desirous afterward to avoid the Sunday payment, he offered to pay the whole at one time: on what day of the week would this payment come? *Ans.* Friday.

5. Jan. 1, I find myself indebted to John Kennedy in sums as follows: $650 due in 4 months; $725 due in 8 months; and $500 due in 12 months: at what date may I settle by giving my note on interest for the whole amount? *Ans.* Aug. 21.

CASE II.

344. When the terms of credit begin at different dates, and the account has only one side.

345. An **Account** is the statement or record of mercantile transactions in business form.

Give Case II. Define an account.

346. The **Items** of an account may be sums due at the date of the transaction, or on credit for a specified time.

An account may have both a debit and a credit side, the former marked Dr., the latter Cr. Suppose A and B have dealings in which there is an interchange of money or property; A keeps the account, heading it with B's name; the Dr. side of the account shows what B has received from A; the Cr. side shows what he has parted with to A.

347. The **Balance** of account is the difference of the two sides, and may be in favor of either party.

If, in the transactions, one party has received nothing from the other, the balance is simply the whole amount, and the account has but one side. Bills of purchase are of this class.

NOTE. Book accounts bear interest after the expiration of the term of credit, and notes after they become due.

348. To **Average an Account** is to find the mean or equitable time of payment of the balance.

349. A **Focal Date** is a date to which all the others are compared in averaging an account.

1. When does the amount of the following bill become due, by averaging?

J. C. SMITH,

1859.		To C. E. BORDEN,	Dr.
June	1.	To Cash,	$450
"	12.	" Mdse. on 4 mos.,	500
Aug.	16.	" Mdse.,	250

FIRST OPERATION.

Due.	da.	Items.	Prod.
June 1	0	450	
Oct. 12	133	500	66500
Aug. 16	76	250	19000
		1200	85500

85500 ÷ 1200 = 71 da.

Ans. { 71 da. after June 1, or Aug. 11.

SECOND OPERATION.

Due.	da.	Items.	Prod.
June 1	133	450	59850
Oct. 12	0	500	
Aug. 16	57	250	14250
		1200	74100

74100 ÷ 1200 = 62 da.

Ans. { 62 da. before Oct. 12, or Aug. 11.

Define items. Balance. To average an account. A focal date.

ANALYSIS. By reference to the example, it will be seen that the items are due June 1, Oct. 12, and Aug. 16, as shown in the two operations. In the first operation we use the *earliest* date, June 1, as a focal date, and find the difference in days between this date and each of the others, regard being had to the number of days in calendar months. From June 1 to Oct. 12 is 133 da.; from June 1 to Aug. 16 is 76 da. Hence the first item has no credit from June 1, the second item has 133 days' credit from June 1, and the third item has 76 days' credit from June 1, as appears in the column marked da. After this we proceed precisely as in Case I, and find the average credit, 71 da., and the equated time, Aug. 11.

In the second operation, the *latest* date, Oct. 12, is taken for a focal date; the work is explained thus: Suppose the account to be settled Oct. 12. At that time the first item has been due 133 days, and must therefore draw interest for this time. But interest on $450 for 133 days = the interest on $59850 for 1 da. The second item draws no interest, because it falls due Oct. 12. The third item must draw interest 57 days. But interest on $250 for 57 days = the interest on $14250 for 1 day. Taking the sum of the products, we find the whole amount of interest due on the account, at Oct. 12, equals the interest on $74100 for 1 day; and this, by division, is found to be equal to the interest on $1200 for 62 days, which time is the average term of interest. Hence the account would be settled Oct. 12, by paying $1200 with interest on the same for 62 days. This shows that 1200 has been due 62 days; that is, it falls due Aug. 11, *without interest.* Hence the following

RULE. I. *Find the time at which each item becomes due, by adding to the date of each transaction the term of credit, if any be specified, and write these dates in a column.*

II. *Assume either the earliest or the latest date for a focal date, and find the difference in days between the focal date and each of the other dates, and write the results in a second column.*

III. *Write the items of the account in a third column, and multiply each sum by the corresponding number of days in the preceding column, writing the products in a final column.*

IV. *Divide the sum of the products by the sum of the items. The quotient will be the average term of credit when the*

Give analysis. Rule.

earliest date is the focal date, or the average term of interest when the latest date is the focal date; in either case always reckon from the focal date toward the other dates, to find the equated time of payment.

EXAMPLES FOR PRACTICE.

2. JOHN BROWN,

1859.				To JAMES GREIGG,		Dr.
Jan. 1.	To	50 yds.	Broadcloth,	@	$3.00, . . .	$150
" 16.	"	2000 "	Calico,	"	.10, . . .	200
Feb. 4.	"	75 "	Carpeting,	"	$1.33\frac{1}{3}$, . .	100
March 3.	"	400 "	Oil Cloth,	"	.40, . . .	160

If James Greigg wishes to settle the above bill by giving his note, from what date shall the note draw interest?

Ans. Jan. 27.

3. ABRAM RUSSEL,

1859.		To WYNKOOP & BRO., Dr.
March 1.	To Cash, ...	$300
April 4.	" Mdse., ...	240
June 18.	" " on 2 mo., ...	100
Aug. 8.	" Cash, ...	400

What is the equated time of payment of the above account?

Ans. May 26.

4. JOHN OTIS,

1858.				To JAMES LADD,	Dr.
June 1.	To	500 bu.	Wheat,	@ $1.20, ...	$600
" 12.	"	200 "	"	" 1.50, ...	300
" 15.	"	640 "	"	" 1.30, ...	832
" 25.	"	760 "	"	" 1.00, ...	760
" 30.	"	500 "	"	" 1.50, ...	750

When is the whole amount of the above bill due, per average? *Ans.* June 18.

5. My expenditures in building a house, in the year 1856, were as follows: Jan. 16, $536.78; Feb. 20, $425.36; March 4, $259.25; April 24, $786.36. If at the last date I agree to

sell the house for exactly what it cost, with reference to interest on the money expended, and take the purchaser's note for the amount, what shall be the face of the note, and what its date?

Ans. { Face, $2007.75. Date, March 8, 1856.

6. THOMAS WHITING,

1859.				To ISRAEL PALMER, Dr.
Jan. 1.	To	60 bbls. Flour,	@ $7.00,	$420
" 28.	"	90 bu. Wheat,	" 1.50,	135
Mar. 15.	"	300 bbls. Flour,	" 6.00,	1800

If credit of 3 months be given to each item, when will the above account become due? *Ans.* May 30.

CASE III.

350. When the terms of credit begin at different times, and the account has both a debt and a credit side.

1. Average the following account.

DAVID WARE.

Dr.									*Cr.*
1858.					1858.				
June	1	To Mdse.	400	00	July	4	By Mdse.	200	00
"	16	" Draft, 3 mo.	800	00	Aug.	20	" Cash	150	00
Oct.	20	" Cash,	250	00	Sept.	20	" "	500	00

OPERATION.

	Dr. Due	da.	Items.	Prod.	*Cr.* Due	da.	Items.	Prod.
	June 1	141	400	56400	July 4	108	200	21600
	Sept. 19	31	800	24800	Aug. 20	61	150	9150
Focal date.	Oct. 20	0	250		Sept. 20	30	500	15000
			1450	81200			850	45750
			850	45750				
Balances.			600	35450				

35450 ÷ 600 = 59 da., average term of interest.

Oct. 20 — 59 da. = Aug. 22, balance due.

What is Case III? Explain operation.

ANALYSIS. In the above operation we have written the dates, showing when the items become due on either side of the account, adding 3 days' grace to the time allowed to the draft. The latest date, Oct. 20, is assumed as the focal date for both sides, and the two columns marked da. show the difference in days between each date and the focal date. The products are obtained as in the last case, and a balance is struck between the items charged and the products. These balances, being on the Dr. side, show that David Ware, on the day of the focal date, Oct. 20, owes $600 with interest on $35450 for 1 day. By division, this interest is found to be equal to the interest on $600 for 59 days. The balance, $600, therefore, has been due 59 days. Reckoning back from Oct. 12, we find the date when the balance fell due, Aug. 22. Hence the following

RULE. I. *Find the time when each item of the account is due; and write the dates, in two columns, on the sides of the account to which they respectively belong.*

II. *Use either the earliest or the latest of these dates as the focal date for both sides, and find the products as in the last case.*

III. *Divide the balance of the products by the balance of the account; the quotient will be the interval of time, which must be reckoned from the focal date* TOWARD *the other dates when both balances are on the same side of the account, but* FROM *the other dates when the balances are on opposite sides of the account.*

2. What is the balance of the following account, and when is it due?

JOHN WILSON.

Dr. *Cr.*

1859.					1859.				
Jan.	1	To Mdse. .	448	00	Jan.	20	By Am't bro't forward	560	00
Feb.	4	" Cash. .	364	00	Feb.	16	" 1 Carriage	264	00
"	20	" " . .	232	00	"	25	" Cash	900	00

Ans. { Balance, $680. Due March 13.

3. If the following account be settled by giving a note, what shall be the face of the note, and what its date?

Give analysis. Rule.

Isaac Foster.

Dr *Cr.*

1858.					1858.				
Jan.	1	To Mdse. on 3 mo.	145	86	May	11	By Cash	11	00
"	12	" " " 5 "	37	48	July	12	" "	15	00
June	3	" " " 3 "	12	25	Oct.	12	" "	82	00
Aug.	4	" " " 2 "	66	48					

Ans. { $154.07, face of note. Mar. 26, 1858, date.

RATIO.

351. Ratio is the comparison with each other of two numbers of the same kind. It is of two kinds — arithmetical and geometrical.

352. Arithmetical Ratio is the difference of the two numbers.

353. Geometrical Ratio is the quotient of one number divided by the other.

354. When we use the word *ratio* alone, it implies geometrical ratio, and is expressed by the quotient arising from dividing one number by the other. Thus, the ratio of 4 to 8 is 2, of 10 to 5 is $\frac{1}{2}$, &c.

355. Ratio is indicated in two ways.

1st. By placing two points between the numbers compared, writing the divisor before and the dividend after the points. Thus, the ratio of 5 to 7 is written 5 : 7; the ratio of 9 to 4 is written 9 : 4.

2d. In the form of a fraction; thus, the ratio of 9 to 3 is $\frac{3}{9}$; the ratio of 4 to 6 is $\frac{6}{4}$.

356. The **Terms** are the two numbers compared.

357. The **Antecedent** is the first term.

358. The **Consequent** is the second term.

359. No comparison of two numbers can be fully explained but by instituting *another* comparison; thus, the com-

NOTE. It is thought best to omit the questions at the bottom of the pages, in the remaining part of this work, leaving the teacher to use such as may be deemed appropriate.

parison or relation of 4 to 8 cannot be fully expressed by 2, nor of 8 to 4 by $\frac{1}{2}$. If the question were asked, what relation 4 bears to 8, or 8 to 4, in respect to magnitude, the answer 2, or $\frac{1}{2}$, would not be complete nor correct. But if we make *unity* the standard of comparison, and use it as one of the terms in illustrating the relation of the two numbers, and say that the ratio or relation of 4 to 8 is the same as 1 to 2, or the ratio of 8 to 4 is the same as 1 to $\frac{1}{2}$, *unity* in both cases being the standard of comparison, then the whole meaning is conveyed.

360. A **Direct Ratio** arises from dividing the consequent by the antecedent.

261. An **Inverse** or **Reciprocal Ratio** is obtained by dividing the antecedent by the consequent. Thus, the *direct* ratio of 5 to 15 is $\frac{15}{5} = 3$; and the *inverse* ratio of 5 to 15 is $\frac{5}{15} = \frac{1}{3}$.

362. A **Simple Ratio** consists of a single couplet; as 3 : 12.

363. A **Compound Ratio** is the product of two or more simple ratios. Thus, the compound ratio formed from the simple ratios of 3 : 6 and 8 : 2 is $\frac{6}{3} \times \frac{2}{8} = 3 \times 8 : 6 \times 2 = \frac{12}{24} = \frac{1}{2}$.

364. In comparing numbers with each other, they must be of the same *kind*, and of the same *denomination.*

365. The ratio of two *fractions* is obtained by dividing the second by the first; or by reducing them to a common denominator, when they are to each other as their numerators. Thus, the ratio of $\frac{3}{10} : \frac{3}{5}$ is $\frac{3}{5} \div \frac{3}{10} = \frac{30}{15} = 2$, which is the same as the ratio of the numerator 3 to the numerator 6 of the equivalent fractions $\frac{3}{10}$ and $\frac{6}{10}$.

Since the antecedent is a divisor and the consequent a dividend, any change in either or both terms will be governed by the general principles of division, (**87.**) We have only to substitute the terms *antecedent, consequent,* and *ratio,* for *divisor, dividend,* and *quotient,* and these principles become

GENERAL PRINCIPLES OF RATIO.

PRIN. I. *Multiplying the consequent multiplies the ratio; dividing the consequent divides the ratio.*

PRIN. II. *Multiplying the antecedent divides the ratio; dividing the antecedent multiplies the ratio.*

PRIN. III. *Multiplying or dividing both antecedent and consequent by the same number does not alter the ratio.*

These three principles may be embraced in one

GENERAL LAW.

A change in the consequent produces a LIKE *change in the ratio; but a change in the antecedent produces an* OPPOSITE *change in the ratio.*

366. Since the *ratio* of two numbers is equal to the consequent divided by the antecedent, it follows, that

1. The *antecedent* is equal to the consequent divided by the ratio; and that,

2. The *consequent* is equal to the antecedent multiplied by the ratio.

EXAMPLES FOR PRACTICE.

1. What part of 9 is 3?

$\frac{3}{9}=\frac{1}{3}$; or, 9 : 3 as 1 : $\frac{1}{3}$, that is, 9 has the same ratio to 3 that 1 has to $\frac{1}{3}$.

2. What part of 20 is 5? *Ans.* $\frac{1}{4}$.
3. What part of 36 is 4? *Ans.* $\frac{1}{9}$.
4. What part of 7 is 49? *Ans.* 7 times.
5. What is the ratio of 16 to 88? *Ans.* $5\frac{1}{2}$.
6. What is the ratio of 6 to $8\frac{1}{2}$? *Ans.* $\frac{17}{12}$.
7. What is the ratio of $6\frac{1}{2}$ to 78? *Ans.* 12.
8. What is the ratio of 16 to 66? *Ans.* $4\frac{1}{8}$.
9. What is the ratio of $\frac{3}{4}$ to $\frac{3}{5}$? *Ans.* $\frac{4}{5}$.
10. What is the ratio of $\frac{5}{8}$ to $\frac{4}{16}$? *Ans.* $\frac{2}{5}$.
11. What is the ratio of $3\frac{1}{3}$ to $16\frac{2}{3}$? *Ans.* 5.
12. What is the ratio of 3 gal. to 2 qt. 1 pt.? *Ans.* $\frac{5}{24}$.

13. What is the ratio of 6.3 s to 8 s. 6 d.? *Ans.* $1\frac{22}{63}$

14. What is the ratio of 5.6 to .56? *Ans.* $\frac{1}{10}$.

15. What is the ratio of 19 lbs. 5 oz. 8 pwts. to 25 lbs. 11 oz. 4 pwts.? *Ans.* $1\frac{1}{3}$.

16. What is the inverse ratio of 12 to 16? *Ans.* $\frac{3}{4}$.

17. What is the inverse ratio of $\frac{2}{7}$ to $\frac{4}{9}$? *Ans.* $\frac{9}{14}$.

18. What is the inverse ratio of $5\frac{3}{4}$ to $17\frac{1}{4}$? *Ans.* $\frac{1}{3}$.

19. If the consequent be 16 and the ratio $2\frac{2}{7}$, what is the antecedent? *Ans.* 7.

20. If the antecedent be 14.5 and the ratio 3, what is the consequent? *Ans.* 43.5.

21. If the consequent be $\frac{7}{8}$ and the ratio $\frac{3}{4}$, what is the antecedent? *Ans.* $1\frac{1}{6}$.

22. If the antecedent be $\frac{3}{5}$ and the ratio $\frac{1}{6}$, what is the consequent? *Ans.* $\frac{1}{10}$.

PROPORTION.

367. **Proportion** is an equality of ratios. Thus, the ratios 6 : 4 and 12 : 8, each being equal to $\frac{2}{3}$, form a proportion.

368. Proportion is indicated in two ways.

1st. By a double colon placed between the two ratios; thus, 2 : 5 : : 4 : 10.

2d. By the sign of equality placed between the two ratios; thus, 2 : 5 = 4 : 10.

369. Since each ratio consists of two terms, every proportion must consist of at least *four terms.*

370. The **Extremes** are the first and fourth terms.

371. The **Means** are the second and third terms.

372. Three numbers may be in proportion when the first is to the second as the second is to the third. Thus, the numbers 3, 9, and 27 are in proportion since 3 : 9 : : 9 : 27, the ratio of each couplet being 3.

In such a proportion the second term is said to be a *mean proportional* between the other two.

373. In every proportion the product of the extremes is equal to the product of the means. Thus, in the proportion *3 : 5 : :* 6 : 10 we have 3 × 10 = 5 × 6.

374. Four numbers that are proportional in the direct order are proportional by *inversion*, and also by *alternation*, or by inverting the means. Thus, the proportion 2 : 3 :: 6 : 9, by *inversion* becomes 3 : 2 :: 9 : 6, and by *alternation* 2 : 6 :: 3 : 9.

375. From the preceding principles and illustrations, it follows that, any three terms of a proportion being given, the fourth may readily be found by the following

RULE. I. *Divide the product of the extremes by one of the means, and the quotient will be the other mean.* Or,

II. *Divide the product of the means by one of the extremes, and the quotient will be the other extreme.*

EXAMPLES FOR PRACTICE.

Find the term not given in each of the following proportions.

1. 48 : 20 :: ( ) : 50. *Ans.* 120.
2. 42 : 70 :: 3 : ( ). *Ans.* 5.
3. ( ) : 30 :: 20 : 100. *Ans.* 6.
4. 1 : ( ) :: 7 : 84. *Ans.* 12.
5. 48 yd. : ( ) :: \$67.25 : \$201.75. *Ans.* 144 yd.
6. 3 lb. 12 oz. : ( ) :: \$3.50 : \$10.50. *Ans.* 11 lb. 4 oz.
7. ( ) : \$38.25 :: 8 bu. 2 pk. : 76 bu. 2 pk. *Ans.* \$4.25.
8. $4\frac{1}{4}$: $38\frac{1}{4}$ :: ( ) : $76\frac{1}{2}$. *Ans.* $8\frac{1}{2}$.
9. ( ) : 12 :: $\frac{3}{4}$: $1\frac{2}{7}$. *Ans.* 7.
10. $\frac{5}{16}$: ( ) :: $\frac{1}{3}$: $\frac{2}{5}$. *Ans.* $\frac{3}{8}$.

SIMPLE PROPORTION.

376. Simple Proportion is an equality of two simple ratios, and consists of four terms, any three of which being given, the fourth may readily be found.

377. Every question in simple proportion involves the principle of *cause and effect.*

378. Causes may be regarded as *action*, of whatever kind, the producer, the consumer, men, animals, time, distance, weight, goods bought or sold, money at interest, &c.

379. Effects may be regarded as whatever is accomplished by action of any kind, the thing produced or consumed, money paid, &c.

380. Causes and effects are of two kinds — simple and compound.

381. A **Simple Cause**, or **Effect**, contains but one element; as goods purchased or sold, and the money paid or received for them.

382. A **Compound Cause**, or **Effect**, is the product of two or more elements; as men at work taken in connection with time, and the result produced by them taken in connection with dimensions, length and breadth, &c.

383. Causes and effects that admit of computation, that is, involve the *idea of quantity*, may be represented by numbers, which will have the same relation to each other as the things they represent. And since it is a principle of philosophy that *like causes* produce *like effects*, and that effects are always *in proportion* to their causes, we have the following proportions:

1st Cause : 2d Cause : : 1st Effect : 2d Effect.

Or, 1st Effect : 2d Effect : : 1st Cause : 2d Cause;

in which the two causes, or the two effects forming one couplet, must be *like* numbers, and of the same denomination.

Considering all the terms of the proportion as *abstract numbers*, we may say that

1st Cause : 1st Effect : : 2d Cause : 2d Effect,

which will produce the same numerical result.

But as ratio is the result of comparing two numbers or things of the *same kind* (**364**), the first form is regarded as the most natural and philosophical.

384. Simple causes and simple effects give rise to simple ratios; compound causes and compound effects to compound ratios.

385. 1. If 5 tons of coal cost $30, what will 3 tons cost?

NOTE. The required term will be denoted by a ( ), and designated "blank."

STATEMENT.

tons.		tons.		$		$
5	:	3	::	30	:	( )
1st cause.		2d cause.		1st effect.		2d effect.

OPERATION.

$$5 \times (\quad) = 3 \times 30$$

$$(\quad) = \frac{3 \times \not{3}\not{0}^{6}}{\not{5}} = \$18, \textit{ Ans.}$$

Analysis. In this example an *effect* is required, and 5 tons must have the same ratio to 3 tons, as $30, the cost of 5 tons, to (blank) dollars, the cost of 3 tons.

Since the product of the extremes is equal to the product of the means (**373**), and the product of the means divided by one of the extremes will give the other; (blank) dollars will be equal to the product of 3 × 30 divided by 5, which is $18, *Ans.*

2. If 15 barrels of flour cost $90, how many barrels can be bought for $30?

STATEMENT.

bar.		bar.		$		$
15	:	( )	::	90	:	30
1st cause.		2d cause.		1st effect.		2d effect.

OPERATION.

$\not{9}\not{0}$	$\not{3}\not{0}$
( )	$\not{1}\not{5}^{5}$

( ) = 5 bar., *Ans.*

Analysis. In this example a *cause* is required, and the statement may be read thus: If 15 barrels cost $90, how many or (blank) barrels will cost $30? The product of the extremes, 30 × 15, divided by the given mean, 90, will give the required term, 5, as shown in the operation. Hence we deduce the following

Rule. I. *Arrange the terms in the statement so that the causes shall compose one couplet, and the effects the other, putting ( ) in the place of the required term.*

II. *If the required term be an extreme, divide the product of the means by the given extreme; if the required term be a mean, divide the product of the extremes by the given mean.*

Notes. 1. If the terms of any couplet be of different denominations, they must be reduced to the same unit value.

2. If the odd term be a compound number, it must be reduced to its lowest unit.

3. If the divisor and dividend contain one or more factors common to both, they should be canceled. If any of the terms of a proportion contain mixed numbers, they should first be changed to improper fractions, or the fractional part to a decimal.

4. When the vertical line is used, the divisor and the required term are written on the left, and the terms of the dividend on the right.

386. We will now give another method of solving questions in simple proportion, without making the statement, and which may be used, by those who prefer it, to the one already given. We will term it the

SECOND METHOD.

Every question which properly belongs to simple proportion must contain *four* numbers, at least *three* of which must be given (**376**). Of the three given numbers, one must always be of the same denomination as the required number. The remaining two will be *like* numbers, and bear the same relation to each other that the third does to the required number; in other words, the ratio of the third to the required number will be the same as the ratio of the other two numbers.

Regarding the third or odd term as the antecedent of the second couplet of a proportion, we find the consequent or required term by multiplying the antecedent by the ratio (**366**).

By comparing the two *like* numbers, in any given question, with the third, we may readily determine whether the answer, or required term, will be greater or less than the third term; if greater, then the ratio will be greater than 1, and the two *like* numbers may be arranged in the form of an improper fraction as a multiplier; if the answer, or required term, is to be less than the third term, then the ratio will be less than 1, and the two *like* numbers may be arranged in the form of a proper fraction, as a multiplier.

1. If 4 cords of wood cost $12, what will 20 cords cost?

OPERATION.

$$12 \times \tfrac{20}{4}, \text{ written } \frac{\not{1}\not{2}^{3} \times 20}{\not{4}} = \$60.$$

ANALYSIS. It will be readily seen in this example, that 4 cords and 20 cords are the *like* terms, and that $12 is the third term, and of the same denomination as the answer or required term.

If 4 cords cost $12, will 20 cords cost more, or less, than 4 cords? evidently more; then the answer or required term will be greater than the third term, and the ratio greater than 1. The ratio of 4 cords to 20 cords is $\frac{20}{4}$, or 5; hence the ratio of $12 to the answer must be 5, and the answer will be $\frac{20}{4}$ or 5 times $12, which is $60.

2. If 12 yards of cloth cost $48, what will 4 yards cost?

OPERATION.

$48 \times \frac{4}{12} = \$16$, *Ans.*

ANALYSIS. In this example we see that 12 yards and 4 yards are the *like* terms and $48 the third term, and of the same denomination as the required answer.

If 12 yards cost $48, will 4 yards cost more or less than 12 yards? less: then the ratio will be less than 1, and the multiplier a proper fraction. The ratio of 12 yards to 4 yards is $\frac{4}{12}$; hence the ratio of $48 to the answer is $\frac{4}{12}$, and the answer will be $\frac{4}{12}$ times $48, which is $16. Hence the following

RULE. I. *With the two given numbers, which are of the same name or kind, form a ratio greater or less than* 1, *according as the answer is to be greater or less than the third given number.*

II. *Multiply the third number by this ratio, and the product will be the required number or answer.*

NOTE. 1. Mixed numbers should first be reduced to improper fractions, and the ratio of the fractions found according to (**365**).

2. Reductions and cancellation may be applied as in the first method.

The following examples may be solved by either of the foregoing methods.

EXAMPLES FOR PRACTICE.

1. If 48 cords of wood cost $120, how much will 20 cords cost? *Ans.* $50.

2. If 6 bushels of corn cost $4.75, how much will 75 bushels cost? *Ans.* $59.37½.

3. If 8 yards of cloth cost $3½, how many yards can be bought for $50? *Ans.* 114$\frac{2}{7}$ yds.

4. If 12 horses consume 42 bushels of oats in 3 weeks, how many bushels will 20 horses consume in the same time?

5. If 7 pounds of sugar cost 75 cents, how many pounds can be bought for $9? *Ans.* 84 lbs.

6. What will 11 lb. 4 oz. of tea cost, if 3 lb. 12 oz. cost $3.50? *Ans.* $10.50.

7. If a staff 3 ft. 8 in. long cast a shadow 1 ft. 6 in., what is the height of a steeple that casts a shadow 75 feet at the same time? *Ans.* 183 ft. 4 in.

8. At \$2.75 for 14 pounds of sugar, what will be the cost of 100 pounds? *Ans.* \$19.64$\frac{2}{7}$.

9. How many bushels of wheat can be bought for \$51.06, if 12 bushels can be bought for \$13.32?

10. What will be the cost of 28$\frac{1}{2}$ gallons of molasses, if 15 hogsheads cost \$236.25? *Ans.* \$7.12$\frac{1}{2}$.

11. If 7 barrels of flour are sufficient for a family 6 months, how many barrels will they require for 11 months?

12. At the rate of 9 yards for £5 12 s., how many yards of cloth can be bought for £44 16 s.? *Ans.* 72 yds.

13. An insolvent debtor fails for \$7560, of which he is able to pay only \$3100; how much will A receive, whose claim is \$756? *Ans.* \$310.

14. If 2 pounds of sugar cost 25 cents, and 8 pounds of sugar are worth 5 pounds of coffee, what will 100 pounds of coffee cost? *Ans.* \$20.

15. If the moon move 13° 10′ 35″ in 1 day, in what time will it perform one revolution?

16. If 8$\frac{3}{4}$ bushels of corn cost \$4.20, what will be the cost of 13$\frac{1}{2}$ bushels at the same rate? *Ans.* \$6.48.

17. If 1$\frac{3}{4}$ yards of cotton cloth cost 6$\frac{1}{4}$ pence, how many yards can be bought for £10 6 s. 8 d.? *Ans.* 694$\frac{2}{5}$ yds.

18. If 12$\frac{1}{2}$ cwt. of iron cost \$42$\frac{1}{4}$, how much will 48$\frac{3}{8}$ cwt. cost? *Ans.* \$163.50+.

19. What quantity of tobacco can be bought for \$317.23, if 8$\frac{2}{5}$ lbs. cost \$1$\frac{3}{4}$? *Ans.* 15 cwt. 22.7+ lbs.

20. If 15$\frac{5}{8}$ bushels of clover seed cost \$156$\frac{1}{4}$, how much can be bought for \$95.75? *Ans.* 9 bu. 2 pk. 2$\frac{2}{5}$ qt.

21. If $\frac{5}{6}$ of a barrel of cider cost \$$\frac{60}{77}$, how much will $\frac{7}{8}$ of a barrel cost? *Ans.* \$$\frac{9}{11}$.

22. If a piece of land of a certain length, and 4 rods in breadth, contain $\frac{3}{4}$ of an acre, how much would there be if it were 11$\frac{3}{5}$ rods wide? *Ans.* 2 A. 28 rods.

23. If 13 cwt. of iron cost \$42$\frac{1}{4}$, what will 12 cwt. cost?

24. A grocer has a false balance, by which 1 pound will weigh but 12 oz.; what is the real value of a barrel of sugar that he sells for $28? *Ans.* $21.

25. A butcher in selling meat sells $14\frac{11}{16}$ oz. for a pound; how much does he cheat a customer, who buys of him to the amount of $30? *Ans.* $2.46 +.

26. If a man clear $750 by his business in 1 yr. 6 mo., how much would he gain in 3 yr. 9 mo. at the same rate?

27. If a certain business yield $350 net profits in 10 mo., in what time would the same business yield $1050 profits?

28. B and C have each a farm; B's farm is worth $25 an acre, and C's $30½; if in trading B values his land at $28 an acre, what value should C put upon his? *Ans.* $34.16.

29. If I borrow $500, and keep it 1 yr. 4 mo., for how long a time should I lend $240 as an equivalent for the favor? *Ans.* 2 yr. 9 mo. 10 da.

COMPOUND PROPORTION.

387. Compound Proportion embraces that class of questions in which the causes, or the effects, or both, are compound.

The required term may be a cause, or a single element of a cause; or it may be an effect, or a single element of an effect.

1. If 16 horses consume 128 bushels of oats in 50 days, how many bushels will 5 horses consume in 90 days?

STATEMENT.

1st cause.		2d cause.		1st effect.		2d effect
$\left\{\begin{array}{c}16\\50\end{array}\right.$	:	$\left\{\begin{array}{c}5\\90\end{array}\right.$	: :	128	:	( )

Or, $16 \times 50 : 5 \times 90 :: 128 : (\ )$

OPERATION.

$$\frac{\not{5} \times \not{9}\not{0}^{9} \times \not{1}\not{2}\not{8}^{8}}{\not{1}\not{6} \times \not{5}\not{0}} = 72 \text{ bu.}$$

ANALYSIS. In this example the required term is the second effect; and the question may be read, If 16 horses in 50 days consume 128 bushels of oats, 5 horses in 90 days will consume how many, or (blank) bushels?

NOTE. These questions are most readily performed by cancellation.

2. If \$480 gain \$84 interest in 30 months, what sum will gain \$21 in 15 months?

STATEMENT.

$$\begin{matrix}\text{1st cause.} & & \text{2d cause.} & & \text{1st effect.} & & \text{2d effect.}\\ \left\{\begin{matrix}480\\30\end{matrix}\right. & : & \left\{\begin{matrix}(\ \ )\\15\end{matrix}\right. & :: & 84 & : & 21\end{matrix}$$

OPERATION.

$$\frac{\not{4}\not{8}\not{0}^{120}\times\not{3}\not{0}^{2}\times\not{2}\not{1}}{\not{8}\not{4}\times\not{1}\not{5}}=\$240,\ \textit{Ans.}$$

ANALYSIS. The required term in this example is an element of the second cause; and the question may be read, If \$480 in 30 months gain \$84, what principal in 15 months will gain \$21?

3. If 7 men dig a ditch 60 feet long, 8 feet wide, and 6 feet deep, in 12 days, what length of ditch can 21 men dig in $2\frac{2}{3}$ days, if it be 3 feet wide and 8 feet deep?

STATEMENT.

$$\left\{\begin{matrix}7\\12\end{matrix}\right. : \left\{\begin{matrix}21\\2\frac{2}{3}\end{matrix}\right. :: \left\{\begin{matrix}60\\8\\6\end{matrix}\right. : \left\{\begin{matrix}(\ \ )\\3\\8\end{matrix}\right.$$

$$\text{Or, } 7\times12 : 21\times\tfrac{8}{3} :: 60\times8\times6 : (\ \ )\times3\times8$$

OPERATION.

$$\frac{\not{2}\not{1}\times\ 8\times\not{6}\not{0}^{5}\times\not{8}\times\not{6}^{2}}{\not{7}\times\not{1}\not{2}\times\not{3}\ \ \times\not{8}\times\not{3}}=80\text{ ft., }\textit{Ans.}$$

$$\text{Or, }\begin{array}{r|l}\not{3} & 8\\ \not{7} & \not{2}\not{1}\\ \not{1}\not{2} & \not{6}\not{0}^{5}\\ \not{8} & \not{8}\\ \not{3} & \not{6}^{2}\\ (\ \ ) & \\ \hline \end{array}$$

$$(\ \ )=80\text{ ft., }\textit{Ans.}$$

ANALYSIS. In this example the required term is the *length* of the ditch, and is an element of the second effect. The question, as stated, will read thus: if 7 men, in 12 days, dig a ditch 60 feet long, 8 feet wide, and 6 feet deep, 21 men, in $2\frac{2}{3}$ days, will dig a ditch how many, or (blank) feet long, 3 feet wide, and 8 feet deep?

Hence we have the following

RULE. I. *Of the given terms, select those which constitute the causes, and those which constitute the effects, and arrange them in couplets, putting ( ) in place of the required term.*

II. *Then, if the blank term ( ) occur in either of the extremes, make the product of the means a dividend, and the product of the extremes a divisor; but if the blank term occur in either mean, make the product of the extremes a dividend, and the product of the means a divisor.*

NOTES. 1. The causes must be exactly alike in the *number* and *kind* of their terms; the same is true of the effects.

2. The same preparation of the terms by reduction is to be observed as in simple proportion.

388. We will now solve an example according to the Second Method given in Simple Proportion.

1. If 18 men can build 42 rods of wall in 16 days, how many men can build 28 rods in 8 days?

OPERATION.

$$\not{1}\not{8}^{3} \times \frac{\not{2}\not{8}^{4}}{\not{4}\not{2}} \times \frac{\not{1}\not{6}^{2}}{\not{8}} = 24 \text{ men.}$$

ANALYSIS. We see in this example that all the terms appear in couplets, except one, which is 18 men, and that is of the same kind as the required answer.

Since compound proportion is made up of two or more simple proportions, if this third or odd term be multiplied by the compound ratio, or by the simple ratio of each couplet successively, the product will be the required term.

By comparing the terms of each couplet with the third term we may readily determine whether the answer, or term sought, will be greater or less than the third term; if greater, then the ratio will be greater than 1, and the multiplier an improper fraction; if less, the ratio will be less than 1, and the multiplier a proper fraction.

First we will compare the terms composing the first couplet, 42 rods and 28 rods, with the third term, 18 men. If 42 rods require 18 men, how many men will 28 rods require? less men; hence the ratio is less than 1, and the multiplier a proper fraction, $\frac{28}{42}$; next, if 16 days require 18 men, how many men will 8 days require? more men; hence the ratio is greater than 1, and the multiplier an improper fraction, $\frac{16}{8}$. Regarding the third term as the antecedent of a couplet, the consequent being the term sought, if we multiply this third term by the simple ratios, or by their product, we shall have the required term or answer, thus: $18 \times \frac{28}{42} \times \frac{16}{8} = 24$, as shown in the operation.

2. 5 compositors, in 16 days, of 14 hours each, can compose 20 sheets of 24 pages in each sheet, 50 lines in a page, and

40 letters in a line; in how many days, of 7 hours each, will 10 compositors compose a volume to be printed in the same letter, containing 40 sheets, 16 pages in a sheet, 60 lines in a page, and 50 letters in a line? *Ans.* 32 days.

OPERATION.

days. comp. hours. sheets. pages. lines. letters.

$$16 \times \frac{5}{10} \times \frac{14}{7} \times \frac{40}{20} \times \frac{16}{24} \times \frac{60}{50} \times \frac{50}{40} = 32 \text{ days.}$$

BY CANCELLATION.

	16
10	5
7	14
20	40
24	16[2]
50	60
40	50

32 days, *Ans.*

ANALYSIS. The required term or answer is to be in *days*; and we see that all the terms appear in pairs or couplets, except the 16 days, which is of the same kind as the answer sought.

We will proceed to compare the terms of each couplet with the 16 days. First, if 5 compositors require 16 days, how many days will 10 compositors require? less days; hence the multiplier is the proper fraction $\frac{5}{10}$, and we have $16 \times \frac{5}{10}$. Next, if 14 hours a day require 16 days, how many days will 7 hours a day require? more days; hence the multiplier is the improper fraction $\frac{14}{7}$, and we have $16 \times \frac{5}{10} \times \frac{14}{7}$. Next, if 20 sheets require 16 days, how many days will 40 sheets require? more days; hence the multiplier is the improper fraction $\frac{40}{20}$, and we have $16 \times \frac{5}{10} \times \frac{14}{7} \times \frac{40}{20}$. Pursuing the same method with the other couplets, we obtain the result as shown in the operation. Hence we have the following

RULE. I. *Of the terms composing each couplet form a ratio greater or less than* 1, *in the same manner as if the answer depended on those two and the third or odd term.*

II. *Multiply the third or odd term by these ratios successively, and the product will be the answer sought.*

NOTE. By the *odd* term is meant the one that is of the same kind as the answer.

The following examples may be solved by either of the given methods.

EXAMPLES FOR PRACTICE.

1. If 16 horses consume 128 bushels of oats in 50 days, how many bushels will 5 horses consume in 90 days?

2. If a man travel 120 miles in 3 days when the days are 12 hours long, in how many days of 10 hours each will he require to travel 360 miles? *Ans.* $10\frac{4}{5}$ days.

3. If 6 laborers dig a ditch 34 yards long in 10 days, how many yards can 20 laborers dig in 15 days? *Ans.* 170 yds.

4. If 450 tiles, each 12 inches square, will pave a cellar, how many tiles that are 9 inches long and 8 inches wide will pave the same? *Ans.* 900.

5. If it require 1200 yards of cloth $\frac{5}{4}$ wide to clothe 500 men, how many yards which is $\frac{7}{8}$ wide will it take to clothe 960 men? *Ans.* $3291\frac{3}{7}$ yds.

6. If 8 men will mow 36 acres of grass in 9 days, of 9 hours each day, how many men will be required to mow 48 acres in 12 days, working 12 hours each day? *Ans.* 6 men.

7. If 4 men, in $2\frac{1}{2}$ days, mow $6\frac{2}{3}$ acres of grass by working $8\frac{1}{4}$ hours a day, how many acres will 15 men mow in $3\frac{3}{4}$ days by working 9 hours a day? *Ans.* $40\frac{10}{11}$ acres.

8. If, by traveling 6 hours a day at the rate of $4\frac{1}{2}$ miles an hour, a man perform a journey of 540 miles in 20 days, in how many days, traveling 9 hours a day at the rate of $4\frac{2}{3}$ miles an hour, will he travel 600 miles? *Ans.* $14\frac{2}{7}$ days.

9. If $2\frac{1}{2}$ yards of cloth $1\frac{2}{5}$ yards wide cost \$3.37$\frac{1}{2}$, what cost $36\frac{1}{2}$ yards, $1\frac{1}{2}$ yards wide? *Ans.* \$52.79 +.

10. If 5 men reap 52.2 acres in 6 days, how many men will reap 417.6 acres in 12 days? *Ans.* 20 men.

11. If 6 men dig a cellar 22.5 feet long, 17.3 feet wide, and 10.25 feet deep, in 2.5 days, of 12.3 hours, in how many days, of 8.2 hours, will 9 men take to dig another, measuring 45 feet long, 34.6 wide, and 12.3 deep? *Ans.* 12 days.

12. If 54 men can build a fort in $24\frac{1}{2}$ days, working $12\frac{1}{2}$ hours each day, in how many days will 75 men do the same, when they work but $10\frac{1}{2}$ hours each day? *Ans.* 21 days.

13. If 24 men dig a trench $33\frac{3}{4}$ yards long, $5\frac{2}{3}$ wide, and $3\frac{1}{2}$ deep, in 189 days, working 14 hours each day, how many hours per day must 217 men work, to dig a trench $23\frac{1}{4}$ yards long, $3\frac{2}{3}$ wide, and $2\frac{1}{3}$ deep, in $5\frac{1}{2}$ days? *Ans.* 16 hours.

PARTNERSHIP.

389. **Partnership** is a relation established between two or more persons in trade, by which they agree to share the profits and losses of business.

390. The **Partners** are the individuals thus associated.

391. **Capital**, or **Stock**, is the money or property invested in trade.

392. A **Dividend** is the profit to be divided.

393. An **Assessment** is a tax to meet losses sustained.

CASE I.

394. To find each partner's share of the profit or loss, when their capital is employed for *equal* periods of time.

1. A and B engage in trade; A furnishes $300, and B $400 of the capital; they gain $182; what is each one's share of the profit?

OPERATION.

$300
$400
$700, whole stock.

$\frac{300}{700} = \frac{3}{7}$, A's share of the stock.

$\frac{400}{700} = \frac{4}{7}$, B's " " "

$182 × $\frac{3}{7}$ = $78, A's share of the gain.

$182 × $\frac{4}{7}$ = $104, B's " " "

ANALYSIS. Since the whole capital employed is $300 + $400 = $700, it is evident that A furnishes $\frac{300}{700} = \frac{3}{7}$ of the capital, and B $\frac{400}{700} = \frac{4}{7}$ of the capital. And since each man's share of the profit or loss will have the same ratio to the whole profit or loss that his share of the stock has to the whole stock, A will have $\frac{3}{7}$ of the entire profit, and B $\frac{4}{7}$, as shown in the operation.

We may also regard the whole capital as the *first cause*, and each man's share of the capital as the *second cause*, the whole profit or loss as the *first effect*, and each man's share of the profit or loss as the *second effect*, and solve by proportion thus:

1st cause.		2d cause.		1st effect.		2d effect.
$700	:	$300	: :	$182	:	( )
$700	:	$400	: :	$182	:	( )

$$\begin{array}{c|l} \not{7}\not{0}\not{0} & \not{3}\not{0}\not{0}^{3} \\ (\ ) & \not{1}\not{8}\not{2}^{26} \\ \hline \end{array} \qquad \begin{array}{c|l} \not{7}\not{0}\not{0} & \not{4}\not{0}\not{0}^{4} \\ (\ ) & \not{1}\not{8}\not{2}^{26} \\ \hline \end{array}$$

( ) = $78, A's profit. ( ) = $104, B's profit.

Hence we have the following

RULE. *Multiply the whole profit or loss by the ratio of the whole capital to each man's share of the capital.* Or,

The whole capital is to each man's share of the capital as the whole profit or loss is to each man's share of the profit or loss.

2\. Three men trade in company; A furnishes $8000, B $12000, and C 20000 of the capital; their gain is $1680; what is each man's share?

Ans. A's $336; B's $504; C's $840.

3\. Three persons purchased a house for $2800, of which A paid $1200, B $1000, and C $600; they rented it for $224 a year; how much of the rent should each receive?

4\. A man failed in business for $20000, and his available means amounted to only $13654; how much will two of his creditors respectively receive, to one of whom he owes $3060, and to the other $1530? *Ans.* $2089.062; $1044.531.

5\. Four men hired a coach for $13, to convey them to their respective homes, which were at distances from the place of starting as follows: A's 16 miles, B's 24 miles, C's 28 miles, and D's 36 miles; what ought each to pay?

Ans. { A $2. C. $3.50.
B $3. D $4.50. }

6\. A captain, mate, and 12 sailors took a prize of $2240, of which the captain took 14 shares, the mate 6 shares, and each sailor 1 share; how much did each receive?

7\. A cargo of corn, valued at $3475.60, was entirely lost; $\frac{1}{8}$ of it belonged to A, $\frac{1}{4}$ of it to B, and the remainder to C; how much was the loss of each, there being an insurance of $2512? *Ans.* $120.45, A's. $240.90, B's. $602.25, C's.

8. Three persons engaged in the lumber trade; two of the persons furnished the capital, and the third managed the business; they gained $2571.24, of which C received $6 as often as D $4, and E had $\frac{1}{5}$ as much as the other two for taking care of the business; how much was each one's share of the gain?

Ans. $1285.62, C's. $857.08, D's. $428.54, E's.

9. Four persons engage in the coal trade; D puts in $3042 capital; they gain $7500, of which A takes $2000, B $2800.75, and C $1685.25; how much capital did A, B, and C put in, and how much is D's share of the gain?

Ans. { A, $6000. C, $5055.75.
B, $8402.25. D's gain, $1014.

CASE II.

395. To find each partner's share of the profit or loss when their capital is employed for *unequal* periods of time.

It is evident that the respective shares of profit and loss will depend upon two conditions, viz.: *the amount of capital* invested by each, and the *time* it is employed.

1. Two persons form a partnership; A puts in $450 for 7 months, and B $300 for 9 months; they lose $156; how much is each man's share of the loss?

OPERATION.

$450 × 7 = $3150, A's capital for 1 mo.
$300 × 9 = $2700, B's " " "
$5850, entire " " "

$\frac{3150}{5850} = \frac{7}{13}$, A's share of the entire capital.
$\frac{2700}{5850} = \frac{6}{13}$, B's " " " "
$156 × $\frac{7}{13}$ = $84, A's loss.
$156 × $\frac{6}{13}$ = $72, B's "

ANALYSIS. The use of $450 capital for 7 months is the same as the use of 7 times $450, or $3150 for 1 month; and of $300 for 9 months is the same as the use of 9 times $300, or $2700 for 1 month. The entire capital for 1 month is equivalent to $3150 + $2700 = $5850. If the loss, $156, be divided between the two partners, according to Case I, the results will be the loss of each as shown in the operation.

Examples of this kind may also be solved by proportion as in Case I, the *causes* being compounded of *capital* and *time*; thus,

$5850 : $3150 : : $156 : ( )
$5850 : $2700 : : $156 : ( )

5850	3150 7
( )	156 12

( ) = $84, A's loss.

5850	2700 6
( )	156 12

( ) = $72, B's loss.

Hence the following

RULE. *Multiply each man's capital by the time it is employed in trade, and add the products. Then multiply the entire profit or loss by the ratio of the sum of the products to each product, and the results will be the respective shares of profit or loss of each partner.* Or,

Multiply each man's capital by the time it is employed in trade, and regard each product as his capital, and the sum of the products as the entire capital, and solve by proportion, as in Case I.

EXAMPLES FOR PRACTICE.

2. Three persons traded together; B put in $250 for 6 months, C $275 for 8 months, and D $450 for 4 months; they gained $825; how much was each man's share of the gain?

3. Two merchants formed a partnership for 18 months. A at first put in $1000, and at the end of 8 months he put in $600 more; B at first put in $1500, but at the end of 4 months he drew out $300; at the expiration of the time they found that they had gained $1394.64; how much was each man's share of the gain? *Ans.* A's $715.20; B's $679.44.

4. Three men took a field of grain to harvest and thresh for $\frac{1}{4}$ of the crop; A furnished 4 hands 5 days, B 3 hands 6 days, and C 6 hands 4 days; the whole crop amounted to 372 bushels; how much was each one's share?

5. William Gallup began trade January 1, 1856, with a capital of $3000, and, succeeding in business, took in M. H. Decker as a partner on the first day of March following, with

a capital of $2000; four months after they admitted J. Newman as third partner, who put in $1800 capital; they continued their partnership until April 1, 1858, when they found that $4388.80 had been gained since Jan. 1, 1856; how much was each one's share?

Ans. { $2106, Gallup's. $1300, Decker's. $ 982.80, Newman's.

6. Two persons engaged in partnership with a capital of $5600; A's capital was in trade 8 months, and his share of the profits was $560; B's capital was in 10 months, and his share of the profits was $800; what amount of capital had each in the firm? *Ans.* A, $2613.33⅓; B, $2986.66⅔.

7. A, B, and C, engaged in trade with $1930 capital; A's money was in 3 months, B's 5, and C's 7; they gained $117, which was so divided that ½ of A's share was equal to ⅓ of B's and to ¼ of C's; how much did each put in, and what did each gain?

Ans. { A, $700 capital; $26 gain. B, $630 " $39 " C, $600 " $52 "

ANALYSIS.

396. **Analysis**, in arithmetic, is the process of solving problems independently of set rules, by tracing the relations of the given numbers and the reasons of the separate steps of the operation according to the special conditions of each question.

397. In solving questions by analysis, we generally reason from the *given number* to *unity*, or 1, and then from unity, or 1, to the *required number*.

398. United States money is reckoned in dollars, dimes, cents, and mills (**180**), one dollar being uniformly valued in all the States at 100 cents; but in most of the States money is sometimes still reckoned in pounds, shillings, and pence.

NOTE. At the time of the adoption of our decimal currency by Congress, in 1786, the *colonial currency*, or *bills of credit*, issued by the colonies, had depreciated in value, and this depreciation, being unequal in the different colonies, gave rise to the different values of the State currencies; and this variation continues wherever the denominations of shillings and pence are in use.

399. In New England, Indiana, Illinois, Missouri, Virginia, Kentucky, Tennessee, Mississippi, Texas, ... } $1 = 6 s. = 72 d.

New York, Ohio, Michigan, ... $1 = 8 s. = 96 d.

New Jersey, Pennsylvania, Delaware, Maryland, ... } $1 = 7 s. 6 d. = 90 d

South Carolina, Georgia, ... } $1 = 4 s. 8 d. = 56 d.

Canada, Nova Scotia, ... } $1 = 5 s. = 60 d.

EXAMPLES FOR PRACTICE.

1. What will be the cost of 42 bushels of oats, at 3 shillings per bushel, New England currency?

OPERATION.

$42 \times 3 = 126$ s.

$126 \div 6 = \$21$ Or,

	~~42~~ 7
~~6~~	3
	$21, *Ans.*

ANALYSIS. Since 1 bushel costs 3 shillings, 42 bushels will cost 42 times 3 s., or $42 \times 3 = 126$ s.; and as 6 s. make 1 dollar New England currency, there are as many dollars in 126 s. as 6 is contained times in 126, or $21.

2. What will 180 bushels of wheat cost at 9 s. 4 d. per bushel, Pennsylvania currency?

OPERATION.

	~~180~~ 2
~~90~~	112
	$224

Or,

	~~180~~ 4
~~3~~	28
~~15~~	2
	$224, *Ans.*

ANALYSIS. Multiplying the number of bushels by the price, and dividing by the value of 1 dollar reduced to *pence*, we have $224. Or, when the pence in the given price is an aliquot part of a shilling, the price may be reduced to an improper fraction for a multiplier, thus: 9 s. 4 d. $= 9\frac{1}{3}$ s. $= \frac{28}{3}$ s., the multiplier. The value of the dollar being 7 s. 6 d. $= 7\frac{1}{2}$ s. $= \frac{15}{2}$, we divide by $\frac{15}{2}$, as in the operation.

3. What will be the cost of 3 hhd. of molasses, at 1 s. 3 d. per quart, Georgia currency?

OPERATION.

	3
	~~63~~ 9
	~~4~~
2 ~~56~~	15
2	405.00
	$202.50

ANALYSIS. In this example we first reduce 3 hhd. to quarts, by multiplying by 63 and 4, and then multiply by the price, either reduced to pence or to an improper fraction, and divide by the value of 1 dollar reduced to the same denomination as the price.

4. Sold 9 firkins of butter, each containing 56 lb., at 1 s. 6 d. per pound, and received in payment carpeting at 6 s. 9 d. per yard; how many yards of carpeting would pay for the butter?

OPERATION.

	~~9~~
	56
~~81~~	~~18~~ 2
	112 yd.

ANALYSIS. The operation in this is similar to the preceding examples, except that we divide the cost of the butter by the price of *a unit* of the article received in payment, reduced to the same denominational unit as the price of *a unit* of the article sold. The result will be the same in whatever currency.

5. What will 3 casks of rice cost, each weighing 126 pounds, at 4 d. per pound, South Carolina currency? *Ans.* $27.

6. How many pounds of tea, at 7 s. per pound, must be given for 28 lb. of butter, at 1 s. 7 d. per pound? *Ans.* $6\frac{1}{3}$.

7. Bought 2 casks of Catawba wine, each containing 72 gallons, for $648, and sold it at the rate of 10 s. 6 d. per quart, Ohio currency; how much was my whole gain? *Ans.* $108.

8. What will be the expense of keeping 2 horses 3 weeks if the expense of keeping 1 horse 1 day be 2 s. 6 d., Canada currency? *Ans.* $21.

9. How many days' work, at 6 s. 3 d. per day, must be given for 20 bushels of apples at 3 s. per bushel? *Ans.* $9\frac{3}{5}$.

10. Bought 160 lb. of dried fruit, at 1 s. 6 d. a pound, in New York, and sold it for 2 s. a pound in Philadelphia; how much was my whole gain? *Ans.* 12.66\frac{2}{3}$.

11. A merchant exchanged $43\frac{1}{2}$ yards of cloth, worth 10 s. 6 d. per yard, for other cloth worth 8 s. 3 d. per yard; how many yards did he receive? *Ans.* $55\frac{4}{11}$.

12. What will be the cost of 300 bushels of wheat at 9 s. 4 d. per bushel, Michigan currency? *Ans.* \$350.

13. If $\frac{3}{4}$ of $\frac{6}{7}$ of a ton of coal cost $\$2\frac{2}{5}$, how much will $\frac{5}{7}$ of 6 tons cost?

OPERATION.

5	12^2
18	28^4
7	30^2

\$16, *Ans.*

ANALYSIS.. Since $\frac{3}{4}$ of $\frac{6}{7} = \frac{18}{28}$ of a ton costs $\$2\frac{2}{5} = \$\frac{12}{5}$, 1 ton will cost 28 times $\frac{1}{18}$ of $\$\frac{12}{5}$, or $\$\frac{12}{5} \times \frac{28}{18}$; and $\frac{5}{7}$ of 6 tons $= \frac{30}{7}$ tons, will cost $\frac{30}{7}$ times $\frac{28}{18}$ of $\$\frac{12}{5} = \$16$.

14. If 8 men can build a wall 20 ft. long, 6 ft. high, and 4 ft. thick, in 12 days, working 10 hours a day, in how many days can 24 men build a wall 200 ft. long, 8 ft. high, and 6 ft. thick, working 8 hours a day?

OPERATION.

$$\frac{12}{1} \times \frac{8}{24} \times \frac{10}{8} \times \frac{200^{10}}{20} \times \frac{8}{6} \times \frac{6}{4} = 100 \text{ da.}$$

ANALYSIS. Since 8 men require 12 days of 10 hours each to build the wall, 1 man would require 8 times 12 days of 10 hours each, and 10 times (12×8) days of 1 hour each. To build a wall 1 ft. long would require $\frac{1}{20}$ as much time as to build a wall 20 ft. long; to build a wall 1 ft. high would require $\frac{1}{6}$ as much time as to build a wall 6 ft. high; to build a wall 1 ft. thick, $\frac{1}{4}$ as much time as to build a wall 4 ft. thick. Now, 24 men could build this wall in $\frac{1}{24}$ as many days, by working 1 hour a day, as 1 man could build it, and in $\frac{1}{8}$ as many days by working 8 hours a day, as by working 1 hour a day; but to build a wall 200 ft. long would require 200 times as many days as to build a wall 1 ft. long; to build a wall 8 ft. high would require 8 times as many days as to build a wall 1 ft. high; and to build a wall 6 ft. thick would require 6 times as many days as to build a wall 1 ft. thick.

15. If 2 pounds of tea are worth 11 pounds of coffee, and 3 pounds of coffee are worth 5 pounds of sugar, and 18 pounds of sugar are worth 21 pounds of rice, how many pounds of rice can be purchased with 12 pounds of tea?

OPERATION.

	~~21~~ 7
3 ~~18~~	5
~~3~~	11
~~2~~	~~12~~
3	385
Ans.	$128\frac{1}{3}$ lb.

ANALYSIS. Since 18 lb. of sugar are equal in value to 21 lb. of rice, 1 lb. of sugar is equal to $\frac{1}{18}$ of 21 lb. of rice, or $\frac{21}{18} = \frac{7}{6}$ lb. of rice, and 5 lb. of sugar are equal to 5 times $\frac{7}{6}$ lb. of rice, or $\frac{35}{6}$ lb.; if 3 lb. of coffee are equal to 5 lb. of sugar, or $\frac{35}{6}$ lb. of rice, 1 lb. of coffee is equal to $\frac{1}{3}$ of $\frac{35}{6}$ lb. of rice, or $\frac{35}{18}$ lb., and 11 lb. of coffee are equal to 11 times $\frac{35}{18}$ lb. of rice, or $\frac{385}{18}$ lb.; if 2 lb. of tea are equal to 11 lb. of coffee, or $\frac{385}{18}$ lb. of rice, 1 lb of tea is equal to $\frac{1}{2}$ of $\frac{385}{18}$ lb. of rice, or $\frac{385}{36}$ lb., and 12 lb. of tea are equal to 12 times $\frac{385}{36}$ lb. of rice, or $\frac{385}{3}$ lb. $= 128\frac{1}{3}$ lb.

16. If 16 horses consume 128 bushels of oats in 50 days, how many bushels will 5 horses consume in 90 days? *Ans.* 72.

17. If $\$10\frac{1}{2}$ will buy $4\frac{2}{3}$ cords of wood, how many cords can be bought for $\$24\frac{3}{4}$? *Ans.* 11.

18: Gave 52 barrels of potatoes, each containing 3 bushels, worth $33\frac{1}{3}$ cents a bushel, for 65 yards of cloth; how much was the cloth worth per yard? *Ans.* \$.80.

19. If a staff 3 ft. long cast a shadow 5 ft. in length, what is the height of an object that casts a shadow of $46\frac{2}{3}$ ft. at the same time of day? *Ans.* 28 ft.

20. Three men hired a pasture for \$63; A put in 8 sheep $7\frac{1}{2}$ months, B put in 12 sheep $4\frac{1}{6}$ months, and C put in 15 sheep $6\frac{2}{3}$ months; how much must each pay?

21. If 7 bushels of wheat are worth 10 bushels of rye, and 5 bushels of rye are worth 14 bushels of oats, and 6 bushels of oats are worth \$3, how many bushels of wheat will \$30 buy? *Ans.* 15.

22. If \$480 gain \$84 in 30 months, what capital will gain \$21 in 15 months? *Ans.* \$240.

23. How many yards of carpeting $\frac{2}{3}$ of a yard wide are equal to 28 yards $\frac{3}{4}$ of a yard wide? *Ans.* $31\frac{1}{2}$.

24. If a footman travel 130 miles in 3 days, when the days are 14 hours long, in how many days of 7 hours each will he travel 390 miles? *Ans.* 18.

25. If 6 men can cut 45 cords of wood in 3 days, how many cords can 8 men cut in 9 days? *Ans.* 180.

26. B's age is $1\frac{1}{2}$ times the age of A, and C's is $2\frac{1}{10}$ times the age of both, and the sum of their ages is 93; what is the age of each? *Ans.* A's age, 12 yrs.

27. If A can do as much work in 3 days as B can do in $4\frac{1}{2}$ days, and B can do as much in 9 days as C in 12 days, and C as much in 10 days as D in 8, how many days' work done by D are equal to 5 days' done by A? *Ans.* 8.

28. The hour and minute hands of a watch are together at 12 o'clock, M.; when will they be exactly together the third time after this?

OPERATION.

$12 \times \frac{1}{11} \times 3 = 3\frac{3}{11}$ h.

Ans. 3 h. 16 min. $21\frac{9}{11}$ sec., P. M.

ANALYSIS. Since the minute hand passes the hour hand 11 times in 12 hours, if both are together at 12, the minute hand will pass the hour hand the first time in $\frac{1}{11}$ of 12 hours, or $1\frac{1}{11}$ hours; it will pass the hour hand the second time in $\frac{2}{11}$ of 12 hours, and the third time in $\frac{3}{11}$ of 12 hours, or $3\frac{3}{11}$ hours, which would occur at 16 min. $21\frac{9}{11}$ sec. past 3 o'clock, P. M.

29. A flour merchant paid \$164 for 20 barrels of flour, giving \$9 for first quality, and \$7 for second quality; how many barrels were there of each?

OPERATION.

$9 × 20 = $180;
$180 — $164 = $16.
$9 — $7 = $2;
16 ÷ 2 = 8 bbl., 2d quality.
20 — 8 = 12 bbl., 1st "

ANALYSIS. If all had been first quality, he would have paid \$180, or \$16 more than he did pay. Every barrel of second quality made a difference of \$2 in the cost; hence there were as many barrels of second quality as \$2, the difference in the cost of one barrel, is contained times in \$16, &c.

30. A boy bought a certain number of oranges at the rate of 3 for 4 cents, and as many more at the rate of 5 for 8 cents; he sold them again at the rate of 3 for 8 cents, and gained on the whole 108 cents; how many oranges did he buy?

OPERATION.

$\frac{4}{3} + \frac{8}{5} = \frac{44}{15}$; $\frac{44}{15} \div 2 = \frac{22}{15}$, average cost.
$\frac{8}{3} - \frac{22}{15} = \frac{18}{15} = 1\frac{1}{5}$ cts., gain on each.
$108 \div 1\frac{1}{5} = 90$, number of oranges.

ANALYSIS. For those he bought at the rate of 3 for 4 cents he paid $\frac{4}{3}$ of a cent each, and for those he bought at the rate of 5 for 8 cents he paid $\frac{8}{5}$ of a cent each; and $\frac{4}{3} + \frac{8}{5} = \frac{44}{15}$ cents, what he paid for 1 of each kind, which divided by 2 gives $\frac{22}{15}$ cents, the average price of all he bought. He sold them at the rate of 3 for 8 cents, or $\frac{8}{3}$ cents each; the difference between the average cost and the price he sold them for, or $\frac{8}{3} - \frac{22}{15} = \frac{18}{15} = 1\frac{1}{5}$ cents, is the gain on each; and he bought as many oranges as the gain on one orange is contained times in the whole gain, &c.

31. A man bought 10 bushels of wheat and 25 bushels of corn for $30, and 12 bushels of wheat and 5 bushels of corn for $20; how much a bushel did he give for each?

OPERATION.

	W.	C.	
1st lot,	10	25	$30
2d "	12	5	$20
1st ÷ 5 =	2	5	$6
	10	.....	$14
1 bu. W. =			$1.40
1 bu. C. =			$ .64

ANALYSIS. We may divide or multiply either of the expressions by such a number as will render one of the commodities purchased, alike in both expressions. In this example we divide the first by 5 to make the numbers denoting the corn alike, (the same result would be produced by multiplying the second by 5,) and we have the cost of 2 bushels of wheat and 5 bushels of corn, equal to $6. Subtracting this from 12 bushels of wheat and 5 bushels of corn, which cost $20, we find the cost of 10 bushels of wheat to be $14; therefore the cost of 1 bushel is $\frac{1}{10}$ of $14, or $1.40. From any one of the expressions containing both wheat and corn, we readily find the cost of 1 bushel of corn to be 64 cents.

32. A, B, and C agree to build a barn for $270. A and B can do the work in 16 days, B and C in $13\frac{1}{3}$ days, and A and C in $11\frac{3}{7}$ days. In how many days can all do it working together? In how many days can each do it alone? What part of the pay ought each to receive?

OPERATION.

$\frac{1}{16} = \frac{5}{80}$, what A and B do in 1 day.
$\frac{3}{40} = \frac{6}{80}$, " B and C " "
$\frac{7}{80} = \frac{7}{80}$, " A and C " "
$\frac{5}{80} + \frac{6}{80} + \frac{7}{80} = \frac{18}{80}$, what A, B, and C do in 2 days.
$\frac{18}{80} \div 2 = \frac{9}{80}$, what A, B, and C do in 1 day.
$1 \div \frac{9}{80} = 8\frac{8}{9}$ days, time A, B, and C, will do the whole work together.

$\frac{9}{80} - \frac{5}{80} = \frac{4}{80}$; $1 \div \frac{4}{80} = 20$ da., C alone.
$\frac{9}{80} - \frac{6}{80} = \frac{3}{80}$; $1 \div \frac{3}{80} = 26\frac{2}{3}$ da., A "
$\frac{9}{80} - \frac{7}{80} = \frac{2}{80}$; $1 \div \frac{2}{80} = 40$ da., B "
$\frac{4}{80} \times 8\frac{8}{9} = \frac{4}{9}$, the part of the whole C did.
$\frac{3}{80} \times 8\frac{8}{9} = \frac{3}{9}$, " " " A "
$\frac{2}{80} \times 8\frac{8}{9} = \frac{2}{9}$, " " " B "

$\$270 \times \frac{4}{9} = \$120$, C's share.
$\$270 \times \frac{3}{9} = \$90$, A's "
$\$270 \times \frac{2}{9} = \$60$, B's "

ANALYSIS. Since A and B can do the work in 16 days, they can do $\frac{1}{16}$ of it in 1 day; B and C, in $13\frac{1}{3}$ or $\frac{40}{3}$ days, they can do $\frac{3}{40}$ of it in 1 day; A and C, in $11\frac{3}{7}$ or $\frac{80}{7}$ days, they can do $\frac{7}{80}$ of it in 1 day. Then A, B, and C, by working 2 days each, can do $\frac{1}{16} + \frac{3}{40} + \frac{7}{80} = \frac{18}{80}$ of the work, and by working 1 day each they can do $\frac{1}{2}$ of $\frac{18}{80}$, or $\frac{9}{80}$ of the work; and it will take them as many days working together to do the whole work as $\frac{9}{80}$ is contained times in 1, or $8\frac{8}{9}$ days.

Now, if we take what any two of them do in 1 day from what the three do in 1 day, the remainder will be what the third does; we thus find that A does $\frac{3}{80}$, B $\frac{2}{80}$, and C $\frac{4}{80}$.

Next, if we denote the whole work by 1, and divide it by the part each does in 1 day, we have the number of days that it will take each to do it alone, viz.: A $26\frac{2}{3}$ days, B 40 days, and C 20 days. And each should receive such a part of \$270 as would be expressed by the part he does in 1 day, multiplied by the number of days he works, which will give to A \$90, B \$60, and C \$120.

33. If 6 oranges and 7 lemons cost 33 cents, and 12 oranges and 10 lemons cost 54 cents, what is the price of 1 of each?
Ans. Oranges, 2 cents; lemons, 3 cents.

34. If an army of 1000 men have provisions for 20 days, at the rate of 18 oz. a day to each man, and they be reinforced by 600 men, upon what allowance per day must each man be put, that the same provisions may last 30 days? *Ans.* $7\frac{1}{2}$ oz.

35. There are 54 bushels of grain in 2 bins; and in one bin are 6 bushels less than $\frac{1}{2}$ as much as there is in the other; how many bushels in the larger bin? *Ans.* 40.

36. The sum of two numbers is 20, and their difference is equal to $\frac{1}{3}$ of the greater number; what is the greater number? *Ans.* 12.

37. If A can do as much work in 2 days as C in 3 days, and B as much in 5 days as C in 4 days; what time will B require to execute a piece of work which A can do in 6 weeks? *Ans.* $11\frac{1}{4}$ weeks.

38. How many yards of cloth, $\frac{3}{4}$ of a yard wide, will line 36 yards $1\frac{1}{4}$ yards wide? *Ans.* 60.

39. How many sacks of coffee, each containing 104 lbs, at 10 d. per pound N, Y. currency, will pay for 80 yards of broadcloth at $\$3\frac{1}{4}$ per yard? *Ans.* 24.

40. A person, being asked the time of day, replied, the time past noon is equal to $\frac{1}{5}$ of the time to midnight; what was the hour? *Ans.* 2, P. M.

41. A market woman bought a number of peaches at the rate of 2 for 1 cent, and as many more at the rate of 3 for 1 cent, and sold them at the rate of 5 for 3 cents, gaining 55 cents; how many peaches did she buy? *Ans.* 300.

42. A can build a boat in 18 days, working 10 hours a day, and B can build it in 9 days, working 8 hours a day; in how many days can both together build it, working 6 hours a day?

43. A man, after spending $\frac{1}{2}$ of his money, and $\frac{1}{3}$ of the remainder, had \$10 left; how much had he at first?

44. If 30 men can perform a piece of work in 11 days, how many men can accomplish another piece of work, 4 times as large, in $\frac{1}{5}$ of the time? *Ans.* 600.

45. If $16\frac{1}{4}$ lb. of coffee cost $\$3\frac{1}{4}$, how much can be bought for \$1.25? *Ans.* $6\frac{1}{4}$ lb.

46. A man engaged to write for 20 days, receiving \$2.50 for every day he labored, and forfeiting \$1 for every day he was idle; at the end of the time he received \$43; how many days did he labor? *Ans.* 18.

47. A, B, and C can perform a piece of work in 12 hours; A and B can do it in 16 hours, and A and C in 18 hours; what part of the work can B and C do in $9\frac{1}{7}$ hours? *Ans.* $\frac{4}{9}$.

ALLIGATION.

400. Alligation treats of mixing or compounding two or more ingredients of different values. It is of two kinds — *Alligation Medial* and *Alligation Alternate.*

401. Alligation Medial is the process of finding the *average* price or quality of a compound of several simple ingredients whose prices or qualities are known.

1. A miller mixes 40 bushels of rye worth 80 cents a bushel, and 25 bushels of corn worth 70 cents a bushel, with 15 bushels of wheat worth $1.50 a bushel; what is the value of a bushel of the mixture?

OPERATION.

$$\begin{array}{r} 80 \times 40 = \$32.00 \\ 70 \times 25 = \quad 17.50 \\ 1.50 \times \underline{15} = \quad \underline{22.50} \\ 80 \quad)\ 72.00 \\ \hline \$.90, \textit{ Ans.} \end{array}$$

ANALYSIS. Since 40 bushels of rye at 80 cents a bushel is worth $32, and 25 bushels of corn at 70 cents a bushel is worth $17.50, and 15 bushels of wheat at $1.50 a bushel is worth $22.50, therefore the entire mixture, consisting of 80 bushels, is worth $72, and one bushel is worth $\frac{1}{80}$ of $72, or $72 \div 80 = \$.90$. Hence the following

RULE. *Divide the entire cost or value of the ingredients by the sum of the simples.*

EXAMPLES FOR PRACTICE.

2. A wine merchant mixes 12 gallons of wine, at $1 per gallon, with 5 gallons of brandy worth $1.50 per gallon, and 3 gallons of water of no value; what is the worth of one gallon of the mixture? *Ans.* $.975.

3. An innkeeper mixed 13 gallons of water with 52 gallons of brandy, which cost him $1.25 per gallon; what is the value of 1 gallon of the mixture, and what his profit on the sale of the whole at $6\frac{1}{4}$ cents per gill? *Ans.* $1 a gallon; $65 profit.

4. A grocer mixed 10 pounds of sugar at 8 cts. with 12 pounds at 9 cts. and 16 pounds at 11 cts., and sold the mixture at 10 cents per pound; did he gain or lose by the sale, and how much? *Ans.* He gained 16 cts.

5. A grocer bought $7\frac{1}{2}$ dozen of eggs at 12 cents a dozen, 8 dozen at $10\frac{1}{2}$ cents a dozen, 9 dozen at 11 cents a dozen, and $10\frac{1}{2}$ dozen at 10 cents a dozen. He sells them so as to make 50 per cent. on the cost; how much did he receive per dozen? *Ans.* $16\frac{1}{8}$ cents.

6. Bought 4 cheeses, each weighing 50 pounds, at 13 cents a pound; 10, weighing 40 pounds each, at 10 cents a pound; and 24, weighing 25 pounds each, at 7 cents a pound; I sold the whole at an average price of $9\frac{1}{2}$ cents a pound; how much was my whole gain? *Ans.* \$6.

402. Alligation Alternate is the process of finding the proportional quantities to be taken of several ingredients, whose prices or qualities are known, to form a mixture of a required price or quality.

CASE I.

403. To find the proportional quantity to be used of each ingredient, when the mean price or quality of the mixture is given.

1. What relative quantities of timothy seed worth \$2 a bushel, and clover seed worth \$7 a bushel, must be used to form a mixture worth \$5 a bushel?

OPERATION.

$$5\left\{\begin{array}{c|c|c} 2 & \frac{1}{3} & 2 \\ 7 & \frac{1}{2} & 3 \end{array}\right\} \textit{Ans.}$$

ANALYSIS. Since on every ingredient used whose price or quality is *less* than the mean rate there will be a *gain*, and on every ingredient whose price or quality is *greater* than the mean rate there will be a *loss*, and since the gains and losses must be exactly equal, the relative quantities used of each should be such as represent the unit of *value*. By selling one bushel of timothy seed worth \$2, for \$5, there is a gain of \$3; and to gain \$1 would require $\frac{1}{3}$ of a bushel, which we place opposite the 2. By selling one bushel of clover seed worth \$7, for \$5, there is a loss of \$2; and to lose \$1 would require $\frac{1}{2}$ of a bushel, which we place opposite the 7.

In every case, to find the unit of value we must divide \$1 by the gain or loss per bushel or pound, &c. Hence, if, every time we take $\frac{1}{3}$ of a bushel of timothy seed, we take $\frac{1}{2}$ of a bushel of clover seed, *the gain* and loss will be exactly equal, and we shall have $\frac{1}{3}$ and $\frac{1}{2}$ *for the proportional quantities.*

If we wish to express the proportional numbers in integers, we may reduce these fractions to a common denominator, and use their numerators, since fractions having a common denominator are to each other as their numerators. (**365**) thus, $\frac{1}{3}$ and $\frac{1}{2}$ are equal to $\frac{2}{6}$ and $\frac{3}{6}$, and the proportional quantities are 2 bushels of timothy seed to 3 bushels of clover seed.

2. What proportions of teas worth respectively 3, 4, 7 and 10 shillings a pound, must be taken to form a mixture worth 6 shillings a pound?

OPERATION.

		1	2	3	4	5
6	3	$\frac{1}{3}$		4		4
	4		$\frac{1}{2}$		1	1
	7		1		2	2
	10	$\frac{1}{4}$		3		3

ANALYSIS. To preserve the equality of gains and losses, we must always compare two prices or simples, one *greater* and one *less* than the mean rate, and treat each pair or couplet as a separate example. In the given example we form two couplets, and may compare either 3 and 10, 4 and 7, or 3 and 7, 4 and 10.

We find that $\frac{1}{3}$ of a lb. at 3 s. must be taken to gain 1 shilling, and $\frac{1}{4}$ of a lb. at 10 s. to lose 1 shilling; also $\frac{1}{2}$ of a lb. at 4 s. to gain 1 shilling, and 1 lb. at 7 s. to lose 1 shilling. These proportional numbers, obtained by comparing the two couplets, are placed in columns 1 and 2. If, now, we reduce the numbers in columns 1 and 2 to a common denominator, and use their numerators, we obtain the integral numbers in columns 3 and 4, which, being arranged in column 5, give the proportional quantities to be taken of each.*

It will be seen that in comparing the simples of any couplet, one of which is greater, and the other less than the mean rate, the proportional number finally obtained for either term is the difference between the mean rate and the other term. Thus, in comparing 3 and 10, the proportional number of the former is 4, which is the difference between 10 and the mean rate 6; and the proportional number of the latter is 3, which is the difference between 3 and the mean rate. The same is true of every other couplet. Hence, when the simples and the mean rate are integers, the intermediate steps taken to obtain the final proportional numbers as in columns 1, 2, 3, and 4, may be omitted, and the same results readily found by taking the difference between each simple and the mean rate, and placing it opposite the one with which it is compared.

---

* Prof. A. B. Canfield, of Oneida Conference Seminary, N. Y., used this method of Alligation, essentially, in the instruction of his classes as early as 1846, and he was doubtless the author of it.

From the foregoing examples and analyses we derive the following

RULE. I. *Write the several prices or qualities in a column, and the mean price or quality of the mixture at the left.*

II. *Form couplets by comparing any price or quality less, with one that is greater than the mean rate, placing the part which must be used to gain 1 of the mean rate opposite the less simple, and the part that must be used to lose 1 opposite the greater simple, and do the same for each simple in every couplet.*

III. *If the proportional numbers are fractional, they may be reduced to integers, and if two or more stand in the same horizontal line, they must be added; the final results will be the proportional quantities required.*

NOTES. 1. If the numbers in any couplet or column have a common factor, it may be rejected.

2. We may also multiply the numbers in any couplet or column by any multiplier we choose, without affecting the equality of the gains and losses, and thus obtain an indefinite number of results, any one of which being taken will give a correct final result.

EXAMPLES FOR PRACTICE.

3. A grocer has sugars worth 10 cents, 11 cents, and 14 cents per pound; in what proportions may he mix them to form a mixture worth 12 cents per pound?

Ans. 1 lb. at 10 cts., and 2 lbs. at 11 and 14 cts.

4. What proportions of water at no value, and wine worth $1.20 a gallon, must be used to form a mixture worth 90 cents a gallon? *Ans.* 1 gal. of water to 3 gals. of wine.

5. A farmer had sheep worth $2, $2½, $3, and $4 per head; what number could he sell of each, and realize an average price of $2¾ per head?

Ans. 3 of the 1st kind, and 1 each of the 2d and 3d, and 5 of the 4th kind.

6. What relative quantities of alcohol 80, 84, 87, 94, and 96 per cent. strong must be used to form a mixture 90 per cent. strong?

Ans. 6 of the first two kinds, four of the 3d, 3 of the 4th, and 16 of the 5th.

CASE II.

404. When the quantity of one of the simples is limited.

1. A miller has oats worth 30 cents, corn worth 45 cents, and barley worth 84 cents per bushel; he desires to form a mixture worth 60 cents per bushel, and which shall contain 40 bushels of corn; how many bushels of oats and barley must he take?

OPERATION.

	30	$\frac{1}{30}$		4		4	20	
60	45		$\frac{1}{15}$		8	8	40	*Ans.*
	84	$\frac{1}{24}$	$\frac{1}{24}$	5	5	10	50	

ANALYSIS. By the same process as in Case I we find the proportional quantities of each to be 4 bushels of oats, 8 of corn, and 10 of barley. But we wish to use 40 bushels of corn, which is 5 times the proportional number 8, and to preserve the equality of gain and loss we must take 5 times the proportional quantity of each of the other simples, or $5 \times 4 = 20$ bushels of oats, and $5 \times 10 = 50$ bushels of barley. Hence the following

RULE. *Find the proportional quantities as in Case I. Divide the given quantity by the proportional quantity of the same ingredient, and multiply each of the other proportional quantities by the quotient thus obtained.*

EXAMPLES FOR PRACTICE.

2. A merchant has teas worth 40, 60, 75, and 90 cents per pound; how many pounds of each must he use with 20 pounds of that worth 75 cents, to form a mixture at 80 cents.

Ans. 20 lbs. each of the first three kinds, and 130 lbs. of the fourth.

3. A farmer bought 24 sheep at $2 a head; how many must he buy at $3 and $5 a head, that he may sell the whole at an average price of $4 a head, without loss?

Ans. 24 at $3, and 72 at $5.

4. How much alcohol worth 60 cents a gallon, and how much water, must be mixed with 180 gallons of rum worth $1.30 a gallon, that the mixture may be worth 90 cents a gallon? *Ans.* 60 gallons each of alcohol and water.

5. How many acres of land worth 35 dollars an acre must be added to a farm of 75 acres, worth $50 an acre, that the average value may be $40 an acre? *Ans.* 150 acres.

6. A merchant mixed 80 pounds of sugar worth $6\frac{1}{4}$ cents per pound with some worth $8\frac{1}{3}$ cents and 10 cents per pound, so that the mixture was worth $7\frac{1}{2}$ cents per pound; how much of each kind did he use?

CASE III.

405. When the quantity of the whole compound is limited.

1. A grocer has sugars worth 6 cents, 7 cents, 12 cents, and 13 cents per pound. He wishes to make a mixture of 120 pounds worth 10 cents a pound; how many pounds of each kind must he use?

OPERATION.

10	6	$\frac{1}{4}$		3		3	30
	7		$\frac{1}{3}$		2	2	20
	12		$\frac{1}{2}$		3	3	30
	13	$\frac{1}{3}$		4		4	40
						12	120

ANALYSIS. By Case I we find the proportional quantities of each to be 3 lbs. at 6 cts., 2 lbs. at 7 cts., 3 lbs at 12 cts., and 4 lbs. at 13 cts. By adding the proportional quantities, we find that the mixture would be but 12 lbs. while the required mixture is 120, or 10 times 12. If the whole mixture is to be 10 times as much as the *sum* of the proportional quantities, then the quantity of each simple used must be 10 times as much as its respective proportional, which would require 30 lbs. at 6 cts., 20 lbs. at 7 cts., 30 lbs. at 12 cts., and 40 lbs. at 13 cts. Hence we deduce the following

RULE. *Find the proportional numbers as in Case I. Divide the given quantity by the sum of the proportional quantities, and multiply each of the proportional quantities by the quotient thus obtained.*

EXAMPLES FOR PRACTICE.

2. A farmer sold 170 sheep at an average price of 14 shillings a head; for some he received 9 s., for some 12 s., for some 18 s., and for others 20 s.; how many of each did he sell? *Ans.* 60 at 9 s., 40 at 12 s., 20 at 18 s., and 50 at 20 s.

3. A jeweler melted together gold 16, 18, 21, and 24 carats fine, so as to make a compound of 51 ounces 22 carats fine; how much of each sort did he take? *Ans.* 6 ounces each of the first three, and 33 ounces of the last.

4. A man bought 210 bushels of oats, corn, and wheat, and paid for the whole $178.50; for the oats he paid $\$\frac{1}{2}$, for the corn $\$\frac{3}{4}$, and for the wheat $\$1\frac{1}{2}$ per bushel; how many bushels of each kind did he buy? *Ans.* 78 bushels each of oats and corn, and 54 bushels of wheat.

5. A, B, and C are under a joint contract to furnish 6000 bushels of corn, at 48 cts. a bushel; A's corn is worth 45 cts., B's 51 cts., and C's 54 cts.; how many bushels must each put into the mixture that the contract may be fulfilled?

6. One man and 3 boys received $84 for 56 days' labor; the man received $3 per day, and the boys $\$\frac{1}{2}$, $\$\frac{3}{4}$, and $\$1\frac{3}{4}$ respectively; how many days did each labor? *Ans.* The man 16 days, and the boys 24, 4, and 12 days respectively.

INVOLUTION.

406. A **Power** is the product arising from multiplying a number by itself, or repeating it several times as a factor; thus, in $2 \times 2 \times 2 = 8$, the product, 8, is a power of 2.

407. The **Exponent** of a power is the number denoting how many times the factor is repeated to produce the power, and is written above and a little to the right of the factor; thus, $2 \times 2 \times 2$ is written 2^3, in which 3 is the exponent. Exponents likewise give names to the powers, as will be seen in the following illustrations:

$3 = 3^1 = 3$, the first power of 3;
$3 \times 3 = 3^2 = 9$, the second power of 3
$3 \times 3 \times 3 = 3^3 = 27$, the third power of 3.

408. The **Square** of a number is its second power.

409. The **Cube** of a number is its third power.

410. **Involution** is the process of raising a number to a given power.

411. A **Perfect Power** is a number that can be exactly produced by the involution of some number as a root; thus, 25 and 32 are perfect powers, since $25 = 5 \times 5$, and $32 = 2 \times 2 \times 2 \times 2 \times 2$.

1. What is the cube of 15?

OPERATION.

$15 \times 15 \times 15 = 3375$. *Ans.*

ANALYSIS. We multiply 15 by 15, and the product by 15, and obtain 3375, which is the 3d power, or cube of 15, since 15 has been taken 3 times as a factor. Hence, we have the following

RULE. *Multiply the number by itself as many times, less 1, as there are units in the exponent of the required power.*

EXAMPLES FOR PRACTICE.

2. What is the square of 25? *Ans.* 625.
3. What is the square of 135? *Ans.* 18225.
4. What is the cube of 72? *Ans.* 373248.
5. What is the 4th power of 24? *Ans.* 331776.
6. Raise 7.2 to the third power. *Ans.* 373.248.
7. Involve 1.06 to the 4th power. *Ans.* 1.26247696.
8. Involve .12 to the 5th power. *Ans.* .0000248832.
9. Involve 1.0002 to the 2d power. *Ans.* 1.00040004.
10. What is the cube of $\frac{2}{5}$?

OPERATION.

$$\frac{2}{5} \times \frac{2}{5} \times \frac{2}{5} = \frac{2 \times 2 \times 2}{5 \times 5 \times 5} = \frac{2^3}{5^3} = \frac{8}{125}$$

It is evident from the above operation, that

A common fraction may be raised to any power, by raising each of its terms, separately, to the required power.

11. What is the square of $\frac{3}{8}$? *Ans.* $\frac{9}{64}$.
12. What is the cube of $\frac{13}{14}$? *Ans.* $\frac{2197}{2744}$.
13. Raise $24\frac{3}{4}$ to the 2d power. *Ans.* $612\frac{9}{16}$.

EVOLUTION.

412. A **Root** is a factor repeated to produce a power; thus, in the expression $5 \times 5 \times 5 = 125$, 5 is the root from which the power, 125, is produced.

413. **Evolution** is the process of extracting the root of a number considered as a power, and is the reverse of Involution.

414. The **Radical Sign** is the character, $\sqrt{}$, which, placed before a number, denotes that its root is to be extracted.

415. The **Index** of the root is the figure placed above the radical sign, to denote what root is to be taken. When no index is written, the index 2 is always understood.

416. A **Surd** is the indicated root of an imperfect power.

417. Roots are named from the corresponding powers, as will be seen in the following illustrations:

The square root of 9 is 3, written $\sqrt{9} = 3$.
The cube root of 27 is 3, written $\sqrt[3]{27} = 3$.
The fourth root of 81 is 3, written $\sqrt[4]{81} = 3$.

418. Any number whatever may be considered a power whose root is to be extracted; but only the perfect powers can have *exact* roots.

SQUARE ROOT.

419. The **Square Root** of a number is one of the two equal factors that produce the number; thus the square root of 49 is 7, for $7 \times 7 = 49$.

420. In extracting the square root, the first thing to be determined is the relative number of places in a given number and its square root. The law governing this relation is exhibited in the following examples: —

Roots.	Squares.	Roots.	Squares.
1	1	1	1
9	81	10	1,00
99	98,01	100	1,00,00
999	99,80,01	1000	1,00,00,00

From these examples we perceive

1st. That a root consisting of 1 place may have 1 or 2 places in the square.

2d. That in all cases the addition of 1 place to the root adds 2 places to the square. Hence,

If we point off a number into two-figure periods, commencing at the right hand, the number of full periods and the left hand full or partial period will indicate the number of places in the square root; the highest period answering to the highest figure of the root.

421. 1. What is the length of one side of a square plat containing an area of 5417 sq. ft.?

OPERATION.

	54,17	73.6
	49	
140	517	
143	429	
146.0	88.00	
146.6	87.96	
	4	

ANALYSIS. Since the given figure is a square, its side will be the square root of its area, which we will proceed to compute. Pointing off the given number, the 2 periods show that there will be two integral figures, tens and units, in the root. The tens of the root must be extracted from the first or left hand period, 54 hundreds. The greatest square in 54 hundreds is 49 hundreds, the square of 7 tens; we therefore write 7 tens in the root, at the right of the given number.

Since the entire root is to be the side of a square, let us form a square (Fig. I), the side of which is 70 feet long. The area of this square is $70 \times 70 = 4900$ sq. ft., which we subtract from the given number. This is done in the operation by subtracting the square number, 49, from the first period, 54, and to the remainder bringing down the second period, making the entire remainder 517.

Fig. I.

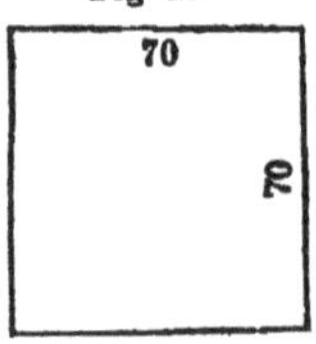

If we now enlarge our square (Fig. I) by the addition of 517 square feet, in such a manner as to preserve the square form, its sise will be that of the required square. To preserve the square form, the addition must be so made as to extend the square equally in two directions; it will therefore be composed of 2 oblong figures at the sides, and a little square at the corner (Fig. II). Now, the *width* of this addition will be the additional length to the side of the square, and consequently *the next figure in the root.* To find *width* we divide square contents, or area, by *length.* But the length of one side of the little square cannot be found till the width of the addition be determined, because it is equal to this width. We will therefore add the lengths of the 2 oblong figures, and the sum will be sufficiently near the whole length to be used as a trial divisor.

Each of the oblong figures is equal in length to the side of the square first formed; and their united length is $70 + 70 = 140$ ft. (Fig. III). This number is obtained in the operation by doubling the 7 and annexing 1 cipher, the result being written at the left of the dividend. Dividing 517, the area, by 140, the approximate length, we obtain 3, the probable width of the addition, and second figure of the root. Since 3 is also the side of the little square, we can now find the entire length of the addition, or the complete divisor, which is $70 + 70 + 3 = 143$ (Fig. III).

Fig. II.

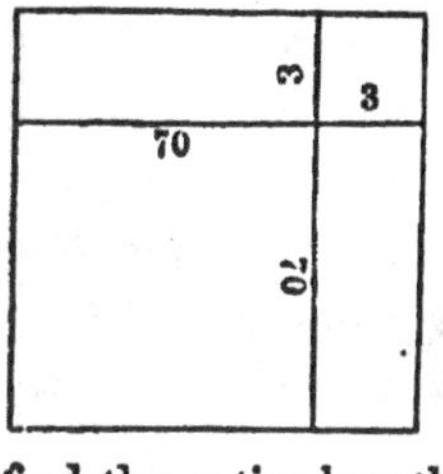

Fig. III.

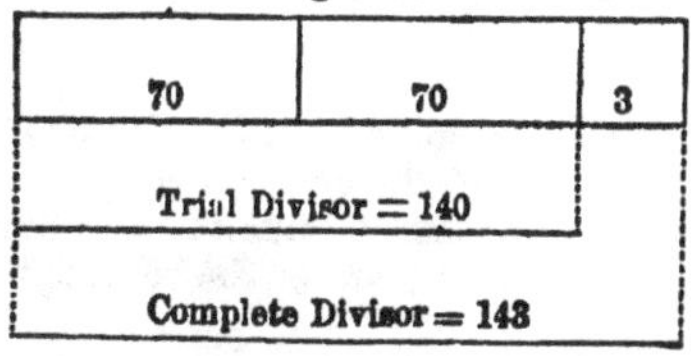

This number is found in the operation by adding 3 to the trial divisor, and writing the result underneath. Multiplying the complete divisor, 143, by the trial quotient figure, 3, and subtracting the product from the dividend, we obtain another remainder of 88 square feet. With this remainder, for the same reason as before, we must proceed to make a new enlargement; and we bring down two decimal ciphers, because the next figure of the root, being tenths, its square will be hundredths. The trial divisor to obtain the width of this new enlargement, or the next figure in the root, will be, for the same reason as before, twice 73, the root already found, with one cipher annexed. But since the 7 has already been doubled in the operation, we have only to double the last figure of the complete divisor, 143, and annex a cipher, to obtain the new trial divisor, 146.0. Dividing, we obtain .6 for the trial figure of the root; then proceeding as before, we obtain 146.6 for a complete divisor, 87.96 for a product; and there is still a remainder of .04. Hence, the side of the given square plat is 73.6 feet, nearly. From this example and analysis we deduce the following

RULE. I. *Point off the given number into periods of two figures each, counting from unit's place toward the left and right.*

II. *Find the greatest square number in the left hand period, and write its root for the first figure in the root; subtract the square number from the left hand period, and to the remainder bring down the next period for a dividend.*

III. *At the left of the dividend write twice the first figure of the root, and annex one cipher, for a trial divisor; divide the dividend by the trial divisor, and write the quotient for a trial figure in the root.*

IV. *Add the trial figure of the root to the trial divisor for a complete divisor; multiply the complete divisor by the trial figure in the root, and subtract the product from the dividend, and to the remainder bring down the next period for a new dividend.*

V. *To the last complete divisor add the last figure of the root, and to the sum annex one cipher, for a new trial divisor, with which proceed as before.*

NOTES. 1. If at any time the product be greater than the dividend, diminish the trial figure of the root, and correct the erroneous work.

2. If a cipher occur in the root, annex another cipher to the trial divisor, and another period to the dividend, and proceed as before.

EXAMPLES FOR PRACTICE.

2. What is the square root of 406457.2516?

OPERATION.

		40,64,57.25,16	637.54, *Ans.*
		36	
Trial divisor,	120	464	
Complete "	123	369	
Trial "	1260	9557	
Complete "	1267	8869	
Trial "	1274.0	688.25	
Complete "	1274.5	637.25	
Trial "	1275.00	51.0016	
Complete "	1275.04	51.0016	

NOTES. 3. The decimal points in the work may be omitted, care being taken to point off in the root according to the number of decimal periods used.

4. The pupil will acquire greater facility, and secure greater accuracy, by keeping units of like order under each other, and each divisor opposite the corresponding dividend, by the use of the lines, as shown in the operation.

3. What is the square root of 576? *Ans.* 24.

4. What is the square root of 6561? *Ans.* 81.
5. What is the square root of 444889? *Ans.* 667.
6. What is the square root of 994009? *Ans.* 997.
7. What is the square root of 29855296? *Ans.* 5464.
8. What is the square root of 3486784401? *Ans.* 59049.
9. What is the square root of 54819198225?

NOTE. The cipher in the trial divisor may be omitted, and its place, after division, occupied by the trial root figure, thus forming in succession only *complete divisors*.

10. What is the square root of 2?

	2.	1.4142 +, *Ans.*
	1	
	100	
24	96	
	400	
281	281	
	11900	
2824	11296	
	60400	
28282	56564	

11. Extract the square roots of the following numbers:

$\sqrt{3} = 1.7320508+$	$\sqrt{7} = 2.6457513+$
$\sqrt{5} = 2.2360679+$	$\sqrt{8} = 2.8284271+$
$\sqrt{6} = 2.4494897+$	$\sqrt{10} = 3.1622776+$

12. What is the square root of .00008836? *Ans.* .0094.
13. What is the square root of .0043046721? *Ans.* .06561.

NOTES. 5. The square root of a common fraction may be obtained by extracting the square roots of the numerator and denominator separately, provided the terms are perfect squares; otherwise, the fraction may first be reduced to a decimal.

6. Mixed numbers may be reduced to the decimal form before extracting the root; or, if the denominator of the fraction is a perfect square, to an improper fraction.

14. Extract the square root of $\frac{625}{6561}$. *Ans.* $\frac{25}{81}$.
15. Extract the square root of $\frac{7056}{9216}$. *Ans.* $\frac{7}{8}$.
16. Extract the square root of $\frac{2}{3}$. *Ans.* .816496 +.
17. Extract the square root of $17\frac{3}{8}$. *Ans.* 4.1683 +.

APPLICATIONS.

422. An **Angle** is the opening between two lines that meet each other; thus, the two lines, A B and A C, meeting, form an angle at A.

423. A **Triangle** is a figure having three sides and three angles, as A, B, C.

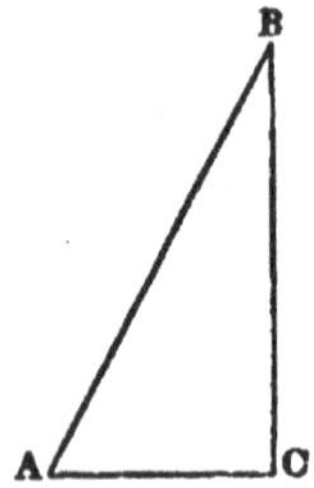

424. A **Right-Angled Triangle** is a triangle having one right angle, as at C.

425. The **Base** is the side on which it stands, as A, C.

426. The **Perpendicular** is the side forming a right angle with the base, as B, C.

427. The **Hypotenuse** is the side opposite the right angle, as A, B.

428. Those examples given below, which relate to triangles and circles, may be solved by the use of the two following principles, which are demonstrated in geometry.

1st. *The square of the hypotenuse of a right-angled triangle is equal to the sum of the squares of the other two sides.*

2d. *The areas of two circles are to each other as the squares of their radii, diameters, or circumferences.*

1. The two sides of a right-angled triangle are 3 and 4 feet; what is the length of the hypotenuse?

OPERATION.

$3^2 = 9$, square of one side.
$4^2 = 16$, square of the other side.
25, square of hypotenuse.
$\sqrt{25} = 5$, *Ans.*

ANALYSIS. Squaring the two sides and adding, we find the sum to be 25; and since the sum is equal to the square of the hypotenuse, we extract the square root, and obtain 5 feet, the hypotenuse. Hence,

To find the hypotenuse. *Add the squares of the two sides, and extract the square root of the sum.*

To find either of the shorter sides. *Subtract the square of the given side from the square of the hypotenuse, and extract the square root of the remainder.*

EXAMPLES FOR PRACTICE.

2. If an army of 55225 men be drawn up in the form of a square, how many men will there be on a side? *Ans.* 235.

3. A man has 200 yards of carpeting $1\frac{1}{8}$ yards wide; what is the length of one side of the square room which this carpet will cover? *Ans.* 45 feet.

4. How many rods of fence will be required to inclose 10 acres of land in the form of a square? *Ans.* 160 rods.

5. The top of a castle is 45 yards high, and the castle is surrounded by a ditch 60 yards wide; required the length of a rope that will reach from the outside of the ditch to the top of the castle. *Ans.* 75 yards.

6. Required the height of a May-pole, which being broken 39 feet from the top, the end struck the ground 15 feet from the foot. *Ans.* 75 feet.

7. A ladder 40 feet long is so placed in a street, that without being moved at the foot, it will reach a window on one side 33 feet, and on the other side 21 feet, from the ground; what is the breadth of the street? *Ans.* 56.64 + ft.

8. A ladder 52 feet long stands close against the side of a building; how many feet must it be drawn out at the bottom, that the top may be lowered 4 feet? *Ans.* 20 feet.

9. Two men start from one corner of a park one mile square, and travel at the same rate. A goes by the walk around the park, and B takes the diagonal path to the opposite corner, and turns to meet A at the side. How many rods from the corner will the meeting take place? *Ans.* 93.7 + rods.

10. A room is 20 feet long, 16 feet wide, and 12 feet high; what is the distance from one of the lower corners to the opposite upper corner? *Ans.* 28.284271 + feet.

11. It requires 63.39 rods of fence to inclose a circular field of 2 acres; what length will be required to inclose 3 acres in circular form? *Ans.* 77.63 + rods.

12. The radius of a certain circle is 5 feet; what will be the radius of another circle containing twice the area of the first? *Ans.* 7.07106 + feet.

CUBE ROOT.

429. The **Cube Root** of a number is one of the three equal factors that produce the number. Thus, the cube root of 27 is 3, since $3 \times 3 \times 3 = 27$.

430. In extracting the cube root, the first thing to be determined is the relative number of places in a cube and its root. The law governing this relation is exhibited in the following examples: —

Roots.	Cubes.	Roots.	Cubes.
1	1	1	1
9	729	10	1,000
99	907,299	100	1,000,000
999	997,002,999	1000	1,000,000,000

From these examples, we perceive,

1st. That a root consisting of 1 place may have from 1 to 3 places in the cube.

2d. That in all cases the addition of 1 place to the root adds three places to the cube. Hence,

If we point off a number into three-figure periods, commencing at the right hand, the number of full periods and the left hand full or partial period will indicate the number of places in the cube root, the highest period answering to the highest figure of the root.

431. 1. What is the length of one side of a cubical block containing 413494 solid inches?

OPERATION — COMMENCED.

```
      413494 | 74
      343
  ------------
14700  70494
```

ANALYSIS. Since the block is a cube, its side will be the cube root of its solid contents, which we will proceed to compute. Pointing off the given number, the two periods show that there will be two figures, tens and units, in the root. The tens of the root must be extracted from the first period, 413 thousands. The greatest cube in 413 thousands is 343 thousands, the cube of 7 tens; we therefore write 7 tens in the root at the right of the given number.

Since the entire root is to be the side of a cube, let us form a cubical block (Fig. I), the side of which is 70 inches in length. The contents of this cube are $70 \times 70 \times 70 = 343,000$ solid inches, which we subtract from the given number. This is done in the operation by subtracting the cube number, 343, from the first period, 413, and to the remainder bringing down the second period, making the entire remainder 70494.

Fig. I.

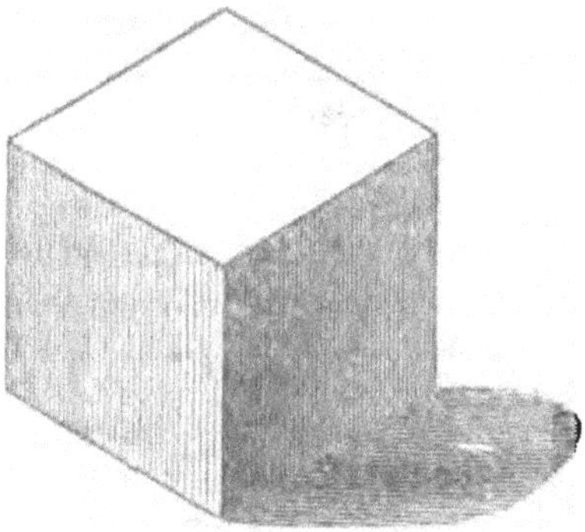

If we now enlarge our cubical block, (Fig. I), by the addition of 70494 solid inches, in such a manner as to preserve the cubical form, its size will be that of the required block. To preserve the cubical form, the addition must be made upon three adjacent sides or faces. The addition will therefore be composed of 3 flat blocks to cover the 3 faces, (Fig. II); 3 oblong blocks to fill the vacancies at the edges, (Fig. III); and 1 small cubical block to fill the vacancy at the corner, (Fig. IV). Now, the *thickness* of this enlargement will be the *additional length* of the *side of the cube*, and, consequently, the *second figure in the root.* To find *thickness*, we may divide solid contents by *surface*, or *area*. But the area of the 3 oblong blocks and little cube cannot be found till the thickness of the addition be determined, because their common breadth is equal to this thickness. We will therefore find the area of the three flat blocks, which is sufficiently near the whole area to be used as a *trial divisor*. As these are each equal in length and breadth to the side of the cube whose faces they cover, the whole area of the three is $70 \times 70 \times 3 = 14700$ square inches. This number is obtained in the operation by annexing 2 ciphers to three times the square of 7; the result being written at the left hand of the dividend. Dividing, we obtain

Fig. II.

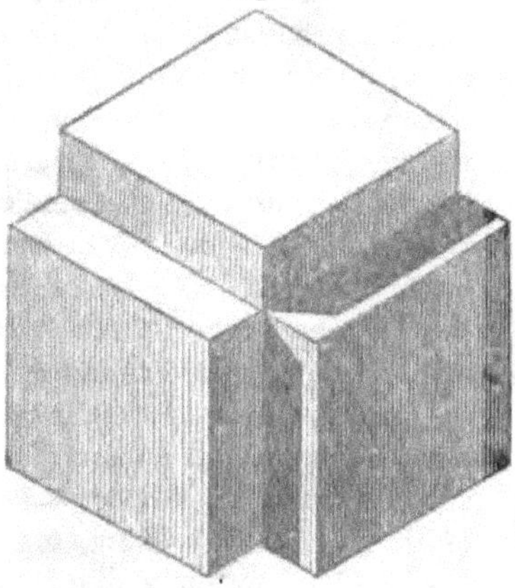

4, the probable thickness of the addition, and second figure of the root. With this assumed figure, we will *complete* our divisor by adding the area of the 4 blocks, before undetermined. The 3 oblong blocks are each 70 inches long; and the little cube, being equal in each of its dimensions to the thickness of the addition, must be 4 inches long. Hence, their united length is 70 + 70 + 70 + 4 = 214. This number is obtained in the operation by multiplying the 7 by 3, and annexing the 4 to the product, the result being written in column I, on the next line below the trial divisor. Multiplying 214, the length, by 4, the common width, we obtain 856, the area of the four blocks, which added to 14700, the trial divisor, makes 15556, the *complete divisor*; and multiplying this by 4, the second figure in the root, and subtracting the product from the dividend, we obtain a remainder of 8270 solid inches. With this remainder, for the same reason as before, we must proceed to make a new enlargement. But since we have already two figures in the root, answering to the two periods of the given number, the next figure of the root must be a decimal; and we therefore annex to the remainder a period of three decimal ciphers, making 8270.000 for a new dividend.

Fig. III

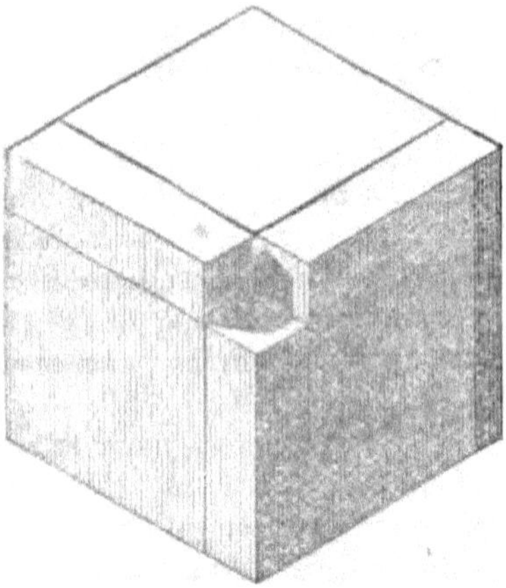

OPERATION — CONTINUED.

I.	II.			
			413494	74
			343	
		14700	70494	
214	856	15556	62224	
			8270.000	

Fig. IV.

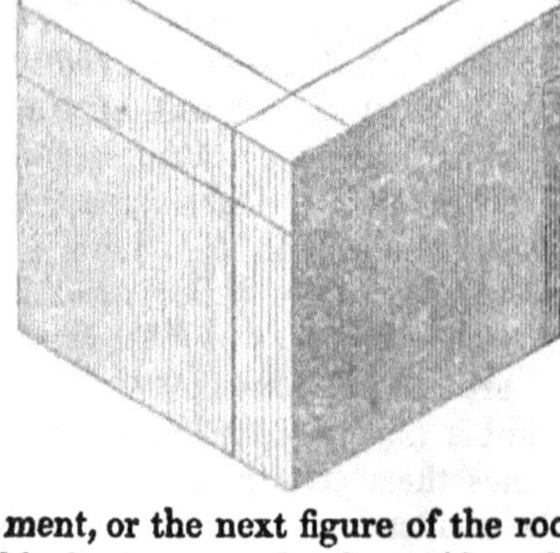

The trial divisor to obtain the thickness of this second enlargement, or the next figure of the root, will be the area of three new flat blocks to cover the three sides of the cube already formed; and this surface, (Fig. IV,) is composed of 1 face of each of the flat blocks already used, 2 faces of each of the oblong blocks, and 3 faces of the little cube. But we have in the complete divisor, 15556, 1 face of each of the flat blocks, oblong blocks, and little cube; and in the correction of the trial divisor, 856, 1 face of each of the oblong blocks and of the little cube; and in the square of the last root figure, 16, a third face of the little cube. Hence, 16 + 856 + 15556 = 16428, the significant figures of the new trial divisor. This number is obtained in the operation by adding the square of the last root figure mentally, and combining units of like order,

OPERATION — CONTINUED.

I.	II.		413494 | 74.5
			343
		14700	70494
214	856	15556	62224
		1642800	8270.000
222.5	111.25	16539.25	8269.625
			.375

thus: 16, 6, and 6 are 28, and we write the unit figure in the new trial divisor; then 2 to carry, and 5 and 5 are 12, &c. We annex 2 ciphers to this trial divisor, as to the former, and dividing, obtain 5, the third figure in the root. To complete the second trial divisor, after the manner of the first, the correction may be found by annexing .5 to 3 times the former figures, 74, and multiplying this number by .5. But as we have, in column I, 3 times 7, with 4 annexed, or 214, we need only multiply the last figure, 4, by 3, and annex .5, making 222.5, which multiplied by .5 gives 111.25, the correction required. Then we obtain the complete divisor, 16539.25, the product, 8269.625, and the remainder, .375, in the manner shown by the former steps. From this example and analysis we deduce the following

RULE. I. *Point off the given number into periods of three figures each, counting from units' place toward the left and right.*

II. *Find the greatest cube that does not exceed the left hand period, and write its root for the first figure in the required root; subtract the cube from the left hand period, and to the remainder bring down the next period for a dividend.*

III. *At the left of the dividend write three times the square of the first figure of the root, and annex two ciphers, for a trial divisor; divide the dividend by the trial divisor, and write the quotient for a trial figure in the root.*

IV. *Annex the trial figure to three times the former figure, and write the result in a column marked* I, *one line below the trial divisor; multiply this term by the trial figure, and write the product on the same line in a column marked* II; *add this term as a correction to the trial divisor, and the result will be the complete divisor.*

V. *Multiply the complete divisor by the trial figure, and subtract the product from the dividend, and to the remainder bring down the next period for a new dividend.*

VI. *Add the square of the last figure of the root, the last term in column* II, *and the complete divisor together, and annex two ciphers, for a new trial divisor; with which obtain another trial figure in the root.*

VII. *Multiply the unit figure of the last term in column* I *by* 3, *and annex the trial figure of the root for the next term of column* I; *multiply this result by the trial figure of the root for the next term of column* II; *add this term to the trial divisor for a complete divisor, with which proceed as before.*

NOTES. 1. If at any time the product be greater than the dividend, diminish the trial figure of the root, and correct the erroneous work.

2. If a cipher occur in the root, annex two more ciphers to the trial divisor, and another period to the dividend; then proceed as before with column I, annexing both cipher and trial figure.

EXAMPLES FOR PRACTICE.

1. What is the cube root of 79.112?

OPERATION.

			79.112	4.2928 +, *Ans.*
			64.	
		4800	15112	
122	244	5044	10088	
		529200	5024000	
1269	11421	540621	4865589	
		55212300	158411000	
12872	25744	55238044	110476088	
		5526379200	47934912000	
128768	1030144	5527409344	44219274752	
			3714637248 rem.	

2. What is the cube root of 84604519? *Ans.* 439.
3. What is the cube root of 2357947691? *Ans.* 1331.
4. What is the cube root of 10963240788375? *Ans.* 22215.
5. What is the cube root of 270671777032189896? *Ans.* 646866.
6. What is the cube root of .091125? *Ans.* .45.
7. What is the cube root of .000529475129? *Ans.* .0809.
8. What is the approximate cube root of .008649? *Ans.* .2052+.

Extract the cube roots of the following numbers:—

$\sqrt[3]{2} = 1.259921+$	$\sqrt[3]{5} = 1.709975+$
$\sqrt[3]{3} = 1.442249+$	$\sqrt[3]{6} = 1.817120+$
$\sqrt[3]{4} = 1.587401+$	$\sqrt[3]{7} = 1.912931+$

APPLICATIONS IN CUBE ROOT.

1. What is the length of one side of a cistern of cubical form, containing 1331 solid feet? *Ans.* 11 feet.

2. The pedestal of a certain monument is a square block of granite, containing 373248 solid inches; what is the length of one of its sides? *Ans.* 6 feet.

3. A cubical box contains 474552 solid inches; what is the area of one of its sides? *Ans.* $42\frac{1}{4}$ sq. ft.

4. How much paper will be required to make a cubical box which shall contain $\frac{27}{64}$ of a solid foot? *Ans.* $\frac{3}{8}$ of a yard.

5. A man wishes to make a bin to contain 125 bushels, of equal width and depth, and length double the width; what must be its dimensions? *Ans.* Width and depth, 51.223+ inches; length, 102.446+ inches.

NOTE. Spheres are to each other as the cubes of their diameters or circumferences.

6. There are two spheres whose solid contents are to each other as 27 to 343; what is the ratio of their diameters?

ANALYSIS. Since spheres are to each other as the cubes of their diameters, the diameters will be to each other as the cube roots of the spheres; and $\sqrt[3]{27} = 3$, $\sqrt[3]{343} = 7$; hence the diameters required are as 3 to 7.

7. The diameter of a sphere containing 1 solid foot is 14.9 inches; what is the diameter of a sphere containing 2 solid feet? *Ans.* 18.7 + inches.

8. If a cable 4in. in circumference, will support a sphere 2ft. in diameter, what is the diameter of that sphere which will be supported by a cable 5in. in circumference? *Ans.* 2.32 + ft.

ARITHMETICAL PROGRESSION.

432. An **Arithmetical Progression,** or **Series,** is a series of numbers increasing or decreasing by a common difference. Thus, 3, 5, 9, 11, &c., is an arithmetical progression with an ascending series, and 13, 10, 7, 4, &c., is an arithmetical progression with a descending series.

433. The **Terms** of a series are the numbers of which it is composed.

434. The **Extremes** are the first and last terms.

435. The **Means** are the intermediate terms.

436. The **Common Difference** is the difference between any two adjacent terms.

437. There are *five parts* in an arithmetical series, any *three* of which being given, the other *two* may be found. They are as follows: the *first term, last term, common difference, number of terms,* and *sum of all the terms.*

CASE I.

438. To find the last term when the first term, common difference, and number of terms are given.

Let 2 be the first term of an ascending series, and 3 the common difference; then the series will be written, 2, 5, 8, 11, 14, or analyzed thus: 2, 2 + 3, 2 + 3 + 3, 2 + 3 + 3 + 3, 2 + 3 + 3 + 3 + 3.

Here we see that, in an *ascending* series, we obtain the *second* term by *adding* the common difference *once* to the first term; the *third* term, by adding the common difference *twice* to the first term; and, in general, we obtain *any* term by adding the common difference *as many times* to the first term as there are terms less *one.*

NOTE. The analysis for a descending series would be similar. Hence,

RULE. *Multiply the common difference by the number of terms less one, and add the product to the first term, if the series be ascending, and subtract it if the series be descending.*

EXAMPLES.

1. The first term of an ascending series is 4, the common difference 3, and the number of terms 19; what is the last term? *Ans.* 58.

2. What is the 13th term of a descending series whose first term is 75, and common difference 5? *Ans.* 15.

3. A boy bought 18 hens, paying 2 cents for the first, 5 cents for the second, and 8 cents for the third, in arithmetical progression; what did he pay for the last hen?

4. What is the 40th term of the series $\frac{1}{2}$, $\frac{3}{4}$, 1, $1\frac{1}{4}$, &c.? *Ans.* $10\frac{1}{4}$.

5. A man travels 9 days; the first day he goes 20 miles, the second 25 miles, increasing 5 miles each day; how far does he travel the last day of his journey? *Ans.* 60 miles.

6. What is the amount of $100, at 7 per cent., for 45 years? $\$100 + \$7 \times 45 = \$415$, *Ans.*

CASE II.

439. To find the common difference when the extremes and number of terms are given.

Referring to the series, 2, 5, 8, 11, 14, analyzed in **438**, we readily see that, by subtracting the *first term* from any term, we have left the *common difference* taken as many times as there are terms less one; thus, by taking away 2 in the fifth term, $2 + 3 + 3 + 3 + 3$, we have 3 taken 4 times. Hence,

RULE. *Divide the difference of the extremes by the number of terms less one.*

EXAMPLES.

1. The first term is 2, the last term is 17, and the number of terms is 6; what is the common difference? *Ans.* 3.

2. A man has seven children, whose ages are in arithmetical progression; the youngest is 2 years old, and the eldest 14; what is the common difference of their ages? *Ans.* 2 years.

3. The extremes of an arithmetical series are 1 and 50½, and the number of terms is 34; what is the common difference?

4. An invalid commenced to walk for exercise, increasing the distance daily by a common difference; the first day he walked 3 miles, and the 14th day 9½ miles; how many miles did he walk each day?

NOTE. When we have found the common difference we may add it once, twice, &c., to the first term, and we have the series, and consequently the *means.*

Ans. 3, 3½, 4, 4½, 5, 5½, &c.

CASE III.

440. To find the number of terms when the extremes and common difference are given.

Examining the series, 2, 5, 8, 11, 14, analyzed in **438**, we also see that after taking away the *first* term from any term, we have left the common difference taken as many times as the *number of terms,* less 1. Hence,

RULE. *Divide the difference of the extremes by the common difference, and add* 1 *to the quotient.*

EXAMPLES.

1. The extremes are 7 and 43, and the common difference is 4; what is the number of terms? *Ans.* 10.

2. The first term is 2½, the last term is 40, and the common difference is 7½; what is the number of terms? *Ans.* 6.

3. A laborer agreed to build a fence on the following conditions: for the first rod he was to have 6 cents, with an increase of 4 cents on each successive rod; the last rod came to 226 cents; how many rods did he build? *Ans.* 56 rods.

CASE IV.

441. To find the sum of all the terms when the extremes and number of terms are given.

To deduce a rule for finding the *sum of all the terms*, we will take the series 2, 5, 8, 11, 14, writing it under itself in an inverse order, and add each term; thus,

$$2 + 5 + 8 + 11 + 14 = 40, \text{ once the sum.}$$
$$14 + 11 + 8 + 5 + 2 = 40, \text{ “ “ “}$$
$$16 + 16 + 16 + 16 + 16 = 80, \text{ twice the sum.}$$

Here we perceive that 16, the sum of the extremes, multiplied by 5, the number of terms, equals 80, which is *twice the sum of the series*. Dividing 80 by 2 gives 40, which is the sum required. Hence,

RULE. *Multiply the sum of the extremes by the number of terms, and divide the product by 2.*

EXAMPLES.

1. The extremes are 5 and 32, and the number of terms 12; what is the sum of all the terms? *Ans.* 222.

2. How many strokes does a common clock make in 12 hours? *Ans.* 78 strokes.

3. What debt can be discharged in a year by weekly payments in arithmetical progression, the first being $24, and the last $1224? *Ans.* $32448.

4. Suppose 100 apples were placed in a line 2 yards apart, and a basket 2 yards from the first apple; how far would a boy travel to gather them up singly, and return with each separately to the basket? *Ans.* 20200 yards.

GEOMETRICAL PROGRESSION.

442. A **Geometrical Progression** is a series of numbers increasing or decreasing by a constant multiplier.

When the multiplier is *greater* than a unit, the series is

ascending; thus, 2, 6, 18, 54, 162, is an *ascending* series, in which 3 is the multiplier.

When the multiplier is *less* than a unit, the series is *descending*; thus, 162, 54, 18, 6, 2, is a *descending* series, in which $\frac{1}{3}$ is the multiplier.

443. The **Ratio** is the constant multiplier.

444. In every geometrical progression there are five *parts* to be considered, any *three* of which being given, the other *two* may be determined. They are as follows: The *first term, last term, ratio, number of terms*, and the *sum of all the terms.*

The first and last terms are the *extremes*, and the intermediate terms are the *means.*

CASE I.

445. To find any term, the first term, the ratio, and number of terms being given.

The first term is supposed to exist independently of the ratio. Using the ratio *once* as a factor, we have the second term; using it *twice*, or its *second power*, we have the *third* term; using it *three times*, or its *third power*, we have the fourth term; and, in general, the *power* of the ratio in any term is *one less* than the number of the term. The ascending series, 2, 6, 18, 54, may be analyzed thus: 2, 2×3, $2 \times 3 \times 3$, $2 \times 3 \times 3 \times 3$.

In this illustration we see that

1st term, 2, is independent of the ratio.

2d " $6 = 2 \times 3 =$ the first term into the 1st power of the ratio.

3d term, $18 = 2 \times 3^2 =$ the first term into the 2d power of the ratio.

4th term, $54 = 2 \times 3^3 =$ the first term into the 3d power of the ratio. Hence

RULE. *Multiply the first term by that power of the ratio denoted by the number of terms less* 1.

EXAMPLES.

1. The first term of a geometrical series is 4, the ratio is 3; what is the 9th term? *Ans.* $4 \times 3^8 = 26244$.

2. The first term is 1024, the ratio $\frac{1}{4}$, and the number of terms 8; what is the last term? *Ans.* $\frac{1}{16}$.

3. A boy bought 9 oranges, agreeing to pay 1 mill for the first orange, 2 mills for the second, and so on; what did the last orange cost him? *Ans.* \$.256.

4. The first term is 7, the ratio $\frac{1}{7}$, and the number of terms 7; what is the last term? *Ans.* $\frac{1}{16807}$.

5. What is the amount of \$1 at compound interest for 5 years, at 7 per cent. per annum? *Ans.* \$1.40255 +.

NOTE. In the above example the first term is \$1, the ratio is \$1.07, and the number of terms is 6.

6. A drover bought 7 oxen, agreeing to pay \$3 for the first ox, \$9 for the second, \$27 for the third, and so on; what did the last ox cost him? *Ans.* \$2187.

CASE II.

446. To find the sum of all the terms, the extremes and ratio being given.

If we take the series 2, 8, 32, 128, 512, in which the ratio is 4, multiply each term by the ratio, and add the terms thus multiplied, we shall have

$8 + 32 + 128 + 512 + 2048 = 2728 =$ { *Four times* the sum of all the terms.

But $2 + 8 + 32 + 128 + 512 = \quad 682 =$ { *Once* the sum of all the terms.

Hence, by subtracting, we get $2048 - 2 = 2046 =$ { *Three times* the sum of all the terms.

Dividing by 3, the ratio less one, $2046 \div 3 = 682 =$ { *Once* the sum of all the terms.

The subtraction is performed by taking the *lower line* or series from the *upper*. All the terms cancel except 2048 and 2. Taking their difference, which is 3 times the sum, and dividing by 3, the ratio less one, we must have the sum of all the terms. Hence

RULE. *Multiply the greater extreme by the ratio, subtract the less extreme from the product, and divide the remainder by the ratio less* 1.

NOTE. Let every *decreasing* series be inverted, and the first term called the last; then the ratio will be *greater* than a unit. If the series be *infinite*, the first term is a cipher.

EXAMPLES.

1. The first term is 2, the last term 512, and the ratio 3; what is the sum of all the terms? *Ans.* 767.

2. The first term is 4, the last term is 262144, and the ratio is 4; what is the sum of the series? *Ans.* 349524.

3. The first term of a descending series is 162, the last term 2, and the ratio $\frac{1}{3}$; what is the sum? *Ans.* 242.

4. What is the value of $\frac{1}{5}$, $\frac{1}{25}$, $\frac{1}{125}$, &c., to infinity? *Ans.* $\frac{1}{4}$.

NOTE. In the following examples we first find the *last term* by the Rule under Case I.

5. What yearly debt can be discharged by monthly payments, the first being $2, the second $6, and the third $18, and so on, in geometrical progression? *Ans.* $531440.

6. If a grain of wheat produce 7 grains, and these be sown the second year, each yielding the same increase, how many bushels will be produced at this rate in 12 years, if 1000 grains make a pint? *Ans.* 252315 bu. $4\frac{1}{8}$ qt.

7. Six persons of the Morse family came to this country 200 years ago; suppose that their number has doubled every 20 years since, what would be their number now?

NOTE. The other cases in Progression will be found in the Higher Arithmetic.

PROMISCUOUS EXAMPLES.

1. One half the sum of two numbers is 800, and one half the difference of the same numbers is 200; what are the numbers? *Ans.* 1000 and 600.

2. What number is that to which, if you add $\frac{2}{5}$ of $\frac{3}{11}$ of itself, the sum will be 61? *Ans.* 55.

3. What part of a day is 3 h. 21 min. 15 sec.? *Ans.* $\frac{161}{1152}$.

4. A commission merchant received 70 bags of wheat, each containing 3 bu. 3 pk. 3 qt.; how many bushels did he receive?

5. Four men, A, B, C, and D, are in possession of $1100; A has a certain sum, B has twice as much as A, C has $300, and D has $200 more than C; how many dollars has A? *Ans.* $100.

6. At a certain election, 3000 votes were cast for three candidates, A, B, and C; B had 200 more votes than A, and C had 800 more than B; how many votes were cast for A? *Ans.* 600.

7. What part of $17\frac{1}{2}$ is $3\frac{1}{4}$? *Ans.* $\frac{13}{70}$.

8. The difference between $\frac{6}{7}$ and $\frac{7}{8}$ of a number is 10; what is the number? *Ans.* 560.

9. A merchant bought a hogshead of rum for $28.35; how much water must be added to reduce the first cost to 35 cents per gallon? *Ans.* 18 gal.

10. A and B traded with equal sums of money; A gained a sum equal to $\frac{1}{5}$ of his stock; B lost $200, and then he had $\frac{1}{2}$ as much as A; how much was the original stock of each? *Ans.* $500.

11. A farmer sold 17 bushels of barley, and 13 bushels of wheat, for $31.55; he received for the wheat 35 cents a bushel more than for the barley; what was the price of each per bushel?

Ans. Barley, $.90; wheat, $1.25.

12. What is the interval of time between March 20, 21 minutes past 3 o'clock, P. M., and April 11th, 5 minutes past 7 o'clock, A. M.? *Ans.* 21 da. 15 h. 44 min.

13. What o'clock is it when the time from noon is $\frac{9}{11}$ of the time to midnight? *Ans.* 5 o'clock 24 min. P. M.

14. What is the least number of gallons of wine that can be shipped in either hogsheads, tierces, or barrels, just filling the vessels, without deficit or excess? *Ans.* 126 gal.

15. A ferryman has four boats; one will carry 8 barrels, another 9, another 15, and another 16; what is the smallest number of barrels that will make full freight for any one, and all of the boats?

16. A and B have the same income; A saves $\frac{1}{8}$ of his, but B, by spending $30 a year more than A, at the end of four years finds himself $40 in debt; what is their income, and how much does each spend a year?

Ans. { Income, $160. A spends $140. B spends $170. }

17. If a load of plaster weighing 1825 pounds cost $2.19, how much is that per ton of 2000 pounds? *Ans.* $2.40.

18. If $2\frac{1}{2}$ yards of cloth $1\frac{3}{5}$ yards wide cost $$3.37\frac{3}{5}$, what will be the cost of $36\frac{1}{2}$ yards $1\frac{1}{2}$ yards wide? *Ans.* $52.779.

19. I lend my neighbor $200 for 6 months; how long ought he to lend me $1000 to balance the favor?

20. Bought railroad stock to the amount of $2356.80, and found that the sum invested was 40 per cent of what I had left; what sum had I at first? *Ans.* $8248.80.

21. 20 per cent. of $\frac{1}{2}$ of a number is what per cent. of $\frac{4}{5}$ of it?

Ans. $12\frac{1}{2}$.

22. Divide a prize of $10200 among 60 privates, 6 subaltern officers, 3 lieutenants, and a commander, giving to each subaltern double the share of a private, each lieutenant 3 times as much as the subaltern, and to the commander double that of a lieutenant; how much is each man's share? *Ans.* Com. $1200; each man, $100.

23. A is 51 miles in advance of B, who is in pursuit of him; A travels 16 miles per hour, and B 19; in how many hours will B overtake A?

24. How much wool, at 20, 30, and 54 cents per pound, must be mixed with 95 pounds at 50 cents, to make the whole mixture worth 40 cents per pound?

Ans. 133 lb. at 20; 95 lb. at 30; 190 lb. at 54 cents.

25. If 240 bushels of wheat are purchased at the rate of 18 bushels for $$22\frac{1}{2}$, and sold at the rate of $22\frac{1}{2}$ bushels for $33.75, what is the profit on the whole? *Ans.* $60.

26. My horse, wagon, and harness together are worth $169; the wagon is worth 4 times the harness, and the horse is worth double the wagon; what is the value of each?

Ans. Horse, $104. Wagon, $ 52. Harness, $ 13.

27. The shadow of a tree measures 42 feet; a staff 40 inches in length casts a shadow 18 inches at the same time; what is the height of the tree? *Ans.* $93\frac{1}{3}$ ft.

28. If a piece of land 40 rods long and 4 rods wide make an acre, how wide must it be to contain the same if it be but 25 rods long? *Ans.* $6\frac{2}{5}$ rods.

29. A, B, and C are employed to do a piece of work for $26.45; A and B together are supposed to do $\frac{4}{5}$ of it, A and C $\frac{9}{10}$, and B and C $\frac{13}{20}$, and paid proportionally; how much must each receive?

30. If 12 ounces of wool make $2\frac{1}{2}$ yards of cloth that is 6 quarters wide, how many pounds of wool will it take for 150 yards of cloth 4 quarters wide?

31. Six persons, A, B, C, D, E, and F, are to share among them $6300: A is to have $\frac{1}{7}$ of it, B $\frac{1}{5}$, C $\frac{2}{5}$, D is to have as much as A and C together, and the remainder is to be divided between E and F in the proportion of 3 to 5; how much does each one receive?

32. What is the amount of $200 for 8 years at 6 per cent. compound interest? *Ans.* $318.769.

33. A garrison, consisting of 360 men, was provisioned for 6 months; but at the end of 5 months they dismissed so many of the men that the remaining provision lasted 5 months longer; how many men were sent away?

34. A certain principal, at compound interest for 5 years, at 6 per cent., will amount to $669.113; in what time will the same principal amount to the same sum, at 6 per cent. simple interest?

Ans. 5 yr. 7 mo. 19.3+da.

35. Paid $148.352 for 9728 feet of pine lumber; how much was that per thousand?

36. Comparing two numbers, 483 was found to be their least common multiple, and 23 their greatest common divisor; what is the product of the numbers compared? *Ans.* 11,109.

37. Eight workmen, laboring 7 hours a day for 15 days, were able to execute $\frac{1}{3}$ of a job; in how many days can they complete the residue, by working 9 hours a day, if 4 workmen are added to their number? *Ans.* $15\frac{5}{9}$ days.

38. If a hall 36 feet long and 9 feet wide require 36 yards of carpeting 1 yard wide to cover the floor, how many yards $1\frac{1}{4}$ yards wide will cover a floor 60 feet long and 27 feet wide?

Ans. 144 yards.

39. A, B, and C traded in company; A put in \$1 as often as B put in \$3, and B put in \$2 as often as C put in \$5; B's money was in twice as long as C's, and A's twice as long as B's; they gained \$52.50; how much was each man's share of the gain?

Ans. A's, \$12. B's, \$18. C's, \$22.50.

40. A and B found a watch worth \$45, and agreed to divide the value of it in the ratio of $\frac{2}{3}$ to $\frac{5}{6}$; how much was each one's share?

Ans. \$20, A's. \$25, B's.

41. A man received \$33.25 interest on a sum of money, loaned 5 years previous, at 7 per cent.; what was the sum lent?

Ans. \$95.

42. The diameter of a ball weighing 32 pounds is 6 inches; what is the diameter of a ball weighing 4 pounds? *Ans.* 3 inches.

43. Divide \$360 in the proportion of 2, 3, and 4.

Ans. \$80, \$120, \$160.

44. If by working $6\frac{2}{5}$ hours a day a man can accomplish a job in $12\frac{1}{2}$ days, how many days will be required if he work $8\frac{1}{3}$ hours per day? *Ans.* $9\frac{9}{10}$ days.

45. An open court contains 40 square yards; how many stones, 9 inches square, will be required to pave it? *Ans.* 640.

46. A drover paid \$76 for calves and sheep, paying \$3 for calves, and \$2 for sheep; he sold $\frac{1}{4}$ of his calves and $\frac{2}{5}$ of his sheep for \$23, and in so doing lost 8 per cent. on their cost; how many of each did he purchase? *Ans.* 12 calves; 20 sheep.

47. If a cistern, $17\frac{1}{2}$ feet long, $10\frac{1}{2}$ broad, and 13 deep, hold 546 barrels, how many barrels will that cistern hold that is 16 feet long, 7 broad, and 15 deep? *Ans.* 384 bbls.

48. If 12 men, working 9 hours a day, for $15\frac{3}{4}$ days, were able to execute $\frac{3}{8}$ of a job, how many men may be withdrawn, and the residue be finished in 15 days more, if the laborers are employed only 7 hours a day? *Ans.* 4 men.

49. A general formed his men into a square, that is, an equal number in rank and file, and found that he had 59 men over; and increasing the number in both rank and file by 1 man, he wanted 84 men to complete the square; how many men had he? *Ans.* 5100.

50. Bought wheat at $1.50 per bushel, corn at $.75 per bushel, and barley at $.60 per bushel; the wheat cost twice as much as the corn, and the corn twice as much as the barley; of the sum paid, $243 and $\frac{1}{4}$ of the whole was for wheat, and $153 and $\frac{1}{12}$ of the whole was for the corn; how many bushels of grain did I purchase?

Ans. 756.

51. Divide $630 among 3 persons, so that the second shall have $\frac{3}{4}$ as much as the first, and the third $\frac{1}{2}$ as much as the other two; what is the share of each?

Ans. { 1st, $240. 2d, $180. 3d, $210.

52. Bought a hogshead of molasses for $28, and 7 gallons leaked out; at what rate per gallon must the remainder be sold to gain 20 per cent.?

53. 20 per cent. of $\frac{4}{5}$ of a number is how many per cent. of 2 times $\frac{3}{4}$ of $1\frac{1}{2}$ times the number? *Ans.* $7\frac{1}{9}$.

54. B and C, trading together, find their stock to be worth $3500, of which C owns $2100; they have gained 40 per cent. on their first capital; what did each put in?

Ans. { B, $1000. C, $1500.

55. If the ridge of a building be 8 feet above the beams, and the building be 32 feet wide, what must be the length of rafters?

56. If 12 workmen, in 12 days, working 12 hours a day, can make up 75 yards of cloth, $\frac{3}{4}$ of a yard wide, into articles of clothing: how many yards, 1 yard wide, can be made up into like articles, by 10 men, working 9 days, 8 hours each day? *Ans.* $23\frac{7}{16}$.

57. A grocer sells a farmer 100 pounds of sugar, at 12 cents a pound, and makes a profit of 9 per cent.; the farmer sells him 100 pounds of beef, at 6 cents a pound, and makes a profit of 10 per cent.; who gains the more by the trade, and how much?

Ans. The grocer gains $.445 + more.

58. In 1 yr. 4 mo. $311.50 amounted to $336.42, at simple interest; what was the rate per cent.? *Ans.* 6.

59. Three persons engage to do a piece of work for $20; A and B estimate that they do $\frac{4}{5}$ of it, A and C that they do $\frac{2}{3}$ of it, and B and C that they do $\frac{2}{5}$ of it; according to this estimate, what part of the $20 should each man receive? *Ans.* A's, $$11\frac{3}{7}$; B's, $$5\frac{5}{7}$; C's, $$2\frac{6}{7}$.

60. Paid $375, at the rate of $2\frac{1}{2}$ per cent., for insurance on a cotton factory and the machinery; for what amount was the policy given?

61. A merchant bought goods in Boston to the amount of $1000, and gave his note, dated Jan. 1, 1857, on interest after 3 months; six months after the note was given he paid $560, and 5 months after the first payment he paid $406; what was due Aug. 23, 1859?

Ans. $66.63+

62. If $\frac{2}{3}$ of A's money be equal to $\frac{3}{4}$ of B's, and $\frac{3}{7}$ of B's be equal to $\frac{2}{5}$ of C's, and $\frac{3}{4}$ of C's be equal to $\frac{2}{3}$ of D's, and D has $45 more than C, how much has each?

Ans. { A, $378; C, $360; B, $336; D, $405.

63. A owed B \$900, to be paid in 3 years; but at the expiration of 9 months, A agreed to pay \$300 if B would wait long enough for the balance to compensate for the advance; how long should B wait after the expiration of the 3 years? *Ans.* $13\frac{1}{2}$ mo.

64. A certain clerk receives \$800 a year; his expenses equal $\frac{5}{11}$ of what he saves; how much of his salary does he save yearly?

65. A merchant sold cloth at \$1 per yard, and made 10 per cent. profit; what would have been his gain or loss had he sold it at \$.$87\frac{1}{2}$ per yard? *Ans.* Loss, $3\frac{3}{4}$ per cent.

66. What is the cube of $\dfrac{21\frac{9}{11}}{29\frac{1}{11}}$ *Ans.* $\frac{27}{64}$.

67. What is the cube root of $\dfrac{63}{149\frac{1}{3}}$ *Ans.* $\frac{3}{4}$.

68. A miller is required to grind 100 bushels of provender worth 50 cents a bushel, from oats worth 20 cents, corn worth 35 cents, rye worth 60 cents, and wheat worth 70 cents per bushel; how many bushels of each may he take?

69. A man owes \$6480 to his creditors; his debts are in arithmetical progression, the least being \$40, and the greatest \$500; required the number of creditors and the common difference between the debts.

Ans. { 24 creditors.
\$20 difference.

70. Two ships sail from the same port; one goes due north 128 miles, and the other due east 72 miles; how far are the ships from each other? *Ans.* 146.86 + miles.

71. If 10 pounds of cheese be equal in value to 7 pounds of butter, and 11 pounds of butter to 2 bushels of corn, and 14 bushels of corn to 8 bushels of rye, and 4 bushels of rye to 1 cord of wood; how many pounds of cheese are equal in value to 10 cords of wood? *Ans.* 550.

72. A and B traded until they gained 6 per cent. on their stock; then $\frac{2}{5}$ of A's gain was \$18; if A's stock was to B's as $\frac{2}{5}$ to $\frac{1}{3}$, how much did each gain, and what was the original stock of each?

Ans. { A's gain, \$45; stock, \$750.
B's " \$37.50; " \$625.

73. If 20 men, in 21 days, by working 10 hours a day, can dig a trench 30 ft. long, 15 ft. wide, and 12 ft. deep, when the ground is called 3 degrees of hardness, how many men, in 25 days, by working 8 hours a day, can dig another trench 45 ft. long, 16 ft. wide, and 18 ft. deep, when the ground is estimated at 5 degrees of hardness? *Ans.* 84.

74. Wishing to know the height of a certain steeple, I measured the shadow of the same on a horizontal plane, $27\frac{1}{2}$ feet; I then erected a 10 feet pole on the same plane, and it cast a shadow of $2\frac{2}{3}$ feet; what was the height of the steeple? *Ans.* $103\frac{1}{8}$ ft.

75. A can do a piece of work in 3 days, B can do 3 times as much in 8 days, and C 5 times as much in 12 days; in what time can they all do the first piece of work? *Ans.* $\frac{8}{9}$ da.

76. A person sold two farms for $1890 each; for one he received 25 per cent. more than its true value, and for the other 25 per cent. less than its true value; did he gain or lose by the sale, and how much? *Ans.* Lost $252.

77. Three men paid $100 for a pasture; A put in 9 horses, B 12 cows for twice the time, and C some sheep for $2\frac{1}{2}$ times as long as B's cows; C paid one half the cost; how many sheep had he, and how much did A and B each pay, provided 6 cows eat as much as 4 horses, and 10 sheep as much as 3 cows?

Ans. C had 25 sheep.
A paid $18.
B " $32.

78. A man purchased goods for $10500, to be paid in three equal installments, without interest; the first in 3 months, the second in 4 months, the third in 8 months; how much ready money will pay the debt, money being worth 7 per cent.? *Ans.* $10203.94+.

79. A farmer sold 50 fowls, consisting of geese and turkeys; for the geese he received $.75 apiece, and for the turkeys $1.25 apiece, and for the whole he received $52.50; how many were there of each? *Ans.* 20 geese, 30 turkeys.

80. There is an island 73 miles in circumference, and 3 footmen start together and travel around it in the same direction; A goes 5 miles an hour, B 8, and C 10; in what time will they all come together again if they travel 12 hours a day? *Ans.* 6 da. 1 h.

81. A, B and C are to share $100000 in the proportion of $\frac{1}{3}$, $\frac{1}{4}$, and $\frac{1}{5}$, respectively; but C dying, it is required to divide the whole sum proportionally between the other two; how much is each one's share?

Ans. A's, 57142.85\frac{5}{7}$.
B's, 42857.14\frac{2}{7}$.

82. A, B, and C have 135 sheep; A's plus B's are to B's plus C's as 5 to 7, and C's minus B's to C's plus B's as 1 to 7; how many has each? *Ans.* A, 30; B, 45; C, 60.

83. A man sold one hog, weighing 250 pounds, at 4 cents per pound; a second, weighing 300 pounds, at $4\frac{1}{2}$ cents; and a third, weighing 369 pounds, at 5 cents; what was the average price per pound for the whole? *Ans.* $4\frac{519}{919}$ cents.

84. In a certain factory are employed men, women and boys; the boys receive 3 cents an hour, the women 4, and the men 6; the boys work 8 hours a day, the women 9, and the men 12; the boys receive $5 as often as the women $10, and for every $10 paid to the women, $24 are paid to the men; how many men, women, and boys are there, the whole number being 59?

Ans. 24 men, 20 women, 15 boys.

85. A fountain has 4 receiving pipes, A, B, C, and D; A, B, and C will fill it in 6 hours, B, C, and D in 8 hours, C, D, and A in 10 hours, and D, A, and B in 12 hours; it has also 4 discharging pipes, W, X, Y, and Z; W, X, and Y will empty it in 6 hours, X, Y, and Z in 5 hours, Y, Z, and W in 4 hours, and Z, W, and X in 3 hours; suppose the pipes all open, and the fountain full, in what time would it be emptied? *Ans.* $6\frac{6}{19}$ h.

86. How many building lots, each 75 feet by 125 feet, can be laid out on 1 A. 1 R. 6 P. $18\frac{1}{2}$ sq. yd.? *Ans.* 6.

87. A man bought a house, and agreed to pay for it $1 on the first day of January, $2 on the first day of February, $4 on the first day March, and so on, in geometrical progression, through the year; what was the cost of the house, and what the average time of payment?

Ans. { $4095. Average time, Nov. 1.

88. A man sold a rectangular piece of ground, measuring 44 chains 32 links long by 36 chains wide; how many acres did it contain? *Ans.* 159 A. 2 R. 8.32 P.

89. What number is that which being increased by its half, its third, and 18 more, will be doubled? *Ans.* 108.

90. A merchant has 200 lb. of tea, worth $$.62\frac{1}{2}$ per pound, which he will sell at $.56 per pound, provided the purchaser will pay in coffee at 22 cents, which is worth 25 cents per pound; does the merchant gain or lose by the sale of the tea, and how much per cent.? *Ans.* gained $1\frac{9}{11}$ per cent.

91. A man owes a debt to be paid in 4 equal installments at 4, 9, 12, and 20 months, respectively; discount being allowed at 5 per cent., he finds that $750 ready money will pay the debt; how much did he owe? *Ans.* $784.74 +.

92. A and B traded upon equal capitals; A gained a sum equal to $\frac{2}{5}$ of his capital, and B a sum equal to $\frac{11}{40}$ of his; B's gain was $500 less than A's; what was the capital of each? *Ans.* $4000.

93. I purchase goods in bills as follows: June 4, 1859, $240.75; Aug. 9, 1859, $137.25; Aug. 29, 1859, $65.64; Sept. 4, 1859, $230.36; Nov. 12, 1859, $36. If the merchant agree to allow credit of 6 mo. on each bill, when may I settle by paying the whole amount? *Ans.* Feb. 1, 1860.

94. A young man inherited a fortune, $\frac{1}{4}$ of which he spent in 3 months, and $\frac{4}{7}$ of the remainder in 10 months, when he had only $2524 left; how much had he at first? *Ans.* $5889.33 +.

95. A man bought a piece of land for $3000, agreeing to pay 7 per cent. interest, and to pay principal and interest in 5 equal annual installments; how much was the annual payment?

Ans. $731.67 +.

96. I have three notes payable as follows: one for $200, due Jan. 1. 1859, another for $350, due Sept. 1, and another for $500, due April 1, 1860; what is the average of maturity?

Ans. Oct. 24, 1859.

97. A man held three notes, the first for $600, due July 7, 1859; the second for $530, due Oct. 4, 1859; and the third for $400, due Feb. 20, 1860; he made an equitable exchange of these with a speculator for two other notes, one of which was for $730, due Nov. 15, 1859; what was the face of the other, and when due?

Ans. { Face, $800. Due Aug. 29, 1859.

MENSURATION OF LINES AND SUPERFICIES.

447. In taking the measure of any line, surface, or solid, we are always governed by some denomination, a unit of which is called the *Unit of Measure.* Thus, if any lineal measure be estimated in feet, the unit of measure is 1 foot; if in inches, the unit is 1 inch. If any superficial measure be estimated in feet, the unit of measure is 1 square foot; if in yards, the unit is 1 square yard.

448. If any solid or cubic measure be estimated in feet, the unit of measure is 1 cubic foot; if in yards, the unit is 1 cubic yard.

449. The area of a figure is its superficial contents, or the surface included within any given lines, without regard to thickness.

450. An **Oblique Angle** is an angle greater or less than a right angle; thus, A B C and C B D are oblique angles.

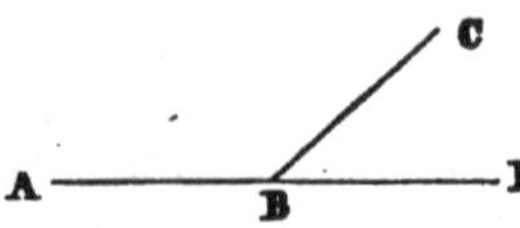

CASE I.

451. To find the area of a square or a rectangle.

452. A **Square** is a figure having four equal sides and four right angles.

453. A **Rectangle** is a figure having four right angles, and its opposite sides equal.

RULE. *Multiply the length by the breadth, and the product will be the square contents.*

EXAMPLES FOR PRACTICE.

1. How many square inches in a board 3 feet long and 20 inches wide? *Ans.* 720.

2. A man bought a farm 198 rods long and 150 rods wide, and agreed to give $32 an acre; how much did the farm cost him? *Ans.* $5940.

3. A certain rectangular piece of land measures 1000 links by 100; how many acres does it contain? *Ans.* 1 A.

CASE II.

454. To find the area of a rhombus or a rhomboid.

455. A **Rhombus** is a figure having four equal sides and four oblique angles.

456. A **Rhomboid** is a figure having its opposite sides equal and parallel, and its angles oblique.

NOTE. The square, rectangle, rhombus, and rhomboid, having their opposite sides parallel, are called by the general name, *parallelogram.*

It is proved in geometry that any parallelogram is equal to a rectangle of the same length and width; hence the

RULE. *Multiply the length by the shortest or perpendicular distance between two opposite sides.*

EXAMPLES FOR PRACTICE.

1. A meadow in the form of a rhomboid is 20 chains long, and the shortest distance between its longest sides is 12 chains; how many days of 10 hours each will it take a man to mow the grass on this meadow, at the rate of 1 square rod a minute? *Ans.* 6 da. 4 h.

2. The side of a plat in the form of a rhombus is 15 feet, and a perpendicular drawn from one oblique angle to the side opposite, will meet this side 9 feet from the adjacent angle; what is the area of the plat? *Ans.* 180 sq. ft.

CASE III.

457. To find the area of a trapezoid.

458. A **Trapezoid** is a figure having four sides, of which two are parallel.

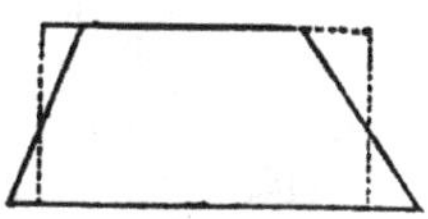

The mean length of a trapezoid is one half the sum of the parallel sides; hence the

RULE. *Multiply one half the sum of the parallel sides by the perpendicular distance between them.*

EXAMPLES FOR PRACTICE.

1. What are the square contents of a board 12 feet long, 16 inches wide at one end, and 9 at the other? *Ans.* $12\frac{1}{2}$ sq. ft.

2. What is the area of a board 8 feet long, 16 inches wide at each end, and 8 in the middle? *Ans.* 8 sq. ft.

3. One side of a field is 40 chains long, the side parallel to it is 22 chains, and the perpendicular distance between these two sides is 25 chains; how many acres in the field? *Ans.* 77 A. 5 sq. ch.

CASE IV.

459. To find the area of a triangle.

460. The **Base** of a triangle is the side on which it is supposed to stand.

461. The **Altitude** of a triangle is the perpendicular distance from the angle opposite the base to the base, or to the base produced or extended.

462. A **Triangle** is one half of a parallelogram of the same base and altitude; hence the

RULE. *Multiply one half the base by the altitude, or one half the altitude by the base.* Or, *Multiply the base by the altitude, and divide the product by 2.*

EXAMPLES FOR PRACTICE.

1. How many square yards in a triangle whose base is 148 feet, and perpendicular 45 feet? Ans. 370 yds.

2. The gable ends of a barn are each 28 feet wide, and the perpendicular height of the ridge above the eaves is 7 feet; how many feet of boards will be required to board up both gables?

Ans. 196 feet.

CASE V.

463. To find the circumference or the diameter of a circle.

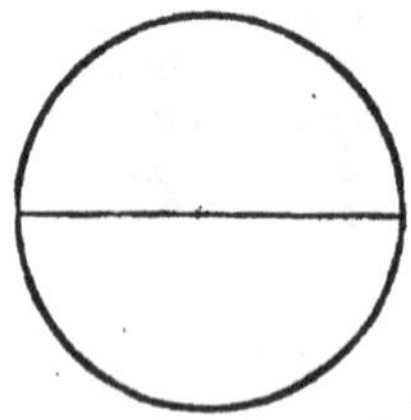

464. A **Circle** is a figure bounded by one uniform curved line.

465. The **Circumference** of a circle is the curved line bounding it.

466. The **Diameter** of a circle is a straight line passing through the center, and terminating in the circumference.

It is proved in geometry that in every circle the ratio between the diameter and the circumference is 3.1416 +. Hence the

RULE. I. To find the circumference. — *Multiply the diameter by* 3.1416.

II. To find the diameter. — *Multiply the circumference by* .3183.

EXAMPLES FOR PRACTICE.

1. What length of tire will it take to band a carriage wheel 5 feet in diameter? *Ans.* 15 ft. 8.4 + in.
2. What is the circumference of a circular lake 721 rods in diameter? *Ans.* 7 mi. 25 rds. 1.54 + ft.
3. What is the diameter of a circle 33 yards in circumference? *Ans.* 10.5 + yards.

CASE VI.

467. To find the area of a circle.

From the principles of geometry is derived the following

RULE. I. When both diameter and circumference are given; — *Multiply the diameter by the circumference, and divide the product by* 4.

II. When the diameter is given; — *Multiply the square of the diameter by* .7854.

III. When the circumference is given; — *Multiply the square of the circumference by* .07958.

EXAMPLES FOR PRACTICE.

1. The diameter of a circle is 113, and the circumference 355; what is the area? *Ans.* 10028.75.
2. What is the diameter of a circular island containing 1 square mile of land? *Ans.* 1 mi. 41 rd. 1.4 + ft.
3. A man has a circular garden requiring 84 rods of fencing to inclose it; how much land in the garden? *Ans.* 3 A. 81.5 + P.

MENSURATION OF SOLIDS.

468. A **Solid** or **Body** is a magnitude which has length, breadth, and thickness.

CASE I.

469. To find the cubic contents of a prism, cube, or cylinder.

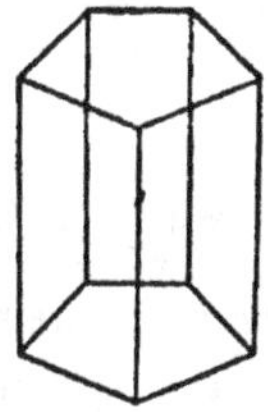

470. A **Prism** is a solid whose bases or ends are any similar, equal, and parallel plane figures, and whose sides are parallelograms.

471. A **Cylinder** is a body whose bases or ends are equal and parallel circles, and whose side is a uniform curved surface.

472. The **Altitude** of a prism, cube, or cylinder, is the perpendicular distance between the two bases; it is the *length* of the body.

To estimate the solid contents of any one of the bodies defined under this case

RULE. *Multiply the area of the base by the altitude.*

EXAMPLES FOR PRACTICE.

1. The side of a cubic block measures 8 inches; how many cubic inches does it contain? *Ans.* 512.

2. The end of a prism 20 feet long is a right-angled triangle, the two shorter sides of which measure 9 and 12 inches; what are the cubic contents of the prism? *Ans.* $7\frac{1}{2}$ cu. ft.

3. A stick of timber is 25 ft. 3 in. long, 1 ft. 8 in. wide, and 18 in. thick; how much will it come to at 8 cents per cubic foot? *Ans.* $5.05.

4. A cistern is $5\frac{1}{2}$ feet in diameter, and 8 feet deep; how many standard wine gallons will it contain? *Ans.* 1421.7984 gal.

NOTES. 1. The mean or average diameter of a barrel or cask may be found by adding to the head diameter $\frac{2}{3}$, or, if the staves be but little curving, $\frac{6}{10}$ of the difference between the head and bung diameters. The cask will then be reduced to a cylinder, and its contents found by the above rule.
2. The process of estimating the capacity of barrels or casks is called *gauging*.

5. The head diameter of a cask is 22 inches, the bung diameter 28 inches, and the length 31 inches; how many wine gallons will it contain? *Ans.* 71.2504.

6. The head diameter of a cask is 30 inches, the bung diameter 35 inches, and the length 40 inches; what is its capacity?

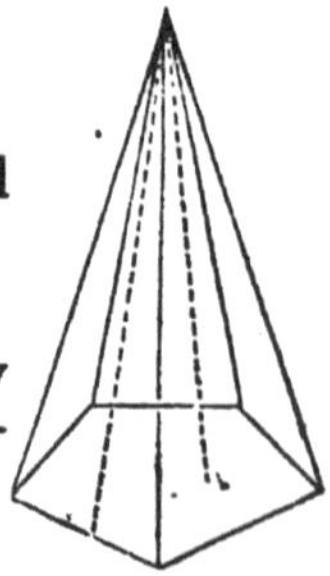

CASE II.

473. To find the cubic contents of a pyramid or a cone.

474. A **Pyramid** is a solid whose base is any plane figure, and whose sides are triangles terminating in a point at the top.

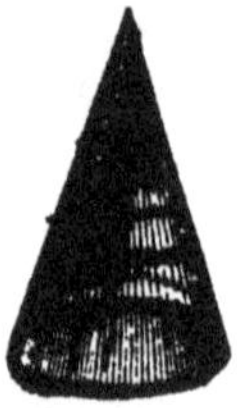

475. A **Cone** is a solid whose base is a circle, and whose side is a curved surface terminating in a point at the top.

RULE. *Multiply the area of the base by $\frac{1}{3}$ of the altitude.*

EXAMPLES FOR PRACTICE.

1. What are the solid contents of a pyramid 15 feet square at the base and 40 feet high? *Ans.* 3000 cu. ft.
2. A pyramid has a triangular base, each side of which is 30 inches, and the altitude of the pyramid is 4 feet; what are the cubic contents? *Ans.* 3.6 + cu. ft.
3. The base of a cone is 7 feet in diameter, and the altitude 16 feet 9 inches; what are the solid contents? *Ans.* 214.87 + cu. ft.
4. A heap of grain, in the form of a cone, is 4 feet high, and measures 15 feet round the base; how many bushels does it contain? *Ans.* 19 bu. 5.9 + qt.

CASE III.

476. To find the surface or the solid contents of a sphere.

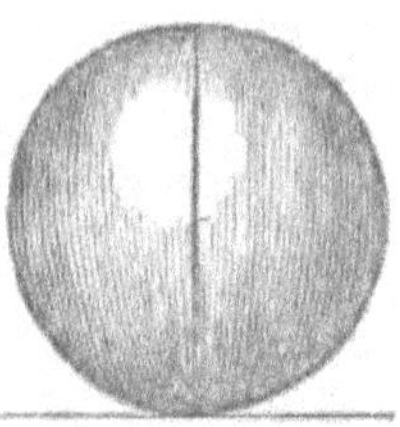

477. A **Sphere** or **Globe** is a solid bounded by a single curved surface, which in every part is equally distant from a point within called its center. Hence

RULE. I. To find the surface;—*Multiply the square of the diameter by* 3.1416.

II. To find the solid contents;—*Multiply the cube of the diameter by* .5236.

EXAMPLES FOR PRACTICE.

1. How many square inches on the surface of a globe 15 inches in diameter? *Ans.* 706.86.
2. The diameter of a sphere is 18 inches; what is its solidity?
3. What is the solidity of a ball that can just be put into a cylindrical cup 5 inches in diameter and 5 inches deep? *Ans.* 65.45 cu. in.

CPSIA information can be obtained
at www.ICGtesting.com
Printed in the USA
LVHW040027180422
716440LV00005B/383